She pushed her bottom further up, ensuring that her two holes were as close to the vertical as possible. Sale's hands went to her bottom and she felt a candle butt touch her vagina, greasy with butter. It went in, sliding deep up inside her. Fingers spread her bottom and the second butt touched her anus, making her wince and tighten, only for it to pop suddenly past her sphincter and into the chamber beyond. Judith's mouth came open as the candle filled her rectum, then she had begun to purr as her holes squeezed on the intruding butts.

Sale lit the candles with a taper, and Judith held exactly still, waiting for the pain of the wax. She knew what to expect, but still flinched and cried out when the first drop of wax fell to catch her sex lips. More followed quickly, rolling down to cake on her vaginal and anal skin or dropping to fall hot and stinging on her bottom, sex and thighs. Her purring had quickly turned to whimpering, then to gasps as the pain grew and her self-control threatened to break. A drop hit her clitoris and her mouth came open to scream, only to have an orange thrust into it.

By the same author:

THE RAKE
MAIDEN
TIGER, TIGER
DEVON CREAM

PURITY

Aishling Morgan

Dedicated to Felix for his knowledge,
and to Judith, for her dirty mind.

This book is a work of fiction.
In real life, make sure you practise safe sex.

First published in 2000 by
Nexus
Thames Wharf Studios
Rainville Road
London W6 9HA

www.nexus-books.co.uk

Typeset by TW Typesetting, Plymouth, Devon

Printed and bound by
Cox & Wyman Ltd, Reading, Berks

ISBN 0 352 33510 6

Glossary

Bantling – literally a child, but more commonly used to describe a young, inexperienced adult.

Biter – a wench whose cunt is ready to bite her arse – meaning a rampantly lascivious girl. 'Biter' might be deemed complimentary in some circumstances, 'bitch biter' definitely would not, much as a highly sexed modern girl might enjoy being called dirty, but not a dirty dog.

Bobtail – any willing girl, but especially one who wiggles her bottom to excite male admiration.

Bubble – a person cheated, literally one who has been filled with empty words, i.e. hot air.

Bull – one crown.

Carib – a member of a cannibalistic tribe originally from South America, and from whom the word cannibal derives. When discovered by Europeans, they were eating their way slowly up the chain of the Antilles islands, devouring the local Arawaks. They were extremely warlike and resisted both Spanish and British for over two hundred years before being pacified.

Crop – to hang someone, or to break their neck.

Dell – a young, but ripe girl, in some contexts a virgin. 'No deeper than a dell's doodle sack' – the depth of a vagina with hymen intact, i.e. very shallow.

Douser – a boxer, literally someone who puts an opponent's lights out.

Dust – money, especially in the form of winnings.

Fart catchers – servants, especially footmen, from their habit of walking directly behind their master.

Flashman – a generic term for a madam's bully, hence the name of the notorious bully from *Tom Brown's Schooldays* and the modern *Flashman* series.

Flyer – sexual intercourse with the clothes still on, often standing.

Galimaufrey – originally a hash made up of whatever happens to be in the larder, later a rather complicated recipe served at the original Kettner's restaurant.

Green gown – a dress smeared green at the back from its wearer having been mounted while lying on grass.

Green seal – basic claret, not from a named château and probably equivalent in quality to modern generic Médoc. A gentleman who served green seal to guests would be considered mean.

Lascar – an Indian, especially an Indian sailor, but often used as a wider term for non-white foreigners.

Miss Laycock – the vagina.

Mort – a woman, generally of the lower classes.

Mr Sharps – any con artist, but particularly one adept at cards or billiards. To 'sharp' was not necessarily to cheat, but more often to pretend ineptitude in order to lull the mark into making high bets.

Partridge Eye – pale red or dark pink wine from the Loire valley.

Stay close – keep a secret.

Trade – any substance, particularly those not well known or readily understood. A dismissive term when applied to goods for sale, suggesting worthlessness.

Traps – watchmen and thief takers in general. The term 'pigs' was also in use at the time, but later disappeared from common slang, only to re-emerge after about a century.

For a more detailed study of period slang see *A Classical Dictionary of the Vulgar Tongue* (Captain Francis Grose, 1785, 2nd ed., 1788) and *1811 Dictionary of the Vulgar Tongue* (various inc. 'Hell Fire Dick', 1811, unabridged reprint 1984, Bibliophile Books).

One

Henry Truscott lowered his eyes as the first spadeful of earth fell into the dank hole before him. The soil struck the coffin lid with a dull thump, obscuring the brass plaque that bore his father's name and the date of 1791. His sadness was genuine, yet tempered by a sense of relief. John Truscott had been the victim of rapidly advancing senility and a poor shadow of the father Henry remembered from his childhood. As the earth continued to fall on the coffin and the rector's voice droned on in prayer, Henry cast his mind back to the best of his times with the old man: learning to ride, being introduced to the pleasures of wine, their secret trip to a brothel in Plymouth . . .

Henry's thoughts ran on to the girl whom he had enjoyed that day. His father had fondly imagined that she was Henry's first, a misapprehension that Henry had never had the heart to break. The girl's name escaped him, but he remembered her as plump, dark-haired and vivacious, also genuinely enthusiastic about sex. Her breasts had been large and round, with the same defiant pout as those of Eloise, his wife. At the thought of Eloise he lifted his gaze from the coffin lid to the graveside. She stood to one side of the knot of more immediate relatives, immaculate in black satin and with her hair and face obscured beneath bonnet and veil. Only a stray wisp of her red-gold hair was visible, but

1

Henry had no difficulty in remembering its full glory, or the beauty of her face. Although he knew that her features would be set in an expression of formal sorrow, in his imagination they showed the blend of impudence and excitement that she wore to bed.

To enjoy the sight of her breasts needed little or no imagination. They pushed out the front of her dress, large and heavy, shockingly sexual in the sombre environment of the graveyard despite Eloise's best efforts to restrain them. In their normal state they were large enough, two ample handfuls of soft flesh, but Eloise was now in her seventh month of pregnancy and they had begun to swell along with her abdomen. Although he had always admired the trimness of her waist and the way it exaggerated the curves above and below, he had found to his surprise that he took equal pleasure in the very different contours of her pregnant belly. Now it bulged out the waist of her dress, as blatantly fecund as her breasts were sexual, an enhancement to her femininity and proof of his own virility.

Eloise's lower body was hidden beneath her skirts, and although these hinted at the magnificence of her hips and bottom Henry found his eyes once more rising to her bosom. As his gaze returned to her breasts he found himself wetting his lips at the sight and imagining them bare, with the nipples straining in erection and the cream-smooth skin flushed pink with arousal. With the shock of his father's sudden death and the subsequent sorrow, he had not had her for some days, and as his eyes lingered on her chest he felt his cock twinge in sympathy.

The rector's loud amen brought Henry sharply back to reality and he quickly resumed an expression of suitable gravity.

'He is in a better place,' Henry's elder brother, Stephen, remarked quietly as the knot of people around the grave began to break up.

Henry gave a forlorn nod in response, resisting the temptation to point out that if there was any truth whatsoever in Christian teaching then his father was hardly likely to have earned himself a place in heaven. Indeed, bearing in mind the old man's lifetime of drunken debauchery, not to mention adultery, the killing of two men in duels and a penchant for sodomy, for John Truscott even to arrive in front of St Peter was likely to be regarded as the most extraordinary piece of effrontery. Henry suppressed a chuckle at the image, only to realise that Stephen might have been expressing a more mundane sentiment in that there was no doubt that John Truscott's death would spare the family considerable embarrassment.

His brief amusement turned to a feeling of annoyance. Stephen was the most prim of men, austere and sober, the very opposite of both Henry and their father. It had always astonished Henry that his brother's character was so different from his own, yet other relatives showed the same traits. To them, as to Stephen, John Truscott had always been a source of vexation, Henry also.

Putting aside his ill feeling, he cast his eyes around for Eloise, finding her making polite conversation with a group of aunts and cousins. She was in profile to him, and the swell of her chest and belly once more turned his thoughts to lust. He caught the conversation as he approached, someone making a suitably respectful remark, which immediately struck Henry as hypocritical. In life John Truscott had excited little but disapproval from the family and would doubtless have been outraged by the mock solemnity of his own funeral.

Moving up to the group, he gave a polite nod and took Eloise's arm, excusing himself as he drew her gently away. She responded and followed as he led her from the graveside. At first relieved to be spared the somewhat awkward conversation of Henry's relatives, she began to hesitate as he marched her towards the older part of the graveyard.

'Should we not stay a while?' she queried. 'They will think us rude.'

'To the devil with them,' Henry answered. 'I'll mourn the guv'nor as I see fit.'

'How do you mean?' she demanded as Henry pulled her in among a thick screen of overhanging yew.

'By tupping you over this handy tomb,' Henry answered and pushed Eloise forward across the flat slab of lichen-encrusted slate.

'Henry!' Eloise squeaked as his hands fumbled at her skirts. 'Not here! Not now! Someone might see! What of your father! Have you no respect?'

'He'll not see, not from under six feet of sod,' Henry answered, 'but by God he'd have liked to. He always admired your backside, and not without reason.'

'Henry!' Eloise squeaked once more and made to rise, but he had one hand in the small of her back and held her firmly down with her swollen belly pressed to the lid of the tomb as he pulled her overskirt high around her waist, the lower coming with it.

With the heavy black material of her skirts piled on to her back and her petticoats showing Eloise increased her efforts to break free, squealing in a mixture of pleasure and genuine alarm as she frantically tried to smooth her skirts back down over her hips. He paid little attention, merely catching one arm and twisting it into the small of her back, then using it to pin her outer petticoat in place as it joined her skirts. The outrage in her protests redoubled as her two inner petticoats came up and Henry was rewarded with the sight of her neatly turned legs in their silk casings. A final smart tug revealed her bottom, with the chubby, pear-shaped cheeks thrust up and out. Having it bare broke her resistance and she gave a resigned sob, then a sigh as he pressed the hard lump of his crotch between her fleshy cheeks.

4

'Must you, here?' she said in a final, hopeless protest.

Henry didn't trouble to respond, but when he let go of her arm to get at the fastenings of his breeches she made no move to escape, instead taking a grip on her own skirts and petticoats to keep her bottom bare for him.

'That's my little puppy,' Henry declared as his cock sprang free of restraint.

Eloise gave a grunt of pleasure as the bulbous tip of his penis nudged the pouted rear of her vulva. Henry felt her wetness on his cock and laughed, realising that she must have been juicing from the moment she discovered what was going to happen to her. Taking his cock in hand he began to pull at it and rub the tip in the soft cleft of her bottom, quickly gaining full erection. Briefly he lodged it between the fullest part of her fleshy pear, directly over her anus.

'Not that, not here!' Eloise moaned.

'You tempt your own sodomy,' Henry said, laughing, 'but I'll leave your bud tight for now and watch her make moue as I ride that ripe cunt.'

A shiver went right through Eloise at the crudeness of his words and Henry laughed again, then prodded his cock between the swollen lips of her sex. She was wet and open, allowing the full length of his shaft to slide in easily after only a couple of trial pushes. She sighed as her vagina filled, then hung her head down to the slab beneath her as his balls nudged her vulva. Henry took her by the hips, enjoying the feel of his fingers sinking into the soft, ripe flesh and the way the bulge of her pregnancy altered the contours of her body. For a moment he held his cock deep inside her, then began to move it, fucking her with short, fierce pushes that quickly had her crying out with pleasure.

As he moved inside her he admired her bottom, its naked curves on full display beneath the lace ruffles of her lifted petticoats. Her cheeks were full but well

5

spread by her position, allowing him a view of the puckered hole of her anus, with its ring of flesh a tone pinker than that of her bottom cleft and the tiny, dark hole at the centre. Her buttocks would squash out with each of his pushes, the soft flesh wobbling delightfully.

Looking up, he found that she was busy with the buttons at the front of her dress, fumbling at them in her eagerness to get out her breasts. They soon spilled free, the plump globes falling into her hands to be squeezed and stroked, her shame and embarrassment forgotten in her ecstasy. Henry threw a quick glance over his shoulder, but could see little beyond the screen of yew branches that hid them from view. Increasing his pace, he determined to come in her without delay.

Eloise's moans became louder at the extra friction and he concentrated on his view of her bottom. Her anus had begun to contract and loosen rhythmically, producing a lewd, winking motion and once more tempting him to force his prick into her back passage. Yet her vagina felt wet and hot, but quite tight enough, and as she pulled up her head and began to gasp he felt himself coming. It happened in a rush, his cock rigid, his vision swimming red and his legs burning as his sperm erupted. His teeth were gritted as he emptied himself deep inside her, keeping his cock jammed in to the hilt and making short shoves to rub his unbearably sensitive penis tip on her internal flesh. He felt the hot moisture on his balls as the come squeezed from her hole.

Henry's eyes were shut in bliss and the whole world seemed centred on the junction between his cock and his wife's vagina. As the orgasm faded his thoughts returned to his father, and the way the old man's boozy, bloodshot eyes had always followed Eloise as she walked. Yet there was no guilt in his recollection, nor distaste, but simply a regret that he had never talked his beautiful young wife into allowing his father one last, glorious sexual encounter. He recalled the details of his father's demise and his mouth turned up into an ironic smile as he pulled his cock slowly from Eloise's dripping vagina.

If he had come, then she was still badly in need, and no sooner had the head of his penis fallen free of her sticky hole than she had cocked a leg on to the top of the tomb and was scrambling up with desperate agility. Henry chuckled at her eagerness and took a step back to peer between the yew branches. Nobody was coming their way, although a knot of mourners were gathered no more than a hundred yards distant, by the church door. Turning to watch Eloise masturbate, he found that she had already spread herself out on the tomb with her thighs wide and her arm curled around the bulge of her belly to get at the sopping flesh of her sex. Her breasts were out, squeezed together by her open bodice-neck to form a fine cleavage with the large, dark nipples proudly erect and pointed skywards. One hand was on a breast, tweaking the nipple between forefinger and thumb. Her eyes were shut and her head laid to one side with her face set in an expression of bliss. The hole of her vagina was open and pulsing, with a mixture of his come and her own juice trickling out and running down between her bottom cheeks in waves with each contraction. She pulled her thighs higher and wider still as she started to come, exposing her anus with the white fluid pooled in the tight hole and the place where her buttocks met the dark stone of the tomb, both flesh and slate glistening with their juices.

Henry watched Eloise's orgasm in delight, enjoying the blatant, open exposure of every detail of her body. There was also an added pleasure from their circum-stances, his wife's wanton display being made not among the white linen of their bed but on the lid of an old tomb in the cool, dim light of a Devon graveyard. She screamed when she came and her vagina contracted hard, squeezing more thick, white come from the

7

mouth. The muscles of her abdomen contracted too, and for one awful moment Henry thought that his firstborn was about to be delivered then and there.

Her scream of ecstasy had been quite loud and Henry found himself torn between his alarm at the possibility of her giving birth and the need to check that she had not attracted the attention of the other mourners. Only when her contractions had begun to die without any dramatic consequences did he look round, peering carefully between the yews to see a puzzled glance thrown in their direction by the rector himself.

'Damn!' he swore. 'You've roused old Bamford with your squealing. Can't you learn to keep it down?'

'You are a goat, Henry Truscott!' she retorted. 'A satyr! Taking advantage of me in such a place, at such a time!'

'You're the one who left a puddle atop this fellow's grave,' Henry answered. 'Who was he, anyway? I suppose we ought to thank him for choosing such a handy shape for it.'

Eloise's only answer was an indignant snort, but as he checked the graveyard once more he found that the rector had begun to walk slowly in their direction.

'My dress,' Eloise was saying, 'it is covered with green and quite spoilt!'

'The devil with your dress,' Henry replied. 'Old Bamford's headed this way. You'd better climb the wall and make away over the field.'

'I shall do no such thing!' Eloise snapped, even as Henry caught her by the arm and began to hustle her towards the high granite wall that bordered the grave-yard.

Despite her protests he managed to push her up and over the top, only then remembering that the drop on the far side was considerably greater than the near. He heard her squeak of alarm and a dull thump, feeling genuine concern until her description of him as the bastard of a bastard reassured him that she had come to no harm.

After a hurried adjustment of his clothing he walked out from the shelter of the trees, doing his best to look solemn and somewhat distressed. Bamford was approaching, but at the sight of Henry turned aside with an embarrassed half-smile. Hoping that the rector had mistaken Eloise's scream of ecstasy for Henry's own private distress, Henry returned the acknowledgement and made for where the mourners were beginning to disperse towards the carriages.

Stephen was towards the back of the group, his pale hair evident beneath the rear of his hat, and as Henry approached he glanced back. The brothers' eyes met and Stephen raised a finger, then halted, waiting for Henry to catch up and the others to move ahead.

'A sad day, brother,' Henry said as they came together.

'True indeed,' Stephen replied, 'yet the Lord's action in taking our dear father when he did must surely have been for a purpose.'

'D'you suppose?' Henry asked cautiously.

'I do,' Stephen answered, 'for as you know I have been advancing in the political sphere, and with full control of the family estates I may now reasonably expect to enter Parliament.'

Henry made no response, astonished by his brother's arrogance in assuming that his political yearnings might warrant divine intervention. Stephen Truscott steepled his fingers and placed them to his chin, a mannerism which Henry had always found irritating.

'And indeed,' Stephen continued, 'it is with respect to the estate that I wish to speak to you.'

'Ah, yes,' Henry answered, 'I was hoping you would bring that up.'

'Quite so,' Stephen went on. 'As you are aware, my responsibilities are considerable, yet I have no intention of shirking them. Nor do I wish any of the family to be forced to undergo the disgrace of penury.'

'Good, good,' Henry put in. 'A most Christian attitude, dear brother.'

'So,' Stephen said ponderously, 'I have chosen to award each member of the family who has no separate income the sum of one thousand pounds each year.'

'One thousand pounds!' Henry echoed.

'Do you think it too much?' Stephen queried.

'Too much! Why, it's well enough for the aunts, I dare say, but it wouldn't keep Eloise in petticoats! Damn it, man, I've a household to support and soon enough I'm to be a father!'

'I would consider one thousand pounds a quite ample sum,' Stephen responded. 'Indeed, I fear that to provide more would tempt your propensity to the more worldly pleasures.'

'Come, come, dear brother,' Henry wheedled, 'all that's in the past. From now on I intend to lead a life of dignified sobriety, as befits a father . . .'

'Hardly our own father's attitude, may the Lord keep him,' Stephen broke in.

'Well, true,' Henry admitted, 'but the guv'nor was always something of a rakehell . . .'

'An element of his character to be deplored,' Stephen interrupted again, 'and one of which you have inherited a considerable share. Indeed, in many ways your acts exceed his, outrages I might even be forced to call them.'

Stephen finished with a sorrowful shake of his head and Henry realised that pretence of reformation was pointless.

'Come, come, dear brother,' he said, doing his best to maintain a bluff, open manner, 'what did the estate make last year: seventeen thousand pounds? Surely you can afford your own brother's household the half, or better still ten thousand – a fine, round figure.'

'The income was closer to nineteen thousand,' Stephen answered, 'in large part due to my introduction of more modern agricultural practice. No, Henry, I am not to be swayed. Indeed, it is only from sympathy to your poor dispossessed wife that I am prepared to allow such a generous sum.'

'Precisely my point,' Henry retorted, deciding to use Eloise's status in a last desperate effort to change his brother's mind. 'Eloise is the daughter of a count, a member of the French nobility, cruelly torn from her possessions by the greed and envy of the revolutionaries. Surely the least you can do is provide her with an income that goes some way to reflecting her high estate?'

'I fear not,' Stephen answered. 'One thousand pounds is quite enough to live on and more than many gentlemen receive. Besides, you may supplement your income by taking up some gainful employment. Indeed, I expect it of you.'

'Work?' Henry responded in horror.

'In a manner suitable for a gentleman, of course,' Stephen went on. 'The priesthood would hardly be suitable, I think, but I would be prepared to purchase you a cornetcy in some suitable regiment. War with France would seem inevitable, so the prospects for advancement should be fine.'

'Damned if you will,' Henry retorted. 'You know the army's not for me. Orders and whatnot. I couldn't abide it. As for getting shot at by a load of bloodthirsty Frogs, why, I had my fill of that bringing Eloise out of France.'

'The navy?'

'Never! Worse than the army, where at least there'd be a wench or two around. I'll be damned if I'll take to the use of a cabin boy's breech.'

'The wine trade then,' Stephen continued after giving a distasteful sniff. 'It is considered a gentlemen's profession, and your knowledge of the subject is excellent by all accounts.'

'In trade?' Henry demanded in response. 'Can you imagine Eloise's reaction?'

'In these times we must all learn to make sacrifices,' Stephen answered him. 'In any case, the choice is yours, but you must make it.'

Henry sighed and forced himself not to answer, realising that to do so would be to risk even the sum he had been offered. Long experience had taught him that his brother was unlikely to be swayed. Stephen, several years Henry's senior, had always seen his younger brother as an unruly, wilful child. Undoubtedly there would be a smug pleasure in denying him the means to take his full enjoyment of life, while there was no denying that political ambitions were likely to come expensive.[1] Then came the thought of Eloise's likely reaction to the news and his anger and consternation were joined by a strong sense of discomfort.

Taking a gentle sip from her glass of champagne, Judith Cates settled back in her chair and wondered how she might break the sombre mood of the company. Never having met Henry's father, the funeral had held little meaning for her. Not only that, but as the mistress of Charles Finch, who himself had attended largely as a friend of Henry's, she had felt herself the object of disapproval from the less tolerant of the mourners. That uncomfortable sensation had passed with time, for the company now consisted only of those few intent on providing the dead man with a wake of which he would have approved. Stephen Truscott had long retired to bed, allowing Henry to relax sufficiently to invite those of his friends whom his brother did not consider suitable in from the kitchen parlour. These were the massive Todd Gurney, a blacksmith and occasional pacifier for Henry, Todd's tiny, Catalan wife Natalie, and Peggy Wray, Eloise's maid. They, along with herself, Charles and Henry would normally have made the merriest company, but Henry's announcement of the allowance Stephen intended to settle on him had soured the mood

12

more than the funeral itself. Eloise had been so discom-
fited by the news that she had delivered her spate of
invective in her native French and then fled the room.
Since then the atmosphere had been morose in the
extreme and Judith's hopes of an evening of merry
debauchery were beginning to fade.

'The fellow actually suggested that I should go into
trade,' Henry was saying. 'I mean, damn it all, my own
brother!'

'Disgraceful,' Charles agreed, taking a swallow of
port from his glass.

'But I must do something,' Henry went on. 'What of
the City, Charles? I understand there's good money to
be made on stocks for the clever man.'

'True enough,' Charles answered, 'but you need to be
in the know to make the best of it. Those who ain't are
more likely to end up with no more than the clothes on
their backs, if those.'

'Like any gaming, I dare say,' Henry answered, 'with
a few sharps skinning any number of marks. I know
better than to risk a game when I haven't the knack of
it, but still . . .'

Henry thoughtfully sank a swallow of his port and
lapsed into silence.

'The art is to know what's going to happen before it
does,' Charles began to explain. 'At present it seems
clear that we shall soon be at war with the French, so
the prices of iron, tin, copper are likely to rise, as they'll
be needed for the war. That's easy to see, but harder is
how the prices of fine goods, like silk and pepper, will
fair. They may rise because they're hard to come by, or
fall as nobody has the time for them. There's money to
be made either way, for the clever man, but an equal
amount to be lost. Even then it is all down to how the
war proceeds, if war there is . . .'

Bored by the conversation, Judith began to study the
men in the room, once more wondering if they might

not be persuaded into some more exciting pastime, preferably one that would involve her paying court to one or more cocks. Charles was, as ever, languid, elegant, perfectly dressed. He made a good lover, handsome, wealthy and tractable, also happy to indulge her sexual preferences. If he lacked a certain fire, it was more than compensated for by an accommodating nature and the free rein she was given for her frequent dalliances.

Then there was Henry Truscott, who had an undoubted attraction. This came partly from his somewhat boyish good looks, but more because of the ease of his manner, which suggested to her an almost animal virility very far from the poised, civilised manner of the majority of her male acquaintances. Also there was Charles' assertion that Henry's sexual preferences focused firmly on girls' bottoms, and in particular on the tight, sensitive holes between their cheeks. This reflected Judith's own needs closely enough to make her shiver each time she glanced at the conspicuous bulge in the crotch of his breeches.

Todd Gurney's attraction was more obvious: great height and heavy, rolling muscles that spoke of enough strength to handle her like a doll. Yet he was gentle and self-assured in the way only a truly powerful man can be, and she had no doubt that he would be capable of bringing her to a most satisfactory head of ecstasy.

As for her fellow females, both Natalie and Peggy had been Eloise's maids in France, and if Charles was to be believed they had willingly provided their mistress with the most intimate of services. Despite their physical differences – Natalie tiny and dark, Peggy full and soft and blonde – both carried a sexual air, sultry yet shy in the one case, sweet and boisterous in the other. Of the two, Peggy, a merchant's daughter, was intent on the conversation. Natalie, with little English and no interest

14

in commercial matters, seemed as bored as Judith herself. Choosing her tactic, Judith leaned forward to where a pack of cards lay by a cribbage board.

'Would you care for a game, my dear?' she offered, holding out the cards towards Natalie to make sure that her meaning was clear.

Natalie looked puzzled for an instant and then smiled and nodded.

'Do you know cribbage?' Judith went on as she carelessly disarranged the pegs that Henry's aunts had left in place for the future resumption of their game.

'I have been shown,' Natalie answered uncertainly.

'Good,' Judith replied. 'Well, let us try a rubber, and how about a shilling each boundary to make it more interesting?'

'A shilling?' Natalie queried.

'A penny then,' Judith said merrily, knowing full well that Natalie had no money whatever on her person.

'I . . .' Natalie began, casting a glance to where Todd Gurney was growling his disapproval of the whole concept of credit and capital.

'We must have some stake!' Judith declared gaily. 'A game is so dull with nothing to play for. Come, let us make it our clothes and perhaps the boys might give us some attention.'

Natalie's answering giggle, both shy and conspiratorial, told Judith all she needed to know. With her spirits rising as rapidly as her pulse she dealt out the cards, her fingers moving with practised motions as she placed each upon another. She felt that her skill, honed in a combination of brothel and gambling hell, was sure to exceed Natalie's, and was looking forward to having the petite Frenchwoman stripped to blushing nudity before she herself had removed more than her gloves. It also seemed likely that with Natalie's tiny size she was likely to be showing the effects of the champagne they had both been drinking.

15

They cut and began to play, Judith using her long nails to make tiny and dexterous marks on each card as it came into her hand. The first went Natalie's way, six points putting her peg over the first boundary and resulting in her delighted giggles as Judith kicked off a shoe with a look of mock resignation. Judith took a swallow of wine and picked up the cards, shuffling and cutting to leave those already used close to the top of the pack. On dealing again she found herself knowing two of the three cards in Natalie's hand but by ill luck secured only four points while her opponent managed a further single.

Again she had marked each card, and she dealt the third hand out with greater confidence, only to have Natalie immediately make her pair a triple and jump six holes to cross the second boundary. Feeling rather less sure of herself, she pulled off her second shoe and laid it neatly by the first, then turned back to the play. A good hand gave her three and she was rewarded with the sight of Natalie taking off one tiny boot, while the crib yielded a mere two points.

Judith glanced to the side as she took up the cards. All three men were deep in conversation but Peggy cast her a single, curious glance to which Judith returned a wink. With the cards dealt, she took them up, intent on making the most of her crib and forcing Natalie to expose something that would create a little more chagrin than her stockinged feet. Indeed, with no gloves on and probably only a single petticoat, it would not take much at all until the French girl's exposure had become not only thoroughly embarrassing but also arousing.

The hand went well, securing her ten points to Natalie's none and putting her peg across two boundaries but leaving it a frustrating single hole short of the third. Natalie gave only the smallest of blushes and reached behind her back to undo the pinny she had been wearing in order to assist in the preparation of dinner.

16

Her mop cap followed and as she threw out a cloud of glossy black hair Judith found her pulse quickening. Nobody else took the least notice and Judith scooped up the cards with a determination to have the small woman's breasts naked before the next hand was over.

As Judith shuffled the cards Natalie turned aside to reach for the champagne. Clearly half-drunk, she made a poor effort at pouring, giggling wildly as more spilled from the edge in froth than settled in the glass. For a moment Natalie was distracted with the wine and Judith took the chance to make a few quick adjustments to the pack, slipping a choice selection of eights and sevens to the right places.

By the time Natalie turned back the pack had been arranged to provide Judith with a hand that would in all likelihood leave Natalie with every detail of her trim curves on show, and possibly even allow Judith to demand some suitable forfeit. That, she was certain, the men would be unable to ignore.

'I must cut, I think,' Natalie said as she offered Judith the bottle.

Judith could do nothing, and watched in alarm as Natalie took the pack and, rather than cut it at the middle, simply peeled off the top card and placed it at the bottom. As the cards were passed back Judith swallowed and returned Natalie's suddenly bright smile as best she could. With no option but to go ahead she dealt and found herself with the main part of the truly dreadful hand she had intended for Natalie. The cut only added to her woes, and her toes had begun to twitch uncomfortably in her stockings as they began to play.

Natalie played artlessly, and Judith's hope rose as the play secured Natalie only a single point. Carefully she removed one glove and laid it on the table in full view of the men, then spread out her hand. It contained two points, enough to take her across the border but no more. Yet it was enough, for Natalie was already throwing shy glances around the room as she reached up beneath her skirts. Judith watched Natalie peel off a stocking with delight, enjoying the woman's blushes as much as the brief glimpse of a neatly turned leg. The action was too clear to be mistaken, and Charles noticed and nudged Henry. They had been discussing the money to be made by investing in Cornish mines, an increasingly loud conversation of which Judith had been half-aware. Henry had been losing the argument, his drink and desperation-inspired optimism fading in the face of Todd Gurney's practical objection. As he turned to see what the girls were doing Judith saw a hint of relief in his expression from being able to drop the argument, then pleasure as he saw what was happening. Even Gurney turned to the girls, but ignored them and continued speaking.

'Let me tell you this,' he was saying. 'Mining's a chancy game, chancier perhaps than your stocks business and a sight more dangerous to a man's life. There's a dozen minerals as look the same, save to the most knowing of eyes, and most of them worthless. Then if it is the right stuff there's a chance the vein'll go down no more than a few feet. Don't touch it, that's my advice.'

'I thought it was largely a question of who owned the right land,' Henry put in vaguely, with his attention fixed firmly on Natalie's discarded stocking.

'There's that as well,' Todd agreed. 'I'll tell you a tale, and I'll wager it'll put the idea clean out of your mind. My grandfather was a miner, of sorts, leastways, he was the smith at a minecamp, which is the better job. Wheal Purity it was called, on account of the quality they thought they'd take out. They found black stone in plough out along to the east of Climsland Hill and took a piece of land on rent from the Cunningham family. Ruinous rate it was, but they thought it'd be worth it. So they cut a shaft and hit a vein twelve feet wide, but

18

they couldn't keep the water out so they had to cut an adit. By then there was a great heap of ore building up outside of the mine, but when the assay came back it wasn't black tin at all, but some old trade called schorl, worthless. By that time they had hardly two farthings to rub together, so the camp broke up and the main part of them went off to fight for Marlborough. Not too many came back, as I recall, so let's put such fool's play aside and give our attention to the wenches.'

'A capital suggestion,' Charles agreed. 'Come, Henry, d'you think old John would have sat here arguing with three fine girls on hand?'

'Damned if he would,' Henry agreed. 'So what's the game, girls? Cribbage, is it? And each inlay on the board means a piece of clothing shed? By God, that'd be a game to make the aunts' eyes start!'

'We felt it might lighten the mood,' Judith explained, finding herself blushing now that all eyes were on her.

'So how's the game running?' Charles asked.

'It is Natalie's crib,' Judith responded, 'and in her hand she has, let me see, three eights and a seven turned up . . .'

She stopped talking as she realised just how good a hand it was and that the attention of the entire company was now firmly focused on her.

'Twelve!' Natalie declared, clapping her hands with joy.

'Two boundaries,' Henry said happily, 'but I say, Charles, Judith here has twice the finery of Natalie, that is hardly fair play.'

'Far from it,' Charles agreed, 'but what is to be done?'

'We must assume they started with neither showing an advantage,' Henry replied. 'What would your total have been, Talia, my dear?'

'How many clothes?' Natalie responded. 'I think, yes, nine.'

'And Judith?' Charles demanded.

19

'Eleven,' Judith admitted. 'No, thirteen, if my garters are to count.'

'Whether they do or not, it is only fair that you are on even terms with your opponent. Is that not so, Henry, Todd?'

'Certain sure it's fair,' Todd Gurney replied.

'I feel I must agree, my dear,' Henry put in. 'You must remove six items in all, if fair play is to be maintained.'

'Six!' Judith exclaimed.

'Including your garters,' Charles said fairly.

Judith swallowed as she calculated. She had planned to end naked or near naked in due time, but had not bargained for stripping while the others watched and remained fully dressed. Still, six items meant stockings, gloves and garters, so in fact revealed little, allowing her to tease while retaining at least some modesty.

With slow, elegant motions she removed her gloves, rolled her garters off each leg and then peeled off her stockings, taking care to allow a full display of her bare arms and legs but not to show the ruder details hidden by her full skirts. With her shoes gone five items remained to her, while Natalie had only four. With the next hand the crib came back to her, and so it still seemed likely that she would not be the first to reveal the more intimate details of her body.

'What of your crib, my dear?' Charles asked Natalie.

The cards were spread out and Judith immediately felt the blood rising to her cheeks. With the seven turned up, the seven and ace she herself had discarded became dangerous, but Natalie had added a further seven and the last of the eights. There was a moment of silence while each calculated the score, then Charles spoke up.

'Eighteen, I declare!' he said.

'I agree,' Henry added.

'A further three boundaries!' Charles announced in high delight, 'and a mere peg from a fourth. Come, my

20

dear, you must play better than this. Where is the skill that used to fleece the marks at Mother Agie's?'

Judith shook her head sadly, but as she began to undo her buttons she was already feeling the thrill of having to expose herself while others stayed covered. Her dress was a single piece, with stays, a chemise and two petticoats beneath, forcing her to go close to naked. The obvious choice was to leave herself in the chemise and a single petticoat, yet she had begun to tremble and found herself taking the front of the chemise down with her bodice. As her breasts lolled free she gave a sigh of pleasure. Her nipples were already hard and sensitive, and as all three of the men made noises of appreciation her excitement and vanity came to the fore. Pushing her breasts out she cupped one in each hand and held them up, then looked to her admirers from beneath half-lowered eyelids.

'Are these what you gentlemen had hoped to see?' she enquired softly and then squeezed them together to enhance her cleavage.

'By God they'll do!' Henry declared. 'You're a lucky man, Charles!'

Gurney gave a gruff noise of agreement and Judith turned to push her breasts out in his direction, keen not to exclude him from the group. He grinned and Judith thought to offer them to his touch, only to catch a warning look from Natalie. Not intending to spoil the increasingly sexual atmosphere, she contented herself with a coy smile and stood to push her dress down over her hips. Turning her back to them as if from a sense of modesty, she deliberately wiggled her bottom as the thick material slid down over her petticoats, then bent to take the dress to the floor. For Charles to have pulled up her petticoats and taken advantage of her bottom would have been easy, but he held back and allowed her to straighten.

Her fingers were trembling as she worked on her stays and the laces of her chemise. Both fell open and she

21

pulled each garment up over her head, leaving her bare from the waist up. As she turned she put her hands behind her head and stuck out her chest, giving the company a full view of her bare breasts.

With only two petticoats left she took her seat again, now with the men crowding round. All intention of having Natalie stripped was gone. She was eager to lose and be forced to strip – better yet to take some rude and painful forfeit that might be used as an excuse to bring herself to ecstasy. With her fingers shaking she fumbled the cards out and cut, her heart giving a delighted jump at the sight of a jack.

'One for his knob!' Charles crowed. 'Which I'll be bound is what you'll be getting presently, my little bobtail!'

Henry laughed and moved to place Natalie's peg across the boundary. Judith rose and tweaked open the tie of her outer petticoat, letting it fall to the floor. With trembling hands she chose two cards for her crib and began to play, intent on losing as fast as possible. The play yielded two points for herself, and Natalie's hand only four, leaving the peg a frustrating single place from the boundary. Her own scores pushed the next boundary and she waited as Natalie was obliged to remove another item of clothing. With her cheeks blushing crimson under the men's attention, the Frenchwoman peeled off her remaining stocking. For an instant the dark mound of Natalie's well-furred sex was showing and Judith felt her pulse quicken as she caught a faint hint of aroused female scent.

Once more she dealt the cards, now certain that it was the last hand and full of expectation for what would come once she was nude. Sure enough, the play had not been completed when Natalie crossed the final boundary and Judith found herself obliged to stand and let her final petticoat slip away, leaving her nude. The men were eyeing her, none troubling to hide their delight in her body. The women's interest was less open, but both

Natalie and Peggy showed pleased smiles that showed as much simple lust as amusement that it was Judith who was stripped down.

'How about a late supper, my dear?' Charles asked. 'Bread and plums.'

'A fine notion all round,' Henry agreed, 'and a hued arse for the last to make her man spend.'

'Across the face to show it's done!' Charles added, and lowered himself into a chair.

Judith sank quickly to her knees and crawled to Charles, starting to pull at his breeches' buttons even as the other girls followed her example. Both Henry and Todd responded with deliberate sloth and exchanged amused glances as Peggy and Natalie scrabbled at their respective crotches, neither girl disputing the bet. Soon all three men were seated and each girl had a rapidly stiffening penis in her mouth. Judith watched the room as she sucked on Charles, enjoying the view as well as her arousal and the urgency of the stiff erection in her mouth. She could see both Natalie and Peggy, each with her cheeks puffed out as she worked on her man's cock. Their bottoms were pushed out, balling the seats of their skirts into round, tempting shapes. The sight increased Judith's awareness of her own nudity. She was in the same kneeling position, but not just the shape of her bottom was showing. Instead it was in its full naked glory, with the cheeks apart to show the ginger puff of hair on her pouted sex and the tight dimple of her anus.

Each girl sucked urgently, using her full skill to bring forward the moment she received her man's come in her face and so avoided a whipped bottom. In her heart Judith knew that the greatest pleasure would come from losing the game, but it was hard to deliberately give herself up for a thrashing. As she continued to suck she thought of how Peggy's broad white bottom might look decorated by a dozen welts, or perhaps Natalie's trim, dusky behind.

23

'Old Catchpole's hanging a beef in the barn,' Henry said between grunts. 'As this is a day for religion we shall christen it across one girl's backside or another!'

Judith redoubled her efforts on Charles' cock at the thought of the stretched and dried bull's cock being used on her bottom. She had seen the thing earlier, a two-foot length of drying gristle with a pound weight hung from the end. Even without knowing that it was intended for laying across girls' bottoms it had seemed both obscene and virile, especially with the smell of badly cured leather and bull's cock. The thought of being the first to be beaten with it now sent a shiver the full length of her spine.

The three girls had visited the barn together, and a glance to the side showed that they were also scared. Natalie had burrowed a hand down Todd Gurney's breeches and seemed to have a finger in his anus, while Peggy had pulled out her fat breasts and was rubbing them against Henry while she sucked. Both men were breathing heavily and clearly excited, while Charles seemed calmer than either. Cursing herself for not paying attention to the task in hand, she took hold of his balls and began to knead, also moving her lips up to the head of his erection so that she could masturbate him into her mouth. His answering groan of pleasure gave her new energy, only for Gurney to grunt aloud. Judith turned her head in alarm, letting Charles' cock slip from her mouth. Todd had Natalie by the hair and was pulling her head back. His cock came free, and as it did so he came, sending a thick ejaculation full into Natalie's face. The come landed in a long, sticky streamer, running from Natalie's forehead, down across one eye and on to her nose. Her mouth had remained open, perhaps in the hope of catching the sperm in it, perhaps in shock at the sensation of it splashing in her face.

For a moment Judith found her gaze fixed on Natalie's heavily soiled face, then went quickly back to sucking. Now desperate, she pushed a hand down into Charles' breeches, seeking his anus and hoping to make him come by putting a finger in the hole. He grunted as she penetrated him, but the sound was echoed by Henry and as she turned her eyes in despair she found Peggy in the same filthy state as Natalie.

'Don't stop,' Charles said through gritted teeth.

Judith went back to sucking, less eagerly now that both her rivals had come on their faces to signal their success. Yet Charles' cock felt bloated in her mouth and his anal ring had already began to contract on her finger, so she made a purse of her lips and pushed them down on his cock, which jerked as they parted. She sighed as his come erupted directly into her mouth, tasting the salt and feeling the slimy texture even as he pulled back and took his cock in his own hand to deliver the second spurt directly between her eyes. She shut them as come splashed on one lid, leaving her blind. She sank to floor in defeat, raising her bottom for the coming whipping.

'Damned eager, that one,' Henry remarked. 'Well, let's not disappoint her. Who'll fetch the pizzle?'

'I shall,' Peggy chirped up brightly.

Judith remained in position, breathing heavily and bracing herself for her punishment, all the while with her desire fighting her fear. Her pose left her entirely exposed, with both vagina and anus pushed skywards between the naked cheeks of her bottom.

'Is that not a truly beautiful sight?' Charles commented. 'One that would have quickened your father's heart, I'll warrant.'

'Not so different from the one that stopped it,' Henry replied, 'but you say she does a trick with a candle. That I'd like to see.'

Judith squirmed at the remark, embarrassed despite already having made a show of herself. At Mother Agie's the girls had been punished by having a candle

25

inserted into vagina, anus or both. With the candle lit they would be made to recite a lengthy apology, all the while with hot wax running on to the most sensitive areas of their skin. The punishment was called the burning shame, and was most often inflicted on over-willing girls. Judith had acquired a taste for it, until Agie had reverted to simple whippings in despair at her charge's depravity. Since then Judith had pursuaded each of her lovers to indulge her quirk, but had never before had it done in front of so large an audience.

Charles heartily agreed to her torture, and when she made no dispute of their right a thick candle was greased with butter and put to her anus. She felt her hole stretch and take the wax shaft well up, leaving it sticking obscenely from between her buttocks. Her bottom skin sensed the heat as a brand was brought from the fire and put to the wick, leaving the candle burning in her anus. Before the first drop of wax had touched her she had reached back to masturbate, surrendering her last shred of dignity in her need to reach orgasm. The men gave grunts of pleasure or amusement at the sight, and she cried out as the first drip of hot wax rolled down the candle and pooled in her vagina. The second caught the taught ring of her anus and the third her fingers as she rubbed at herself and squealed out her pain and ecstasy. With her dangling breasts swinging against the pile of the carpet and the wet come running slowly down over her face, in addition to having her anus full and the hot feel of the wax, she knew her orgasm would not be far away.

She never heard Peggy return, but felt the first blow of the bull's pizzle as it was brought down hard across her naked rear end. The blow stung and made her jump, spraying droplets of molten wax across her rear and into the crease of her buttocks. She screamed and somebody laughed, then the second came, harder still as her body jolted and the flesh of her bottom jumped in response.

The third blow struck and a trickle of wax ran full into the open hole of her vagina, making her scream and claw at her sex as her anus began to clamp down on the candle. She felt the thick shaft start to squeeze out of her hole, only for someone to grip it and push it firmly back up her rectum. The whip struck again, lower, across the soft flesh of her thighs, then once more, plumb across the crease of her buttocks to catch the lips of her sex. Another blow fell, across the same line, once more spraying hot wax over her bottom and catching her cunny, then she was coming in earnest, screaming and thrashing as she clawed and chewed at the carpet.

Charles laughed and she felt the thick end of the pizzle pushed at her vagina. It went in, filling her with hard, leathery bull's cock. Her knees slid apart as she lost control of her body. The candle once more started to exude from her anus, with her fingers working wax and her own come into her clitoris. Her mouth was full of carpet, her nipples sore against the rough fibres, her whole bottom a fat, burning ball of pain, huge in front of her laughing audience. At the very peak of her orgasm the candle was once more rammed back home in her anus and a piece of molten wax caught in the vee of her sex lips, directly beneath her clitoris. For a moment the sensation was unbearable and she felt her senses slipping. Then strong arms were taking hold of her and she heard a puff of breath as the candle was extinguished.

Unable to do more than slump to the carpet, she lay prone, her bottom still raised with the candle sticking out from between her cheeks. Something soft touched her face and the come was wiped from her eyes and nose, allowing her at last to open her eyes. Charles was crouched beside her, smiling yet concerned, while beyond kneeled Peggy Wray with a silver flask in one hand.

Judith accepted the brandy and crawled to a chair, faint with reaction and the fierce, bruising ache of her hindquarters. The pizzle slipped from her vagina as she went, falling to the floor behind her. Reaching back she drew the candle slowly from her bottom, finding it more painful than when it had gone in. Finally, slumped in a chair with Peggy holding the brandy flask to her lips, she managed a weak smile.

Two

Henry Truscott raised his tankard to his mouth and took a swallow of the strong ale it contained. The action was performed with his left arm as the right was held across his front in a sling. Charles Finch and Judith Cates stood to his side. Before them a game of billiards was in progress, with Saunder Cunningham making easy work of a young man in a jacket of brown velvet. Cunningham had pushed the stakes to a guinea a ball, and a fair crowd had gathered to see the sport. Most of these were Cunningham's cronies, along with Henry's group and a handful who were hoping for a show when the young man realised he had been cheated.

Cunningham had got to the point of making deliberate mistakes in order to have the balls replaced on the table and so increase his eventual winnings. At first this had been done carefully, but as it became apparent that the young man was alone the fleecing had become increasingly outrageous, until Cunningham's friends were catcalling and laughing at each missed shot. Finally the last ball was sunk and the white-faced youngster was forced to disgorge the contents of his purse on to the table and write a note for the balance.

'Well played, Saunder!' one of the men declared. 'You've the eye for billiards and no mistake!'

'Easy enough, against a greenhorn with his mama's milk still wet on his lips,' Henry said loudly. 'I'll wager he'd not make so brave a show against Mr Sharps, nor even your little bobtail, eh, Charles?'

Charles laughed in response, as did more than one of the men who had been watching the game. Henry saw Saunder Cunningham's face colour in anger.

'Be fair, Henry,' Charles called out. 'Saunder'd not lose to a woman. He'd not dare play for fear of it!'

Cunningham turned, pretending to notice them for the first time. His annoyance at being so openly taunted was evident in his expression, yet he held his poise, meeting Henry's gaze and then letting his eyes travel slowly down Judith's body.

'I'll play her,' he drawled, 'if she'll put her cunt up against a ha'penny.'

It was a calculated response, designed to insult and humiliate Judith while avoiding the challenge.

'A ha'penny?' Henry answered. 'A touch mean, ain't that, from a man who's just taken the youngster here for nine guineas and a note? It should be on the same terms, or else a friendly game.'

'We must not oblige the gentleman,' Judith added. 'Perhaps he does not care to take a risk?'

Murmurs went up from the crowd, while Cunningham paused, evidently suspicious but also angry. Henry could see how the man's mind was running, suspicious that he was being cheated yet inwardly sure he could beat Judith. The position was awkward, as even to play her was to risk being laughed at, while to refuse invited ridicule even more quickly.

'I'll play then,' he said, suddenly bluff and friendly, 'a friendly game, but at a bull a ball to keep my interest up while I show how it's done.'

Judith responded with a nod and took a cue from one of the bystanders as Cunningham began to replace the balls. The game went fast, Henry not even troubling to watch the balls but admiring the roundness of Judith's bottom or the depth of her cleavage as she bent over the table to place her shots. Only towards the end did his attention go elsewhere, partly in admiration of the smoothness of her play and partly to watch Saunder Cunningham's increasing fury as the game went against him. It finished with Cunningham losing by a greater margin than the one he had taken over the young man, and with the onlookers howling with amusement at his expense. Cunningham hurled his cue to the ground as Judith rose and gave him a mocking half-bow.

'Don't take it hard, Saunder,' Henry laughed as Cunningham counted out crown pieces on to the table. 'She used to fleece the marks at Mother Agie's, and you're not the best she's taken.'

'Damn you, Truscott!' Cunningham swore. 'You've sharped me! I thought I'd seen her before!'

'Hold your temper, Saunder,' Henry answered back. 'There was no money in it, leastways not until you insisted. I was just too keen to take a puff of wind from your sails after you skinned the greenhorn.'

'Well, I may not have the measure of a sharp,' Cunningham retorted, 'but I do of you, in billiards, or any style you'd care to name.'

'That I don't doubt,' Henry answered, 'while I've a game arm, but if you're keen to make a bet I'll play you the garter run for anything you'd care to name.'

'That I'll take! Ten guineas and a bull a piece to the winner.'

'I don't want your money, Saunder, for I've plenty of my own,' Henry lied. 'I've more in mind the chance to buy one of those pheasant coverts of which you boast, say at fifty guineas. Will you put that up?'

'Against what?' Cunningham demanded.

'Anything you care to name, as I said.'

'Done then. I've a covert named Trethaw Wood. I'll wager it against the ten guineas, a plate of galimaufrey and the clothes on your back, to show you for a fool.

31

And this time I want the wench's cunt in the bargain, if she has the courage for it?'

Charles cast a questioning glance at Judith, who replied with a demure nod. Some of the men called out in delight, others merely smirked. It was clear to Henry that they were amused by more than just the bet, but he paid no attention.

'Taken,' Henry called.

Judith Cates felt her stomach fluttering as she and Charles watched Henry ascend the steps to Mother Agie's brothel. In the five years since she had left she had never dared come within a half-mile of Dallington Alley, in which it was situated. Her departure with the New Year's takings and one of the customers would not have been forgotten, of that she was certain. Yet she knew Agie well, and her habits: running away was punished by the cane, as was theft, while the sum involved would have to be repaid on her back. It would also be done with the crudest and most debauched clients, yet Judith's plans extended only as far as the caning.

Henry was admitted and she gave Charles a kiss, then started forward, steeling herself to the coming encounter. Inside, hidden deep, was the knowledge that the beating she had chosen to accept, ostensibly for the sake of Henry and Charles' complicated machinations, would be both cathartic and arousing for her. This made no difference to her fear at the prospect of exposure and pain, yet as she reached the door she found it easier to apply her hand to the knocker than she had expected.

One of Mother Agie's bullies opened the door, a burly lascar who had not been there in her time. He gave her a condescending, lust-filled look, conveying both desire and contempt. The reaction brought her old memories to the fore and she hesitated, then pushed in as he allowed the door to swing open.

No sooner had she entered the room than she found herself faced with Mother Agie herself. Her one time madam was as formidable as ever, tall, heavy set and running to fat, with her full-cheeked, pleasant face heavy with make-up and her massive chest lifted to display close to a foot of deep, pink cleavage. The old bawd's expression had been one of welcome, the face she always wore to customers as they entered. On seeing Judith it changed to anger and then to outright disbelief.

'Mother,' Judith greeted her quietly.

There was a pause as Mother Agie struggled to find her voice.

'By heaven but you've a nerve showing your face in here, Judy Cates!' she finally managed. 'I suppose that Jenks has dropped you back in the gutter where you came from, and now you're come crawling back to Mother Agie for a place.'

Judith nodded, doing her best to look contrite and pathetic.

'Well, who's to say I want you?' Agie continued. 'You thought the foolish old woman had a soft spot for you, I dare say, just on account of how you . . . Well, never mind, be that as it may, these old fingers have been itching to take a rod to your backside these last years and by heaven I aims to do it now. Then we'll see if you're to come back or not. Where are my men? Tom! John!'

The lascar turned to Judith with a grin that was now cruel as well as lustful. From the small room where the bullies took their meals two other men emerged, both big, hard-faced types. One of these Judith recognised as Tom, who had been the first man to put a candle in her anus and subsequently his cock. He gave a knowing leer as he saw her, which made Judith blush as she remembered just how aware he was of the way punishment aroused her.

Mother Agie moved into the main room and Judith followed, the bullies coming behind. The room was as

Judith remembered it, only somewhat more shabby in parts and more ornate in others. Benches heavily upholstered in red plush stood against three of the walls, the fourth being open to the gambling room, from which the sounds of the games in progress could be heard. Chairs and tables were set out in the middle of the room, while a stair rose from one side to a balcony, from which the doors to the girls' rooms on the first floor could be glimpsed.

It was clearly a busy evening, as some dozen men were present and as many girls. Most of these were in states of undress, many of the girls with their breasts bare and one or two in nothing but their stockings. Judith recognised only one of the girls, who returned her wan smile with a look of shock and pity. Henry was among the men, talking to a petite blonde and paying no attention whatever to Judith. Agie moved to the centre of the room and raised her arms, the gesture producing immediate attention.

'There's to be a treat tonight for you gentlemen,' she announced. 'A caning, at a bull a look for those who want to see.'

'Who's the lucky wench?' one of the men called out, a stick-thin individual in a fancy waistcoat.

'Judy Cates here,' Agie replied, pulling Judith forward by the arm, 'who a few of you may recall skipped off with a night's purse some few years back. She'll be getting twenty and they'll be hard ones. Also she'll be as nature intended, stark.'

'And how displayed, Mother?' the thin man called.

'Spread across my Tom's back with her legs akimbo,' Agie answered.

'That I'll pay to see,' he replied, with several others agreeing and more laughing at the thought of how Judith was to be beaten.

Nine men paid their crown pieces to watch Judith's punishment, leaving their tarts looking sulky in the main room. Henry held back, declaring that seeing a girl beaten was not his thing, an admission that drew disparaging remarks from several of the others. With the men following behind, Judith allowed herself to be led through the gambling den and into the one beyond. It was a room she knew well, and as the door closed firmly behind her she found the old familiar fear rising into her throat. As with the main room, benches stood around the walls. They were not upholstered though but simple wood, while the floor was bare. The lower part of an elephant's leg stood in one corner, stuffed with canes ranging from tiny whalebones designed for whipping girls' breasts to heavy lengths of malacca for the most severe punishments.

It was the punishment room, the place were girls were flogged or given the burning shame for breaking Mother Agie's house rules. It was also where those clients who enjoyed beating were brought, either to see it done to a girl or to take it themselves. Judith was trembling hard as she remembered her previous visits, the feel of thick candles in her vagina and anus, the sting of hot wax on her flesh, the bite of the cane across her buttocks, the groans of men as they masturbated over her pain.

'Strip her down,' Mother Agie ordered as the door clicked to behind the last of the men.

Rough hands encircled her, gripping the fabric of her bodice. She shut her eyes as it was torn open and her breasts fell out, then meekly allowed her gown to be pulled down off her arms and over her hips. Her petticoats were taken with it, the strings wrenched open in passing as if her total exposure were of no more significance than the removal of a bonnet. The bully let go of her dress and petticoats and they fell to the floor, leaving her to step out of the puddle of cloth, stark naked but for her boots, knee stockings and garters. Several of the men gave noises of appreciation at the sight of her naked body and she opened her eyes to find Mother Agie admiring her with frank enjoyment.

'Scrawny little dell you was when first I got you,' the old woman remarked, 'but I see you've not been starving yourself. A guinea a throw I could ask, just with your bubbies on show, never mind your arse. Maybe I will take you back, but you've a lesson to learn first, my girl, a sharp one. Horse her up, boys.'

Judith went forward obediently as Tom turned his back to her. Placing her hands over his shoulders she allowed him to grip her wrists. As he bent forward and her feet lifted clear of the ground she saw Mother Agie to one side, in the act of selecting a thick malacca from the cane stand. Judith shut her eyes again, tightly, as her body began to shiver with expectation. The other bullies took hold of her legs, stretching her across the breadth of Tom's back. As he bent down her bottom was forced up and out, naked and spread for Agie's attention. With the three men gripping her she could manage only a feeble wriggling, enough to make her bottom cheeks wobble but far too little to give any respite from the cane. The air on her open cunny felt cool, bringing home to her how blatantly she was spread for the onlookers, with every detail of quim and even her anus on clear show.

Trembling hard, she waited for the beating to start, all the while knowing that Agie would do it slowly and so draw out her terrified anticipation. She kept her mouth hard shut, determined not to break and call out for it. The silence was close to absolute, the sole sound the ticking of an especially loud clock that she knew had been chosen to add to the torment of beaten girls. Then it came, suddenly, the swish of the cane through the air and an explosion of pain across her bottom as the wicked thing bit home into her soft cheeks. She screamed, unable to hold back, and tried to kick out against the powerful hands that held her legs. The effort was useless and she only managed to wobble her buttocks at the onlookers, drawing delighted calls and crude suggestions.

Even before she had time to recover herself the second stroke came whistling down, then the third as Mother Agie's long-pent-up desire for revenge found full expression across the vulnerable meat of Judith's bottom. It was impossible to hold herself and she thrashed and squealed as the beating continued, much to the delight of the audience. Twice she farted and both times the act was greeted by guffaws of coarse laughter and suggestions that her anus should be plugged, preferably with a cock. Her tears came at that, bursting from her tight-shut eyes to run hot down her cheeks and spatter against the cloth that covered Tom's broad back.

As she lost count of the number of strokes that had been inflicted on her poor bottom her senses went entirely. Screaming, blubbering and thrashing wildly in the bullies' grip, she was lost in a haze of pain through which the men's raucous laughter and filthy suggestions seemed to come from a great distance. Offers were made to put cocks in her while she was hot from beating, several calling for the use of her vagina and some for her anus. Others called for Mother Agie to make the strokes harder while a lone voice was calling for odds that she would wet herself.

Suddenly it was over, the agonising blows breaking off abruptly to leave Judith gasping for breath and shaking her head in a desperate effort to make the pain go away. Tom relaxed his grip and she sank slowly to the floor, snivelling brokenly in between great sobs that sent spasms through her body. Her bottom was up high, spread for all to see, while she could feel the wet of her juices running down the insides of her thighs to betray her excitement to the jeering audience.

A big hand began to stroke her hair, gently, soothing away the agony of the beating. A strange, pathetic sense of gratitude began to well up inside her. Dimly she was aware of Mother Agie ordering the onlookers out of the room and telling the bullies to watch the door. The stroking continued as the men left, still laughing and passing comments on Judith's display during punishment. As the door clicked shut once more the gentle soothing motions of Agie's hand stopped and changed abruptly to a hard grip among Judith's curls. She knew what was going to happen and surrendered herself to it as she was dragged forward by the hair.

For the first time since the beating had started she opened her eyes, just in time to see Agie's great thighs spreading in front of her to expose a fat, swollen sex. She could only stare as her head was pulled in with the smell of aroused female rich in her nostrils and her mouth coming open of its own accord. The grip in her hair was irresistible, pulling deliberately slowly to make her understand what she was about to do. Her forehead touched the lace ruff of lifted petticoats, her nose bumped on the plump, hairy pubic mound, and then her lips were touching the wet flesh of Mother Agie's vulva.

'Lick it,' Agie ordered, 'lick my cunt, and as you do think of your hued backside and what the boys'll want from you when I'm done.'

Judith shivered, thinking of the three hulking men who were now watching her humiliate herself and how they would use her afterwards.

'That's right,' Mother Agie sighed, her voice suddenly soft. 'You always were a brazen baggage, and you always did like the taste of cunt.'

Judith had began to lick, enjoying the sensation of pleasuring the woman who had beaten her despite herself. It had been the same in her days as one of the big woman's girls, punishment followed by repentance and in the form of applying her mouth to her mistress's sex. Giving girls to the bullies had been less usual, and reserved for especially rebellious girls. Judith knew that she would be well used. Tom's trick had been to bugger her while he dripped hot wax on her upturned buttocks and she shivered at the prospect and began to lick harder. Agie sighed and the grip on Judith's hair weakened.

As Judith concentrated on the task of bringing Mother Agie to orgasm her pain and bewilderment faded. She became aware of the world other than the fleshy vulva under her mouth, her smarting buttocks and the four people who had control of her. Noises could be heard beyond the door, the sounds of the gaming room, faint shrieks of laughter and girlish squeals, then more shrieks, with a new, urgent tone. Suddenly the door burst open. Judith pulled her head round to see a dishevelled blonde girl standing in the doorway. She was nude but for her stockings, both of which were well down her calves, while her breath was coming in gasps.

'Trouble, Ma!' she burst out. 'There's a man on the garter game!'

'Who is it?' Agie demanded.

'Don't know, Ma,' the girl gasped. 'Not a regular, the cull what come in before your new piece here. Ellie says she saw them together, from the top window.'

'You've made a bubble of me, you little bitch biter!' Agie swore at Judith as she realised the deception. 'I'll drub the hide from you for that! Hold her hard, Tom. Dan'l, John, see to the trouble then fetch the cat. I'm going to learn this wicked little mort how a real beating feels!'

Judith was still on her knees, her hair gripped in the fat woman's powerful fist. Even as the grip tightened she had grabbed Agie's ankles and heaved with all her strength, catching the fat woman off balance and sending woman and bench backwards. There was a sharp pain as the false part of her hair was pulled out, along with some of the real, then a crash as Mother Agie hit the floor. Leaping backwards she sent the blonde girl staggering into John and lashed the tip of

39

her boot into Tom's crotch. He went down and she was through the door with John's hand clutching at her bare shoulder but failing to find purchase.

Henry Truscott hurled the bolster down the stairs and laughed as it caught two of his pursuers and knocked them into a tangle of gaudy skirts and flounced petticoats, with all four legs and one plump bottom showing at the centre. With sixteen garters in his possession he felt confident of victory, while sounds from further down in the building suggested that Mother Agie's bullies had finally been alerted.

It had been easy, mainly due to Judith's diversion but also because of the simplicity of his technique. On choosing a girl he would grab her by the ankles and tip her up, forcing her to use her hands to protect herself while her skirts flew up around her head. Her garters could then be pulled off before she had a chance to recover, then it was on to the next one with the outraged complaints of his victim ringing out behind. Eight times he had gone through the motions, leaving Mother Agie's in a ferment of squealing girls and angry customers. Three of the bolder spirits among the girls were now in pursuit, making further gains less easy.

His main difficulty was that the game had carried him to the third floor of the house and that his escape was blocked. Yet this too he had allowed for, and as he darted up to the next landing he was waiting expectantly for the chaos that Charles was supposed to provoke in the house by claiming it was being raided. With two of his pursuers in a tangle on the landing and the third struggling to climb over the mess of kicking legs and disordered petticoats he had won valuable seconds. Determined to add to his score he piled through the nearest door and slammed it behind him.

The view that greeted him was of a thrusting male bottom, with a plump white leg kicked up to either side, each decorated with a pretty blue garter. In an instant he had seized both garters and pulled them from the girl's legs, resulting in fresh squeals and then a furious bellow from the man. Apologising hastily, he made a dash for the open window, only to find himself looking down over a sheer drop into the blackness of an unlit yard. To the side were roofs and gable ends, frustratingly close yet out of reach. The idea of climbing on to the ledge and making a leap for it lasted only a second before he had turned back. The couple were still disentangling themselves and both were looking at him, the girl in shock, the man in red-faced anger.

Again Henry gave a polite nod, despite an inclination to laugh. The man's penis was waving to and fro as he struggled with his breeches, creating a ludicrous sight, while the girl had covered her breasts with her hands but still had one leg beneath her partner and so was providing a fine view of spread cunny. Doing his best to ignore the sight he scrambled for the door, only to hesitate at the sound of screams and aggressive male voices. He bunched a fist and took hold of the door knob, hurled the door wide and struck out at the first figure he saw.

His punch took the man in the jaw, sending him sprawling even as Henry took in the rich blue velvet coat and the much larger man beyond. The bully's surprise lasted a fraction of a second and then he was coming for Henry with his massive arms outstretched. Cursing his luck Henry dashed for the stairs, only to hear his name called in a shrill female voice. Judith was on the upward stair beyond the bully, naked but for her stockings and with her bottom dark with cane welts. Another bully was beside her, gripping her by the ankle. He was fully dressed and carried a short whip. On the stairs below him were the three girls who had been chasing him, now gathered in an accusing knot. The biggest of them called out as she saw him, yelling at the bullies to take him. Both turned, their expressions turning to malign pleasure as they realised that their prey was trapped. Henry braced himself to fight despite the cold certainty of being unable to handle two experienced roughs.

'Come on, flashman, let's see your mettle!' Henry taunted as he judged his chances of reaching the stairs and breaking through the three girls before he was caught.

A feint at the nearest bully drew no response whatever, and then screams and shouts were coming from below, angry, frightened or demanding, creating a cacophony of sound from which he caught the words traps and pigs. The bully hesitated, listening, and then Henry had planted a fist into his groin with all his force.

'It's the traps!' Henry bellowed as he clambered over the prone bully and grabbed for Judith.

He caught her and for a moment he thought they were free, only for a hand to catch his ankle and lock on it. Cursing the man's tenacity he kicked out, missed, lost his balance and sprawled on the stairs. From the edge of one eye he saw Judith's knee come up against the bully's chin. The grip on his ankle slackened and he tore his leg free even as the doors above them burst open and disgorged frightened customers and wide-eyed tarts on to the landing. Henry managed to find his feet, but the second bully had a firm grip on Judith and was pulling her down despite her furious struggles.

'Damn it, you fellows!' he roared, pointing at the bullies. 'Have at the traps, or we're all done for!'

The trick worked only partially as all the girls and some of their customers recognised the bullies. Yet a burly man in the upper part of a sailor's uniform did not and planted a vicious kick in the back of the man who was down before anybody else could react.

'Thank you, my man!' Henry called. 'Now down, quick, while this brave fellow and I hold them!'

The command was nonsensical, but with the whole house resounding with screams and cries of panic the

42

group on the landing were in no mood to dispute him and made a rush for the stairs as one. One bully was still down while the other was holding a struggling Judith around the waist. For an instant he considered abandoning his companion, only to dismiss it as the sailor made for the man with fists flying. Seeing what was coming, the bully dropped Judith and put his fists up. She caught Henry's hand as he reached down for her and he pulled her hard towards the stairs, dragging her through the press of frightened bodies by main force.

More people were coming down from the upper flights, but they ran on, gaining the fourth floor and then the fifth and highest. Furious shouts were coming from below as they struggled with a window, and the voice of Mother Agie herself came clear, pouring a string of obscenities after Judith and demanding that she come down. The window gave and Henry and Judith exchanged triumphant grins.

Outside the night was cool and oddly quiet despite the hubbub below and the general noise of the city. There was a bright moon in the sky, illuminating the jumbled rooftops, and as Judith moved off confidently Henry followed her. She obviously knew the route well, and for a space they went in silence, reaching a flat area among a tangle of gables before they stopped. Judith turned to him and smiled, then burst into laughter. Henry responded, hugging her to him and joining in her mirth as the excitement and tension of the raid drained away.

'By God, but you're the game one, aren't you?' he exclaimed when he finally managed to catch his breath. 'And after taking a thrashing and all.'

Judith answered with a shy grin, then made a face as she turned to show off her heavily discoloured bottom. It was the gesture of a comrade, showing off the wounds taken in their daring exploit. Judith herself had planned the expedition, accepting a certain thrashing to distract Mother Agie's bullies while Henry raided the brothel for garters. It was her knowledge of how Mother Agie gave out punishment that had allowed the plan to succeed. As he admired the curves of her well-punished bottom he had an idea of the pain she must have suffered and wondered if she had the same taste for flagellation that drove Eloise's sexuality.

Certainly she seemed pleased with herself, proud even. She made no move to cover herself, but allowed him to inspect her, all the while watching over her shoulder. Henry swallowed, his rising lust causing his penis to twitch. The actual raid had been too chaotic and fraught to allow him to think of sex. Yet each time he had divested a girl of her garters he had been given a fine and involuntary display of her charms, thighs, bottoms and cunnies all shown off in the most immodest poses. While most of the girls had reacted to being upended with outrage, some had giggled, and one had not even troubled to close her thighs, evidently expecting to be mounted and enjoying the prospect. It had hardly been practical, but now it was different, with just the quiet of the night and Judith's pretty bottom bare for him to admire.

'Do you think we've time for a flyer? If you'd care for it?' he asked carefully.

Judith was on him in an instant, pressing her mouth to his and tearing at the flap of his breeches. He responded, opening his mouth under hers and curling his arms around the narrow span of her waist to knead her bottom. No sooner had his fingers come to squeeze one roughened cheek than her passion became stronger still. She worked open his breeches' buttons with frantic fingers, all the while kissing with urgent, bruising lust. His cock responded quickly, stiffening even before she had pulled it free and begun to tug hard at the shaft. With his hands full of hot, soft bottom he came erect fast, and she was pulling his penis towards her belly even as he lifted her from beneath. Her arms came around his shoulders as she realised his intent and he settled her on to his penis, the full length of it sliding up her well-lubricated vagina without the slightest difficulty. They were still kissing as she began to bounce on his cock and grind her naked belly into him. His hands were under her bottom, cupping it, and as she rode he slipped his fingers into her crease, finding her anus and popping into the tight hole. Judith sighed as his finger pushed up into the hot, wet tube of her rectum and he began to use the purchase to control the pace of their sex.

With her full weight on his shoulders and cock he was beginning to flag, and sank down on to the flat lead of the roof, taking her with him. As his buttocks touched the surface he lay back but she stayed upright, letting her arms slip from his shoulders. Throwing her head back to the night sky she began to masturbate, tossing her hair and moaning as she rubbed hard at her sex. Henry's finger was still in her anus and he began to work it around as she rode him. Her movements were frantic, a wild, uncontrolled bucking that jerked his cock from side to side within her. He knew she was coming when she began to shriek and gasp and tried to get the rhythm to come himself as her vagina began to tighten on his cock. With her hair flying and her breasts bouncing in front of him she was an ideal sight to help his orgasm, but so wild were her movements that he found himself unable to get there, even as her vagina squeezed and pulsed on his cock as she came.

She slumped forward as she finished and his erection slipped from her hole, but Henry was in no mood to stop. Putting an arm around her back to hold her still, he pulled his finger from her bottom hole and took hold of his cock. As he masturbated he began to rub the head of his penis on her bottom, getting friction first against the beaten flesh, then in the slick, wet crease between the cheeks and lastly against the anus itself.

'You can put it in,' Judith sighed weakly as his knob brushed her sphincter.

Henry needed no more prompting and put his cock to her bottom hole, forcing it into the greasy opening and then once more beginning to tug at the shaft. Judith began to contract her anus on his cock as he masturbated into her bottom hole, squeezing the tip so that it felt as if it was her lips and not her anus that was pouted around his cock. The sensation was far more than he could resist. He came, feeling the sperm erupt into her rectum as his cock jerked in his hand, spurt after spurt until it had begun to ooze out. His hand caught it and began to slip in the wet, only for Judith to abruptly sit up. Henry cried out as her anus slid down the full length of his shaft, taking his cock to the hilt in her bottom with the hole well lubricated by his come.

She sank down again as he finished off inside her, his cock once more drawing from her body with a sticky sound. For a while they lay together, listening to the sounds of London around them, Henry half-concerned that the bullies might be searching the roofs and come across their hiding place. Nothing suspicious could be heard, and after a while Judith rolled off him.

'So,' he remarked, 'I imagine you might wish to borrow my coat. I assume you know a way down from here, but first, if I might trouble you for your garters.'

Saunder Cunningham was already back at the billiards hall. He was sporting a black eye and his coat was gone, but he was grinning and holding out a fist in which was clutched a bunch of garters. News of the bet had spread and the room was crowded, with a good number of Henry's friends and acquaintances present. As Henry approached, Cunningham threw his spoils out on to the table.

'Eight?' Henry remarked. 'And six in pairs, not a bad haul, I'll warrant.'

'And your own?' Cunningham demanded.

46

'Twenty,' Henry answered casually, 'and ten pairs to boot. My game, I believe.'

'Twenty?' Cunningham echoed. 'You've not a scratch on you! You must have cheated!'

'If you doubt my word ask at Mother Agie's in Dallington Alley,' Henry answered, 'but be sure to take a round dozen of your boys with you; garters are not likely to be a popular subject.'

'Some trick, no doubt,' Cunningham went on. 'No man gathers twenty so fast, not without a merry fight. Still, I pay my bets. Fifty guineas for Trethaw Wood, was it not? Will you accept my note on it and the deeds tomorrow?'

'Certainly,' Henry answered, ignoring the surprising grace with which Cunningham had given in.

Having collected his note he called for port and went to a table to toast his success and wait for Charles and Judith to return. They had stopped at Charles' town house to find Judith new clothes and soothe her injured bottom, a process that Henry suspected might take some time. Offering port to his friends and well-wishers with an even hand he settled down to enjoy what remained of the night, only to see the bulky form of Squire Robson pushing towards him with a look of concern.

'Bertie!' Henry hailed him. 'Don't look so sour. Come, take a glass with me.'

'Gladly,' Robson answered, pompously, 'though you may find your celebration somewhat premature.'

'Why so?' Henry demanded.

'I fear you have been duped most soundly,' Robson said earnestly. 'Trethaw Wood is a covert, it's true, but a small one and on a slope a goat would think twice before mounting. What's more there's an old mine that spoils a half portion of what little good cover there is.'

'I know,' Henry replied happily.

* * *

47

High on the slope of Kit Hill Todd Gurney and Peggy Wray stood looking down to the scarred and broken top of Hingston Down. Four mines were visible, each with its engine house and chimney, shaft gear and sheds along with piles of ore and slag. Beyond, a wooded slope stretched down towards the valley and the slate grey waters of the Tamar estuary.

'There's the track they take the ore wagons along,' Gurney was saying, 'down to the barges at Calstock, then to Plymouth. I've made repairs for them, a time or two, when it was called for, and smelted black stone for assay. Sevenstones' the best, and Wheal Ann. Wheal Hope's for silver and lead, while Dolcombe's near worked out.'

'And which is ours?' Peggy enquired.

'Sevenstones,' Gurney replied. 'Ned Tooze is watchman. He'd likely not notice you if you went and sat on his head. Now the man at Wheal Ann is Luke Annaferd, who was in the regiment with me. He's sharp, and while there's more ore it's not so fine, which is our concern. No, Sevenstones is our mark.'

'That's the closest,' Peggy replied, 'with the tallest chimney?'

'That's the one. Now the big buildings are the engine houses, and if you follow down from them you'll see the counting house with the watchman's hut beside. Keep clear of that and well up the hill and you can come down over the top to where the ore's stacked before the stamps. Now there'll not be many about, it being a Sunday, but stay clear of the topmost engine house: he works the pumps and there'll likely be some fellows about. When you reach the stacks choose pieces that're black right through, with a fine grain. If any do ask, you're looking for William Snell. He was put off a fortnight back and'll be half way to the Americas by now, so there's no fear of finding him. So long as you can get the ore in your pockets without being seen you should be clear. I'd come, but I'd be recognised, certain sure, so it's down to you. Do you think you can do it?'

'I'll try my best,' Peggy promised. 'After all, if it hadn't been for me, old John Truscott would still be with us and there'd be no such trouble.'

'Nonsense, girl,' Gurney answered, 'that was no fault of yours but of his alone, and perhaps of that fool Stephen, stirring the old man up with his talk of reform and what not. That was why he asked for it, was it not?'

'Yes,' Peggy admitted. 'Perhaps, in a way you are right, but you mustn't call Mister Stephen a fool. Why, he's full of clever ideas.'

'Fool, as I say,' Gurney said emphatically. 'Look at this agricultural reform business. The estate may do better, but it's left half the men of three parishes without work. Very clever idea, I'd call that. Now old John, he was happy so long as the local maids were willing, and if that meant keeping the rents low and forgetting arrears now and again, then so it was. Henry would be the same if he was squire.'

'John Truscott never showed much interest in the village girls,' Peggy answered. 'More in me, I'd say.'

'Ah,' Todd replied, 'well that's because latterly a good half of them are likely to be his daughters, and he could never be sure which half. Now you'd best get on, there's no sense in waiting.'

Peggy nodded and set off down the slope, aiming for the buildings of Sevenstones Mine. The plan seemed simple and, as Gurney said, so long as she managed to get the ore into the large pockets sewn inside her petticoats there was little chance of discovery. Nevertheless she found her stomach fluttering as she approached the mine and had to make a conscious effort to continue. The feeling of unease also affected her bladder, and by the time she drew level with the ridge of broken ground that ran along the top of the mine she was desperate to pee.

She paused, wondering if it would be possible to squat down and quickly relieve herself beneath the shelter of her skirts. Nobody was visible, yet the down was distressingly open and exposed. She knew that Gurney would be watching from the hill, while the upper windows in the buildings of Wheal Ann seemed to be staring right at her. Too embarrassed to pee on the ground and determined that she could make it if she tried, she pushed on along the ridge until she judged that she was above the ore stacks of Sevenstones Mine.

Circling wide of the chimney tops that marked where the engine houses stood, she came out directly above the stamps. The slope down was rough and exposed, sending agonising jolts through her bladder but never providing enough cover to allow her to relieve herself. By the time she made the bottom she was wriggling her toes in her need to pee, but she was among the ore stacks. She chose the ore pieces in a frenzied hurry born more of the painful, swollen feeling in her belly than the danger of being seen. The large pockets she had sewn into the inside of her petticoat worked perfectly, allowing her to conceal several large pieces of the finest grained black stone.

Only when she was fully laden did she discover that it was hard enough to walk with her burden, and that climbing back up the slope was out of the question, at least without wetting herself. She hesitated, listening, but heard no more than the rhythmic thump of the engines. The pain had become a sharp, insistent sting in her vulva along with the dull ache of her belly and she knew that she could hold no longer. Ducking down into a squat behind an ore stack she struggled to lift her petticoats, pushing the ore pockets aside among the folds of cotton until her naked cunny was poised over the ground.

With a sigh of pure bliss she let go, feeling the pee erupt from her cunny and hearing the patter as it struck the ground. Some splashed her petticoats but she went on, letting the stream run out beneath her as the awful pressure drained slowly away. For a moment nothing mattered save the delicious feeling of release as the pee squirted from her body, only for a sudden growl from behind her to bring her sharply back to earth.

Peggy spun around, caught a heel on a piece on projecting rock and went over with her petticoats flying up and her pee spraying out in a long, golden arc. The stream flew high and splashed down into her petticoats and over her midriff, even in her face and hair as she struggled to right herself. It was still coming as she pulled her body up, soaking her petticoats as she looked around frantically for the dog.

It emerged from behind an ore heap, a great shaggy black animal of no obvious breed. Terrified, Peggy could do nothing, only sit with her legs spread and her cunny on plain view as the pee trickled out to form a yellow pool in her sodden petticoats and under her bottom. The dog came on, sniffling and growling, its eyes seemingly focused on the plump mound between her thighs.

Her fear faded as it failed to attack her, but only when its nose was within inches of her cunny did she find the courage to push its head gently away. It resisted, and for a moment she felt the wet nose nuzzle her vulva, actually touching her clitoris. That was too much and she pushed it back.

'Get away with you, you filthy animal!' she hissed and to her surprise the dog responded, going back on to its haunches.

As it sat down Peggy noticed that it was male, with an ample pair of balls and a big, black furred cock sticking up with the pink tip showing. She hastily covered her cunny, concerned that it might try to mount her and not sure that she would be able to resist it. The idea made her feel both silly and dirty, although the dog stayed still, simply watching her from large, soulful eyes.

'There's a good boy,' she said softly. 'Now why don't you run along to your master?'

Even as she said it she realised that the dog's appearance might well presage that of Ned Tooze, who might be as big a fool as Gurney said, but could hardly fail to notice that something was amiss with the ore pockets making huge lumps beneath her skirts. Nor did she wish him to catch her sitting in a puddle of her own pee, so she got quickly to her feet. The dog watched as she began to struggle up the rough slope, its expression now strangely regretful but making no effort to follow or give a warning. Looking back, with the sunlight striking from its coat, she realised that its hair was brown with age and that for all its size it was fat, stiff-legged and undoubtedly elderly.

The climb back to the ridge was difficult with the ore pockets weighing her down and her pee-soaked petticoats making her uncomfortable. The wet had also soaked through into her dress, which was of blue wool and sure to spoil if she failed to wash it quickly. That was bad, but the thought of having to explain how she had wet herself to Gurney and then ride back the twenty odd miles to the Truscott estate in the Torridge valley was unendurable. From Kit Hill a gully had been visible, with a stream running down between high banks past the mine Gurney had called Dolcombe. Recalling that it was supposed to be nearly worked out and so would hopefully be quiet, she altered course, striking across the down in what she hoped was the right direction.

The stream proved ideal, running down between overgrown spoil heaps in pools and tiny waterfalls. A larger pool had formed where the ancient spoil heaps gave way to newer ones, with great banks of bramble and thorn shielding it from three directions. Peggy scrambled down with some difficulty, arriving by the pool hot and breathless, also extremely uncomfortable.

The sense of loneliness was absolute, and she began to strip with no more than a touch of nervousness.

Climbing out of her wet dress and then the petticoats provided a sense of relief close to that she had enjoyed when she had finally let go her pee. Her stockings were wet and some urine had even got into her boots, forcing her to strip down to her stays. Given that her bottom and cunny were already bare and that the stays supported her big breasts but did nothing to conceal them, she decided to shed her final garment and go nude. Being bare felt lovely, with her soft, plump flesh unrestricted by garments and the sunlight hot on her skin.

She had stripped on a patch of grass beneath the shelter of a pair of rowans, but was obliged to move out into the open to wash her clothes in the stream. As she stepped out from cover her feeling of vulnerability increased, yet there was no sign whatever of other people and as she sorted her clothes her nervousness faded until it was no more than an added excitement to the pleasure of being nude. With all her clothes in the water and the ore samples washed and spread out on the bank she climbed in herself, enjoying the cool water as soon as the initial shock of immersion had gone. The pool was fairly deep, with fine sand at the bottom, allowing her to kneel with her breasts only just above the level of the surface. Her position brought back the way she had squatted to pee and made her bottom and breasts feel prominent, drawing a giggle from her lips as she rubbed at her clothes. When each garment was clean to her satisfaction she spread it out on the grass, then climbed back into the pool to enjoy bathing properly.

With little chance of being seen she was beginning to truly enjoy the improper feeling of being naked and began to wonder if she dared touch herself beneath the water. It was entirely safe, with no chance that anyone would know how dirty she was being even if they did chance on her hiding place. The cool water had brought her nipples to erection and it was more than she could resist not to take a breast in each hand and run her fingers across them. Their size was normally awkward, each being big enough to spill over her spread fingers. Yet men adored them, and when she masturbated it was always nice to cup them and feel their weight, remembering how lovers had done the same and murmured compliments on their shape and the smoothness of their skin.

Several times old John Truscott had caught her in her room or about to bathe. She had always protested, but he had usually persuaded her to allow him to put his cock between her breasts to make him come, sometimes more. The thought brought her mind back to the funeral and she forced herself to think of happier things, all the while caressing her breasts, stomach and thighs. Her flesh felt plump and soft beneath her fingers. Fat, Eloise said, yet her mistress enjoyed her often enough when Henry was away, cuddled together in bed, hands straying over the full contours of each other's bodies. It often happened after punishments, Eloise taking as much pleasure in beating her maid as she did in Henry thrashing her own bottom. Or if it amused Eloise Peggy's face would go in the chamber pot while she was beaten, a humiliation that always left Peggy trembling and eager to satisfy her mistress.

Her hands had gone to her bottom, caressing the plump globes of heavy flesh and pulling them open to get the cool water to her anus. The cheeks felt big in her hands, wobbling mounds of female flesh parted by a deep crease with her bottom hole a tight, sensitive spot at the very heart. She touched it, feeling ruder still as her finger caressed the tight knot of flesh and she remembered how it felt to have Henry's cock pushed up her bottom. It hurt but it was worth it, and as she thought of the hot, breathless sensation and the feeling of utter wantonness that came with being buggered she realised that she had to come.

Slipping a finger into her anus she put her other hand to her cunny, finding her clitoris. She began to bounce in the water, making her breasts slap against the surface and masturbating to the rhythm of her movements. Her eyes were shut, her mouth wide and her mind fixed on the pleasure of her sex. With one finger in the hot embrace of her rectum she concentrated on the dirty, abandoned pleasure of taking a penis in the same place. She remembered Henry, tipping her up and throwing her skirts high to bare her bottom, laughing at her squeal of surprise and then laying the length of his erection between her ample buttocks. He had opened her with a spit-wet finger and then buggered her across her own bed, but the initial exposure had been no ruder than what she had shown when she slipped in the quarry, and that had been to a dog . . .

Peggy came, aghast at her own dirty thoughts even as she imagined how the dog might have taken advantage of her and quickly turning her mind back to Henry as soon as she had the control. But it was too late, her orgasm had come over the unspeakable idea of the big, black dog mounting her as she sat with her cunny on show in the pool of pee.

Blushing furiously, she got quickly to her feet, only to sink back down as she realised that there was a man among the spoil heaps further down the stream. She could not be sure he had seen her, yet it was not unlikely that he had and that he might even have realised that she was masturbating. After only an instant's hesitation she scrambled from the pool and into the shelter of the rowan trees, pulling her wet clothes after her.

Shocked at her own filthy thoughts and scared of what the man might do if he caught her nude, she pulled her damp clothes on as fast as she could, yet even in her panic did not forget to replace the precious ore in her petticoat pockets.

Three

'So,' Henry stated, 'we have Trethaw Wood and with it the mine, and as I paid well over what might fairly have been asked for the land our possession cannot be held in doubt. Should it come to court, and let us pray it never does, there'll be two score men who'll vouch I won the right to buy a pheasant covert in a fair bet. So now we must find some gentlemen to invest their money in our venture.'

'Yet she'll need to seem a proper mine,' Gurney. 'Not the blindest of fools'll pay good money for an over-grown hole.'

'Many have before now,' Henry quipped. 'But you're right, it must seem a working mine should any choose to inspect it. You may hire men as you see fit, Gurney, and build what seems right. Don't let the bills run away, but do nothing that might raise doubts. Meanwhile, Charles and I, along with you, Judith, will be in London.'

'With prices rising the way they are it should be easy to find investors,' Charles remarked.

'It won't do to seem over eager,' Henry went on, 'so rather than trying to raise money directly we'll let a rumour leak that the mine's rich. That way we can't be said to have led the pack if all goes awry, and it should raise the buyer's greed nicely. Now that's your part, Judith; you can act giddy and thoughtless, I've no doubt.'

Judith nodded.

'Choose rich men, of course,' Henry went on, 'but not those who've made their pile by their brains, nor any who might know mines, nor engineers and such.'

'I shall go carefully,' Judith assured him.

'You don't need too many,' Charles put in, 'after all, once the rumour's out it'll spread fast enough.'

'True,' Henry answered him, 'the knack is to get it to the right people.'

'And why might I not do the same?' Eloise spoke up.

'You?' Henry demanded. 'Well, damn it girl, you're my wife for one and heavy with our child for another. A fine condition to be whoring all over town, I think, not to say that I don't care to be taken for a cuckold.'

'It's no work for a lady, begging you pardon, Miss Judith,' Gurney put in, 'not a married one, any roads.'

'I'm bored,' Eloise answered with a sulky pout, 'and besides, who better to draw in the French emigrants. They have all lost land, but many have brought out fine fortunes and will be looking to make the best of them.'

'There is that,' Charles spoke up, 'why, only the last time I was at Le Roy's some seigneur or other was seeking to buy stock.'

'Now look here . . .' Henry began, only to be interrupted by Eloise.

'I will not be dissuaded,' she said firmly. 'I stand to gain, or lose, as we all do, and I'll not have it said that I sat by while others took the risks . . . and, and, I'm bored with sitting here and doing nothing. I'm bored with being pampered and told I must not ride and I must not do this, and I must not do that, and . . .'

Her voice had risen in pitch and her face was beginning to turn red, sure signs that her temper was flaring. Henry hesitated, knowing that short of turning her across his knee and spanking the temper out of her he had little choice but to allow her to get her way. Normally she would have been head down across his legs with her bare bottom dancing to his slaps for all to see, but he hesitated, concerned for the effect a sound spanking might have on her condition.

'Besides,' she was saying, 'it is wrong of you to think I would stray. How can you say such a thing indeed? No, I shall flirt, no more, and they will run to give you money, just see.'

'Oh, very well,' Henry snapped, 'you may come to London, but heaven help me, if you so much as let your bubbies out I'll tan your behind in the middle of St James, baby or no baby!'

Standing on the ridge that overlooked Trethaw Wood, Henry was unable to suppress a smile. Directly below him the steep slope of the wood was scarred by the remnants of what had once been the Wheal Purity mine and now was going to be again. An area of scrub had already been cleared and work had begun on the old engine house, restoring it to working condition.

In the mine Gurney was salting the adit with ore taken from Sevenstones Mine while Henry kept an eye out for unwelcome visitors. His thoughts were pleasant, remembering the way he had gained the land while leaving Saunder Cunningham with the impression that it was he, Henry, who had come off worst. Since then things had gone well, with Peggy securing the ore samples they needed without incident and everybody agreeing that it should be easy to promote the mine in London. Wheal Purity had already been registered as a company, with himself as the majority shareholder and lesser stakes going to Charles and Judith. The sole annoyance was Eloise's insistence on coming to London. He had little faith in her declaration of fidelity, having experience of the strength of her lust. Not that it was possible for her to have a child fathered by somebody else, as she was already pregnant, yet the thought of her infidelities becoming known and of his set branding him a cuckold was irritating. His mind had begun to dwell on the pros and cons of carrying out his threat and spanking her in public when a movement caught his eye among the trees.

His initial wariness faded as he saw that it was a horse, a small, grey mare with a woman riding. She was side-saddle, with the full skirts of a russet-coloured riding dress on the side towards him. As she approached he recognised the trim figure and glossy brown hair of May Cunningham, Saunder's wife. His interest quickened, as she had flirted with him more than once although he had never had the opportunity to do more than give her bottom a brief squeeze. At the time she had responded with a sidelong look and a gesture of her fan, while the shape and texture of her buttock had been promising.

He stood straight as she approached, greeting her with a friendly wave as soon as it became apparent that she was making in his direction. An expanse of low scrub and larger trees separated them and he admired her figure as she picked her way across it. The tension of her bodice was fine, hinting at fair-sized breasts if nothing to compare with the magnificence of Eloise's bosom. Her waist was slender and the curve of her hips beneath her full skirt suggested a compact if not lavish figure.

'Mrs Cunningham!' he hailed her as she drew near. 'A fine day for a ride.'

'Quite so, Mr Truscott,' she replied. 'I understand that you are to be our new neighbour?'

'In a manner of speaking,' Henry answered. 'Saunder was kind enough to sell me Trethaw Wood to provide us with a little shooting.'

'And these buildings? Shelter for the parties?' she asked as she dismounted.

'Mine buildings, but nothing of interest. Tell me, with Saunder in London so often you must be alone a great deal of the time.'

'You must call, of course,' she said, colouring slightly at his direct approach. 'Saunder's sisters live with us, as you may know, so we are quite a little party even while he is away. Have you met them? Miss Alice and Miss Caroline.'

'I haven't had the pleasure,' Henry answered, wondering if the sisters were as toothsome as the wife.

'Caroline only came out last season,' May Cunningham continued, 'and Alice is but a year older. You must have met them at a ball, surely?'

'I was in France much of the time,' Henry admitted.

'I have heard of your adventure, it is quite the talk. How exciting it must have been. You have a young wife, I believe?'

'Eloise, daughter of the Comte Saonnois,' Henry answered.

May paused, looking down over the wood and out across the valley, then glancing back the way she had come as if concerned that someone might be following.

'Is Saunder with you?' Henry asked.

'Somewhere,' she answered. 'He had heard there is a new fox's earth in Gibbet Wood and is eager to inspect it. It is a lively gallop from here.'

'Indeed,' Henry answered, deciding to take her words as an invitation and reaching out to tweak open one button of her bodice.

'Mr Truscott!' she exclaimed, but it was half-hearted. Henry undid a second button.

'Really, we shall be seen!' she protested.

'Then come down here,' he answered, taking her arm. 'We shall be quite secure.'

She responded to the pressure of his hand, looking around nervously as she was drawn gently down on to the grass. Seated beside her he leaned over and kissed her, all the while busy with her dress. At first she resisted but as his hand slid inside her bodice to cup the roundness of one breast she opened her mouth under

60

his. He caught her nipple between two fingers and squeezed it gently, bringing the bud to erection. Their tongues met and he pressed her slowly down to the grass, now certain of success. She made no more than a token show of reluctance, allowing him to pull her bodice open and free her breasts, then to haul her skirts and petticoats high and slip a hand down between her thighs. As he began to knead her cunny she gave in, pulling her knees up and open to let him get his hand to the hole of her vagina. His fingers slipped inside, finding her wet and open.

He began to masturbate her, allowing her pleasure to rise without pushing the issue until her hand sought his crotch and began to work on the fastenings of his breeches' flap. The buttons gave easily and his cock was soon out, standing proud in her hand as she stroked him to full erection. Henry lifted his head for one final glance at the surrounding woods and then mounted May, his cock slipping inside her easily. He began to fuck her, pushing urgently as she started to moan and then grunt in response.

With her thighs spread beneath him and his cock squeezed into her surprisingly tight vagina he quickly found himself approaching orgasm and slowed to avoid coming too quickly and so spoiling the treat. Going up on to his hands, he began to fuck her with long, slow strokes, his cock penetrating the mouth of her vagina over and over with each push. Her grunts stopped, to be replaced by a low purring noise as she lifted her hands to her breasts and began to massage them. Her nipples were engorged with blood and a pale red, each poking up from between her fingers. Henry admired the sight as he rode her and wondered what she would make of being turned over and entered from the rear. Yet she seemed to be enjoying her breasts and had cocked her legs up and apart as far as they would go, allowing his balls to slap against the tuck of her bottom each time he pushed his cock into her.

Deciding to postpone the joys of her bottom, he pulled his cock from her vagina, intent on ensuring that this was not their only time together. May gave a disappointed sigh as his erection left her hole but then gasped as he put the head of his cock to her clitoris and began to rub it in the wet flesh. Henry chuckled as she began to push her pubic mound up to meet his cock. Her kneading had become harder and she had begun to dig her nails into the soft flesh of her breasts, leaving short red scratches across them. As her mouth came open in a scream of pleasure he stopped it with his own, continuing to rub as they kissed. He felt her body buck beneath his and her hips rise to his cock, wriggling beneath him to get more friction to her clitoris. Henry obliged, rubbing harder as her thighs clamped tight around his body.

May's back arched and every muscle in her body locked around his as she came, writhing and squirming beneath him as he rubbed his penis hard across her clitoris. When it became too much she tried to pull away but he kept on, mercilessly grinding his flesh against hers while she thrashed beneath him. Only when he felt himself coming did he stop, nudging his cock down and filling her vagina just as the sperm erupted from the tip. He let it happen, deep inside her as her contractions milked the come from his cock.

Allowing his body to collapse on to hers he felt her arms come around him. They kissed and then broke apart, May sighing and babbling her thanks.

'Don't mention it,' Henry answered, 'the pleasure was mine, I assure you.'

'No,' she gasped, 'that was, was, wonderful, like nothing Saunder has ever done . . .'

'Don't tell me he's never brought you off before?' Henry demanded, astonished by the implications of what she was saying.

May answered with a long sigh and Henry realised that not only had she probably never come before but

62

that she might not even have understood what had happened. Smiling to himself he sat up, wiped his cock on a convenient corner of her petticoats and looked around. As before the woods were quiet but a wood-pigeon was rising some way to the north.

'Best get decent,' he remarked. 'It wouldn't do to have Saunder come upon us like this.'

May responded by pulling herself up and starting to rearrange her clothes. Henry stood, looking down towards the mine to find Todd Gurney working on the stones of the engine house. Putting a finger to his lips, Henry indicated the need for silence as the big man looked up. Todd responded with a nod and went back to his work. As Henry helped May to her feet she saw Gurney and blushed, realising that they had not been as alone as she had imagined.

'Don't mind Todd Gurney,' Henry assured her. 'The safer man's not yet born. Now, you were saying I should call.'

'Whenever you wish, Mr Truscott,' she answered, once more cool and poised but with a smile that showed exactly what she meant.

'Excellent,' he answered and reached out with the intention of giving her breasts a parting fondle only to stop abruptly at the sound of a voice calling her name.

'It's Saunder!' she exclaimed.

'No matter,' Henry answered, glancing quickly around and then squeezing both her breasts an instant before a large bay gelding appeared across the scrub with Saunder Cunningham on its back. May Cunningham pulled quickly back and turned to wave to her husband, who was approaching at a fast trot.

'Afternoon, Saunder,' Henry called. 'Your lovely wife tells me you've been out cubbing. I see you're dressed for it.'

'Inspecting an earth, as it happens,' Cunningham replied with no great warmth and then glanced down at his obviously expensive clothes with a touch of annoyance.

'I was just looking over my new covert,' Henry went on, 'and seeing to one or two improvements.'

'What's this here?' Cunningham demanded, looking down at the mine works.

'It's a mine,' Henry answered, unable to resist the opportunity for sarcasm.

'That I can see,' Cunningham answered. 'What are you about?'

'We plan to drain it,' Henry replied.

'Whatever for? It's no more than a scratch, and heaven knows how old. Why, it's been there all my lifetime. You don't think there's worth in it, do you?'

'I hired a mining fellow to see if it might be made safe,' Henry answered casually. 'He came up to see the work and says there are scraps of ore as rich as any he's seen.'

'Nonsense, why wasn't it worked out then?'

'Blessed if I know, after all it's on your family land, or rather, it was on your family land.'

Cunningham bridled, passing Henry a black look and then making a stiff bow and extending his arm to his wife. May took it and with a final glance at Henry from beneath half-lowered eyelids followed her husband.

As the Cunninghams departed Henry noted with amusement that not only did May Cunningham have several pieces of grass in her hair but that there was a distinct green colour on those parts of her dress that had been pressed to the ground. He watched him help her mount up and responded to Cunningham's sudden, questioning look with the blandest of smiles.

Judith sipped her drink and allowed her gaze to wander over the faces below as Charles pointed out possible investors. They sat together in Charles' phaeton, a high perch model that allowed them to watch both the crowds and the races. Newmarket was busy, with crowds boosted by the recent sale of the Prince's stud and the scandal of the previous autumn.[2] Charles had judged it the ideal place to find potential investors for Wheal Purity, in addition to enjoying several days' sport.

'Bertie Robson you know,' he was saying, 'and heaven knows he's rich enough. You probably wouldn't even end up on your back.'

For a brief moment Judith considered the portly figure of Robson and then shook her head, remembering his earnest, puffing efforts to seduce her on a previous occasion.

'What of Lord Farrow?' she suggested, nodding towards a distant figure in a coat of fine grey cloth. 'He is notoriously free with his money.'

'Careless would be a better word,' Charles answered. 'He is already heavily in debt. Money from him would not be safe. I advise against his companion also, he is Augustus Barclay, who is certainly rich but has a reputation for breaking young women. He is said to be barred from more than half the bawdy houses in London and the counties.'

'I have met him,' Judith said, 'when I was first at Mother Agie's. He is cruel and vicious, but to take his money would be a joy. Do I dare? I don't know, certainly not until my poor bottom is healed.'

'Sir John Church might serve,' Charles went on. 'He is rash, and takes drink like Hellgate himself.[3] I do not see him, but he holds an establishment and plans a party tonight, so it is said. Perhaps we may secure an invitation.'

'Let us seek him out then,' Judith answered.

'It should be easy,' Charles assured her. 'Thomas Grattan, who won the last race on Blue Boy, is his jockey and doubtless will seek his master out.'

Charles' logic proved accurate and before long they had found Sir John Church. He was in high spirits, his stable already having collected two victories, and on being introduced to Judith quickly issued an invitation to the party, pausing only to check with Charles that she was not overly respectable.

Having chosen a mark they spent the rest of the day enjoying the races and then set off for Sir John Church's turf establishment. This proved to be a tangle of low, yellow stone structures in the shelter of a wood and it was quickly apparent why respectable ladies had not been welcome at the planned entertainment. The majority of the company were patrons of the local races, with several jockeys and a scattering of others. Judith and Charles arrived to the sound of encouragement and calls for odds, which surprised them until they managed to push through the crowd and discovered four girls crawling across the floor of the main hall, each with a jockey on her back. The riders were wielding their whips with vigour, lashing them down on the out-thrust posteriors of their mounts and calling for more speed, while the girls squealed and giggled their way down the course. A tall, dark-haired girl won and the volume of noise immediately doubled with the sound of applause, disappointment and demands for a new race.

'Will you venture on it?' Charles asked Judith. 'It would serve well to draw attention, especially if you should win.'

'I doubt I could win,' Judith answered. 'The dark girl looks strong and has some five inches of height on me.'

'You'll race though?'

'Certainly I shall, but place no money on me!'

'Here's a fine filly for the next run!' Charles called out, pushing Judith forward. 'Who'll ride her?'

His voice was largely drowned out by the general noise, but Thomas Grattan was nearby. Judith smiled at him and he responded immediately, striding over to take her by the hand.

'Miss Cates, Mr Grattan,' Charles said formally.

66

Judith gave a curtsy, to which the jockey replied with an equally precise bow.

'Would you do me the honour, Miss Cates?' he asked, as if suggesting that they be partners in a dance.

'It would my pleasure, Mr Grattan,' Judith replied.

Their brief pastiche had drawn amused looks from those nearby and, as the jockey led her out into the space cleared for racing, Judith heard several voices offering money on her or demanding to know at what odds she stood. For a moment she imagined she recognised one as that of Augustus Barclay, but on turning she could not see him. She was still trying to find him among the crowd when the call came for the girls to get down on all fours and she put the thought aside as she prepared for the race.

Sir John Church called out for the race to start and she began to crawl, moving as fast as possible with her skirts catching at her knees and the weight of the jockey across her back. It was harder than she expected, and despite her skirts and petticoats each smack of the whip stung her tender bottom, making her squeal and falter. She had quickly lost ground on the leaders, making Tom Grattan apply the whip with greater vigour and thus make the problem worse. By the time the girl in front had reached the wall Judith and her rider were no more than two-thirds the way across the room, leading to a good deal of catcalling and jokes at Grattan's expense.

He took it well, kissing Judith and treating himself to a squeeze of her breasts before accepting a tankard of ale from his sponsor. Judith lingered, hoping for an introduction to Church. Yet there was a press of bodies around him and she decided to postpone her attempt until a quieter moment. Her bottom was smarting as well, distracting her, and so she determined to find something with which to soothe her cheeks. Making her way upstairs she discovered a room with a hip bath and

67

a jug of water laid out; there was also a large gilded mirror that occupied the most part of one wall.

With her bottom turned to the mirror Judith lifted her dress, displaying her cheeks with the cane bruises still evident nearly two weeks after her thrashing. A few new red marks showed among the black, yellow and blue of the old ones, evidence of Grattan's efforts to make her crawl faster. She winced at the sight, but could not resist reaching back and stroking her discoloured skin, thinking of the pain and indignity of the beating and of how she'd been displayed to the laughing audience while she was punished. The race had also been arousing, and as she contemplated her abused buttocks she wondered if she had time to masturbate before returning to the party. It was certainly tempting, and the sorry state her bottom had been beaten into would provide the perfect view while she did it, yet she hesitated, listening for sounds.

For a moment it seemed that she was safe and her hand began to sneak down over her bottom, intent on burrowing down between the cheeks to reach her clitoris from the rear. Twice she stroked the length of her crease, deliberately teasing herself, only to stop abruptly at the sound of footfalls in the corridor. She dropped her dress even as the door swung open, blushed and then gasped as she saw that it was Augustus Barclay.

He moved into the room, glancing at her still ruffled dress with amusement. Every aspect of him spoke of arrogance: his dress, his bearing, and most of all his speech, which managed to convey both condescension and spite. Judith considered a dash for the door, but he was too close.

'Why, if it isn't little Judy Cates,' he drawled. 'Little Tom hued your arse, has he?'

'Sir, I . . .' Judith began, hastily smoothing down her skirts.

'You needn't give yourself airs,' he went on. 'Remember I know what you are. Why, I've seen you often enough with your arse in the air and a candle in each hole.'

Judith blushed and said nothing, knowing that he had been in audiences watching her punished more than once.

'Indeed I had your virginity, didn't I?' he continued. 'Ten guineas, wasn't it, to have you in the box for the night and then to break your purse in the morning?'

'It was false,' Judith said determinedly. 'A trick.'

'Gut and pig's blood?'[4] Barclay demanded, suddenly angry only to regain his poise as quickly as it had gone.

Judith declined to answer his question.

'That fop Finch keeps you now, don't he?' he said. 'A fine billet for a slut, and better than you deserve.'

'Mr Finch is a most kind gentleman and provides very well for me, thank you, sir,' Judith answered.

'He does, does he,' Barclay answered. 'Spoils you I dare say, plenty of comfort and not too much cock, just how you little trollops like it. You'd not be so pampered if you were mine, you may be sure.'

'Of that I have no doubt,' she replied and darted for the door.

He had been edging round her, a motion that had been making her as uneasy as his remarks. As she jumped forward he lunged at her but missed and an instant later she was in the corridor and running for the stairs. He failed to give chase but emerged from the room behind her as she reached the stair head. She caught his sneer and hurried on down the stairs, lifting her skirts to prevent herself from tripping.

The party was as merry as ever, but she could not see Charles and wondered if he had gone to look for her. The only other face she knew at all well was that of Squire Robson, who was egging on his choice in the current girl race. It had changed, and the girls were now in petticoats with their bare breasts swinging beneath their chests as they moved. Judith spared a moment for the sight and then began to push her way towards Robson.

The race finished amid roars of delight and calls for the girls to strip completely. By the time Judith arrived at Robson's side they had been persuaded and she watched as four young women disrobed. Some were clearly enjoying the attention, others were shy or at least feigning shyness, but all went through with it, ending entirely nude and then going down on all fours to be mounted by the jockeys. Robson had been watching the girls strip in fascination but responded to Judith as she laid a hand on his shoulder.

'Have you seen Charles?' she demanded, raising her voice above the din of the room.

'Charles?' Robson replied. 'Why yes, he is here.'

Feeling suddenly foolish, Judith realised that Charles had merely been hidden from view by larger men. With a deep sense of relief she joined him, taking his arm and then craning her neck to watch the finish of the race. Their position provided a prime view, with the girls' bare bottoms wobbling from side to side as they crawled and bouncing from the smacks of the riding whips. All four cunnies also showed, the lips peeping out from between the girls' thighs in a thoroughly rude display that made Judith giggle as she thought of how she herself would look in the same pose.

'Fine!' Charles declared as the tall girl once more took the line. 'Will you race again, my dear?'

'And show the crowd my bruises?' Judith laughed. 'They will think you beat me, Charles.'

'I do,' he answered. 'I suspect you would find another lover if I did not!'

'There is beating and beating,' she answered and kissed him. 'No, I'll not race, especially as the tall girl is sure to win. If you care for a ride of a different sort we might find a quiet room.'

Charles smiled and squeezed her hand. She caught an envious look from Robson as they backed away through the crowd and giggled, now feeling safe and even mischievous. By the time they had made their way to the staircase she was wondering if it might not be possible to find a couple of good-sized candles for her vagina and anus. Aroused by the sight of wiggling female bottoms and bare cunnies she wanted her own sex shown off the same way, then made good use of.

Pulling Charles by the hand, she began to mount the stairs, only for his man Griggs to call out from below. Charles responded and Judith felt a flush of annoyance, then one of sheer mischief as she wondered if the two men might not be persuaded to share her.

'Begging you pardon, sir,' Griggs said as he came up beside them, 'but there's trouble out in the yard. Some fellow says Jinny is his horse and won't take no for an answer. One of Sir John's grooms is holding on for now, but I thought you'd better know.'

'Damn!' Charles swore. 'Look, I . . . Oh, hell, look, Judith, my dear, I had better deal with this. I shan't be a moment.'

Judith followed the two men as they made for the rear of the house. She felt a sense of irritation but also of unease, and determined to stay close to Charles. Yet as she reached the foot of the stair a man took a familiar squeeze of her bottom and she turned to remonstrate. Charles and Griggs had disappeared into the servants quarters by the time she managed to break free of the crowd. She pushed after them, trying to work out which corridor would lead in the direction of the stables as she entered the back house. Her sense of unease grew as she hurried on, then turned abruptly to fright as a man stepped out of the shadows in front of her.

A hand clamped over her mouth from behind, stifling her scream and forcing some foul-tasting rag into her mouth. She kicked out, catching something and drawing a curse, then a bag was being pulled down over her head and she was in blackness with two men holding her writhing body.

Despite her struggles she was dragged outside. Strong hands lifted her and dropped her on to a hard surface that smelled faintly of rotting cabbage. A horse's snicker made her realise that she was in a cart. She heard the men climb in behind her and one settled his weight on her back, making it impossible to move. Helpless, she lay inert as the cart jerked into motion.

The journey was brief, but by the time the cart stopped she had lost all sense of direction and had no idea how far she was from the house. She was dragged from the cart and dumped on the ground, her dress ripped off her body and her petticoats pulled down the length of her legs as she kicked and writhed to try to prevent herself being stripped. It did no good and she was soon nude but for boots and stockings, which they left on as she was dragged by the arms over first damp earth and then a hard, wooden floor.

She was dropped with a bump and she heard voices telling the men to leave. Then the bag was wrenched from her head, leaving her blinking in the light for a moment before her vision cleared. She was sprawled on a bed of dirty straw in a large barn, next to naked and with Augustus Barclay looming over her. In his hand he held a whip: not the light, pig-skin type she was used to being beaten with but a full-length bull whip of braided hide. He was smiling, a grin both malicious and lecherous. Judith pushed herself back with her heels, bumping against stacked bales behind her. More stood to each side, leaving her no escape.

'You played a trick on me, you and that fat bitch Agie,' he snarled. 'So now I intend to take my full ten guineas' worth of pleasure from you, and a measure more perhaps to teach you sluts that I'm no mark.'

'No, please!' Judith stammered as he lifted the whip. 'I carry information worth ten times the sum, a hundred times!'

'I doubt it,' he answered, 'but tell me anyway and maybe I won't give you to my men when I've finished myself.'

'Charles has a mine,' she said, 'in Cornwall, along with Henry Truscott. They need to sell stock, to have it drained or some such thing. They plan to offer it only among friends, but the ore is rich, the richest. Any man who puts money up will make it back a hundredfold!'

'Interesting,' he answered, 'and coming from a frightened slut, probably true. Useless though, as they'll hardly sell to me when you come crawling back. If you do, that is.'

A tremor of fear went through Judith at his words and she felt her body start to shake. He laughed at the sight, then spoke again.

'Don't take fright so. I'll let you live, though it may be as a dog in the kennels on my Galway estate. Now, will you turn your arse up or must I whip your fat dugs first?'

'Charles will call you out,' Judith asserted.

'Over a whipped whore? Hardly, and besides, he hasn't the courage.'

'Henry Truscott will, be sure of it.'

Barclay paused and as he did so Judith hurled herself forward, her head catching him in the crotch with her full weight behind her. He went down with her on top of him but she rolled to the side, jumping free and dashing for the barn door. It was open and the cart stood beyond with the horse still in the traces and her dress in a puddle of dirt by one wheel. The men stood to one side and turned as she burst out into the dim light of a lantern that stood on the tail of the cart. Beyond was blackness and Barclay's angry bellow sounded from behind her as both men came forward.

Judith grabbed for the lantern, caught the handle and hurled it blindly. It flew far wide of the two men, high in the air to strike the ground and burst in a gout of fire directly in front of Barclay as he hobbled to the barn door. For an instant his horrified face was outlined in a red glare and then he had thrown himself backwards with his coat ablaze. The men rushed towards him and Judith dashed for the black mouth of the lane.

At first she ran blindly with her hands before her face, only to have her vision clear as the dancing lights in her eyes faded. The hedges on either side of the lane became visible as black masses against the stars, then the puddles and mud in the lane itself, reflecting dull silver and grey in the moonlight. She slowed, listening for pursuit. A glance behind her showed only darkness and she heard Barclay's voice calling angrily for the other lantern.

Feeling frightened and alone, she looked around, wondering whether to hide until the morning or to attempt to find safety. The night was warm but damp and she found herself shivering, making her decide to go on, naked or not. She kept her ears strained for sounds of pursuit as she walked hurriedly away, expecting to see light moving behind her and hear the horses' hooves. It happened as she came to a place where the lane cut through a high bank. She recognised it as the same man-made ridge through which the race course cut. Scrambling to the top she ran, glancing back again and again at the lantern light moving up the lane. It vanished into the cut, then appeared at the far side, for a moment clear enough for her to make out all three men within.

Judith stopped, crouched low as the light receded and finally vanished. When she at last stood to take her bearings she found herself looking out above the gentle Cambridgeshire countryside with moonlit fields and wood stretching away on every side. The sense of peace was so profound that the terror of only minutes previously began to fade, and as she caught the distant sound of music and laughter on the breeze she managed a smile.

A brisk walk brought her to Sir John Church's establishment, where she sank into a crouch and ran in among the ranked carriages and coaches, dashing from one to another until she reached Charles' phaeton. Crawling in beneath the oilskin she curled herself into a ball and hugged her knees, her fear blending with triumph as she remembered Barclay's face as the lantern had burst at his feet. She laughed, aware that there was a slightly demented quality to the sound yet unable to restrain herself.

Eloise turned her head to the side, admiring her profile and seeking for the slightest imperfection in her appearance. There were none. From the elaborate rolls and ringlets of her high-piled, red-gold hair, through her skilfully powdered face with the single, coquettish beauty spot, to her magnificent dress of gold and green brocade, she was perfect. Even the full swell of her belly looked in place, while her heavy breasts were displayed to advantage without being blatant. The creation had taken Peggy the best part of three hours and the maid now sat on Eloise's bed in the Truscotts' town house in Petty France, exhausted and dishevelled yet proud of her achievement.

'Is my lady pleased?' Peggy asked as Eloise turned her head once more to admire herself in three-quarter face.

'You have excelled yourself,' Eloise answered. 'I cannot fail to attract attention. Now, fetch the chamber-pot.'

'But my lady . . .' Peggy faltered.

'Not a word,' Eloise interrupted. 'You are not being punished for any fault, but simply to remind you of your place and so forestall any flights of fancy or hubris you might undertake. Now, the chamberpot, and hand me my hairbrush.'

'Yes, my lady,' Peggy responded miserably.

'Do not be so miserable,' Eloise chided. 'You know I shall allow your pleasure, and tonight, if Henry is drunk, you may come into my bed.'

'Yes, my lady,' Peggy answered and kneeled to drag the chamberpot from beneath the bed.

Eloise took two delicate steps, the large china vessel vanishing beneath her ample skirts. With some difficulty she squatted down, settling her bottom on to the pot. Peggy reached beneath her mistress's skirts, adjusting the petticoats to prevent them from becoming soiled. Eloise waited patiently, enjoying the sensation of holding back simply because she knew that she could let go when she wished. When Peggy stepped back Eloise relaxed her belly and allowed her pee to gush forth, sighing as it splashed and gurgled into the chamberpot.

The look of alarm on Peggy's face increased as the pee continued to come, the noise of liquid on china changing as the pot filled. Eloise giggled at her maid's discomfort and tensed the muscles of her bottom and belly, ensuring that every last drop was out. Standing, she stepped back, revealing the chamberpot nearly half full of pale gold liquid. Peggy crawled forward, not needing to be told what to do.

The plump blonde pulled up her skirt and petticoats, revealing her broad white bottom, naked and meaty with the golden puff of her pubic hair stuck out between the thighs. Peggy's face was over the chamberpot, one pale ringlet already dangling into the pee, her pretty face screwed up with eyes and mouth tight shut. Leaning forward, she put her face in the pot. Eloise clapped her hands in delight as the maid immersed her face in the urine, then stepped to the dressing table on which her heavy silver hairbrush lay.

Peggy's bottom was trembling, both plump cheeks quivering in anticipation of the coming beating. To Eloise the view was delightful, a pretty maid with her naked bottom lifted for punishment and her face in her mistress's pee. It was amusing and equally arousing, with the full lips of Peggy's sex on show and even the tight pink dimple of her anus, deep down between the meaty cheeks. Eloise paused, waiting until Peggy was forced to lift her face and take a gasp of air. At that instant she reached down and gave the maid a firm shove between the shoulder blades, pushing Peggy's face back into the pee. A spluttering noise signalled that the maid's mouth had still been open and Eloise laughed as she brought the hairbrush down hard across Peggy's bottom.

The big white cheeks jumped and wobbled and Peggy cried out, only for the squeal to turn into a peculiar bubbling noise as Eloise once more thrust the maid's face into the chamberpot and under the surface of the pee. Holding Peggy's head down with one hand, Eloise belaboured the fat white buttocks with the hairbrush, laughing all the while to see the frantic kicking of Peggy's feet and the way the maid's hands clutched at the carpet. Peggy's bottom was a deep pink by the time she gave in to the arousal of her situation. The first sign was when she suddenly tugged down the front of her bodice to let her huge breasts swing free, then she had reached back to find her sex and started to rub as Eloise increased the force of the spanking.

'Drink, my little one, and come as you swallow your lady's pee!' Eloise crowed. 'Is that not fitting? Is that not suitable, that you should take your pleasure in the taste of my piddle!'

A slurping noise signalled that Peggy had begun to drink and swallow. Eloise let go of the maid's neck and stepped back, watching the fingers work in the wet flesh of Peggy's sex. Both big cheeks were red with spanking and Peggy's vagina and anus had begun to pulse, tightening and then slackening over and over. Eloise continued to spank, aiming for the fattest part of her maid's cheeks as Peggy lapped greedily at the pee. The maid was coming, squirming her bottom about and lifting it to the hairbrush, drawing new cries of delight from Eloise. As Peggy's orgasm ran through her Eloise began to apply the brush with all her force. Peggy gasped and for a moment was choking on her mouthful of pee, drawing a long peel of laughter from Eloise. White juice was running from the maid's vagina, down over her busy fingers and on to her inner thighs. With a delighted squeal Eloise turned the hairbrush in her hand and sank the full length of the handle into Peggy's sex, then began to pump it in and out as the maid burbled and gasped her way through orgasm.

As it finished Peggy's thighs slid apart and her face lifted slowly from the pot, dripping pee from nose and mouth and with her blonde curls and the mop cap that constrained her hair both sodden.

'Oh, you are a mess,' Eloise laughed, 'and clumsy too. Why, you have splashed my gown, and my hair is quite out of order. Now clean up quickly, you disgusting girl. I shall need adjustments made. Really, you do get carried away with yourself, you should learn to accept punishment with more grace and less self-display.'

'Yes, my lady,' Peggy managed faintly.

Henry glanced at the clock, finding it no more than five minutes advanced on the last time he had looked. He had come to expect Eloise to take time over getting ready, yet it was close to four hours since she and Peggy had gone upstairs and he was beginning to lose patience. He had also had to endure his brother's conversation, although for once this had not consisted entirely of moralising and reprimands.

'I am surprised by your industry, I must confess,' Stephen was saying. 'Yet I am also impressed with the new improvements of the steam engineers; mining will doubtless become a great industry,[5] while our dear country's advances are sure to mean a high demand for copper.'

'Tin,' Henry corrected him, wondering if Stephen ever actually listened to what other people told him at all.

78

'Tin, of course,' Stephen went on. 'What of investment? Do you have sufficient capital?'

'The money from Eloise suffices for the present,' Henry answered quickly. 'We may need to raise capital at a later stage.'

'Possibly I might consider risking some of the family money,' Stephen said cautiously, 'once your assays are in, of course.'

'No, no, dear brother, I won't hear of it,' Henry said urgently. 'Ah, but here is Eloise. Come, my dear, the carriage is waiting; indeed, it has been this last hour.'

'Do not be petty,' Eloise chided gently, 'rather remark on me. Besides, it does not do to arrive too early.'

'Nor when the hostess wishes to retire to bed,' Henry replied. 'You look magnificent, so I shall say no more.'

She took his arm as he offered it and together they left the house. On announcing their arrival in London it had not been necessary to seek out invitations. Prior to the revolution Eloise had been the toast of the French nobility, both from her beauty and from a number of indiscretions. Paste boards had begun to arrive on their mat within hours of settling in and they had selected a ball given by the Comte and Comtesse de Breuil as the most suitable. It promised to attract the majority of those French nobility currently in England, particularly those who had managed to come away with a respectable amount of their wealth.

The house was one of the grandest of those in the Grosvenor estate, suggesting to Henry a wonderfully casual attitude to expense. Wealth was also evident in the company, with several fine carriages drawn up before the house and no shortage of servants. Eloise was welcomed with a rapture that would normally have caused him jealousy, while he and Stephen were greeted with the minimum of politeness that protocol demanded. He was aware that his marriage to Eloise shocked and angered the French aristocracy, yet was certain that the reaction was born more of jealousy than genuine disapproval.

The cold looks and formal remarks only served to amuse him, while the prominent swell of Eloise's belly said more than any amount of words. Meanwhile a significant number of the ladies in the company were anything but aloof, as if fascinated to know what might have driven one of their number to marry an Englishman. Eloise was quickly swept away in a crowd of admirers eager to gain a place on her dance card. She accepted all with equal amicability, maintaining the same bright cheerfulness that she had shown since the beginning of the evening. As she was drawn beyond Henry's earshot he caught her voice laughingly declining an offer to dance on account of her condition, her tone carrying the perfect blend of the coy and the flirtatious.

He shook his head and rescued a flute of champagne from a passing servant, then began to cast his eye around for a way to amuse himself. So bright had been Eloise's mood that in the absence of Stephen he would have attempted to have her in the carriage, perhaps seated on his lap with her skirts spread out and her bottom bouncing on him to move his cock inside her. It had been impractical and it now looked like being some hours before he would have another opportunity.

As glass followed glass it quickly became apparent that the problem was not so much gaining the attention of a suitably attractive female as separating one out from among her fellows. It seemed to particularly amuse them to flirt with him, possibly because of the annoyance it caused the men, yet each attempt he made to concentrate his charm on one or another met with failure.

By midnight he was drunk, lustful and extremely frustrated, in conversation with three young women any one of whom he would happily have enjoyed yet who could hardly be expected to perform in tandem. Eloise was on the far side of the room, deep in conversation with the Vicomtesse de Blagny, a cousin of hers who had been present at their wedding. For a moment he watched, admiring the Vicomtesse's soft black curls and the way they contrasted with his wife's glorious red-gold ones. Eloise seemed more intent on her friend than the various men around them, and Henry found his trust in her increasing.

A remark from one of his companions drew his attention away from his wife and when he looked again she was dancing with the elderly Marquis d'Aignan. He was a notorious roué and long admirer of Eloise, yet also old, gaunt and far from handsome, so Henry felt little concern and turned back to his conversation. Some minutes later he looked again, only to find Eloise ascending the staircase alone and the Marquis nowhere to be seen. Suddenly concerned, he excused himself and began to make his way across the room, keeping Eloise in view as she reached the landing and started up the next flight of stairs. Certain that all facilities for the guests' personal needs would have been placed conveniently on the first floor, he became worried that she might have accepted an assignation. Increasing his pace he made for the stair, then slowed, determined that if he was to catch her it would be in a sufficiently compromising position to justify striking the man involved and spanking her.

Catching up with her on the stairs would have been easy but he held back, allowing her to ascend to the third floor. The servants' rooms occupied the fourth and so he waited in the shadows until he heard the soft click of a door closing, counted slowly to one hundred and then followed. The first room he tried proved empty, as did the second, and with a rising sense of panic he thrust open the third door, only to stop in astonishment as he crossed the threshold.

Eloise was there, sitting on the bed with her bodice open and both breasts out. Yet rather than some eager

81

man, her companion was female, her own cousin, who was stark naked and cradled in Eloise's arms, suckling one breast. Henry's angry denouncement died on his lips as he took in the sight. Eloise's eyes met his and her mouth opened in shock, but the Vicomtesse was rapt in her sucking and responded only when Eloise stiffened. She turned, the stiff nipple popping from her mouth to stand wet and glistening in the lamplight. Henry swallowed, entranced by the sight as he struggled to gather his wits.

The Vicomtesse had began to get up, covering her breasts and stammering in French, her face crimson with blushes. Eloise's reaction was less coy, a brief look of annoyance and then a smile. Henry was already working on the flap of his breeches.

'Don't be scared, Marie,' Eloise said softly as Henry's cock came free.

The Vicomtesse hesitated. Her hands had gone to cover her breasts and sex but left enough of her petite figure showing to leave Henry in no doubt about her physical appeal. Her inner thighs were also wet with juice, betraying her excitement and what she had been doing when he interrupted them. The idea of the beautiful young woman masturbating while she suckled his wife was too much for him and he came forward with a growl, flourishing his penis at them with obvious intent. The Vicomtesse squeaked aloud and pulled back on the bed, but Eloise had taken hold of her arm and would not let go as Henry closed with them.

Eloise's mouth opened to accept Henry's cock and she began to suck, her cousin watching in fascination from no more than a foot. Henry waited until his cock was fully erect, then pulled it from Eloise's mouth and held it in front of the two women, allowing Eloise to take the lead. He knew how she liked to control the pleasure of other women and was not surprised when she took her cousin gently by the hair. The Vicomtesse gaped wide, allowing herself to be pushed down slowly on Henry's erection. As it went into her mouth she closed her lips and Henry sighed as she began to suck. Eloise leaned forward and kissed her cousin's cheek, then began to lick at Henry's balls and the base of his erection.

He tried to hold back, yet with the two girls attending to his cock it proved impossible. Eloise's was working on his balls with practised skill, teasing the rough skin with her tongue tip and then abruptly sucking one or both into her mouth to produce a jolt of pleasure that would make him gasp. Nor was the Vicomtesse un-skilled, sucking ever more greedily at his cock as her initial inhibition faded. He reached down and took a breast in either hand, one from each girl, Eloise full and heavy, Marie small and pert. Marie sighed deep in her throat as his fingers found her nipple and suddenly it was too much. His cock erupted, deep in Marie's mouth, then again as she pulled abruptly back, spraying both girls' faces with come. As he finished Eloise took him in her mouth, dutifully draining out the last few drops of sperm and swallowing it.

The girls had already come together as Henry stag-gered back and slumped into a chair. Eloise was licking the come from her cousin's face, eagerly seeking out the thick white blobs that were spattered across Marie's cheeks and hung from her nose. The Vicomtesse respon-ded with licks of her own, cleaning up the come that had hit Eloise. She also returned her hand to her sex, starting to masturbate with her trim bottom stuck out towards Henry. Only when both girls' faces were clean did Marie slip back down, once more beginning to suckle Eloise and using her free hand to caress the bulge of her cousin's belly, exploring the contours with obsessive fascination.

Marie came quickly, her mouth locked on Eloise's nipple and her fingers patting her cunny so as to knock on her clitoris over and over again. Eloise held her cousin tight through the climax, allowing Marie the full ecstasy of her suckling. As the girl's orgasm died Henry's cock was already beginning to stiffen, with both the rich scent of female sex and the magnificent view of Marie's spread bottom and Eloise's breasts to stimulate him.

Having come Marie lay back on the bed. Henry expected Eloise to want her own orgasm, perhaps mounting Marie's face and having her cunny licked until she reached a climax, maybe even her anus. As Eloise rose she began to push down her dress, but when she stepped from it, she sank down beside Henry. She took his cock and began to stroke at the half-stiff shaft, then put her mouth to her ear.

'Seven years married and poor Marie has no children,' Eloise whispered. 'Would you?'

Henry glanced at Marie. She was spread out on the bed, her thighs wide to show the swollen, damp centre of her sex. With a nod to his wife he rose, pointing his cock at Marie's vagina even as Eloise crawled quickly on to the bed and swung her leg across her cousin's body. Eloise settled her bottom on to her cousin's face and Henry saw the sharp pink tongue come out and start to lick at his wife's cunny. His cock was hard and he caught hold of Marie's legs, lifting them and then entering her with one, long push. She started at the unexpected penetration but he held her firm and began to fuck her, keeping his grip on her thighs until she once more began to lick at Eloise's sex.

Four

'And the irony of it is,' Henry laughed, 'that the Vicomte is a little short fellow with curly black hair and a nose like a parrot's beak. If she does get a child by me there may be some questions to answer.'

Todd Gurney laughed and Natalie smiled shyly. Henry had returned to the West Country to see how the mine was progressing, leaving Eloise and Judith in Charles' care. Gurney had been living at the mine, Natalie helping the elderly Catchpoles to keep house, but both had been there when Henry arrived. He had expected an air of melancholy with neither Eloise nor his father to share his company, but the absence of Stephen proved to weigh heavily in the other direction. With a free run of the estate he intended to make the most of what Devon had to offer and was unloading cases of burgundy and port from the carriage, assisted by Todd.

'In any case the rumours seem to be spreading,' he went on, 'which is good although the girls seem to have picked the oddest ways to go about it. Judith nearly came a cropper and was wishing you were there but I told her you're needed too badly at the mine.'

'True enough, sir,' Gurney admitted.

'Is it going well?' Henry asked.

'Well enough,' he answered, picking two of the wooden cases from the floor of the carriage. 'The engine house is ready, any roads.'

'Then we'll need an engine,' Henry answered. 'More expense but we can't do without.'

'A Watt's beam engine's the one to have, sir,' Gurney put in. 'She'll get the water out at two, maybe three times the rate of an old Newcomen.'

'Then get a Newcomen,' Henry answered. 'Shiny brass, polished wood, the works, but old and leaky. The last thing we want is someone finding out the vein goes no deeper than a dell's doodle sack.'

'Runs dry to depth is the way it's said, sir,' Gurney replied. 'There's just short of three fathoms of water below where the adit joins in, and if my grandfather told right there's no more than plain rock at the bottom.'

'Take your time then,' Henry advised. 'Charles'll be seeking buyers for stock by next week, so some may well want to come down and look, take samples for assay as well, no doubt. It must look busy.'

'No mistake it looks busy,' Gurney answered. 'I've hired six men, not skilled, just whatever was about to Plymouth docks. The difference don't show though and I've got them working at all sorts of kickshaws.'

'Good,' Henry answered, passing out the final case of burgundy and turning to look at the substantial pile. 'That lot should keep even Eloise content. Now we may declare war on the French at leisure.'[6]

Judith eased her head back, allowing her lips to glide up the full length of the cock she was sucking. Its owner responded with a low groan and she once more took it in, enjoying the feel of the thick, meaty penis as it filled her mouth. She was kneeling on a bear skin, completely naked with the dead animal's fur tickling her thighs and the turn of her bottom. The sensation was pleasant, helping to keep her on heat as she sucked cock.

Luke Hurdon, whose penis she was taking such trouble over, was a man of leisure, living on a comfortable income and spending his time travelling and hunting. The bear skin had come from Bavaria, and part of his efforts in seducing her had involved describing how he had killed the beast. Judith had listened politely, showing what she hoped passed for girlish awe while she admired the breadth of his shoulders and the conspicuous bulge in his breeches. From there it had been simple, allowing him to think he had won her from Charles, accepting the suggestion that they return to his town house and allowing him to tease her out of her clothes while she feigned coyness. She had greeted his demand that she suck his cock with a shocked squeak and had had to have her head forced down on to his genitals. Once his prick had grown hard in her mouth she had given up her pretence of inexperience, a change he seemed not to have noticed.

His balls were in her hand, squirming gently in their sack as she fondled it while her other hand surreptitiously stroked her breasts and stomach. The noises he was making suggested the approach of orgasm and she slowed her pace, wondering if she should make him come in her mouth or risk allowing his impressive cock into her vagina. At that moment he made the decision for her, pulling her head back by the hair to force her to release his penis.

'It was not so terrible, as you see,' he said. 'Now, do not be scared, but obey me and you will come to no harm.'

Judith nodded dumbly, wondering what he intended.

'Kneel,' he ordered her, 'not on the rug but in the centre of the room.'

She obeyed, scrabbling backwards and then crawling across the floor so that he got the best possible view of her bottom and sex. The only light came from a large candelabrum in which a dozen fine, thick-stemmed candles were standing. Judith glanced at this as he rose to his feet. She had judged that he would be best seduced by a pose of relative innocence on her part but felt a strong urge to ask for candles in her holes so that she could enjoy the pain of hot wax and come under the torture.

'You have been beaten,' he remarked as he came to stand over her.

Judith looked back over her shoulder and nodded, trying to look sorry for herself while wondering how best to explain her bruises. They were fading but still showed clear evidence of a heavy beating. Hurdon grunted and prodded the soft flesh of her bottom with a toe, then abruptly turned away. Somewhat sorry that he had not come to focus on her beating, she held her position, lifting her bottom to make the cheeks spread and appear tempting.

Hurdon had crossed to the mantelpiece and for one delicious moment of mingled fear and longing she thought he was going to fetch the candelabrum. Instead he removed the lid from an inlaid box and poked a finger into the interior. It came out glistening with a thick, yellowish grease and Judith caught a new scent, rank and animal yet with a musky undertone that set her lower lip trembling. At the realisation of what was likely to happen to her she put her face to the floor, aware that her anus was showing and sure that it was his intended target. She was whimpering softly as his finger touched between her bottom cheeks, tracing a slow line down between them to grease the cleft. The blob of grease touched her bottom hole, cool and soft, turning her frightened whimpering into a deep sigh.

'Bear's grease,' he remarked, as he began to smear it on to her anus, 'from our friend by the chair.'

Judith shivered, realising what the smell was, then gave a gasp as his finger popped suddenly past the muscular ring and into her rectum. He pushed it well in, Judith feeling each joint of the digit as it was inserted into her bottom. She groaned, abandoning all pretence of innocence in the ecstasy of having her anus probed.

88

The action was bound to precede buggery, of that she was certain, and as her anus opened and relaxed around the intruding finger she thought of the size of his cock and how it was going to feel in her bowels. He continued to open her until she was shivering with pleasure and her anus was gaping and ready, a soft, hot hole with the bear's grease melting and running down over her sex and into her vagina.

'Does Finch sodomise you as well as beat you?' Hurdon asked. 'You seem almost eager.'

She replied with a weak mewl, thinking of the times men had put their cocks in her anus and of how she had so often encouraged it to avoid the risk of pregnancy.

'I had not thought him such a rake,' Hurdon remarked and began to withdraw his finger from her back passage.

Judith sighed as his finger left her anus with a glutinous pop. He rose and once more crossed the room, all the while nursing the erection that protruded from his breeches flap. Wondering what he was doing, she watched him, her eyes fixed to his cock. She could feel the cool air on her greasy bottom cleft and the way her bottom hole had been opened to leave the sensitive flesh at the centre exposed. His cock was large but the sight only increased her need to have it pushed deep up her rectum. She began to buck her hips, feeling the grease ooze in the creases of both vulva and bottom as they were pressed together, then pull wide as they parted, producing a wet, sticky sound.

Hurdon had gone to the bear skin rug and lifted it, giving Judith a sense of gratitude as she thought of how much nicer it would be to be buggered while kneeling in the thick fur than on the hard floor. Then, as he hefted it on to his shoulder she saw what the thick tail had previously concealed and her mouth came open in genuine shock. From the underside of the rug hung a penis, a massive penis, stuffed to full erection with a pair of monstrous balls hanging from the base. She could only gape, at once terrified and delighted as it became clear what he intended. The skin was dumped on her back, weighing her down and covering the body completely. The head hung to the floor in front of her own, which was entirely enveloped in pungent bear leather. She could see nothing and the scent was overpowering, making her gasp for breath. Its penis came to rest between her buttocks, the balls touching her cunny and the head clear of the top of her crease. Hurdon took it and began to rub the obscene thing about in the slime of her crease. Then the vast, straw-filled cock was being pushed to her well-greased anus and every other sensation faded to nothing.

As Judith's anus pressed in she cried out, then once more as a sharp stab of pain caught her straining ring. She begged him to stop, only to realise that it was too late and that her bottom hole had already accepted the head of the bear's cock.

'Relax, my dear,' Hurdon advised. 'It will be easier if you do not resist.'

Judith could not answer, but only managed a groan in a vain attempt to express her depth of emotion at what was being done to her. The thing's grotesque cock was in her anus, stretching the little ring to the point where she was sure it must burst. He began to feed it in, a bit at a time, greasing each inch before pushing it up, then withdrawing it a touch to grease the next piece. Judith grunted and moaned her way through the entry, clutching at the floor and mumbling broken, half-forgotten prayers as her bowels filled with bear's cock.

Her head was spinning by the time it was in, a dizzy, swimming feeling that came from the way the huge penis seemed to invade every part of her body. Dimly she was aware that the whole hideous bulk of the thing was up her bottom and that the bloated testes were lying on her cunny. She felt the air on her buttocks as the tail of the skin was lifted, then on her vagina as the gross scrotum was pushed to the side. Hurdon's cock nudged the mouth of her vagina and slid up, drawing a long, low moan from her lips as she found both holes filled to capacity with penis.

He began to fuck her. With each push he would ram the stuffed bear's cock deep up her rectum, while his own penis moved in synchrony. Gasping and panting, breathing in the thick, leathery scent, she surrendered herself to simultaneous sodomy and fucking. His hands were on her legs, clutching them through the thick hide of the skin to gain purchase for his pushes. Her dangling breasts were touching the ground, the nipples rubbing on the rug with the motion of her body. Lost to any sense of reserve, she sucked in when she found the skin against her face and began to chew, revelling in the taste of bear leather as the great beast's cock worked in her gut and Hurdon kept pace in her vagina.

Moving more by instinct than any deliberate choice, she put her hands back to her vulva, feeling the thick lips where they were parted by Hurdon's cock and beginning to rub at her clitoris. Nothing mattered but the sensations of her body, and she masturbated with urgency, intent only on coming under the overwhelming sensation of what was being done to her. He was taking his time, delighting in her submission, and she began to feel the bubble of her orgasm swelling in her head and sex. Her vagina began to contract on his cock, then her anus, the ring making a futile effort to shut around the monstrous prick that held it wide. She screamed in her throat as she came, thinking of bears and gigantic cocks and of being forced to suck and kneel and spread her buttocks for sodomy. The fucking suddenly became harder, Hurdon jamming his penis to make his balls slap her rubbing fingers. She rode the orgasm, her mouth agape on a wad of bear's leather, her anus pulsing on its filling as Hurdon's sperm erupted inside her and splashed out over her hand.

It was over, with the come trickling down her fingers as she let her muscles give in and collapsed under the rug. His cock pulled free of her vagina and the bear's testicles nudged back into place, covering her gaping hole. She stayed still, too overcome to move, flat on her face with the bear skin on top of her, still with her rectum full of cock and her mouth stuffed full. Not until Hurdon began to pull the penis from her bottom did she start to react, wincing at first and then lifting her bottom to make it easier. It hurt and she was gritting her teeth as the length of the thing slid slowly out. He was careful, yet she could not restrain a gasp of relief when it finally came free and her anus was allowed to close slowly shut. The bear skin was pulled away and with it Hurdon left the room.

Judith stayed on the floor, slowly recovering herself. Her anus stung and the flesh around it felt bruised, yet it was the ecstasy of her orgasm that filled her mind and not the pain. Hurdon did not return immediately and she eventually rose, climbing unsteadily to her feet and collapsing into the chair in which he had sat to have his cock sucked. After a while a servant appeared to tell her that a hip bath had been prepared for her in the scullery. Judith was too exhausted to feign concern for her nudity and followed the man.

When she returned from washing it was to find Hurdon sprawled out on a couch with a jug of claret by his side. He was sipping from a silver flute and gestured for her to join him, all trace of the hard, domineering sexual nature he had displayed gone. For a while they talked, Hurdon seeking her background, Judith trying to ease the conversation around so that she could introduce the subject of the mine. He seemed determined to discuss her enjoyment of sex, and as the level of wine fell in the jug she found herself admitting to enjoying her bottom being beaten and then to taking special pleasure in the burning shame. He listened with rapt attention, making it obvious that he desired her for more than a brief moment of pleasure. She was not surprised when the question of her faith to Charles came up.

'My income is certainly at the level of his, perhaps greater,' Hurdon assured, not troubling to dissemble at all. 'While I am the better man, without doubt.'

'Charles suits me well enough,' Judith answered cautiously.

'Why then do you stray?' Hurdon demanded. 'If you were to become my mistress you would not feel the need, of that I assure you.'

'It is partly because he allows me to stray that I am loyal to him,' Judith admitted, seeing no reason to hide the truth when he was being so open.

Hurdon grunted as if to dismiss her words and Judith saw her chance.

'There is another matter,' she went on. 'In confidence I may say that his wealth will shortly be augmented considerably.'

'How so?' Hurdon enquired.

'He has put money into a mine on land owned by Henry Truscott, near Climsland in Cornwall.'

'Risky business, mining. More like he'll lose every penny he has.'

'Not at all. I understand little of it all, but the ore is said to be of the richest quality. Also they are mining tin, and I am assured that it will be greatly in demand should we enter into a war with France.'

'Bronze for cannon,' Hurdon told her, 'and much else besides. And you are sure of this?'

'As sure as my knowledge permits me,' Judith answered.

Hurdon paused, evidently weighing Judith's remarks in his mind. She stayed silent, hoping he would take the bait.

'This mine,' he said after a while. 'Is it yet in production?'

'It shall be shortly,' she replied, 'Charles and Henry seek to raise money among their friends but have sufficient not to need to make a public call.'

'It is an awkward business, mining,' Hurdon said, 'and not one to be ventured upon lightly. I have a friend, Sir Joseph Snapes, who has a great deal of influence among both the industrial and scientific fellowships. He might be willing to provide advice, although be warned, he is not immune to the charms of young girls and his tastes are, shall we say, peculiar.'

Judith sipped her claret, wondering what Snapes might enjoy if he was considered peculiar by a man who enjoyed sodomising his lovers with a partially stuffed bear.

Sir Joseph Snapes placed the letter he had been reading down on his desk and looked out across the smart new gardens of Bedford Square. His tiny mouth was set in a smile, and after making a minuscule adjustment to his spectacles he picked up the letter and began to read it again. It was from Luke Hurdon, with whom he had recently been in Africa, collecting specimens and studying both human and animal inhabitants of the coasts of the Bight of Benin. The letter was couched in carefully neutral language but the essence of it was that his old friend had met a girl who might allow them to renew their indulgence in some of those pleasures they had enjoyed among the native women. It was a subject they had discussed several times but which had always faltered on the difficulty of finding any woman with the right balance of discretion and perversity. Yet Luke Hurdon insisted that he had found a likely candidate and was bringing her to dinner. It had been some years since he had successfully mounted a girl without a great deal of assistance, yet his cock twitched in his breeches at the thought.

The letter also mentioned a mine in the West Country, a mine with exceptionally rich ore and one run by gentlemen with little or no knowledge of the industry. Both his sexual profligacy and his taste for exotic travel had taken their toll on his wealth and he immediately found himself considering the possibilities of the mine.

He put the letter down once more and allowed his gaze to stray out of the window, expecting to see Hurdon and the remarkable girl at any instant. The bright spring evening had not yet started to fade and despite his failing eyesight he could see to the far side of the square, finding what he was after emerging from Caroline Street. Hurdon was unmistakable, close to a head taller than most of the men in view and well built into the bargain. The girl by his side scarcely reached his shoulder despite the mass of brilliant orange hair piled on to her head. His mouth pursed as the couple approached and with more detail becoming apparent he could not resist licking his lips. She was beautiful, with a tiny pert nose, the palest skin marked by a handful of freckles and large, bright eyes. Her expression suggested a delightfully mischievous character as she laughed at some remark of Hurdon's, while the motion set the upper surfaces of her apple-like breasts quivering.

The couple passed from sight and he rose from his desk, starting down the stairs as the door knocker sounded. He greeted his friend in the hall as his valet ushered them in, then turned to the girl. Close up she was even more appealing than at a distance and it was more than he could resist not to level his eyes at her breasts. She noticed but simply smiled and he felt his pulse quicken.

'Miss Judith Cates,' Hurdon was saying. 'Miss Cates, allow me to introduce Sir Joseph Snapes, Fellow of the Royal Society, a most learned anthropologist and a remarkable man in many ways.'

'Dear Luke exaggerates my abilities, my dear,' Snapes replied. 'I am but a humble worker in the great endeavours of our scientific establishment. But it is

95

seldom indeed that my home is brightened by such lovely company. I am honoured, honoured.'

'You are too kind, sir,' Judith replied, offering one tiny, gloved hand.

Snapes took her hand, feeling the delicacy of it as he once more allowed his eyes to travel slowly over her embonpoint. Hurdon had implied not only that she was willing but actively depraved, yet it was hard to imagine of such a slight, delicate girl. Ushering his guests into his dining room, he followed, watching Judith's reaction as she took in the appointments of the room. The high doors that cut the room in half were open, displaying that portion of it which was normally closed off and which housed his collection of curios. These included carved phalli from India, a vase with a frieze representing the rape of Europa in vivid detail and a length of silk showing women in sexual congress with apes and a bull, but Judith surveyed each with no more than polite remarks as to their rarity and expense. By the time the butler appeared to announce the service of dinner he was convinced that Hurdon was correct in his assessment of her character.

'It is a shame Lord Furlong cannot be here this evening,' he chuckled as he took his seat, drawing a light laugh from Luke Hurdon.

'You are a friend of the Lord Chancellor?' Judith asked.

'To the contrary,' Snapes replied, 'but no matter. I, for one, am famished. Sale, what does cook have for us?'

'Oysters, sir, to begin,' his butler answered, 'with a Mosel. Then ortolans drowned in brandy and served in an aspic of Sauternes wine, as you ordered. I suggest the same wine in accompaniment. A cut of venison follows, well hung and served with its own broth. A Hermitage of the 'seventy-one vintage accompanies it. The dessert is a pudding of suet with mulberries served with cream and Barsac. A round of Stilton completes the menu, with two vintages of port from Messrs Taylor, Fladgate and Yeatman.'

'Splendid, splendid. You must excuse my extravagance, Miss Cates,' Snapes remarked, smiling at Judith's breasts. 'Dining well is one of the few pleasures left to an old man.'

'Not at all,' she answered, 'you spoil me, I am sure.'

'Miss Cates,' Luke Hurdon put in, 'is used to extravagant dinners. Indeed, on more than one occasion she has served as the candlestick. A living sculpture that would put the most voluptuary pieces in your collection to shame.'

Snapes turned to Judith, expecting to find her angry or at least covered in the most furious blushes. She had coloured up, but only slightly, with a pink flush to her cheeks and the upper surfaces of her breasts. Luke Hurdon had hinted of this perversion in his letter, implying that the candles were placed in her body and not in her hands. That it would be her vagina and possibly also her anus which were penetrated he was certain.

'Is this true, my dear?' he asked. 'You need not feel concern, we are quite liberal in this household.'

'I confess a taste for the game,' Judith admitted.

'Well, perhaps you might illuminate us over the port?' Snapes suggested. 'I would count it a favour indeed.'

'The pleasure would be mine,' Judith assured him, smiled and for an instant allowed her eyelids to drop.

Snapes found himself beaming, the muscles around his mouth twitching up into a smile despite his best efforts to control himself. She was indeed as Hurdon as described, happily admitting to the most perverse of pleasures just so long as she felt comfortable with her audience. Even the presence of Sale had not flustered her.

As the butler and valet began to serve Snapes let his mind dwell on the possibilities offered by Judith's acquiescence to his suggestions. Certainly she would be their candlestick over the port, and while all the facilities for his most vicious amusements were at his country seat in Suffolk, there was still plenty to do. Rubbing his hands together in glee he took a last, lingering glance at her breasts and addressed himself to the plate of oysters before him.

Judith swallowed an oyster, not only enjoying the taste and the sensation of the morsel sliding down her throat but the attention of the men as they watched her. Conditions were ideal for her, open flattery and appreciation of her charms and the undivided attention of several men. Hurdon was the only really attractive one, it was true, yet attention was attention and it would be him who ultimately enjoyed her. Her host was a very different prospect and yet Hurdon had explained that Snapes was to all intents and purposes impotent and restricted himself to voyeuristic pleasures. She was glad of this, as although he had obviously once been impressively built time and debauchery had taken a severe toll. Most notable was his head, a great polished dome of bare skin with only a fringe of straggling grey hair at the sides and nape. It struck her as unusual for a man of his generation not to wear a wig when so thoroughly bald, leading her to wonder if the grotesque elements of his appearance were not deliberate. She had met men who liked to frighten girls with their appearance before, and could well believe that Snapes was the same. Certainly the quality of his attention would have scared a less confident woman, with his tiny piggy eyes constantly roving across her cleavage from behind his pebble-like glasses. Although not fat, he was fleshy, with prominent meaty buttocks suspended on spindle-like legs and a sagging paunch barely constricted by his elaborate waistcoat. The prospect of sex with such a man filled Judith with revulsion, although she could recall worse. Yet the idea of being watched by him provoked the very opposite reaction, appealing directly to her joy of misbehaviour and of being forced to behave lewdly in front of an audience.

The prospect of being made a candlestick in front of him provided a tingling sense of anticipation, both erotic and slightly frightening. Also, it was not at all obvious that the servants would be sent from the room when it happened. Judith hoped not, as their presence would add an extra dimension to her erotic shame. The valet was unusual only in being dark skinned, and not the deep olive of an Indian but a rich, glossy brown. Snapes addressed him as John, although it seemed unlikely to be his real name. He also seemed muscular and powerful, although his uniform hid any detail. The butler, Sale, was very different, a large man in every proportion save height. A monstrous belly stretched out the front of his uniform, matched by a round, heavy face, great thick legs and ponderous buttocks. She could also tell that there were further servants below stairs, and from what Hurdon had said of Snapes it seemed entirely possible that they would be called up to watch her mortification. She found herself shivering as the last of her oysters slid down her throat, and wondered whether it should be the duty of a butler or a valet to insert the candles into her cunny and bottom hole.

With the first course finished the valet cleared the table while the butler busied himself with the wine. The ortolans were served, tiny birds rich with the scent of brandy and truffles, each set on a bed of watercress and glistening with its own juices. Unsure how to tackle the delicacy, Judith glanced at Snapes. He had picked up a napkin in one hand and speared the ortolan on a fork. As she watched he placed it whole into his mouth and then covered his face with the napkin. Feeling somewhat uneasy, she imitated the procedure, only to find the flavour so exquisite that her misgivings were swept away. With the napkin still over her face she savoured the delicious morsel, feeling her sense of erotic pleasure rise in response.

By the time she had swallowed and dabbed her mouth clean she was shivering with desire and could feel the response of her cunny, with dampness between her thighs while her nipples were fully erect. Unable to hold back from making the promised display of herself, she wiped her hands carefully on the napkin, cupped both under her breasts and popped them out of her bodice. The butler's eyebrows lifted at the sight but he said nothing, while the valet's mouth merely twitched at one end. Hurdon was watching and gave an indulgent smile, as if at a star pupil who was performing well. Snapes had been savouring his ortolan and still had the napkin over his face, but choked when he removed it and found himself faced not by the teasing swell of Judith's cleavage but by two bare, round breasts with the nipples straining out at each crest. She giggled as the butler hastened to slap his master's back, then very demurely began to fork up her cress.

Henry had instructed her to act giddy and thoughtless, and in the circumstances it was no hardship whatever. Meanwhile, the knowledge that Snapes almost exactly fitted the description of those people she had been told to avoid struck her as amusing and more of a challenge than a problem. The venison passed in a haze, the rich mouthfuls sliding down while gravy ran from her chin and spattered her naked breasts. Her eagerness grew with the wine and the continued attention of the men, and by the time the pudding was served she was itching to strip and present her sex for penetration. At last she swallowed the final mouthful of her serving, and with cream and mulberry jam added to the gravy on her breasts she looked hopefully to her host.

'Up you go then, my dear,' Snapes announced. 'Sale, perhaps if you could be so kind?'

'Very well, sir,' Sale answered.

Judith scrambled on to the table as the butler selected two thick, yellow candles from the sideboard. Both Hurdon and Snapes laughed at her eagerness in stripping off her remaining clothes, while the valet looked on with a quiet smile. She went nude, removing every last vestige of clothing and then kneeling so that her host would be assured of the best possible view of her bottom. Then, putting her face to the smooth polished surface of the dining table and pulling her knees tight in beneath her, she lifted her bottom, offering both vagina and anus for use. The butler had remained impassive throughout her display, moving only to dip the butt of each candle into the butter dish. Looking back, Judith could see them, the thick butter clinging to each, showing only too clearly for what they were intended.

She pushed her bottom further up, ensuring that her two holes were as close to the vertical as possible. Sale's hands went to her bottom and she felt a candle butt touch her vagina, greasy with butter. It went in, sliding deep up inside her. Fingers spread her bottom and the second butt touched her anus, making her wince and tighten at the memory of the bear's cock, only for it to pop suddenly past her sphincter and into the chamber beyond. Judith's mouth came open as the candle filled her rectum, then she had begun to purr as her holes squeezed on the intruding butts.

Sale lit the candles with a taper, then went to the sideboard for the decanter of port. Judith held exactly still, waiting for the pain of the wax and watching Luke Hurdon accept his port. His manner was calm and amused, watching her degradation with a light smile. She knew what to expect, but still flinched and cried out when the first drop of wax fell to catch her sex lips. More followed quickly, rolling down to cake on her vaginal and anal skin or dropping to fall hot and stinging on her bottom, sex and thighs. Her purring had

101

quickly turned to whimpering, then to gasps as the pain grew and her self-control threatened to break. A drop hit her clitoris and her mouth came open to scream, only to have an orange thrust into it.

With that her control started to go, mewling around the orange in her mouth and wriggling her toes as the four men watched her with a casual appreciation bordering on indifference. The wax began to wad in the mouth of her vagina and between her sex lips, bringing her pain to what she knew was the peak beyond which lay utter ecstasy. Sure enough, with the most sensitive parts of her flesh covered the scarcely bearable stinging died. Her buttocks began to open and close rhythmically, squeezing the lump of wax between them. More was running down her cleft and on to her back, renewing the pain. A trickle coursed down the inside of a thigh and on to the table cloth, forming a red pool.

Trembling in pain and ecstasy, she put a hand back to masturbate. Her cunny was sodden, and coated with wax, which had also clotted into her pubic hair. It was thick in the crease of her buttocks, congealed on the hairs around her anus to tug as her bottom squirmed. Her fingers had found her clitoris and she was masturbating, patting her cunny, then rubbing, then touching the lump of wax that covered half her sex. Hurdon's cock was out, stiff and red in the light of the candles inside her. A weak slapping noise from behind showed that Snapes too had freed his penis, and at the thought of him watching her from the rear she started to come.

As she climaxed she began to slip down, her knees coming apart until they would go no further. The wax was no longer hitting her but she was too far gone to care, revelling in the feel of the thick clot that blocked both her holes and was wedged between her bottom cheeks and the lips of her vagina. Her mouth was wide, allowing the orange to roll free even as Hurdon stood and thrust his cock at her face. She took it, sucking hard as wave after wave of orgasm swept through her. For a moment it was perfect, with her wax-fouled cunny clenched tight on one candle and the other deep in her bottom, with a stiff cock in her mouth and Snapes' eyes feasting on her sex. She held the peak, only half aware of her surroundings but totally open to use.

From that exquisite moment the evening became a blur, filled with cocks and candles and food as she was used over and over. Luke Hurdon turned her and pulled the candles free, taking a good deal of her hair with them. She was penetrated, his cock pushed to the hilt in her vagina. As she was fucked Snapes nodded to the servants and in moments she had the butler's cock in her mouth and the valet's in her hand. Sale came quickly, his fat belly bumping her face as his cock erupted down her throat. John replaced him, rubbing a huge, dark erection in her face before taking her hard by the hair and filling her mouth. Hurdon came in her vagina, then finished his orgasm in the sore, sperm-slick cleft of her bottom. The valet came in her face, taking great pleasure in wiping his penis in her hair and across her cheeks, soiling her thoroughly. All the while Sir Joseph Snapes masturbated, watching her with his pig-like eyes.

The men's orgasms did not signal the end. She was rolled in what remained of the dinner, food going into her face and over her breasts, between her bottom cheeks and on to her legs and belly. While held spreadeagled on the table she was mounted by an enormously fat man she took to be the cook. She was made to finish the pudding with her face held into the bowl. What suet she was unable to swallow was forced into her anus and rammed home with a candle butt. She was upended and her vagina filled with port to act as a cup for Hurdon. Finally fresh candles were put in her vagina and anus and lit as she lay exhausted with her bottom stuck meekly up, and it was with that that Snapes finally came.

* * *

103

From the seat of his phaeton Charles Finch scanned the empty heath, his pistols lying loaded beside him. Dusk was falling fast, casting long shadows from the birches and scrub to either side of the post road. Before him Griggs was crouched forward in his seat, urging the horses to greater effort as they pushed west. At Staines there had been talk of a highwayman working the heaths near Farnborough, news that had scared him but not enough to make him turn back.[7]

Judith had arrived shortly before noon, in the company of Sir Joseph Snapes. She had managed to warn him of her mistake, allowing the mine to become known to a man who was not only a fellow of the Royal Society but expressed a specific interest in tin mining. Snapes had been friendly, also effusive, advising on the problems of mining and offering his assistance. He had finished by declaring his intention of driving down to make a survey of Wheal Purity in order to help them promote it.

It had been impossible to decline the offer without raising suspicions, and they had only managed to delay Snapes' departure by having Judith make a fuss of which gowns she should take. Charles had offered to ride ahead in the phaeton, allowing Judith to travel in the greater comfort of Snapes' carriage. The idea had been accepted by Snapes with an ill-concealed leer. Now, despite Charles' casual attitude to her behaviour, he was feeling piqued to the extent that any single rider on Blackdown Heath was likely to be considered a highwayman and fired on.

By riding through the night and with luck in changing the horses at posthouses, he knew he could be in Cornwall by dusk the next day. The carriage was likely to take a full three days, while Judith could be counted on to delay it further. Nevertheless, he was unlikely to gain more than a clear day and the best part of the second in which to bring the mine to a standard that would impress Snapes.

* * *

Henry traced a slow line up the swollen flesh of May Cunningham's sex. Her trips to the mine site had become frequent, with her eager to further explore the pleasures of orgasm. He had responded indulgently, happy to indulge her so long as she would return the favour. The system worked well, with May a willing pupil although of such innocence that Henry began to doubt not only Saunder Cunningham's virility but also his imagination. May Cunningham was attractive beyond doubt, and had a fine, well-fleshed bottom. Yet her husband had never troubled to spank it, nor to bugger her, omissions that Henry found hard to credit.

Her particular joy lay in having her cunny licked and coming to orgasm under Henry's tongue. This was also something that Eloise frequently demanded, and which he was always happy to provide so long as there was no nonsense about swallowing his sperm when the favour was returned. Now she was sitting on a stump in the warm sunlight of the scrubby woodland above the mine. Her skirts and petticoats were high, exposing her cunny for his attention, while her bodice was unlaced with both breasts naked.

Taking his time, he began to dab at her labia, flicking the sensitive flesh to bring her closer to her climax. His cock was in his hand, ready for her when he judged the time right, and by the quality of her moans he knew it would not be long. Somewhere in the wood a call sounded: Henry's name in a tone of urgency. May jumped up, briefly entangling Henry in her skirts.

'Damn!' he swore as he released himself. 'Saunder back early, d'you think?'

'I am not sure,' she answered. 'I had best go.'

'You're right,' he said, wiping his mouth with the back of his hand. 'Doesn't do to be seen together over much.'

May made rapid adjustments to her dress, covering her chest and lacing her bodice, while Henry was still buttoning his breeches as she was mounting her horse. Henry watched with regret as she retreated. He had intended to bring her to the very peak of orgasm and start to use his cock on her cunny in place of her tongue. With the juice running down between her cheeks her anus would have been slick and relaxed, and he had been hoping to slip his cock within when she was at the very edge of orgasm. He would then have buggered her, using his thumb to keep her in ecstasy and so introduce her to the delights of her bottom. Now it seemed that he would have to wait, although he had to admit that it would have been awkward for Saunder Cunningham to discover them while May was being buggered.

The call sounded again and this time Henry recognised the voice and cursed, even as a figure emerged from the trees: not Saunder Cunningham but Charles Finch, with Todd Gurney beside him. Henry hailed them.

'That was a journey,' Charles puffed as he approached, 'not a break from London, save to change horses, and rumours of highwaymen on the Surrey heaths and at Exeter to boot.'

'Why so hurried?' Henry demanded.

'I have bad news,' Charles went on. 'Judith was introduced to a man named Snapes, through no fault of her own. He proves to be a fellow of the Royal Society and insists on taking an interest in the mine. He's coming down and might be here as early as tomorrow evening.'

'Damn!' Henry swore. 'Todd, what of the mine, is it likely to pass muster?'

'The mine's well enough,' Gurney answered. 'She looks half built, but that'll be no surprise. It's the samples that'll trouble us. The mine's salted, but the old heaps are only a quarter part shifted and they're pure schorl.'

'If he picks up a piece we're done,' Henry said. 'Can you shift it in time?'

'Not in a day,' Gurney answered. 'There's many tons, and most of it grown over with bramble. Then there's getting shot of it. We've been scattering it along the stream bed, for all the men think I'm 'mazed. Give me two clear days and I'll have the job done.'

'Hell!' Henry swore. 'But what of the men?'

'As safe as their pay'll make them,' Gurney answered, 'and they've no knowledge, not much, any roads.'

'Give them a holiday, tell them it's my birthday or something,' Henry answered. 'Damn, why couldn't the fool wench keep the man in London? You'd have thought she'd have had enough to occupy him, what with her slut's tricks.'

'She's coming with him,' Charles answered. 'Elseways he'd have been here in hours from now.'

Henry said nothing, looking out, first over the mine and then to the distant loom of Dartmoor where the hills showed dull purple against a bank of cloud.

'Did you say there was a highwayman reported near Exeter?' he said after a while.

'I heard the report in Exeter,' Charles answered. 'He's said to have tried to stop a man near Zeal.'

'Zeal?' Henry replied. 'Lonely country that, where the road comes close in under the moor.'

Judith stared morosely from the carriage window. It was the third day of travel, with stops at coaching inns at Winchester and Exeter. After the dinner at Sir Joseph Snapes' town house she had expected the journey to be one long debauch, with plenty of drink. The presence of the black valet as driver had also suggested a plentiful supply of cock, with Snapes' presence for an audience adding a satisfyingly dirty touch. Instead the journey had been dull, with John sat forward on the driver's perch and Snapes talking interminably of his achievements in science while strangely reluctant to discuss Africa and the Far East. Even at night he had not troubled to demand her services, although at Exeter she had managed to visit John in the stables, sucking his cock but not allowing him to mount her for fear of pregnancy. The heart week of her cycle was just beginning, making her increasingly eager for sex but also wary of conception. Her mind had drifted to the risks she had taken with Hurdon, although she had douched well and felt at least moderately confident.

Outside she could see the same jumble of small hills and fields that had formed the scenery since rising from the Somerset levels. Only as they crossed the Exe valley had it changed, but now a large, round topped hill was visible ahead. She knew this as Cawsand Hill from previous trips, an outlier of Dartmoor near the village of Zeal. Knowing that Dartmoor was visible from the mine site she felt relief, then annoyance at the thought of several more hours in the carriage.

The scenery began to change as Cawsand Hill loomed larger, rocky outcrops appearing, the slopes growing ever steeper and ash and bramble giving way to rowan and gorse. Overhead a bank of cloud was coming in from the west, with long streams of rain hanging beneath it. A fresh breeze caught her cheek, snatching away the warmth of the sun and she moved her hand to the window, only to stop as she caught a call from ahead. The carriage stopped as Judith leaned from the window, Snapes demanding angrily to know what the matter was.

Directly ahead of them the road entered the shadows of a small wood. At its centre stood a man, masked, with his hat pulled well down and with a cocked pistol in either hand. Both were trained on the carriage, and it was clear that the coachman had had no time to bring up his own weapon. Snapes too had seen what was happening and gave a muttered curse, the tone of which showed his fear. With a flick of one pistol the highwayman gestured that they should climb down. Judith obeyed without hesitation, seeing no reason to attempt bravery. Snapes and the valet followed suit, both climbing to the ground.

The man looked at them, both pistols held steady. They were fine pieces, silver chased and obviously expensive, and as the man walked forward Judith recognised them as a set Charles had purchased just months before. Anger and fear started to well up inside her as she wondered if the man had robbed Charles, or worse. He was approaching and stopped level with the lead pair of horses.

'I believe the customary phrase is stand and deliver,' he said. 'Which you will, else I shall fire without compunction.'

The man's voice was hard and grating, but also genteel, which surprised Judith. Snapes had begun to unfasten his purse even before the man had spoken, while the valet had nothing to give. Her own possessions were in the trunk beneath the seats and so she remained still, wondering if she dared demand what had become of Charles.

'Most gracious, and most sensible,' he said as Snapes tossed the purse to the ground. 'Now, you will retire, let us say to that clump of rowan. It appears to threaten rain and you would not wish to get wet.'

Snapes and John began to back away but Judith held her ground despite the violent trembling of her lower lip and the fluttering of her stomach.

'Sir,' she managed, her voice sounding pitiably in her own ears. 'May I enquire: the pistols, from whom did you take them?'

The highwayman had been in the act of sheathing one gun but stopped and looked directly at her, his eyes fixed and hard.

'Please, sir,' Judith begged.

The man continued to look at her, his body exactly still as if unsure what to do. Then, with a slow, deliberate motion of his left eye, he winked. She returned a puzzled look, wondering if he was making fun of her and was about to speak again when he did.

'It does not do to pry into my affairs,' he said coldly. 'For your temerity I shall punish you. Now, stand away, and then strip.'

Judith felt a lump rise in her throat at his words and began to wish she had kept quiet. The man was watching her, his gaze as steady as the pistol in his hand. She found her hands going to the clasp of her cloak in a half-voluntary motion. It fell from her shoulders and she began to undo the laces of her bodice, full of helpless anger and humiliation. Neither Snapes nor the valet spoke up in her defence, let alone acted, and as the dress fell away from her chest she was certain that she was about to be raped.

The man made no move, but watched her as she stripped. With the dress around her ankles she began to unfasten her chemise, letting her breasts free. A single, heavy drop of rain caught one, splashing on the pale skin and running down to hang from a suddenly erect nipple. Still he made no move to touch her and she reached back to find her petticoat strings, telling herself that the stripping might simply be a punishment but not really believing it. The first petticoat fell away, then the second, exposing her belly and the puff of ginger fur that hid her sex. As she kicked the garments off she was left in just her open chemise, bonnet, gloves, stockings and boots, concealing nothing. She shrugged the chemise off and let it fall, feeling the patter of rain on her bare skin as she stood, all but nude in front of him.

'That will do,' he said. 'You are most fine. Now turn. Yes, a trim rump too, and recently beaten. By a cane, and before that a bull's pizzle if I am not mistaken.'

Judith had turned at his order, presenting her bottom and coming to face Snapes and John where they huddled among the rowans. She stiffened at his words but made no reply, unsure if her companions were within earshot. The rain was beginning in earnest, making the leaves tremble and bringing goose-pimples to her naked flesh. From behind her she heard a snap and a snicker from one of the horses, then Snapes finally found his courage.

'Come, sir, have mercy,' he called. 'You have my purse. Enjoy the girl if you must, but leave the horses.'

The man made no answer and Judith turned, finding that he was in the process of cutting the traces with a long, wicked knife. With all four horses free he reached up and took down the coachman's whip, with which he flicked each horse into motion, then gave one animal a resounding crack across the haunch. All four fled, leaving the shaft and trees lying on the ground in a rapidly forming puddle.

Judith watched, shivering as their horses vanished into the wood. The man still held the whip and suddenly flicked it out, the thong wrapping around her waist and the lash catching her side. He began to pull her in, one handed, then suddenly jerked, pulling her legs from beneath her. She managed a squeak of alarm and then she was over, her bottom landing in a puddle of mud and cold water. Her legs were open, with the upper part of her sex on show and the lower hidden in mud. An exclamation of shock and disgust burst from her lips and then she looked up to see that the man had dropped the whip and was working on the buttons of the flap that held his breeches shut.

She stayed still, trembling, thinking not only of the man whose cock was shortly going to be invading her body but also of Sir Joseph Snapes and the joy he took in seeing girls used. The man's prick came free, large and already half-stiff, with the head emerging from the foreskin. Her eyes were fixed on it as he began to tug himself to erection, all the while with the pistol covering them and his gaze flicking from her naked body to the

111

two men cowering beyond. She could imagine Snapes'
delight in watching her, and the valet's indifference, and
knew that she could expect no interference from either
of them.

The man's cock was hard, a thick column of flesh
with the head bloated and shiny with blood. She shook
her head, looking up into his face as he sank to his
knees, never once letting go of the pistol.

'I beg you, sir, not in my cunt,' she managed,
trembling.

'Then you had best grease you breech,' he answered.

Judith turned at once, her bottom pulling from the
muck with a sticky sound. The rain was coming hard,
splashing on her bonnet and soaking her hair, running
down her back and between the cheeks of her bottom as
she moved into a kneeling position. Snapes was watching, also John, the one in horrified fascination, the other
with a cruel, pleased grin. She met their gaze as she
reached back and slid a finger down her bottom crease.
Her anus was cold and slippery with mud from where
she had sat in the puddle. It gave in easily, the mud
helping to lubricate the hole as it opened to her finger.
She began to finger her bottom, closing her eyes in
pleasure despite her efforts to stay aloof. As a sigh
escaped her lips she heard the man chuckle behind her
and then the bulbous head of his penis tapped her
vagina.

For just an instant it slid in, filling her and making
her grunt. His front was against her hand, pushing the
finger deep up her bottom while the pubic hair tickled
her. Twice he pushed himself up her vagina, then
withdrew. Judith pulled her finger from her anus,
surrendering herself to buggery. His knob touched her
bottom hole, warm and slimy with her own juice,
making the little ring tighten and then relax as he began
to push. Judith put her face down as her rectum filled
with cock, heedless of her bonnet and hair as both

touched the puddle beneath her. Inch by inch the cock was pushed up her, stretching her anus and filling her rectum until she was panting and breathless despite her best efforts at control. She felt his balls nudge her empty cunny and knew that it was all in, then a hand took her by the leg and the cock began to move in her bowels.

At first she kept her head down, not wanting Snapes to see the expression on her face as she was buggered. Keeping silent was beyond her, and she quickly found herself panting softly, then starting to grunt as his pace quickened and the sensation of having a thick cock in her back passage became overwhelming. The grip on her leg eased and a firm smack was suddenly planted on her left buttock, then another and she cried out in reaction, overcome by the sheer power of what was happening to her.

No longer able to resist, she looked up. Both Snapes and the valet were staring at her, watching her buggered in the pool of mud and the soiled remnants of her clothes. Her breasts were swinging beneath her in time to his pushes, while her mouth was agape and her eyes wide. The bonnet had half fallen, hanging to one side by its ribbon while her glorious red curls formed a bedraggled mess over her face and half way down her back. Her anus felt as if it was on fire, stretched and hot around the intruding penis, while her buttocks bounced to his pushes and occasional slaps of his hand. All this she knew they could see and could guess their mixed emotions at the way she was being used, sympathy, delight, jealousy and lust, but above all relief that it was she and not they who was kneeling in filth while a cock was repeatedly rammed home in her rectum.

He began to move faster and the pain started to come in Judith's anus, as it always did when a man in her bottom began to approach climax. She gritted her teeth, trying not to cry out. Her arms gave way and her breasts and briefly her face went into the mud. She looked up,

113

rain and muck sliding from her face, then cried out as she felt him jerk inside her and knew that she had received his come in her bowels, only for an ear-splitting roar and a blast of heat to knock her sideways. She landed in the puddle, his cock still inside her as he came down on top. He was still pumping, draining himself into her by instinct even as he cursed and struggled to get up. For a moment Judith's face was pushed firmly into a thick layer of mud, the mixture of water and slime going into her mouth and nostrils. She pulled back, coughing and spitting mud, only to go back in once more as firm hands took hold of her buttocks and the man's cock was pulled from her anus. She squealed and tried to rise, noting the running figures of Snapes and John some way down the road even as she managed to struggle to her elbows.

'You are a bastard, Henry Truscott,' she managed and then once more slumped forward into the mud.

Todd Gurney waited deferentially until the others had filed into the newly completed counting house. For over an hour his nerves had been on edge as Sir Joseph Snapes inspected the mine. The man had arrived no more than an hour after the last of the old ore heaps had been dispersed and the workers had been told to leave. Snapes had been in a foul humour, and it had amused Gurney as Henry and Charles had greeted the story of the highwayman at Zeal with gasps of shock and outrage.

Beer, bread and cheese had calmed Snapes somewhat, until he was explaining how he had intended to stand the highwayman off with his swordstick against two pistols but had refrained for fear of Judith coming to harm. She had said nothing, merely toying with her fan and throwing Henry the occasional glance. At length Snapes had declared himself ready to inspect the mine. The old Newcomen engine had met with a measure of contempt, but Snapes had been impressed by the width of the half-dug vein and the appearance of the scattered pieces of black stone on the floor.

The worst moment had come when Snapes tried to examine a piece of supposed cassiterite that remained in the adit wall, but nothing had been said. When the men had left the mine and rejoined Judith in the counting house, Snapes had been positively jolly.

'You have a good mine here, Mr Truscott,' Snapes announced to Henry as Gurney closed the door. 'Not the best, perhaps, but certainly good. You, my good fellow, Gurney, how much tin do you reckon a ton of your ore will yield?'

'Upwards of a hundred pounds the ton, the best, sir,' Gurney answered. 'Perhaps eighty when all's taken with all.'

'Eighty?' Snapes answered. 'How did you arrive at that figure.'

'By an assay at my forge, to Plymouth,' Gurney answered. 'Five parts in the hundred, I took, from near a hundred weight of ore. Crude, I dare say, to your way of thought, but good enough.'

'Better than I imagined, if accurate,' Snapes replied. 'Yes, subject to my own assay, of course, and certain changes, I would be prepared to invest.'

'What changes are those?' Henry asked.

'Well, the engine for one,' Snapes answered. 'Newcomens were all very well in their day, but lack the power for the sort of deep operation I foresee.'

'She does her job,' Gurney answered.

'Nonsense, nonsense,' Snapes continued. 'We'll have one of the new Watts beam engines installed. It'll have your water out in a trice.'

'And the cost?' Henry asked.

'Ah,' Snapes said, 'as to cost, I have a proposal. On what capital was the company floated?'

'Ten thousand pounds, largely from Mr Finch and myself.'

'Then I propose to add a further nine thousand pounds,' Snapes went on. 'For which I shall take forty-five per cent of the company and the chairmanship in return. You may also retain all right to trade our stock with outsiders. I am a fair man, Mr Truscott, as you see; I do not expect full control. Furthermore, with me as chairman you will find that my reputation carries a great deal of weight.'

'A reasonable offer,' Henry answered, 'although we had been seeking new capital and have several offers.'

'Take them up,' Snapes answered, 'but cautiously. Do not risk overall control passing out of your hands.'

Henry glanced at Charles, trying hard to maintain a serious expression while inside he was laughing. Charles put a thoughtful hand to his chin and then nodded.

'What other changes do you propose?' Charles asked Snapes.

'More advancements than changes,' Snapes went on. 'We need the Watts engine to drain the old shaft efficiently, while we should begin a new adit running in from close to the bottom of the slope for future drainage. That'll mean more men, and while I'm sure your man Gurney is as capable as you say, I'd like my own man to assist him. He's a fellow called Eadie, a coal man, not tin, but broadly capable. I'll send for him directly the assays are in.'

'Fair enough,' Henry answered. 'Gurney?'

'So long as I keep my post and take no cut in wages I've no cause to grouch,' Gurney answered. 'I can manage, but I won't pretend a second man wouldn't come in handy.'

'So be it then,' Henry addressed Snapes.

'Very well,' Snapes finished, 'all this subject to assay, of course, and to be drawn up with the solicitors of all parties back in London. Remembering my unfortunate incident on the way down, I suggest we travel as a party.'

'Absolutely,' Henry agreed. 'Indeed, I'll ride guard myself, and I'll lay you a guinea to a groat the rascal doesn't dare show his face.'

Five

In London, Eloise had been enjoying herself, blissfully unaware of events in the West Country. With Stephen too busy to do more than keep a distant eye on her she had taken to the company, and the bed, of her cousin, Marie, Vicomtesse de Blagny. The affair had been clandestine in the extreme, and restricted to hurried attention to each other's bodies in those few moments of privacy they could find. She had also continued to propagate rumours of the wealth of Wheal Purity, treating the mine as if it were an amusing foible of her husband's and its wealth great but really of no importance. The greedy looks and carefully phrased demands for detail with which this news was usually met delighted her. She gave what was asked, giggling and flirting while she gave away the supposed vital information as if it were no more than the most trivial gossip. In the process she had taken three cocks into her mouth and had allowed herself to be mounted once, from the rear by a particularly handsome young priest.

Aside from her enjoyment of sex and intrigue, she was driven by a determination to outdo Judith. Both were of a similar age, both red-haired and pale-skinned, with figures and features sufficiently similar that they might have passed for sisters. This annoyed Eloise, given that she was the daughter of a count and Judith nothing more than a clever guttersnipe, born in Seven Dials and educated as a whore. If anything the rivalry was worsened by the fact that Eloise found it impossible not to like the girl, and even to find in her a kindred spirit. In her more self-possessed moments her feelings towards Judith filled her with rage and self-disgust, yet in the dark hours of the night she had often found herself wondering how it would feel to take the fiery slut in her arms as an equal. Such feelings she kept carefully hidden, taking out her spite on Peggy with frequent whippings and humiliations. Unfortunately Peggy seemed to thrive on such treatment and only became more loyal and obedient.

Inevitably she had attracted not only those she wished to, but many older and less well favoured men as well. These she handled with practised ease, with only one, the elderly and lecherous Marquis d'Aignan, giving her cause for concern. He had long been a thorn in her side, having discovered that she was free with her favours and being sufficiently arrogant to refuse to accept rejection. At first he had declared love, then offered money. When she had refused he had began to propagate a rumour that she had accepted, but he had only succeeded in provoking her anger.

That had been before her meeting with Henry and the start of the revolution in her home country. The Marquis was now an exile, but seemed no less arrogant for the experience. Twice he had sent representatives to her, and now, as she sat in the drawing room of the Truscotts' town house, a third was waiting in the hall. She had instructed Peggy to have him wait a full half-hour, and had been watching the clock and wondering how to deal with his demands. So persistent had d'Aignan been that she was beginning to wonder if it might not be easier to allow him a brief access to her body in the hope that he would then lose interest. There was also the question of finance, with the prospect of a substantial endowment for the mine should she give in.

Then, when the project collapsed it would be she who was left laughing, and rich.

A voice in the passage signalled the approach of the envoy and Eloise straightened herself in her chair, determined to at least make her feelings clear and bargain for as much as possible in return for her surrender. The door swung open and Peggy appeared, ushering in a tall young man who Eloise recognised as the Seigneur de Poinchy. He was flamboyantly dressed, with an elaborate wig, heavy powder and large beauty spots on both cheeks. Surprised that a fellow noble had been sent rather than a servant, Eloise found herself rising instinctively as he gave a deep bow.

'You know my errand, I am sure,' he began, ignoring further formalities. 'So I will deliver the Marquis' message without delay.'

'Very well,' Eloise replied.

'He offers two thousand English pounds,' he stated, 'on the understanding that you will attend him and allow him the full expression of his love . . .'

'Love!' Eloise broke in, her temper flaring immediately. 'What does he know of love? He is no more than a lecherous toad, crawling after my body for no better reason than wishing to slake his lust on me! I am twenty years of age, married and carrying my husband's child! Has he no decency? Has he no respect, to seek to make a whore of me!'

'Please,' the seigneur stammered, 'I am merely the messenger. Also I come not only to plead my friend's cause, but to tell you of another love, pure and sincere.'

'Whose?' Eloise demanded.

'My own,' he answered and stepped forward to take her in his arms.

'Seigneur!' Eloise exclaimed and pulled back from his clumsy attempt to kiss her.

'I must have you!' he gasped. 'Your beauty drives me to distraction! Please, I beg of you!'

'Now, now, Philippe,' Eloise chided, disengaging herself from his grip. 'Please, you forget yourself.'

'I beg of you!' he repeated. 'Grant me your favour and I shall be your eternal slave. For years I have loved you from afar. Always I was sure that we were destined for one another. How my heart ached when I heard you had taken that man to be your husband. It is too cruel, Eloise, but grant me your favour now! I beg it of you!'

As he spoke Eloise had been struggling not to smile. Her anger at the Marquis' proposal had been genuine, yet she was used to such demands and knew that her status as Henry's wife did not impress her fellow exiles. The seigneur's sudden declaration had caught her only partly by surprise, it being far from the first such incident. Now, seeing the state he was in, she wondered if she might not amuse herself with him, if only so that after the Marquis had paid for her favours she might reveal that the seigneur had enjoyed them for free.

'This is scarcely proper,' she answered him. 'Yet I see that I have aroused you, so I suppose I might offer relief. Purely as a gesture of kindness, you understand.'

He was sweating, desperate in his lust for her. Reaching out, she took a handful of his genitals and gave them a gentle squeeze through his breeches, finding his cock already half-stiff. His desperation amused her, while she found the prospect of satisfying him went some way to soothing her feelings at accepting the Marquis' proposal.

'You may take it out,' she said.

Trying hard to remain cool and poised but laughing within, she sat down and watched as he fumbled with his breeches' buttons. She smiled as he pulled out his penis, then reached for it and took it in hand. He gave a deep groan as she began to masturbate him, keeping his cock pointed carefully away from her body to avoid accidents.

'You are kind indeed,' he sighed, 'but surely if you are willing to touch me so you might grant me more. The

121

sight of your divine breasts, perhaps, or even more exquisite parts.'

'You do presume,' she answered, 'but perhaps my breasts. Yes, why not, you may see my breasts.'

She began to fiddle with the front of her bodice, all the while pulling at his now erect cock. His eyes were fixed on her cleavage, then on the full swell of her naked breasts and she popped first one and then the other free.

'So,' she declared coolly as she continued to masturbate him, 'you may tell d'Aignan that I accept his offer. The money must be sent in advance, in gold and discreetly. Then I will come to him tonight. He is to have a closed carriage waiting at the rear of this house from after midnight.'

'Yes, yes, it will be as you say,' he gasped. 'Now, pray, give me your full attention.'

Eloise smiled. Despite herself the scent and feel of his cock was starting to get to her. Although determined to deny him her cunny, she began to wonder if it might not be enjoyable to take his penis in her mouth. Still tugging hard at his cock, she sank into a squat, gaping to take him in as she pulled him around. The swollen knob was inches in front of her face, bobbing in her hand. She flicked her tongue out, tasting it, then saw a froth of tiny bubbles emerge from the tip, too late as it jerked in her hand and his come erupted into her face.

The bulk of it splashed across her nose and lip, more going into her mouth and on to her chin. She managed a grunt of disgust and let go of his cock, only for him to catch it up and finish himself off over her face and breasts. She shut her eyes, feeling the hot come as it splashed over her cheeks and tasting it in her mouth. Both breasts were soiled, and her neck, while thick blobs hung from her nose and chin, with her make-up running beneath the thick fluid.

'My darling! My beauty!' he exclaimed as he squeezed the final drop from his penis to hang suspended for an instant and then fall on to the lace of her dishevelled bodice.

Eloise could not find words but stayed still, feeling the come running slowly down her face and chest, half-disgusted and half-aroused. A voice sounded beyond the door and she tried to call out to Peggy not to admit anybody, only for another, masculine voice to call her name, Henry's. Her eyes came open in shock and she pushed the seigneur back, but it was too late, the door had opened to reveal Henry, Charles, Judith and, behind them, Peggy.

Henry took an instant to take in the scene, Eloise frozen with her breasts naked and her face spattered with come, de Poinchy frantically attempting to return his penis to his breeches. She rose slowly, her lip trembling.

'By God, I'm going to take my belt to your backside, you little slut,' Henry roared, 'pregnant or otherwise!'

'Not while I have breath!' de Poinchy answered bravely although he had been backing away across the room.

'No, Philippe,' Eloise broke in. 'He is my husband. It is his right.'

'Damned true!' Henry answered. 'Come here, puppy.'

Eloise crossed the room, her head bowed in submission. Henry had pulled the belt from his breeches and taken a seat, his eyes still fixed on the furious seigneur. Beyond were Charles and Judith, one trying to look stern, the other hiding a giggle. Peggy stood in the doorway, looking flustered. Eloise knew none would be asked to leave the room, and that all would enjoy watching her disciplined, yet she gave no resistance as Henry took her hand and drew her down across his knees.

Being laid across Henry's lap and exposed for beating always filled her with an awful sense of indignity and a corresponding arousal. The fact that she, Eloise, daughter of the Comte Saonnois, should have her bottom

123

bared for spanking like any common wench invariably produced a mind-numbing sense of impropriety and injustice. Yet it was done, frequently, and the knowledge of how wet and open it would make her cunny only added to her shame.

It had not happened since her belly began to swell, and as her balance went and her legs flew up she found that her pregnancy added a new intensity to the humiliation of the position. Being bent over inevitably thrust her bottom up, and Henry usually either cocked his leg up or wrapped it around hers, both acts increasing the exposure of her bottom when her skirts were lifted. Now, with her swollen belly pressed to his lap, her bottom was more prominent than ever, with her cheeks wide enough to ensure a display of gaping cunny and winking anus as soon as her skirts came up.

Her head was hanging down, allowing her to look back between the legs of the chair. With her bodice undone her breasts were swinging bare, a rude display she was glad the others could not see clearly, yet nothing to what she was about to show. She saw Henry's hand take hold of the hem of her skirts and then they were being lifted, her petticoats with them, the whole mass of material rising to show her legs and then her bare, spread bottom. A pang of intense shame went through her as she felt the air on her cunny and between her bottom cheeks, while having her skirts lifted meant that she could see not only her stockinged legs but the room beyond. Charles and Judith stood directly behind her, neither troubling to conceal their interest in her naked bottom. Peggy stood behind them, one finger in her mouth. Beyond was de Poinchy, his mouth open, frozen in disbelief, his eyes fixed on what she had denied him.

'That's right, watch her beaten, you French pimp!' Henry declared.

With that the first slap landed, catching Eloise hard on the crest of her bottom and drawing a squeal from

124

her lips. The second followed immediately, then more, until she was kicking and squealing, beating her fists on the floor and thrashing her legs about, all thoughts of dignity or the display she was making of her sex gone in the overwhelming pain of spanking. It was hard, the thick leather belt cracking down on her naked bottom without mercy, to cover both cheeks and the upper surfaces of her thighs. She was squealing incontinently from the start, then began to cry and finally to beg for it to stop, at which Henry relented. She lay inert, her bottom sore and throbbing, still stuck high with the cheeks open to show both cunny and bottom hole to the world. Her face was a mess, streaked with tears and sperm, the make-up ruined and her hair in a wild tangle.

'Now get out, before I take a dog whip to you!' Henry snarled at de Poinchy. 'Damned Frog! And if this gets out I swear you'll end your days at the bottom of the Thames!'

The seigneur left hurriedly, but Henry made no effort to release Eloise from her position across his knee. Instead he began to fondle her reddened bottom, an intimacy she found impossible to resent despite the indignity of having it done in front of an audience.

'So, my little puppy,' he said as she felt a finger trace a line down the crease of her bottom, 'I see you have been becoming too enthusiastic, and as I promised I have given you the beating you so richly deserve. Not in St James, so you may consider yourself fortunate.'

Eloise managed a weak whimper. Between her legs she could see Charles and Judith, now seated together on a couch, while Peggy had gone to close the door behind the Seigneur de Poinchy. A finger touched her anus and she opened her mouth to protest, only to think better of it.

'Yet perhaps I should not be too harsh,' Henry went on. 'Doubtless that French fellow was a potential investor.'

Eloise managed a small, choking sound. Henry still had his thumb on her anus, while his fingers were working on her sex. She could feel her own wet cunny, along with the warm glow of her bottom, and she found herself pushing her bottom out in response even as she gave a sob of pure shame.

'So,' Henry declared, 'Judith, Charles, it seems you must excuse me. As you may see, my wife's cunny is running like a pump. It would be a shame to waste such copious lubrication.'

Sir Joseph Snapes held up the ingot, turning it in his hand to catch the light. It was the product of a single block of Wheal Purity ore, and represented a yield more typical of washed and graded ore than of raw stone. He was in his study, along with Luke Hurdon and three other men, all of whom were in his closest confidence. Among them one stood out as less obviously a gentleman than the others, a thin, sharp-faced man in a simply cut suit of brown cloth and a green waistcoat.

'They have no idea what they have come upon,' he was saying as he admired the block of tin. 'No idea whatever. If the seam runs to depth at the same width it shows at surface we shall be among Cornwall's leading mines within the year. There are fortunes to be made, several fortunes.'

'And you wish us to help back the scheme?' Hurdon enquired.

'Yes,' Snapes answered. 'When more stock is offered, you will buy it, ensuring us a controlling interest. Meanwhile Mr Eadie here will keep an eye on the mine and ensure it is brought into production at best speed.'

'When shall I go down, sir?' the thin man answered.

'Start tomorrow,' Snapes instructed. 'They are really no more than amateurs and your experience will be valuable. I have asked for books to be kept and they are sending down some girl to do it. Check them regularly and make sure expenses do not get out of hand. They had allowed the men a half-holiday when I was down, just on account of this fellow Truscott's birthday. Too slack by half, I'm sure you'll agree.'

Eadie nodded and the others began to ask about their parts in the scheme and what rewards they might expect. Snapes answered each question, occasionally breaking off to take a pull on the long, clay pipe that smouldered on a stand. Eventually they left, each satisfied with his part and Snapes sat back, alone with his thoughts for the first time in days.

The mine offered what seemed a heaven-sent opportunity to renew his fortunes, and he was already considering ways to maximise his gain from the operation. The thought of the naivety of Henry Truscott and Charles Finch brought a smile to his face. Even the frightening and disagreeable experience of being robbed had not been without its rewards. Watching the beautiful Judith Cates forced to strip and raped on her knees in the mud had been one of the most exhilarating experiences of his life.

Eloise stepped carefully to the floor of her bedroom. The household was asleep, of that she was certain. At dinner it had been no great task to ensure that Henry got thoroughly drunk. As usual he had also become amorous, and had given her a gentle spanking and then taken her from the rear before passing out. She had retired to her own room and waited until the last of the servants had gone to bed. With Peggy on her way to the mine to act as bookkeeper she was having to make do with the services of the tweenie, yet this was now an advantage as it made keeping her assignment with the Marquis d'Aignan that much easier.

It was not an assignation she had any great desire to keep, save only for two factors. Firstly a sense of honour as two thousand pounds in gold lay carefully concealed about her room. Secondly, she was determined that she would outdo Judith in supplying investors for the mine. The prospect of finally surrendering to the Marquis was distasteful yet strangely compelling, coming as it did after so many years of resisting his advances. Then there was also the prospect of telling him how many other lovers she had accepted for nothing once he was spent. In addition she intended to compare his physique and abilities with those of others, to his face, casting him in the worst possible light.

She managed to leave the house without incident and the promised carriage was drawn up in Gardener's Lane beside the rear of the house. The coachman she recognised as one of d'Aignan's men and she climbed in, biting her lip with the thrill of what she was doing and her uncertainty about the Marquis. The carriage set off, turning to the east at the park. Eloise sat primly in the back, remembering Henry's cock inside her and wishing he had taken the trouble to help her to her own orgasm.

The driver remained silent until they reached the house d'Aignan had taken in Bruton Street. Here she was helped to alight and escorted into the rear of the house via the garden and so indoors. The interior was ill lit, causing Eloise to stumble as she groped for the wall. Irritation welled up inside her and she rebuked the coachman, at which he reached forward and took a firm handful of her bottom. She squeaked in outrage and lashed out, but missed in the darkness and had to struggle to keep her balance.

'How dare you!' she hissed. 'Your master shall learn of this!'

'Then tell him,' the man answered and pushed open a door to flood the passage with light.

For an instant Eloise was blinded, but she managed a furious protest even before her vision cleared. One quick stride took her into the room and then she stopped, taken aback by what she saw. The Marquis d'Aignan was there, seated in a fine chair among rich furnishings. Between them was a large table, covered in a dark red cloth on which had been laid a number of devices wrought in iron. The nearest was a sort of cage, built approximately to the dimensions of the human head, with hinges and what she guessed to be a gag. The Marquis' face split into an ugly grin as he saw the direction of her gaze.

'A scold's bridle,' he addressed her. 'A most useful item and, I think you'll agree, an appropriate one. Beside it are a few contrivances I had made up to ensure that I gain full value from our coupling.'

Eloise swallowed, her intended angry remarks forgotten in shock.

'I offered love,' he went on, 'and in your arrogance you refused me. Yet you are willing to accept me for base payment. Your are a whore, Eloise de la Tour Romain, nothing better, and so it is as a whore that I intend to use you.'

His voice had risen as he spoke, taking on a demented edge that filled Eloise with terror. Suddenly the teasing she had so enjoyed seemed a dreadful mistake, a thoughtless act for which she was now about to pay.

'I will take my fill of that pretty cunt,' d'Aignan was saying. 'Then I will give you to the servants, of whom there are seven. They have been instructed to make full use of you, and in particular to ensure that you are thoroughly sodomised. The gag in the bridle will muffle your screams, but don't worry, it can be removed to allow you to suck on their penises. Now put it on.'

With trembling fingers Eloise reached for the bridle. The tears were starting in her eyes and she was wishing desperately for Henry, yet knew that she was beyond help. Picking up the bridle, she felt its horrid weight and the cold, unyielding iron. The back was a hinged door, with a clasp and lock, allowing the wearer's head to be locked within. She had seen women made to wear such things and had always imagined the dreadful shame of it, yet never once thought that she herself would be forced to do so. D'Aignan was smiling as she lifted it and raised it slowly to her face, only to stop, realising that once the gag was in her mouth she would be truly helpless.

'My husband will not permit this to go unpunished,' she managed, struggling to keep her voice even.

'And what will he do?' the Marquis sneered. 'Call me out and become a public laughing stock because his wife visited another man? No, if you are foolish enough to tell him he is likely to have the hide off your back himself.'

'Not so,' Eloise answered. 'He may punish me, and rightly, but he will revenge me.'

'Do you think I am scared of some English boy?' d'Aignan demanded. 'I may not have my full power here, but I am well protected, let me assure you. Now put it on, or I will call the servants and have you held down.'

'What of my baby?' she stammered. 'Have you no mercy?'

'More than you,' he answered. 'Since you were little more than a child I have loved you, and you have shown me nothing but contempt. Besides, what do I care for an Englishman's brat? Now put it on.'

Eloise glanced around, thinking the coachman still behind her. He had gone, but she had no doubt that he was within range of his master's call. Biting her lip, she put the mask to her face, opening her mouth to accept the gag. The cold metal touched her chin and she caught the sour smell of the leather, then the taste as it entered her mouth and stopped, with the upper rim pressed to her high-piled hair.

'Stupid girl,' d'Aignan said. 'Take off your wig.'

'I wear no wig,' Eloise answered. 'This is my hair, all my hair.'

The words had been said defiantly, choking back tears as she uttered them.

'Remarkable,' d'Aignan continued, 'you are indeed a beauty, although a whore and a shrew. Yes, that will be an amusing part of your lesson: when you are finished with I shall have your head shaved and send you back to your dolt of a husband as bald as an arse! For now, let it down.'

Eloise's tears started as she lowered the bridle and put her hands to her hair. D'Aignan chuckled at the sight and reached for the decanter of deep red wine that stood to one side. Her fingers searched for the pins that held her hair in place as he poured a glass, his gaunt body hazy through a mist of tears. His hand came to rest on the arm of the chair, his expression setting into a satisfied smile then turning abruptly to agony as Eloise drove a six-inch iron pin through his hand and into the wood of the chair.

He gave a bubbling cry, the wine spilling from his lips, then spraying out as he choked. Seizing the iron mask, Eloise brought it around and down on to his head, knocking his wig askew, then again and a third time, flailing wildly at him through a haze of tears and cursing him with every blow. Only when he slumped to one side did she stop, dropping the mask to the floor. Blood was running from his head and his skin had gone the colour of chalk, while a dribble of red wine ran from one corner of his mouth.

With panic rising inside her she turned for the door, only to hear footsteps in the corridor. Mumbling to herself in terror she forced d'Aignan's wig back on to his blood-stained head and tilted it to one side, then wrenched the pin from his hand. The wine glass fell to the floor, shattering, even as Eloise sank to her knees and scrabbled at the buttons of d'Aignan's breeches. They came loose even as she bent her head down over the unconscious man's cock. A polite tap sounded at the door, then it was opening.

131

Eloise looked around, her mouth open above the Marquis' limp penis. The coachman took one look and withdrew hurriedly, mumbling apologies to his master for intruding. Eloise climbed quickly to her feet. The hair pin lay on the floor, red with blood, and for an instant she considered plunging it into d'Aignan's chest. She bent, thought better of the act and made for the door, waiting until the coachman's footsteps had faded and then letting herself into the passage with her heart in her mouth.

A light was visible down the passage, with voices coming from the room. She caught the coachman saying how servile she had looked sucking d'Aignan's penis and that he would make her do the same. Another voice answered, declaring that he also would make Eloise suck him, but after his erection had been up her bottom. Shivering with fear, Eloise moved away, down the corridor and into a hall where dim light came from a crescent window above what could only be the front door. She found the key in the lock and turned it, drawing a grating noise that seemed like a stove being dragged over cobbles in the silence. The bolts followed and the door came open to the London night and the blessed shape of a cab driving down the street outside.

Reuben Eadie peered out from his hiding place among the ferns of Trethaw Wood. His long face immediately split into a triumphant smile. Below him a plump blonde stood by the stream, already in the first stages of disrobing. He knew her name was Peggy Wray and that she had come down to keep the records at Wheal Purity, but little else.

The amenities at the mine were close to non-existent, but an area upstream from the workings had been screened off to allow the two women who worked there a measure of privacy. Within hours of his arrival Eadie had worked out that this arrangement was likely to provide entertainment and maybe more. When Peggy had left her seat in the counting house he had waited the space of five minutes and then followed.

He had hoped to catch her washing, or perhaps peeing, but it seemed likely that he was in for an even finer display. She had a quantity of linen with her, not all of it her own, and was clearly going to wash this in a deep pool. Rather than wet her own clothes, she had begun to disrobe. With her dress undone she slipped it down, exposing most of two large, white breasts. Her fleshy waist bulged within her stays, while the front was pushed out by a plump belly, yet she was so full at the chest and hips that her middle seemed almost slim. Petticoats followed the dress to the ground, then her stays, allowing the full glory of her flesh to spill out, nude.

Dressed in no more than boots and stockings held up by lacy garters, she hung her clothes on a length of twine that ran between two trees, then completed her disrobing with her back to him. Her bottom was a delight, just the way he liked them. The buttocks were undeniably fat, yet firm and buoyant, two spheres of meaty, wobbling female flesh divided by a deep, high cleft. As he watched she bent to remove her boots, displaying the plump lips of her sex peeping out from between chubby thighs in a nest of gold curls.

His hand was on his cock, stroking the stiff shaft through his breeches and imagining how it would feel inserted between Peggy's meaty sex lips. The urge to move forward and catch her was strong, yet he held back, sure that he could have her if he wished but considering the use of seduction over outright force. In his mind he weighed the risks against the rewards. He had no doubt that Peggy would be an easy conquest. Her plump, soft curves suggested no great strength and he had no doubt whatever that he would be able to overcome her. Indeed, the idea of her ineffectual struggles and vain entreaties while he pushed her down

133

and then mounted her appealed to him as much as did the ultimate goal of getting his cock between the chubby lips of her sex. Certainly there was more pleasure to be gained in forcing her than from her willing submission. Unfortunately she was clearly on close terms with Todd Gurney, whose massive frame and scarred fists were not to be taken lightly. He had learned something of Gurney and knew that he had been a farrier sergeant and served in the colonies before taking over his father's forge in Plymouth. To risk Gurney's wrath was evidently foolish, and yet with Peggy's character it seemed altogether possible that if she were sufficiently shamed she might keep it to herself.

She had begun to wash the clothes, wading into the water with her back still to him and repeatedly bending to show off her sex lips. Also, when each garment had been thoroughly wrung, she would turn and cast it on to the line, making her big breasts bounce and displaying the rich crop of golden curls that covered her lower belly. His cock was rigid in his hand and he decided that he could not wait but had to have her and risk the consequences. Once more he hesitated, thinking of Todd Gurney, then rose as Peggy bent down once more to expose the rear of her sex.

Abruptly he ducked down again, realising that she was not alone. Another woman was approaching along the stream, the tiny, olive-skinned wife of Todd Gurney, who Eadie knew to be French but had only seen briefly. Peggy climbed from the water, hugging Natalie as they met and then beginning to chat merrily. Natalie began to strip, showing no concern whatever at Peggy's presence but revealing her pert, tight body without the least embarrassment. Eadie's interest quickened as he watched, enjoying the contrast between the two women, one plump, soft and blonde, the other, slim, neat and dark. The idea of accosting Peggy was now clearly impractical, and to attempt both was courting disaster,

134

yet Natalie had joined Peggy in the water and so he contented himself with pulling at his cock over the sight of the two naked girls as they bent to their task. When he came it was with a wave of regret that he had not taken his chance, and he made himself a promise to make good the omission as soon as possible.

Henry sat at ease in the drawing room of the house in Petty France. Eloise was beside him, her head curled into his lap as he stroked her hair. For the last few days she had been in a curious mood, desperate to be held and petted but less keen on sex than was normal. In particular she wanted her hair stroked, yet she had refused to allow him to bind and gag her, a game she generally enjoyed. He had put the mood down to her pregnancy, contenting himself with a pair of whores in Covent Garden when she had proved unwilling.

With Snapes' money in the bank and Wheal Purity now worth far more than he and Charles had invested, he found it hard not to be content, despite the risks they had run and the way things were threatening to get out of control. They had even discussed selling out to Snapes, but decided to press on and attempt to secure the full potential of the scheme as the rumour-mongering had worked so well. More and more people were making guarded enquiries and offers to buy stock, and as long as Snapes' man did not discover the true nature of the mine it seemed likely that they would succeed.

Peggy had been sent to the West Country not only to keep the books, but to instruct Gurney to slow the work as much as possible. Thus demand for stock could be brought to a head, with each day gained adding to their prospective fortune. With Snapes now promoting the mine for them it even seemed possible that he and Charles might not be the main targets for recrimination when the inevitable collapse came.

'Did I mention,' he remarked as he continued to stroke Eloise's hair, 'that you no longer need concern yourself with spreading rumours? With Snapes on board we have ample finance for the time being. So no need to suck any more French cocks, eh puppy?'

Six

'Yes, sir, Mr Watt, sir. That is most considerate of you, sir,' Reuben Eadie said, clutching his hat to his chest.

Todd Gurney looked on with ill-concealed disgust. By ill luck the engineer had not only been in Cornwall when he had received Snapes' order for a beam engine, but had been in a position to visit Wheal Purity. Eadie had also managed to negotiate the purchase of one of the Boulton and Watt beam engines lying idle at Dolcombe mine, and was now fawning over James Watt in an effort to get it installed by the firm.[8]

'I might undertake to begin in a fortnight,' Watt was saying. 'Yet if you are as shallow as you say, surely your Newcomen can at least suffice for now?'

'Not with the rain we've been having,' Gurney answered. 'She's no sooner dry than she fills up again.'

'I am surprised,' Watt said. 'Perhaps you would allow me to make an inspection?'

Gurney could think of no reason to refuse and so acquiesced, leading the way into the engine house. Inside, the old Newcomen engine was groaning and shuddering with the great beam moving slowly up and down amid clouds of steam, a most impressive sight which Gurney knew achieved almost nothing.

'This must be the last of these working in Cornwall,' Watt yelled over the racket. 'You just installed it, you say?'

Gurney nodded.

'But not well, I fear,' Watt shouted. 'Your valves are improperly set. You must be losing over half what little pressure you have.'

Gurney nodded again and reluctantly began to assist as the engineer made adjustments. Presently the noise and steam had abated somewhat. Watt shrugged and shook his head, then gestured them outside.

'That should have your mine dry soon enough,' he announced as they came out into the relative quiet of the mine site.

'Thank you, sir, most gracious, sir,' Eadie replied, still clutching his hat.

'Pray don't mention it,' Watt replied. 'Now, I must be on my way, but I shall send a man to supervise the disassembly of the engine at Dolcombe.'

Gurney glanced down the slope as Eadie continued to try and ingratiate himself with Watt. The outflow from the adit, which had been little more than a trickle, was now a rush, which meant the exposure of the end of the schorl seam unless he acted quickly. Glancing to the west, he wished fervently for more rain, then made for the counting house were Peggy was writing out the book for the week's wage bill.

Peggy Wray stood up from her chair and stretched. An hour, Todd had said, or more if she could manage it. That Reuben Eadie would follow her if she went to the washing pool was in little doubt. He had done so twice before, never realising that Gurney had been aware of his every move. When Todd had told her she had been scared, but accepted his reasoning that anything that kept Eadie's attention away from the mine was worthwhile.

Both knew that Eadie might do more than merely watch and Gurney did his best to keep an eye on him in turn. Although she had not admitted it, Peggy found a curious fascination in being spied on, a pleasure that had grown since the day she had been caught masturbating near Dolcombe mine.

Now it was different, with an urgent need for Eadie's attention to be drawn away while Gurney attempted to arrange an accident that would disable the Newcomen. There would be nobody to protect her, and she was trembling as she stepped from the counting house and stretched in the bright spring sunlight. Eadie was visible, down slope, instructing a group of men on the cutting of the new adit. Gurney was with them and Peggy waved and called out, drawing their attention over the noise of the mine. Using hand signals she indicated that she was going up to the washing pool, then made for the living quarters to collect the laundry.

There was too little to really warrant washing, but by adding a few clean petticoats she managed to make a convincing bundle, which she tied and set off with, taking care to stay in view of the men below. Eadie glanced up, his eyes momentarily meeting hers. As she passed into the wood she was thinking of him, of the way he stared at her breasts and bottom, of the way he seemed to undress her with his eyes and of the way his cock always bulged within his breeches. Being watched was one thing, allowing him to touch her quite another. Yet only the previous night when she had brought herself to orgasm it had been over him. At first she had simply thought of him watching her and how it felt to have her naked body caressed by his eyes. Then, as she had neared orgasm the restraints of her self-respect had begun to slip. She had thought of him coming over her as he watched, then of him demanding his cock touched, and finally of being pushed down in the stream and mounted from behind. At that she had come, imagining his erection working fervently in her vagina as he pushed his skinny haunches against her ample bottom.

The memory now made her shiver with shame, yet she knew that if it came to it she would not scream and try to run, nor give more of a fight than was necessary to save face.

Reuben Eadie scrambled up the slope of Trethaw Wood. Now at last he had a clear opportunity to slake his lust with Peggy Wray. Natalie Gurney was in Climsland village, Todd Gurney occupied with the miners and Peggy had taken a large bundle of washing towards the pool. With his mind full of thoughts of her plump white bottom and huge breasts he pushed through the undergrowth, following what was now a familiar path. He was sure she had noticed him on the last occasion and had been taunting him, deliberately bending and adopting lewd poses as she washed. Possibly it had been chance, but in any case he was determined to have her, to make her suck his penis and push her breasts together to make a slide for it. He would make her kneel and display her broad white bottom so that he could take a stick to it. He would roll her on her back and make her play with her fat breasts as her humped her. He would make her masturbate in front of him and come in her face as she hit her own orgasm.

His cock was hard in his breeches as he sank into his watching place among the ferns. Peggy was down by the stream, going through her normal routine of stripping before washing the clothes. Already she was down to her underthings, with her big breasts stretching out a hopelessly inadequate chemise. Normally she undressed quickly, peeling down casually and then giving a wary glance around before taking off her petticoats to go nude. Now it was different. For one thing her nipples were erect, and she seemed to be teasing herself, tugging her laces open bit by bit to let her breasts free. Clearly something had excited her and he found himself smiling at the thought of how her behaviour would change when he accosted her with his erect prick sticking out of his breeches.

He freed it into his hand, watching all the while as she continued to undress. When at last she grew bored of teasing herself she shrugged off her chemise and threw it over the washing line, then began to undo her petticoat strings. With the bows loose she looked over her shoulder, then very deliberately stuck her bottom out and eased both coats down over her hips. Eadie nearly came in his hand as her magnificent bottom came on show and had to hurriedly let go of his cock to prevent it.

Peggy was nude and wading into the water with her bundle of dirty linen in her arms. He watched as she bent to put it down and caught a glimpse of her sex lips. As she began to scrub at a garment he started forward, creeping down the slope from the shelter of one tree to another. She continued to work, singing to herself and keeping her bottom towards him in a pose that made it easy to maintain his erection. In the shadow of the washing line he stopped, took a deep breath and then dashed forward. Peggy heard him as his boot hit the water. She turned, her squeal ringing out loud through the trees even as she lost her footing and went down with a splash in the pool. Her legs had flown up and he grabbed her by the ankles, pulling them wide to display the plump mound of her sex, half covered by the shallow water. As he tipped her up she went backwards, landing in the water with another squeal. Then he was on top of her and his erection was nudging her vulva. Twice he pushed, jamming his prick between her fat buttocks and then against her pubic bone, but found the hole on the third push and slid inside. She groaned as her vagina filled but made none of the effort to get him off for which he had been prepared.

With his body bouncing on her plump curves he began to fuck her, enjoying the warmth of her sex and the cool feel of the water on his balls. At first it was ecstasy, mounted on the woman who had been the

141

subject of his fantasies, and over whom he had come again and again. Yet in his mind she was always reluctant, struggling feebly and begging him not to have her. The reality was different, with her moaning and sighing as his cock worked inside her, showing no inclination to kiss but not trying to fight him either.

Determined to get a reaction other than pleasure, he grabbed her thighs and twisted in order to force her on to her front. She went with the pressure, allowing herself to be manoeuvred into a kneeling position with her huge white bottom thrust out towards him. Pushing forward he sank his cock into her, then began to fuck her once more, only now with her in a more thoroughly undignified position. She took no notice, if anything seeming to enjoy it more.

His cock was on the verge of explosion, rock solid inside her, while his view of her body and the feel of his front against the fat pillows of her bottom were drawing him ever closer to orgasm. With a great effort he pulled out, grasped her cheeks and hauled them apart, spreading her anus to make the little puckered hole stretch and gape.

'Now, you fat slut,' he grunted. 'Let us see how you enjoy sodomy!'

Peggy gave a meek whimper and he saw her bottom hole tense. Going up on to his feet, he mounted her, pressing his erection down between her buttocks. She gave a gasp of shock as the head of his penis found her rear hole. Thinking that she was going to protest he caught her by the hair, then forced his cock hard into her anal ring. With the shaft slick with her lubrication his cock slid in, easing its full length up her back passage to make him groan in ecstasy.

'Please, right in, deep in,' Peggy groaned.

The entirety of his cock was already up her bottom, the head agonisingly sensitive in the hot tube of her flesh. Her ring squeezed on his shaft and she giggled,

142

obviously enjoying being buggered just as she had being caught and mounted. Eadie could wait no longer, but began to move his erection in her rectum as he felt the approach of orgasm. She began to grunt, making oddly pig-like noises in keeping with the plump white flesh of her body. He took her by the waist, his hands filling with soft flesh which he kneaded as he buggered her. She moved, one shoulder dipping, and he realised that she had put a hand back to get at her cunny. He had wanted to make her grovel and beg not to be fucked, then to do it anyway. When he put his prick to her bum-hole he had wanted her to cry out in pain and outrage, then beg and plead for him to stop as his cock invaded her anus. She had done neither, but was rubbing at her cunny even as the full length of his cock was jammed up her bottom. He was coming, unable to hold back from the sheer physical pleasure of her body. A slimy sensation around his penis signalled that he had come in her bowels and then it was squeezing out around the shaft as he pushed his erection in to the hilt and felt her flesh squash against his front. He held it in, drawing out the moment of ecstasy as his own come ran down over his balls.

For him it was over, but not for Peggy. She was still grunting and whimpering, and gave a disappointed moan as he began to pull out. He took no notice, holding her buttocks wide with his thumbs and pulling his erection from her anus. It was glistening with come, wet and shiny as it left the distended ring of deep pink meat. The head popped free but her hole stayed open, a tube of dark red flesh with come running from it and down over her cunny. He sank back on to his haunches, watching in fascination as she masturbated in his sperm. The cool water touched his balls and he began to wash his cock, all the while staring at her rear view.

She was obviously in ecstasy, revelling in the filthy display she was making of her bottom. Her vagina was

gaping wide, her sex spread under her fingers, with the
wet flesh squirming beneath them. With her thighs
spread wide he could glimpse her breasts, the fat spheres
dangling in the water and making ripples as they swung
with her motion. Her anus began to close, expelling
more come on to her sex and over her fingers. The
mouth of her vagina squeezed shut, her anus with it,
both holes starting to contract and her grunting became
higher and more urgent, then changed to a squealing,
piping noise as she came.

Peggy stopped abruptly and sat her fat bottom down
in the pool, then turned, blushing, to smile at Eadie. He
grinned back, astonished by the strength of her lust,
pleased that she had proved so dirty but irritated by her
failure to show the shock and fear he had wanted. As
she began to wash, still smiling and looking shy but
quite unconcerned by her nudity, another possibility
occurred to him.

'I . . . I am sorry I took you unawares,' he said,
deliberately faltering. 'I was overcome by your beauty.
I . . . I could not resist.'

'Please,' she answered softly, 'say nothing. I understand your need. Come, I am becoming chilled. Let us
dry ourselves.'

As he stepped from the water he was thinking of the
possibilities offered by her acquiescence. Throughout his
life he had been frustrated by his inability to bend
women to his will, and Peggy seemed entirely pliable,
not just willing, but eager. The pleasure he took in such
acts as buggering girls unexpectedly when they were
excited by normal sex had the disadvantage that the
trick seldom worked more than once. Also, his reputation for such behaviour quickly spread. Now, with
Peggy, it seemed possible that he might be able to
indulge yet more dirty fantasies.

She had stayed to gather the clothes that remained in
the water and was now emerging with a great armful of

144

dripping linen. He looked at her, admiring her curves and wondering if she was simple, to so readily give in to shameful pleasures. Yet her apparent education and her ability to keep records and figures argued otherwise. He had discovered that her normal occupation was as maid to Eloise Truscott, who had been mentioned as a hard mistress. Possibly, he wondered, her reaction was simply the result of having had all her resistance beaten out of her in service. For her acceptance of him to be cowed submission rather than lust agreed with his preconceptions. He decided it must be the case, and that even the orgasm she had taken must have been for his benefit. Sitting down on the trunk of a fallen beech, he decided to test her pliancy.

'Put those down,' he ordered, 'and come here.'

Peggy obeyed, throwing her bundle haphazardly over the line and walking towards him.

'On your knees,' he continued. 'Stick out that big arse of yours and take my cock in your mouth. Make me hard again or I'll thrash you.'

She did as she was told, showing no hesitation as she got to her knees. As ordered she pushed out her bottom, making a fine display of the fleshy cheeks. Taking his cock in her hand she put it in her mouth and began to suck while also tickling his balls. Eadie sighed and leaned back, enjoying the feel of warm, female mouth on his penis but enjoying even more the fact that his order had been obeyed. Peggy sucked well and he was soon stiffening in her mouth and wondering if more pleasure was to be had by making her swallow his sperm or lick it up from her own breasts.

'Take it deep,' he ordered. 'In your throat, to the back. Yes, now . . .'

He stopped as a shudder passed through the ground beneath him. A great flock of birds took fright, rising in a cloud even as a great, thundering roar swept over them, making the trees shiver and sending more birds skywards in panic-stricken flocks. His cock slipped from Peggy's mouth as together they turned to gape towards the mine.

In his London club, Henry occupied his favourite chair in the library. He held a glass in one hand and a paper in the other, and would alternately sip at his cognac and read a section of one article or another. He had taken to visiting the club each morning and lunching there, allowing people to know where he was and seek him out. The process was predictable, almost routine. A man would approach him and ask for a word in private. Henry would grant it and then listen to an offer of money for shares in Wheal Purity. Some were timid, others serious, still others demanding, yet all met with the same assurance, that in due course they would be invited to Le Roy's coffee house, where a number of shares would be offered for sale.

Augustus Barclay had just left, having taken a tone both hectoring and defensive. The incident with Judith had not been mentioned, although Barclay had clearly been ill at ease in Henry's presence. As always Henry had promised to inform him of the date of the meeting, only changing his tone at the last moment to suggest that Barclay leave the bull whip at home on the day.

Even as Barclay's footsteps faded on the stair Henry heard someone else begin to ascend. He gave a tolerant shake of his head and opened his paper, only to look up in surprise as the door crashed open. Saunder Cunningham stood in the entrance, glaring angrily at Henry. Behind came Squire Robson and two of Cunningham's friends, all looking anxious.

'Ah, Saunder,' Henry called out, 'you look out of sorts. Lost at billiards again? Who was it, some bantling trollop or a blind fellow?'

'Damn you, Truscott!' Cunningham swore. 'You've cheated me!'

146

'I have?' Henry asked mildly, wondering if Cunningham was referring to the mine or had discovered his wife's unfaithfulness.

'You know damned well what I mean!' Cunningham shouted. 'You stole Trethaw Wood from under my nose, knowing all the time how much that mine was worth!'

'This is the club library,' Henry answered. 'It is considered polite to speak quietly, if at all. As to Trethaw Wood, as I recall I won the right to buy it from you as part of a bet. I had intended to use it as a pheasant covert, for which purpose you will admit it is largely useless. The discovery of the potential of Wheal Purity was mere accident.'

'I'll be damned if it was,' Cunningham hissed. 'You knew!'

'Not at all,' Henry replied. 'Only by sheer luck did the man I employed to have the old shaft blocked realise the quality of the ore.'

'Yes,' Cunningham spat. 'Todd Gurney, who is now your mine captain. Don't think I don't know what you're about, Henry Truscott!'

'I merely seek to make the best of my circumstances,' Henry replied. 'You sold me what you thought a worthless piece of land, and now you find it was not worthless after all, you come at me, all wrath and righteous indignation.'

'Robson here says you were damn smug about having bought the wood,' Cunningham went on. 'You knew, and I'll not believe otherwise.'

'Let us assume, then,' Henry answered, 'as you are blind to reason, that I did know. What matter?'

'I own you've a right to the wood,' Cunningham replied. 'Make over half the shares to me and I'll take it no further.'

'My own holding is currently no more than a third part of the shares,' Henry answered, 'and these are

147

conservatively valued at six thousand pounds. As I paid you fifty guineas for the whole concern you must admit I would be a fool to accept your offer. No, if you wish to buy stock we shall be auctioning it at Le Roy's when we have a clearer idea of the total worth of the mine. I bid you good day.'

Henry lifted his paper, purposefully blocking his view of all four men but ready to dodge a punch if Cunningham's temper snapped. A snort of anger sounded from beyond the paper barrier but nothing more. Cunningham had turned on his heel when Henry, unable to resist the temptation, called out after him.

'Do pass my compliments to your charming wife, and mention how delightful she was in her green gown.'

He had expected Cunningham to ignore the insult, given that it would mean revealing that he had been cuckolded to both Robson and the two friends. Instead, after an instant for Cunningham to react Henry found the paper torn away from in front of his face.

'Damn you to hell, Truscott!' Cunningham roared. 'I'll have the satisfaction of you, you debaucher, you villain, you bare-faced thief!'

'Your words give me no choice but to accept,' Henry managed, although somewhat taken aback by the vehemence of the other's reaction. 'Who will be your second?'

'Lord Covehithe, damn you,' Cunningham answered, gesturing at one of his friends.

'Very well,' Henry answered. 'Your lordship, you may expect a call from Mr Charles Finch in good time. I suggest Tuthill fields,[9] Saunder. The view is so hand-some in May, rather like me really.'

Cunningham sprang at him, his hands clutching. Henry dodged to the side as the three others grabbed for Cunningham and hauled him back.

Todd Gurney stared in satisfaction at the ruins of the Wheal Purity engine house. The extension that had housed the boiler was a total wreck, with the roof completely gone and most of one wall blown away. The massive beam had been dislodged and lay half out of the engine house with its supports no more than twisted metal. Bits of slate and iron lay all around, while a thin plume of steam still issued from the pipes in the engine house. Eadie had come up and was staring aghast at the wreckage, with Peggy beyond, while the miners clustered further down the slope.

'What happened?' Eadie demanded.

'Couldn't take the pressure, too old,' Todd replied.

'But Mr Watt himself adjusted it!'

'Too used to new devices, that Mr Watt. Her boiler must have been forty years old or more, and in use for most of that. Still, none hurt, so we'll wait for the new engine and get on with the adit.'

Eadie nodded blankly, apparently oblivious to the fact that his breeches were wet to above the knee and open at the crotch.

Charles Finch raised his cane in lazy salute as he recognised the figure of Lord Covehithe among those walking in St James's Park. They met, linked arms and for a moment exchanged small talk, discussing the fine May weather, the recent meeting at Newmarket and the effects of the act to regulate chimney sweeping. Only when they had crossed to Green Park and began to ascend the relatively empty slope of Constitution Hill did their conversation turn to the quarrel between Henry Truscott and Saunder Cunningham.

'So, Thomas,' Charles remarked, almost casually, 'it seems we must mediate. Henry has no great interest in pursuing the affair and would be prepared to accept an apology.'

'It is unlikely to be forthcoming,' Lord Covehithe replied. 'Saunder is in a fury over this mine affair, and indeed, he has probably done more to bolster your stock than you yourselves. Besides, is there not a certain irony

149

in Henry Truscott demanding an apology for being referred to as a debaucher?'

'Ah, yes,' Charles admitted. 'Perhaps Henry would be prepared to have the apology restricted to those terms "villain" and "bare-faced thief", so long as it is sufficiently public.'

'Has he had May Cunningham?'

'Yes, several times. With Saunder in London so much of the time she becomes bored, as does Henry while at the mine. They take solace in each other's company.'

'How much of that Saunder is aware of I do not know. Still, I doubt he would be prepared to apologise on any terms.'

'Saunder thinks himself a devil of a fellow, does he not?'

'Yes, and with his wealth he is not short of friends eager to encourage that opinion. Indeed, I myself must confess to having egged him on now and again.'

'Fine sport, no doubt, and Henry is rather of the same opinion. So, it seems we must have our duel.'

'I fear so, but we must endeavour to ensure the minimum of bloodshed.'

'Quite. Henry might be persuaded to choose foils and if we were to pull them apart at first blood honour would be satisfied.'

'An ideal solution, Charles, you are as diplomatic as ever. I also suggest they meet at first light, and perhaps at a site less public that Tuthill Fields.'

'No, there Henry is adamant. It is to be Tuthill Fields, by the row of trees near the artillery grounds. He feels three o'clock in the afternoon will be a civilised hour.'

'Three o'clock! Half of London will be there! The duel is already the talk of half the drawing rooms in town, thanks to Bertie Robson's great mouth. Come, Charles, surely we should keep this affair from the vulgar gaze.'

'To the contrary,' Charles replied. 'We wish it to be as public as possible.'

* * *

'I wish to keep my chemise and gloves,' Judith declared. 'The floor is a trifle rough should we take a fall.'

'Sensible girl,' Henry answered. 'Damn painful, I imagine, splinters in your bubbies.'

Judith was already naked from waist to stocking tops, with the low swell of her belly peeping out from beneath the front of her chemise and her buttocks on display behind. Three other girls stood nearby, all in similar states of undress, although two had removed their chemises and stood bare-breasted. All were giggling at the men's attention as they stood in a cleared space at the centre of the wood-floored hall. It was the upper room of the Pheasant, which Henry had hired to celebrate his coming duel with Saunder Cunningham.

With the duel the next day it was an act of deliberate bravado that had been greeted with enthusiasm. Several toasts had already been drunk to Henry, while the atmosphere was heightened by the air of expectation and danger, with everyone determined to make the best of it. Several bets had already been taken, involving either drinking or the removal of pieces of clothing from the handful of girls bold enough to attend. With ten men to each girl Judith had been thoroughly enjoying herself and had already deliberately lost at billiards in order to get spanked across the table.

Two men had held her arms while another lifted her skirts. With her bare bottom stuck high over the edge of the table she had been spanked by Charles, squealing and kicking as the men clapped in time to her beating. It had been her first spanking since the bruises on her bottom had faded and she had thoroughly enjoyed it, making far more fuss than necessary. Her punishment had changed the atmosphere of the party, adding a rude element, and when Henry had suggested a tarts' wheel-barrow race the idea had been taken up with enthusiasm.

The rules were simple, the girl going face down on her hands while the man held her up by the hips with his cock inside her. Each girl was then obliged to crawl forward on her hands while the man walked, aiming to cross the length of the hall. Disqualification was immediate should a cock slip from a vagina. A guinea from each man competing had gone into the pot, which went to the winner.

Judith sank down and began to unbutton Charles' breeches. His cock sprang out, already turgid, and she began to suck, drawing laughter and clapping from the audience. The other three girls were also exciting their men, two in their hands, one between her naked breasts. As Charles came to full erection in her mouth Judith judged their chances. Squire Robson was due to ride a petite blonde, and the two were ludicrously ill matched. It seemed likely that Robson, six foot and portly, would leave his tiny partner hanging almost vertically from his cock, a ludicrous posture that would make any movement at all difficult. More serious opposition was likely to come from Conrad Clive, who now had his cock engulfed in his mistress's cleavage. The girl, Susie, was a friend of Judith's, having been at Mother Agie's together. Although inconveniently busty, Susie was strong, yet Conrad seemed the most drunk of the men racing. The strongest opponent seemed to be Henry himself, who was coming speedily to erection in the hand of a tall, black-haired girl while he fondled her bare breasts.

'We are all ready, it seems?' Henry called out, gesturing to his friend's erection.

'Ready indeed,' Charles called back. 'If you might let go, my dear?'

Judith pulled back, letting his cock slide slowly free of her lips. Staying on her knees, she scrambled over to where a chalk line had been drawn on the floor. Robson was already mounting his partner, his cock easing inside her to leave her dangling almost clear of the floor. Judith giggled at the sight. The blonde girl grinned back through the curtain of hair that had fallen around her face.

'Ready then?' Charles demanded.

Raising herself up on her legs, Judith presented him with her bottom. Charles took hold of her thighs, lifting her, then pulling her back until his balls nudged her cunny. Holding her with a single hand, he took his cock and put it inside her. Judith sighed as she filled and wiggled her hips to make his penis move inside her. Charles held her firmly and began to fuck her with short, gentle motions as they waited for the others. Judith could see them from her upside-down position, Henry just easing himself into his girl while Conrad seemed to be having difficulty entering Susie.

'Gentlemen, are your members secure?' Sir John Church called out, having been appointed referee in view of his experience with racing.

'Hold on, Sir John!' Conrad called out. 'Yes, there, I have it!'

Judith saw the expression on Susie's face change as Conrad's cock was pushed suddenly up her. She opened her mouth to speak, only for Sir John Church to slam the base of a bottle down on to a table and yell for the race to start. Charles pushed forward immediately, catching Judith off balance. She went down on one shoulder, righting herself only for Conrad's leg to catch her as he surged forward. Susie squealed and the four of them went down, collapsing to the floor in a tangle of limbs. Judith had rolled and found herself beneath Conrad, with his cock pressed to her belly. Susie was half underneath her, the softness of her bottom cushioning Judith's head. All four were helpless with laughter, the race forgotten until a sudden bellow of triumph drew their attention back. Judith squirmed around to see Squire Robson cross the finish line, dashing forward with his partner projecting from his cock at the horizontal, her hands entirely clear of the floor.

An uproar immediately began, some calling Robson a cheat, others cheering his technique. Calls went up for an adjudication from Sir John Church, with both Charles and Conrad joining in. Judith stayed down, content to make a pillow of Susie's bottom. The skin felt warm, making her think of her own, freshly spanked cheeks, and she wondered if some new game might not be proposed that would allow more intimate contact between herself and her friend. It had been a while since she had had another girl, and being forced to lick Mother Agie's enormous vulva hardly counted.

'Aren't men so very silly,' she remarked to Susie and patted her friend's bottom. 'As if it matters who won?'

'With four guineas to the winner?' Susie answered. 'Sure it matters.'

'It's not the money they care for, but the sport,' Judith assured her. 'At least that is what Charles always tells me.'

The discussion among the men had grown in volume, with Henry and Squire Robson at its centre and Sir John Church attempting to mediate.

'Do you remember how Mother Agie used to make us fight for the benefit of the men?' Judith asked Susie. 'With flowers in our bottoms and the first to pull the other's free with her teeth the winner?'

Susie giggled in response and Judith jumped to her feet, then blew a piercing whistle to draw the men's attention. Only a few responded, so she marched in among them and climbed on to a chair, then pushed her bottom in between Henry's face and that of Sir John Church. Henry bit her bottom, but all eyes were on her.

'You mustn't squabble so, boys,' she announced. 'Do any of you remember how the girls at Mother Agie's used to fight?'

Several voices were raised in agreement.

'Then,' Judith declared, 'I say that Henry should have won the wheelbarrow race, but if any girl thinks otherwise and can take my flower I will submit to her verdict.'

There was an instant chorus of agreement, many egging her on, others volunteering to fetch flowers from Lincoln's Inn Fields and Bertie Robson calling for a champion. Judith scanned the crowd from her vantage point on the chair. Susie had got up, but was hanging giggling on to Conrad Clive's arm. The small girl who had partnered Robson was looking doubtful, while Henry's partner was whispering together with the remaining two females. They were evidently choosing who should volunteer, and Judith smiled, only to turn at an unexpected shout from the far end of the room.

'I'll do it!' the voice called and Judith immediately felt a lump rise in her throat.

Behind the crude counter beyond which the barrels of ale and bottles were stacked stood not the landlord but his wife. She was a massive, raw-boned woman, handsome in a matronly way. With her huge breasts and wide hips Judith judged her to be at least double her own weight.

'Mrs Figgis is game!' somebody called out. 'Bertie, will you have her as your champion?'

'Certainly I shall!' Robson shouted back. 'Come, my good Mrs Figgis, it is fine that you stand for honour and common sense.'

The landlady replied with a meaningful grin and threw down the greasy cloth with which she had been wiping the counter. Judith swallowed, certain that the big woman had only volunteered in order to enjoy exerting her strength on a smaller fellow female. The men, however, obviously thought the idea highly amusing. Judith had been expecting a playful tussle with Susie, perhaps ending tangled together with their faces in each other's cunnies. That had generally been how the bouts ended at Mother Agie's, and although not entirely averse to losing she was not at all sure what the big woman intended for her.

155

'You're in game fettle tonight, my dear,' Charles said as he lifted her down from the chair. 'Keen for a woman to smack that pretty behind?'

'I had rather set my mind to smacking Susie's,' Judith replied. 'Let Mrs Figgis beat my bottom by all means, but no more.'

'What if she wishes to subdue you, and perhaps to sit up upon your head? That's what she did another time, and fine sport it was for all!'

Judith nodded weakly and began to unlace her chemise. Mrs Figgis had reached the cleared area and was disrobing to the sounds of demands that both women go naked. Judith continued to strip, peeling off stockings and gloves with slow, careful motions so that the audience could appreciate her trim figure and how well it looked beside that of her opponent. Mrs Figgis took little notice, but stripped with a methodical calm, handing each garment to the shocked potboy.

Naked, Judith turned to face her opponent. Mrs Figgis was even more daunting in the nude than she had been dressed. Her forearms seemed to roll with muscle, built strong from years of moving barrels and crates. Nor did she seem to have more than a touch of excess fat, with her ample curves surprisingly firm and muscular. Even her huge breasts sagged less than Judith had expected.

'Courage,' Henry's voice sounded from behind Judith. 'She is big, true, but your speed may yet tell. You need merely duck down between her legs and nip the flower from her arse.'

'She looks as if she could hold a good-sized branch and not let go,' Judith answered. 'What if she simply clenches her buttocks?'

'Then bite her arse, or better still her cunt.'

'She'd thrash me bloody!'

'Oh, don't worry, Charles and I will pull her off before she gets too many strokes in.'

156

'Thank you, Henry. Your advice is a great comfort.'

The door had opened as she spoke, admitting the two men who had gone for flowers. They were laughing and one carried two enormous hollyhocks, both in bloom, one yellow, one deep red and each with a stem as thick as a thumb.

'Splendid!' Henry called out. 'Bottoms up, girls, and then once more into the breech as the bard would have it!'

'What's this?' Mrs Figgis demanded. 'I thought the trollop and I were wrestling, with victory after three falls, or some such rule?'

'No, no,' Robson informed her. 'The rules are simple. Each has a flower in her breech, and the first to pull the other's forth is the winner. Certainly a little rough and tumble is expected, but you must secure the flower, that is the key.'

Mrs Figgis grunted but made no objection, simply taking the red flower. Waddling heavily across to the table at which supper was to be set out, she thrust the stem into a pat of butter and then turned her back to the room. With no more than a slight grimace, she inserted the flower into her bottom, then stood, with the bloom thrust out backwards from between her meaty buttocks.

'Your flower, my dear?' Charles asked, holding it out towards Judith.

'You do it,' she answered, 'although I do think you boys might have had the taste to choose one that goes with my hair.'

She bent and pulled her bottom cheeks apart, resulting in delighted catcalls and lewd remarks from the audience. With her bottom hole showing she immediately felt a fresh tingle of arousal, thinking that losing might not be such a bad thing after all. She stayed in position, with all her rudest details on show while Charles went to grease the hollyhock stem. He came up behind her and the stem touched her anus, making her wince as the tough fibres prodded her hole.

'Relax,' Charles instructed and Judith pushed out her anus, then clenched it as the stem touched, drawing it into the tight hole.

Charles slid the flower well up her bottom, leaving it protruding in a way that she knew from experience looked extraordinarily rude. A good two feet was projecting from her anus, while the tiny hairs of the stem tickled, producing a sensation irritating, yet arousing as it heightened her awareness of her bottom hole and the state she was in.

'Ready then, girls!' Sir John Church called out.

Judith stepped out into the clear area of floor, facing Mrs Figgis. Looking at the big woman with the great hollyhock protruding from her anus made it hard not to laugh. Many of the men were, along with calls of encouragement to one party or the other and offers of odds. So obvious was the mismatch that not even the most dedicated gamblers would take up odds on her, giving Judith a sinking feeling as she faced her opponent.

'Then you may begin!' Church called.

Mrs Figgis came forward with her arms and legs spread, her face set in a determined grin. Knowing that once she was grappled she had lost, Judith decided to follow Henry's advice. She hurled herself down and forward, aiming between Mrs Figgis' knees. The men cheered at the bold move, but an instant later Judith found her head trapped between Mrs Figgis' muscular thighs. With her bottom the highest part of her body and the hollyhock projecting upwards from her anus she knew that she presented a truly ludicrous picture. Yet she could do nothing, and as Mrs Figgis' hands took her by the hips she knew she had lost. She was lifted into the air, her legs kicking wildly. Mrs Figgis' chin bumped her bottom and she heard the crunch of the hollyhock

158

stem in the woman's teeth. Then it was being pulled out of her bottom; she felt her anus close and she had lost. The audience was laughing, both men and women, along with a few declarations of disappointment that the bout had been so short.

'I'll give you something to watch,' Mrs Figgis' voice boomed out from above Judith. 'Just let me get this little bobtail on her back.'

Judith guessed what was coming from the lustful tone of the big woman's voice. She was laid down, Mrs Figgis still holding on to her hips, then the big woman's bottom was over her face, with the hollyhock sticking out from between the cheeks.

'Pull the flower out, little one,' Mrs Figgis ordered, 'and we'll see how you like the taste of me.'

Feeling shamed and helpless, Judith reached for the flower as Mrs Figgis sank down over her. It came free and she threw it aside, then took a deep breath as the huge bottom settled down towards her face. Mrs Figgis' buttocks were wide over her face, spread to show off a remarkably hairy cunny and a broad, wrinkled anus. Judith stuck her tongue out, expecting to be made to lick the woman's clitoris, only to gasp in sudden shock as she realised that it was not the woman's cunny she was expected to lick, but her anus. Then the big buttocks had settled down on her face and it was too late. Mrs Figgis' bottom hole was right over Judith's mouth, still wide from the hollyhock stem and greasy with butter. Unable to breath, she could only writhe her head futilely and wriggle her body in helpless protest.

Her resistance lasted only seconds. Overcome by the experience of being so thoroughly used, she surrendered, poking her tongue out and starting to lick Mrs Figgis' anus. With her head back she could just get air to her nostrils, drawing in deep sniffs, thick with the big woman's scent. The muscular ring of Mrs Figgis' bottom hole was squeezing on Judith's tongue, while her mouth was spread over it. Hands gripped her ankles and pulled her legs up and open, displaying her sex to the room. Raucous laughter greeted the sight, and comments on the ginger colour of her pubic hair and the wetness of her cunny.

Judith knew it was true. She was excited beyond resistance, revelling in being abused on the floor, in having her sex spread out in front of an audience and in the feel of her tongue in the big woman's bottom. It was obvious what she was doing, of that she was certain; some fifty people were watching her lick another woman's anus, a woman who had conquered her and handled her like a toy. Her face was smothered in bottom, and she could see nothing, only feel and taste the open, wet bum-hole over her mouth and hear the laughter and applause of the watchers.

Unable to resist it, Judith reached down, finding her cunny with her fingers. Mrs Figgis laughed and pulled Judith's legs higher. Men began to cheer and clap as Judith started to masturbate, and she heard Susie's squeal of shock and delight. Her own anus was showing and she put a finger into it, determined to give as dirty a show as possible. The little hole opened easily, taking two finger joints, which she began to move about inside. Spreading her cunny, she started to rub, teasing her clitoris towards orgasm.

It came in a rush, almost before she knew it was happening. As the ecstasy hit her she began to burrow her tongue deeper up the big woman's bottom, licking and kissing at the buttery anus. Her legs were kicking in Mrs Figgis' grip, her chest heaving and her buttocks clenching on her fingers. As her climax hit her breathing became impossible, yet she was too far gone to stop and continued, rubbing at her clitty and probing her anus in front of everybody as she came and came while her lungs seemed ready to burst.

People were stamping and clapping, calling out encouragement and ever filthier suggestions. At the very peak of Judith's orgasm it was her absolute exposure that she was thinking of, then nothing as pure, animal pleasure engulfed her. It held, a plateau of bliss lasting until she was on the edge of blacking out, only for the air to rush back as Mrs Figgis lifted her bottom.

The respite was brief, Judith managing only a single gulp of air before the big woman's cunny was planted firmly in her face. Judith knew she was meant to lick and did so, applying her tongue to the clitoris. Her nose was pressed to the woman's anus, her mouth wide, allowing her to breathe with difficulty. Still holding her own sex and with a finger up her bottom, she tongued at the big cunny, waiting until the muscles had started to pulse and then sucking Mrs Figgis' clitoris hard into her mouth. The result was a scream, half pleasure, half shock, and ribald laughter from the audience. Abruptly Mrs Figgis pulled away and Judith was left on the floor, nude, smeared with juice and dirt, exhausted but deeply happy.

She was blushing as Charles helped her to her feet, but more in delight at being so firmly the centre of attention than in shame. As she sank down on a bench she heard Squire Robson loudly claiming his victory and Henry admitting defeat and calling for claret. Lying back, she took a pewter mug from Susie, her fingers trembling as she grasped the handle.

'Pharaoh, compliments of Mrs Figgis,' Susie stated. 'My, what a show!'

Judith smiled weakly and took a swallow of the strong ale. Squire Robson, obviously now thoroughly drunk, had climbed on to a chair.

'Ladies and gentlemen,' he roared, 'I call for a toast – to Harry Truscott!'

The proposal was greeted with a roar of agreement and a crash of mugs and glasses. Judith joined in with another sip of ale.

'A rake of the first water,' Robson was going on, 'and as game a cock as any in England!'

161

More shouting and banging greeted the remark.

'And,' Robson called, 'I'd not have him lose a wager on the eve of a tussle. So I say this, the dust is his if he'll put down a quart pot of any liquor I care to name!'

'Taken, by God!' Henry called back.

A chorus of agreement arose, with men suggesting everything from coffee to brandy until Robson raised his hands.

'None of these!' he declared. 'No, nature's own liquor, straight from the tap!'

'Not water, not Harry!' Conrad Clive called.

'Not so,' Robson answered. 'Girl's piddle.'

'Oh good,' Judith sighed, 'now I needn't get up. Hold the mug, Susie.'

A fresh breeze blew from the river and over the open expanse of Tuthill Fields. Henry Truscott stood facing into it, grateful for the drops of cool rain it brought. His head hurt and his stomach felt a little queasy, making him wish he had not accepted Squire Robson's last bet. Yet the revels had undoubtedly been worth it, for news of his casual attitude to the duel had got round and the meadows were more crowded than he could possibly have expected. A good portion of London society seemed to be there, along with a great rabble of others, including a large contingent of soldiers from the neighbouring barracks. Beyond, alongside the artillery grounds, several carriages were drawn up, their curtains carefully poised to avoid recognition of the occupants.

'How do you feel, Henry?' Charles enquired, coming to stand at his shoulder.

'Raw,' Henry answered.

'Well enough to match Cunningham, I trust?'

'I should hope so. Like a fart, the fellow roars aloud but has no substance.'

'Let us pray you are right; they are coming down the row.'

Henry turned, affecting a nonchalance very different from his true feelings. Cunningham and Lord Covehithe had entered the long row that bisected Tuthill Fields and were approaching, both dressed in sober fashion. In contrast he had selected a scarlet coat faced with gold, black breeches and an elaborate waistcoat of gold and deep red. As he left the house Eloise had complimented him on it and then asked if she should have the cook prepare him one chop or two, showing a confidence that, as far as he could make out, was entirely genuine. She had even told him to be careful not to muddy his boots unduly, an instruction that had caused him to shake his head in disbelief yet which had also done a great deal for his confidence.

As Cunningham approached Henry maintained a casual poise, leaning on a tree and feigning an interest in the clouds that were rolling in from the west. Lord Covehithe split off as the two men came nearer, joining Charles to discuss the final preparations. Charles had been instructed not to accept any last-minute apologies, and from the grim expression on Lord Covehithe's face it was evident that none were going to be offered. Waiting until Cunningham was within hailing distance, Henry broke off his study of the sky and called out to his opponent.

'Do you recall May so wet as this year, Saunder?'

Cunningham gave him an angry look and removed his clock, handing it to Lord Covehithe as the second returned to his side. Henry watched Cunningham select a rapier and begin a series of elaborate flourishes in the air.

'Careful, old fellow, you'll put a prick in someone,' Henry called. 'Which would make a change, I dare say.'

Dancing forward, Cunningham rehearsed a lunging attack, driving the point of his rapier into a tree.

'No, no, over here,' Henry shouted. 'Would you like to go back for some spectacles?'

'Dam't, Harry, have a care,' Charles said as he approached with the remaining rapier. 'Must you taunt the fellow so?'

'Why not?' Henry answered. 'It will make him angry and spoil his concentration.'

'Perhaps,' Charles agreed, 'but it is as likely to make him forget the arrangement. Thomas assures me that Saunder intends to pink you and then allow himself to be pulled back. That way he feels he will retain honour but not lose sympathy.'

'I was not aware he had either in any great measure,' Henry answered. 'At school he used to punch the little ones during prayers so they'd get thrashed for squeaking.'

'You weren't at school with him!'

'Well no, but Bertie Robson tells me that's what he used to do. Dreadful fellow, anyway. Well then, shall we begin?'

Charles gave a regretful shake of his head and signalled to Lord Covehithe. Cunningham stepped out from between the trees and approached Henry, still practising complex cuts and thrusts. Henry shook his head to try and clear the wine fumes, planted his rapier in the ground and shrugged his coat off. Charles took it, then Henry's hat, and stepped away. Retrieving the sword, Henry faced his opponent. Cunningham went into the classic fencing posture, sword arm extended, feet planted, left arm out for balance. Henry imitated the stance, only in exaggerated style to create an image of ludicrous flamboyance.

'You may think this a game, Truscott,' Cunningham hissed as the seconds drew out of earshot, 'but rest assured I mean to kill you.'

Henry allowed his eyebrows to lift a trifle, then tapped his sword against the tip of his opponent's. Cunningham immediately came in with a vicious lunge, forcing Henry to dance quickly back.

164

'Oh, it will seem an accident,' Cunningham went on, 'and doubtless I shall express proper remorse, but you will be in hell for all of that!'

Again Cunningham lunged. Henry swept the oncoming rapier aside and stepped back, now with the blood singing in his ears and all traces of tiredness gone. Cunningham resumed his posture, advancing warily as Henry backed. Their eyes were locked, Cunningham's boring into Henry's with a hate-filled anger.

Henry glanced to the right, then drove his sword in, Cunningham easily slid it away and then retaliated with his own attack. For a moment Henry was defending frantically, also falling back. Cunningham's blade touched Henry's waistcoat, creating a thin slash. Retreating quickly, Henry sank into a defensive posture.

Again their eyes locked. Henry brought his free hand forward, gripping the rapier hilt two-handed as he set his jaw in a tense grin. Cunningham's mouth twitched briefly into a spiteful smile.

'Tired already?' Cunningham spoke.

Henry glanced to the right. Cunningham parried instinctively and Henry drove his rapier, left-handed, into his opponent's shoulder. Immediately a call to stop went up from both seconds. Henry stepped back, raising his sword away from Cunningham and grinning.

'Not so tired, eh, Saunder?' he laughed.

Cunningham was holding his shoulder, with blood running through his fingers, his expression set more in surprise than pain.

'Honour is satisfied, I trust?' Lord Covehithe demanded.

'Oh, entirely, thank you, Thomas,' Henry answered, 'but then I really only came out for a little exercise.'

He had turned and was reaching for his coat when Cunningham lunged. Catching the movement in the corner of his eye he swept around, beating the thin blade aside with his coat.

'No, Saunder, damn you!' Lord Covehithe yelled as a gasp went up from the crowd.

'No, no, please,' Henry managed. 'After all, I may have kissed his wife once or twice. Allow him his tantrum.'

The crowd, which had held silent during the duel, was now buzzing with noise. Henry took his hat from Charles and gave a sweeping bow to each side, then turned to face the Thames. Suddenly he was filled with an overwhelming desire to be sick.

Seven

'Wheal Purity is the talk of London!' Henry declared happily. 'I knew a little bloodshed would excite interest where no amount of dull business talk could reach.'

'True indeed!' Sir Joseph Snapes agreed with enthusiasm.

They had gathered in Snapes' study to discuss the issue of shares, with Henry boasting of his duel and the talk it had created. Not only had the mine and his argument with Cunningham become the gossip of the town, but his conduct before and during the duel had given him almost heroic status. Cunningham's behaviour, in contrast, was considered deplorable.

'So let us call the meeting,' Henry went on. 'Tomorrow at Le Roy's, they will be queuing the length of Thames Street!'

'No, no,' Snapes insisted. 'The time is ripe but not yet fully ripe. In no more than a few days I will be in a position to deliver an address to the Royal Society. My exposition of the mine's worth cannot but help excite interest, not only across London but in the country as a whole.'

'How many is a few days?' Henry demanded. 'You know how it is in London, the gossip will stay warm only until the Prince decides to dress up as his cook again.'[10]

'True,' Snapes answered, 'but I assure you of the virtues of waiting until my presentation. That way we

167

will have secure money, from men of industry and science, men who understand these things. I might be able to arrange the address in a week, no more.'

'The money can come from the devil himself, for all of me,' Henry answered. 'I say we cannot allow this opportunity to slip by. The weight of my vote goes for calling the meeting as soon as word may reasonably be got round. What of you, Charles?'

'I take a middle line,' Charles said thoughtfully. 'We should start to offer stock, but only a limited quantity. Demand is sure to push the price high, with the more reckless investors coming forward as a result of the duel. Many will buy simply to be associated with the sensation. Then, when Sir Joseph makes his presentation the more sober investors will come forward. My supposition is that the price may come off a trifle once the true hotheads all have a slice, and it is they who we lose by waiting.'

'Brilliant,' Henry declared. 'Are you not convinced, Sir Joseph?'

Snapes pursed his mouth, then forced it into a broad smile.

'Very well, gentlemen,' he declared. 'I concede your logic, Mr Finch. Let us offer a tenth of our available stock now, and the remainder after my presentation in perhaps something over a week.'

'Let us say one fifth,' Charles answered. 'I think we may reasonably expect to sell as much. Henry?'

'I am content with a fifth,' Henry answered.

'Then the majority is for a fifth,' Snapes said, 'and I trust your optimism is justified. Now, gentlemen, if you will excuse me I must lose no time in getting to Somerset House[11] in order to book a room and post notice of my presentation. Gentlemen.'

Henry and Charles rose and were shown to the door by Sale, Snapes following. The beaming smile on Snapes' face held until the door closed, then faded abruptly to be replaced by a sour frown. Henry's success in promoting interest in the mine was sure to push stock to prices that would make his intended take-over difficult. Only by delaying the release of the bulk of stock did he stand a chance. Another important matter was taking his full pleasure in Judith, which was clearly going to be impractical after he had successfully deprived Charles Finch of several thousand pounds. That Judith's ultimate loyalty lay with her lover he had no doubt, which gave him only days to complete his preparations.

'Sale,' he addressed the butler. 'I am going to Somerset House. Instruct John to drive down to Suffolk in the gig. Lord Furlong is to be put on a diet of oysters and stout, and Suki is not to visit him. We will follow tomorrow, or perhaps the next day, once I have had a chance to persuade Miss Cates to a visit.'

'Very well, sir,' the butler intoned.

On the slope overlooking Wheal Purity Reuben Eadie sat with a hunch of bread and cheese. A jug of cider stood on a stump to one side, from which he would take an occasional sip. Below, the engine house was in the process of repair, with the remains of the old Newcomen engine being hauled out before work began on the walls. The reason for the explosion was simple, or so it seemed. The ancient boiler, unable to cope with working at full efficiency, had burst. He had known such explosions before, yet two things seemed out of place. First, nobody had been injured. Several people might normally have been expected to be near the engine house, but Todd Gurney had had the entire workforce in the new adit. Peggy had been washing, or more accurately been being mounted by him, and that was the second thing. Being thin and somewhat long in the face he had never been much sought out by women. Most of his sexual encounters had been paid for, and in general his experience of women had soured him against them. Because of this he liked to make them suffer, and had expected Peggy to hate what was done to her. Instead she had welcomed him, despite catching her by surprise and mounting her. She had accepted buggery and sucked his cock when ordered. At first he had thought her submission was simply the result of years of having to do as she was told. Yet the few other women he had met who could be easily manipulated had always been poor, downtrodden creatures. Peggy was anything but, being cheerful and light-hearted by nature.

If it was true that the boiler explosion had been no accident, the only explanation was that Todd Gurney, and Peggy too, did not want the mine drained. That in turn meant they had something to hide, yet it was hard to see what. The mine was rich, that the samples proved. The draining would reveal the flooded portion of the shaft, yet it had been underwater for many years.

Possibilities crowded his mind, each more fanciful than the last. One fact, however, held steady. If Peggy had been deliberately distracting him, then she would not need to do so again, with the boiler blown. It was an experiment he was more than happy to undertake. Thinking of how her pretty, chubby face had looked with his cock in her mouth, he started down the slope towards the counting house. Peggy was there, as usual, carefully marking figures into a ledger. He greeted her and she returned a smile, which seemed entirely without guile.

'We've some matters to finish, I think,' he said as he walked towards her. 'Matters we began down by the washing pool.'

'Not here, Reuben,' she squeaked as he cupped her breasts from behind. 'No, no, someone might see!'

'How about a walk up Climsland Hill?' he queried. 'The view's said to be pretty, and I dare say it'll be a sight prettier by the time I've got you unrigged.'

'Is that what you mean for me, like before?' she asked.

'Yes, and more of the same,' he said, still fondling her heavy breasts through her dress.

He felt her shiver, a passionate reaction surely too strong to be put on. Her nipples were stiff under her dress, two big nubbins of flesh the feel of which set his cock twitching. Taking hold of one of her hands, he pulled it back and put it to the crotch of his breeches. Peggy giggled and squeezed, feeling the hardness of his cock. Certain that her reaction was genuine, he stood, easing her up with him. She responded to the pressure and her stylus dropped to the table.

'Will you pretend to catch me?' she asked. 'Will you make me do it in front of you?'

'You may be sure of it,' he answered.

In the back room of Le Roy's coffee house, Henry Truscott sat with his face set in a stupefied smile. In front of him was a substantial pile of wealth, including coin, notes, bonds and even deeds. It represented enough to keep him in moderate comfort for life, even after the other principal Wheal Purity investors had taken their shares. Yet it was only one fifth of the potential total.

The issue of stock had been an extraordinary success, with investors clamouring to give him their money. Henry had kept the records while Charles had negotiated, allowing each buyer a set amount of stock and a promise of more at the same price. Snapes, meanwhile, had fielded questions and shown off the tin ingot he had made from what he fondly supposed to be Wheal Purity ore.

The French exiles had been particularly insistent, making Henry wonder to what extent Eloise had gone in order to arouse their interest. Only the fact that the most eager of all was the Marquis d'Aignan soothed his suspicions, as he knew that Eloise despised the man.

171

Judith's contacts had also been in evidence, and Henry had tactfully bitten back the remark that came to his mind when Augustus Barclay appeared. There had been several anonymous bidders, at least one of whom Henry suspected of representing Saunder Cunningham. All these had been turned down, Henry declaring that he would accept bids only from the principal parties involved.

Now, with the books closed until after Snapes' presentation to the Royal Society, he felt the first release of tension since they had begun the scheme. At the very least they had made back several times their initial expenses, and barring a disaster in Cornwall it seemed likely that they were home and dry.

'So, Charles,' he declared happily, 'I'd suggest the girls and a case of burgundy, only Eloise is in a damn peculiar mood of late. Getting near to her confinement, I suppose. So how about porter and a brace of Clerkenwell bobtails?'

'I'm game,' Charles replied, 'just as soon as this is safely banked. What of you, Sir Joseph? There's a new wench at Caroline Kay's who's said to have a remarkable trick with milk.'

'At my age I find such sport a trifle faded, I confess,' Snapes replied. 'However, would you consider it presumptuous were I to ask your dear girl, Judith, to dinner?'

'Be my guest,' Charles replied, 'so long as she's game. She comes and goes as she pleases, you know.'

'I thought it polite to ask,' Snapes went on. 'The dinner, you see, is at my Suffolk place.'

'No, no, please do,' Charles insisted.

Snapes gave a polite bow and left. Henry watched him go, thinking of Judith's tale of the last dinner she had attended. She had described in detail not only how she had been given the burning shame over port, but how she had been made to service the entire household.

The image appealed to him, yet stirred an odd feeling combined of envy and a desire to protect her.

'She'd not go if you said the word, you know?' he addressed Charles.

'My dear Harry,' Charles replied. 'If there is one thing I am certain of it is that during the next few days Sir Joseph Snapes is better in Suffolk than London. He may bury himself to his ears in Judith for all of me, and I will rest easier at night for it.'

'True,' Henry admitted. 'So, to Child's then on to Caroline Kay's.'

High on the slope of Climsland Hill Peggy was starting to enjoy the game she was playing with Reuben Eadie. Her emotions were mixed, personal revulsion for him mixed with pleasure in the dirty quality of his attention. It was perverse and filled her with guilty shame, which she managed to overcome by telling herself it was for the good of the mining venture and done out of loyalty to Henry and Eloise. Deep down she knew that with the boiler blown and no prospect of draining the shaft until the new engine arrived her actions were not really necessary.

She had done it anyway, asking him to peep on her and then to run out and do as he liked when the moment was right. Now, as she followed a track through a thick wood of coppiced hazel she knew that he was following her. She had decided what to do, and the idea was making her tremble. Again and again she postponed it, telling herself that she was dirty and wanton and ought to run away. She never did, and once the pressure in her bladder had reached the point that she genuinely wanted to pee she knew that she was really going to do it, however filthy.

With a gentle sob she moved to the side of the path and began to pull up her skirts and petticoats, sure that he would be watching and probably with his cock hanging from his breeches. Even so his sudden appearance from behind a gorse bush no more than a dozen paces away caused her to start and sit back heavily on the ground.

'Not there, girl,' he said. 'Come with me.'

He stepped forward and caught her by the ear, pulling her to her feet despite her protests. Squealing and sobbing, she was led back out into the lane and along to where it ended at a field gate. Inside she was trembling, expecting to be thrown on the ground and mounted at any moment and sure that if he did she would probably wet herself. As it was he simply let go of her ear and stepped away to sit on the bank.

Peggy looked around, feeling very vulnerable despite the sense of absolute solitude. The field the lane led to was small and steep, surrounded by high hedges and with a dozen or so red cows grazing placidly at the far end. Nearby, to either side of the narrow gate, the soil had been churned into a rich slurry from which came a strong, farmyard scent. Eadie nodded at the muck and Peggy felt her mouth come open as she realised what he expected of her.

'Get in it then,' he said.

'That?' Peggy queried.

'What else would I mean?' he asked. 'You wanted to play dirty games, well now's your chance. Do your business in it first, and then we'll see what goes from there.'

Peggy hesitated, looking at the filthy slurry and thinking how it would feel to squat down in it. For all her revulsion she knew the answer.

'I . . . I had better disrobe,' she managed.

'Part, but not all,' he answered. 'Save your dress, and take off your boots.'

Glad to be permitted at least some decency after the event, Peggy began to undress. She did it slowly, uncertain of her feelings, removing first her dress, then

174

her boots and stockings. All the while he watched, stroking his crotch from time to time and pulling on a briar pipe. She hung each garment on the gate, taking care to keep it clear of the mud. Only when she began to unlace her chemise did he raise a hand, then beckon her slowly forward.

The pool of slurry separated them, and Peggy abandoned herself as she stepped in, her bare toes sinking into the warm mud with a soft squelch. Eadie gave a light laugh, tapped his pipe out on a stone and put his hands to the front of his breeches. Taking another step, she again felt her foot sink in, only this time much deeper, until the slurry had risen around her ankle.

'Right deep,' Eadie ordered. 'Where that greenish bit is.'

Peggy saw where he meant, a smooth area of thick mud between two long puddles that had formed in the ruts left by a cart. She guessed it would be deep, and sure enough, as she stretched her foot out she found it sinking well past the ankle. For a moment she almost lost her balance as her foot found a rounded stone beneath the muck. Then she had righted herself and was pulling her back foot free with a sticky sound.

Stood in the mud to half way up her calves, with her petticoats lifted to keep them clear of the surface, she looked at Eadie. He had begun to unbutton his breeches and nodded at her questioning glance. Peggy watched him take his penis out, then hoisted her petticoats high and sank into a squat, spreading her thighs to allow him a full view of her cunny. He took his cock in hand and began to pull at it.

Peggy shut her eyes and let herself relax, feeling the tension in her bladder before letting go with a gasp as the pee splashed out into the mud beneath her. She let it run, knowing that he was masturbating but keeping her eyes closed and concentrating on how rude she was being. The temptation was to put a hand to her cunny

175

and bring herself to climax, yet she held back, what was left of her sense of shame preventing her.

'Now sit in it,' he drawled as her pee died to a trickle.

Without really thinking, Peggy obeyed, lowering her bare bottom. Her skin touched the warm, wet pee puddle, then the firmer, cool mud beneath. Poised with just her cheeks touching she felt deliciously dirty and keener than ever to touch herself. She heard him move and wondered if he wanted his cock sucked. His hand touched her shoulder and she opened her mouth, expecting to have it entered. Instead he gave a sudden, sharp push.

Peggy went back, crying out in shock, her bottom went down in the mud, the thick slurry oozing up between her cheeks and over her cunny before she lost her balance completely and sprawled full length in the filth. For a moment she lay gasping, plastered in muck from her hair to her legs, only her front remaining clean.

In her effort to save herself she had let her petticoats drop, and as she pulled herself up she found herself sitting in them while the mixture of mud and pee was above the level of her cunny. He was standing over her, his boots deep in the mud, masturbating over her filthy body. Unable to help herself, Peggy put a hand down under the mud and began to rub at her cunny. Reuben grinned and began to tug harder at his cock.

Her eyes were glued to his cock as they masturbated together. It was aimed at her face, and she was already imagining the come erupting over her. Taking two big handfuls of slurry, she slapped them to her breasts, squeezing and stroking the heavy globes through her chemise, then pulling it open to spill them out into her filthy hands. Her nipples were hard, bumping under her fingers as she played with herself, rubbing muck over both breasts. Approaching orgasm, she began to squirm her bottom about in the filth, feeling the fat cheeks slide around on her ruined petticoats. More mud went on her belly, then her neck before her hands went to her breasts again. Lifting them, she offered a muddy slide to Reuben's cock, hoping he would come between them. He made no move, but was hammering furiously at his cock and as she once more lifted her breasts he came.

A long string of sperm shot from his cock, catching her in the face and going into her open mouth. More caught her breasts and she began to rub it in as the third spurt landed on her mud-smeared belly. Taking the come in her hands she began to mix it with the slurry, rubbing the filthy mess into her breasts, over her belly and then into her face. She knew that only a few touches to her clitty would be needed to bring her off, but held back, revelling in the sheer rudeness of what she was doing.

'On your knees, do it on your knees,' he ordered, still hoarse from the effort of coming while standing up. 'Stick that fat arse in the air, girl, I've a treat for you.'

Peggy went forward immediately, lifting her bottom as she had been ordered. The filthy petticoats clung to her skin, tight around her ample rear to pull her cheeks together and squeeze muck out from between them. Quickly pulling them up, she exposed herself, spreading her knees to give him an open view of her bottom. Her breasts were now dangling in the slurry and as she put a hand back to her cunny her shoulder and part of her face went under too.

Reuben had stepped back and was retrieving his pipe, the casual action making Peggy feel even more used. She was ready to come, totally abandoned to her dirty pleasure, with her fingers working in the slimy mess of her cunny. He had taken the pipe in his hand, but the wrong way around, and as he stepped back into the slurry pool she realised what he intended.

She could not resist, but only manage a sob as the stem of the pipe was poked into her anus. Smoke was rising from it, a grey curl lifting into the still air above her upturned buttocks. At the sight an overwhelming wave of erotic shame swept through her. With the scents of tobacco, earth and dung strong in her nose she started her orgasm. Her vagina began to contract, squeezing out a thick worm of muck that had been up it. Her anus started to pulse on the pipe stem, drawing it up her bottom and making the smoke come in puffs as if she were smoking it with her hole.

Peggy came, her eyes locked on the obscene sight of her filthy body and the little puffs of smoke rising over her bottom. At the very peak her knees gave way and her belly and sex went into the mud, with her own pee filling her open vagina. She wallowed and squirmed in the slurry as she came, kicking her feet, rubbing muck about over her cunny and crying out over and over again. Only when the pipe squeezed from her bottom hole did she stop masturbating and slump slowly down into pool of filth to lie inert as the shame of what she had done welled up inside her.

As he walked briskly along Fleet Street, Henry Truscott felt both lecherous and irritated. The entertainment at Caroline Kay's had been exciting enough, with a heavily pregnant girl masturbating in her own milk, yet at the end it had failed to appeal. With Eloise disinclined to sex he had found the girls at the brothel too slovenly for his tastes. Prostitutes had always been quite satisfactory before, never the equal of Eloise, yet useful for a change. Now they seemed inadequate, while the sight of the pregnant girl had made it impossible to detach his mind from Eloise as she had been that morning, looking frail and sorry for herself in bed.

Charles had fared better, enjoying the milk scene and then paying for two of the girls to go upstairs with him. Henry had excused himself and set off in a westerly direction with vague thoughts of seeing if Eloise might not be persuaded to indulge him. His mood continued along the length of the Strand, worsening if anything, and by the time he had reached the gate to St James's Park he was ready to swear off harlots for life, if only for ten minutes with Eloise.

In his mind he was already stripping her from the light gown she wore to bed, imagining her kneeling with her swollen belly and breasts swinging beneath her. She was glorious from the rear, with a neat, pursed cunny in a nest of ginger curls and smooth, pink buttocks with her bottom hole a tight rosebud at the centre. It was a very far image from the loose vulvas of the girls at Caroline Kay's, and his cock was hard in his breeches before he had walked half the length of the row. Thinking of Eloise's bottom, he remembered the pleasure of spanking her after catching her sucking the Seigneur de Poinchy. In her room he had completed the spanking with a silver hairbrush and then put the handle up her bottom hole while he mounted her. The feel of the bristles on his balls had been extraordinary, and he was wondering if it would be a good idea to beat her bottom to get her in trim when a voice hailed him.

He recognised it immediately as that of May Cunningham and turned sharply, not at all sure of what kind of reception to expect. She stood not twenty yards distant, on another path, smiling with unmistakable friendliness, as were the two girls by her side. Relieved, Henry made a bow with his hat and altered course, wishing only that she had been alone. Clerkenwell tarts might not rival Eloise, but May was young and pretty and dirty in a way that was not related to how much money she had been paid. The two girls, however, seemed likely to curtail any such thoughts, besides which they were Saunder Cunningham's sisters, Alice and Caroline. Both were younger than their brother, tall with pale brown hair and blue eyes – Alice elegant and poised, Caroline curiously impudent and still with a trace of puppy fat. Approaching them he gave a hearty greeting, still unsure why they appeared so friendly.

179

'Ah, Mr Truscott,' May addressed him. 'We really must thank you.'

'Thank me?' Henry queried.

'Indeed,' May answered, 'you are our benefactor, for all I doubt it was your intention.'

'Well, no, I confess not,' Henry answered after a moment to wonder if there was any way he could pretend his actions to have been for her benefit.

May took his arm and Alice moved to his side, steering him back towards the gates. For a moment Henry wondered if their action was some ghastly trap, but the side of May's breast was pressed to his arm and he found himself deciding to accept the risk.

'Dear Saunder, you see,' May went on, 'has always been inclined to be hot-headed, and although he has his faults he is a good husband, brother and provider. Together we thank you for holding back your own anger.'

'Think nothing of it, please,' Henry answered. 'It was a small enough thing, not really necessary at all, only he would have it that I took Trethaw Wood from him on purpose.'

'How silly,' May said, laughing. 'Still, we should be most grateful if you might allow him at least a share in your good fortune.'

'I might be prepared to offer a little stock,' Henry answered. 'If, that is, you and I are still to be friends as we were before?'

'Certainly,' May answered, colouring slightly.

'And Alice and Caroline?' Henry asked, glancing to the two girls.

It took a moment for May to digest his meaning and then the mild flush of embarrassment that always marked her face during talk of sex became abruptly deeper. For a moment Henry thought he had misjudged the situation and then Caroline giggled. Evidently the two sisters shared at least some knowledge of May's behaviour with Henry.

180

'It serves little to be coy,' he went on, 'although I confess I find your blushes charming.'

There was a pause, Henry waiting in hope that his gamble had paid off. On the previous occasions that he had met Alice and Caroline he had always sensed that they found him appealing and had guessed that they and May shared at least some secrets. He had never pressed the point, not wishing to risk the pleasures he was enjoying with May. Now, with the prospect of mine shares as an excuse, he hoped that they would be able to indulge themselves, one at a time if not all three together.

'Mr Truscott,' May said softly. 'If I understand your meaning correctly then that is quite the most indecent proposal I have ever heard.'

'I could do better,' Henry answered boldly. 'What of the three of you together?'

'Mr Truscott!' May exclaimed but Caroline had begun to giggle openly.

Looking to May he found her blushing, while Alice was wearing a cool smile.

'The question then,' he went on, now thoroughly pleased with himself, 'would seem to be, where?'

'Saunder left for Cornwall this morning,' May answered. 'Bruton Street is empty save for our maids.'

'Which means that we poor girls are quite without protection,' Alice added.

'Who knows what sort of beast might take advantage of such a situation,' Caroline put in.

'I for one,' Henry answered. 'Come, ladies, I am already in mind of a couple of interesting diversions.'

May Cunningham poised the cane over her sister-in-law's bottom, swearing revenge on Henry Truscott despite the pleasure she was taking in his orders. Since arriving at their town house he had controlled the situation with skill, allowing them to overcome their

181

modesty under the pretence of being obliged to do as they were told. All of them knew it was a charade, yet also that what they were doing would never have come about under normal conditions.

On arrival at the Cunningham town house those few servants who had not gone back to Cornwall had been given the afternoon off. Only then had Henry entered the house. After a brief survey he had selected the first-floor music room, which faced out over the mews and was not overlooked. He had ordered brandy, which Caroline had served, and a cigar, which Alice had taken from her brother's humidor.

His first instruction had been for the girls to strip, but not bare. May's initial relief at this choice had quickly vanished when he went on to explain that while they were to retain their stockings, boots and garters, everything else had to come off. She had protested, pleading Caroline's modesty, at which Henry had decided that they might also retain their gloves and bonnets.

As they began to strip he had seated himself in the room's most comfortable chair, glass in one hand and cigar in the other. Despite having been naked in front of him before, and also with her sisters-in-law, May had felt embarrassed. Henry had made no move to hurry them, and she had guessed why as she felt her nervousness gradually replaced by sexual arousal. The act of baring her breasts had made her lip tremble, and by the time she had pushed the last of her petticoats down her legs she had been shivering with anticipation.

Both Alice and Caroline had already undressed. Caroline had stripped with a playful enthusiasm that May found shocking. Her plump breasts had been let free of her bodice with the same lack of concern she might have shown in taking off a cloak. Even when the moment came to ease down her petticoats over her chubby little bottom it had been done with a giggle and a flirtatious glance at Henry. Bare from stocking tops to elbows, she had sat herself on the piano stool and calmly watched May and her sister finish disrobing.

Alice had not been far behind her little sister, undressing with an air of suffering that May was certain was fake. Always given to the theatrical, Alice had made sure the importance of her baring her body was not missed, coyly undoing laces and buttons, and repeatedly turning so as never to reveal her flesh until the last possible moment. Only at the end had it become obvious that she was as excited as her sister. Alice was slim and small-breasted, but proud of her bottom, which May knew. Thus, when Alice turned her back to Henry to take down her petticoats May knew for sure that it was from a desire to display her best feature rather than any sense of modesty.

With the three girls bare for all practical purposes Henry had been sporting a notable bulge in his breeches. Yet he had held back, ordering May to fetch a cane while Alice and Caroline performed a piano duet. May's last view as she hurried from the room had been of the two sisters squeezing together on the piano stool, hips together and bare bottoms stuck out over the edge. It was impossible to deny that it was a charming sight, for all that the thought made her blush.

Running downstairs in the near nude was no less embarrassing. Indeed, she knew that she would have felt less embarrassed had she been completely nude. As it was she was quite clearly dressed to arouse men, which made her self-display that much worse. Most shameful of all was having to fetch a cane which she knew would be used on her own bottom. The only one they had belonged to the cook and was very occasionally applied to the maids' bottoms, in private. For the mistress of the house to be fetching it, let alone be subjected to it, was shocking to say the least.

As she picked the thing up she was imagining the cook looking at her in outrage. The woman was big, and had a no-nonsense manner May had always found intimidating. She was also considerably older than May and had originally been cook to Saunder's mother, who had never approved of May. It was not hard for May to imagine herself thrown over the woman's knee for a few strokes across the bare bottom. The cane was a three-foot length of whalebone with a braided handle for grip. It seemed vicious and May could easily imagine its sting. Yet there was also a crudeness about it, a workmanlike style, as was appropriate for an object used to discipline mere maids. The thought made the prospect of having her own bottom beaten yet more shameful.

By the time May returned to the music room she was flushed and trembling, with her erect nipples betraying her feelings. Caroline had turned as May came in and giggled, spoiling the tune as she did so. Henry had immediately declared that the sisters should be beaten and ordered them to the settee. The instruction had been greeted with genuine nervousness and May guessed that they had thought it was her who was going to be caned. They had crossed the room with their arms about one another's waists and stayed that way on the settee. Henry had told them to kneel, then to put their heads and their bottoms up.

This placed them in an extraordinarily indecent position, with their cunnies showing from behind and their bottom cheeks open to reveal the tight pink dimples of their bumholes. May had swallowed hard at the sight, expecting to be told to join them and present her own sex in the same, lewd manner. Instead Henry had instructed her to cane the girls, which had provoked relief, pleasure and an infuriating stab of disappointment in her. Now, with the cane held over the two quivering, pink behinds, she awaited only Henry's instruction to begin the beating.

'Gently,' Henry instructed, 'just enough to raise the colour.'

184

May tapped the cane across Caroline's bottom, judging that as it was the fleshier of the two it was likely to be better padded. Caroline squeaked, more in surprise than pain and a line appeared, only a tone pinker that the natural colour of her bottom skin.

'A little harder than that,' Henry laughed. 'Come, come, she is a woman. Nature has gifted you with bottoms ideally suited for beating, and Caroline's more so than most.'

Hefting the cane, May planted another stroke, this time hitting both girls' bottoms and drawing squeals from each. A thin line of pale red now crossed the two girlish rears, broken only over their clefts and at the narrow groove where they had pressed together for comfort.

'Better,' Henry announced. 'Pray continue, and watch their cunts as you beat them.'

May shivered at his words but found her attention drawn irresistibly to where it had been directed. Both girls had well-furred sexes, as alike as might be expected of sisters. Caroline's was a trifle plumper in the lips, but both showed signs of arousal, with the centres starting to open and each clitoris peeping out from beneath its fleshy hood. May swallowed hard, knowing that she might have presented a yet more blatant sight in the same rude pose.

Standing a little to the side, she brought down three swift cuts across the girls' bottoms. Caroline squealed and jumped; Alice gave no more than a whimper. May looked around for Henry's approval to find that he was undoing his breeches. He signalled her to continue the beating and she began to plant light, rhythmic cuts of the cane across the girls' bottoms with her eyes glued to Henry's crotch. His cock came free, thick and with the head already clear of the foreskin. He began to masturbate himself and another shiver went through her.

Caroline had begun to dance under the cane, wriggling her toes in her stockinged feet and bouncing on the settee to make her fleshy cheeks quiver. Alice was being more stoic, accepting the caning with an almost serene attitude to the pain and the indignity of her exposure. Guessing that the tip would be more painful than the shaft, May walked behind the girls, allowing the cane tip to trail over the beaten pink cheeks as she went. Using a back-hand stroke, she brought it down once more. Caroline squeaked and shimmied her bottom as before, while Alice gave a soft gasp and an odd little noise from deep in her throat.

Determined to make Alice lose her poise, May gave a harder stroke, then another six in quick succession. At the third Alice broke, and by the last she was squealing and wiggling her bottom with no more reserve or dignity than her sister. May laughed, then remembered that they were supposed to be under coercion and hastily choked the sound back. Both girls' bottoms were now criss-crossed with thin red lines, and as she glanced once more at their cunnies she saw what Henry had meant. Both vulvas were fully swollen, with the vaginas moist and open.

If anything it was Alice who was more aroused, with her hole open enough to admit perhaps a little finger, with the hymen torn although not fully. Caroline's was nearly intact, a reddish membrane that blocked most of her vagina.

'A pretty sight, I'm sure you'll agree,' Henry said. 'Too much riding perhaps. You should stick to side-saddle, my girls, that's the proper way.[12] But I am forgetting my manners. It is quite unfair of me not to allow you to be admired every bit as much as your sisters-in-law.'

'Really, it is quite all right,' May stammered, glancing at his now fully erect cock.

'No, no, I insist,' Henry went on. 'Come, my dear, bottom up, and we shall see if your beating provokes the same charming noises and motions as Alice and Caroline.'

186

May was shivering hard as she kneeled down beside Caroline. Their hips were touching, and she could feel the warmth of the young girl's skin and the softness of her flesh. Sinking her face into the cushions, she lifted her bottom, imagining how she must now look to Henry with her cunny and anus showing as one of a line of three exposed, female bottoms.

'So pretty,' Henry said from behind her and then the cane came down on her bottom.

She squealed in shock, finding the sudden sharp sting far worse than she had anticipated. Caroline giggled and stuck her tongue out at May just as the second stroke hit. Again May cried out in protest.

'Don't be a baby,' Henry said, laughing. 'Why, you never used to squeal so in the woods.'

'You are cruel,' May answered miserably even as she wondered why she could not make less of a fuss in front of the younger girls.

Henry laughed again and May felt Caroline's arm come around her shoulders. She made no resistance, and after the next stroke had made both of them squeak she returned the comforting gesture.

Ten more times the cane cut into her bottom, getting progressively harder, while squeals from Alice and Caroline showed that they were getting the same treatment. Soon she was wiggling her toes and dancing her bottom, just as Caroline had done, with no more thought for her dignity. Yet by the end the stinging pain had given way to a rosy, warm glow that centred on the open, hot mouth of her vagina.

At last the beating stopped and she heard the cane drop to the floor. Feeling at once terribly abused and in heaven, she held her position, looking back between her knees. Henry had stepped back and had his cock in his hand. She could not see his upper half but it was obvious that he was deciding in which tight cunny to sheath his erection.

'Take me, Henry,' she said softly. 'Don't spoil the girls for their wedding nights.'

'Pray do me some justice,' Henry replied. 'No, they need not fear for their precious maidenheads. I shall sodomise the pair.'

May opened her mouth, only for her intended protest to turn to a gasp as Henry's cock was pushed unceremoniously up her vagina. Neither girl had reacted to the threat to enter their bottom holes, but May could feel Caroline shivering.

Henry fucked her with long, firm strokes, holding her hips and pulling himself in again and again until her head was swimming with pleasure. Despite the shame of her position she kept remembering their times in the woods near the mine, and of how he had never sent her home without making sure she had climaxed. As he fucked her she found her hands going back to her breasts, cupping them and stroking the nipples despite being watched by an open-mouthed Caroline. Then, as her pleasure rose beyond wanting to resist a timid hand slid beneath her chest and took one breast. She did nothing to stop it, clutching Caroline's hand to herself. Henry laughed to see them, then pulled his cock out and put it to her clitoris.

'Come, Alice, watch, and touch if you wish,' he declared. 'I shall show you why May has come to visit me so often.'

May was lost, unable to stop herself as the round, firm head of his cock began to rub on her clitoris. She saw Alice rise and walk around behind Henry, then give a little gasp as she saw that her sister was playing with May's breasts. Caroline giggled and blew a kiss to her sister, which drew a look of shock, as if a secret had been betrayed. Then Alice's hands were on May's bottom, stroking and caressing the cheeks, squeezing the flesh and teasing the sensitive skin in the cleft. May could only pant, open-mouthed, into the settee, too far gone to do anything but enjoy the attentions being lavished on her body. She felt her cunny start to tighten, then the rapid tensing of her anus and she was coming, screaming out her pleasure as Henry's cock rubbed her and the girls' hands explored her body.

It lasted for one, long, beautiful moment and then she was slipping down, collapsing off the settee in a welter of shame and exhaustion. Only when she was sat on the floor did she remember that the girls were to be buggered. Before, when she had only had her caned bottom to concern her, it had seemed important to stop Henry from sodomising the two girls. Now, with Caroline giggling over Henry's glistening erection and Alice stroking her sister's bottom, it seemed thoroughly appropriate that both of them should know the same depth of feeling she was going through.

'Alice first, as you are the older,' Henry declared happily. 'May, if I might?'

For a moment May wondered what he was doing, but as he bent and put a hand between her thighs she realised. With a resigned sigh she parted her legs and allowed his fingers to enter her vagina, emerging wet with her juice. Alice was shaking hard as she climbed into position, bent across the settee with her pert rear stuck out. Caroline had sat down and was holding her sister around the waist, though whether the action was intended for comfort or to hold Alice still May could not be sure.

Too fascinated not to watch, May swung herself around to see between Alice's bottom cheeks. The girl's anus was a tight pink ring, seeming ridiculously small to accommodate Henry's cock. Yet May knew her own was no different and Henry had buggered her in the woods three times. Alice winced when his finger touched her anus, but with May's juice to ease the passage it went in easily enough and Henry was soon wriggling the full length of it about inside. Caroline giggled to see her sister with a finger in her bottom hole, then tightened her grip on Alice's waist.

For a space Henry continued to work Alice's anus, sliding his finger in and out to make the little hole swell and become puffy. When he did pull the finger out her ring stayed open, exhibiting a tiny, dark hole into the very rudest cavity of her body. Henry had been masturbating with his free hand and wasted no time in putting his cock to Alice's anus. May saw the ring stretch, push in and then abruptly take the head of the cock as Alice gave a little cry that might have been despair, or pain or simply shock.

With her bottom entered Alice's eyes went round with surprise, as did her mouth. Looking back she began to gasp and shake, her whole body quivering as Henry began to move his penis in her back passage. Her fingers were clutching the settee and her toes wriggling, making May wonder if she herself had looked so utterly wanton with a cock inside her. She knew she had and found her hand going to her cunny as she watched Alice buggered.

Henry's cock was well in, his front pressed to Alice's bottom, making the cheeks spread with each push. Her expression mixed disbelief and ecstasy. Caroline watched, stroking Alice's hair and giggling nervously, her eyes glued to where Henry's penis was easing back and forth in her sister's anus.

Hardly knowing what she was doing, May reached out and slid her hand between Alice's thighs, touching Henry's balls and then the soft wetness of her sister-in-law's cunny. As May began to pat at Alice's clitoris the gasps turned to sighs and then to moans. Between them they concentrated on Alice's pleasure until she began to mumble, then to play with her own breasts and they knew she was coming.

'Yes, deep in me, oh my poor bottom,' Alice stammered as her words became audible. 'Oh, what are you doing to me, oh Carrie . . .'

Alice cried out but May continued to excite her clitoris, patting and flicking it in the same way she herself masturbated. Henry grunted and May knew that Alice's bottom hole would be contracting on his cock, something that had always made him come up her bottom when he had buggered her. Yet he held back, waiting until Alice's squirms and little gagging noises had died down before starting to pull slowly out.

May sat back, her fingers sticky with Alice's juice. Henry's cock was emerging from between Alice's bum-cheeks, long and pink and glistening. Caroline stared entranced, then abruptly scrambled into a kneeling position with her chubby behind thrust out and her bum-hole showing between the cheeks. As the cock left her anus Alice turned, sitting down on the settee with a long sigh. She said nothing, but drew her breath in, then, seeing the indecent haste with which Caroline had got into position she placed a resounding smack on her sister's bottom. Caroline giggled and made as if to slap back, then suddenly took Alice by the hair. Henry laughed as Alice's face was pushed towards his erection. She gave a little cry of protest and then it was in and she was sucking on the penis that had so recently been up her bottom. May swallowed hard, then began to masturbate.

For a long time Henry kept his cock in Alice's mouth, with Caroline holding her sister's head by the hair and rocking it gently back and forth. Alice sucked, at first with her eyes screwed up tightly and then watching the stiff cock as it slid in and out of her own mouth. After a while Henry put his hand between Caroline's chubby bottom cheeks and May saw the girl's expression change as her hole was penetrated. When Caroline began to whimper Henry withdrew from Alice's mouth, his cock now rearing up, slick with saliva. Coming behind Caroline, Henry pushed his erection in between the plump cheeks and May saw the head disappear from

191

view. Alice moved, helpfully spreading her sister's cheeks and May saw the cock go in, popping inside Caroline's tight ring and sliding in half of its length with the first push.

With his hands on Caroline's hips Henry forced the full length of his penis into the girl's rectum. Like her sister, she accepted it with her eyes wide, also making an odd little grunting sound as her bottom filled. May's clitoris was burning under her fingers as Henry began to bugger Caroline. Alice started to stroke her little sister's hair, returning the same, soothing gesture she herself had been given. Henry began to move faster and May knew he would soon come. With her eyes locked on Caroline's bouncing bottom she began to masturbate faster, then felt her climax start as Alice slid a hand under her own sister's belly.

May could see little, but she knew that Alice was masturbating Caroline and doing it in an affectionate, sisterly way that seemed more indecent than the fact that a man's cock was in the younger girl's bottom hole. Caroline responded too, grunting and pushing back her bottom as Henry's front slapped against it again and again. May cried aloud as her orgasm hit her, first one peak, then another as Caroline's lewd grunting became frantic. May knew Caroline had come, then Henry cried out and May hit a third peak at the thought of his come flooding out into Caroline's bowels.

Reuben Eadie pushed open the counting house door, his face set in a broad grin. He had left Peggy washing herself in the stream and was finding it impossible to hide his amusement at what he had made her do. Despite the pleasure she had so obviously taken in it he had begun to feel misgivings as he approached the mine, half-convinced that she would run to Todd Gurney the moment she felt it safe. She had not, and Gurney proved to have gone into the village with a miner who had sustained an injury. Then, as the door swung wide he realised that he was not alone. A man sat at the desk, a tall, lanky individual whom he immediately recognised.

'Does nobody work in this mine, Mr Eadie?' the man greeted him.

'Why, Tom Davey!' Eadie exclaimed. 'What brings you here?'

'I'm hired at Dolcombe,' the man answered, 'to make a study of the spoil heaps and see if they're worth another run. I heard you were buying an engine, so I thought I would pay you a call. Besides, I had to see the mine where the black tin's as fine raw as what Sevenstones can produce after grading. Some of our owners may even be interested and have asked me to take a look around.'

'And welcome,' Eadie replied. 'Here, there's jug of cider somewhere. Will you drink with me?'

Davey accepted the drink and they fell to talking, discussing the prospects of the mines they worked at and old times in the north of England. Only when Peggy reappeared, now decent, to say that she was needed in the village did Tom Davey's flow of stories stop.

'. . . and do you remember old MacPhearson, at Thorpe Pit,' Eadie was saying.

'Hold a moment,' Davey stopped him. 'Who was that?'

'Her name's Peggy Wray,' Eadie answered. 'A fine piece, and, as it goes . . .'

'A fine piece is not wrong,' Davey answered. 'The last time I saw her she was in a pool over the top of Dolcombe, stark naked and playing with her bubbies! I'd put a month's wages to a bent farthing it's the same girl, can't be two alike.'

'Near Dolcombe?' Eadie demanded. 'What was she doing there?'

'Bathing, and diddling herself I think,' Davey answered. 'Up above the tailing dumps. Finest sight I've seen in a while, and not the least strange.'

Eadie didn't answer, thinking of Peggy's behaviour, the boiler explosion and then Davey's remark about the ore quality.

'Sevenstones is hard by Dolcombe, isn't it?' he asked.

'No more than a half-mile across the top of Hingston Down,' Davey answered.

'Could you spare a minute to look at the adit?' Eadie asked. 'You know your work as well as any and I'd like your opinion on the vein.'

'Easy done,' Davey answered.

Collecting lamps and a pick, they made their way to the old adit and inside, then along to the point at which it joined the shaft. Water lay at their feet, the surface of the flooded shaft perfectly still with the images of the lanterns reflected in it. All around the walls glistened black, rich with ore. Eadie hefted his pick and struck at a nodule the size of two fists, which split and fell to the floor. Davey picked it up and turned it over in his hand.

'Try again, Reuben,' he said. 'This piece isn't cassiterite at all. See how long the crystals are, and the glassy lustre. This is no more than a lump of schorl.'

Eight

Todd Gurney awoke to the feel of Natalie's tiny hand around his penis. Outside it was light, with the sky the pale blue of dawn and the clouds still tinged with pink and dull purple. He knew exactly what Natalie wanted to do and made no move to stop her, allowing her to enjoy his morning erection and knowing that her other hand would be on her cunny. She had always enjoyed his cock, touching and sucking it with a desire that approached worship. He found the attention flattering and was always content to let her have her way, coming under her fingers while his erection was in her mouth.

Sure enough, she quickly ducked further down the bed and put her lips to his cock, taking it in and starting to suck. He began to stroke her back, then reached down as she wriggled her body towards him, finding her trim, firm bottom. His cock was rock solid and she was holding the base of it, masturbating him into her mouth. He continued to fondle her bottom, stroking and patting the cheeks. She began to squirm, pushing her bottom into his hand to get his fingers between her cheeks. He responded, rubbing her anus and then slipping a finger inside and another into her cunny. Held firm on his hand she started to come and he felt her holes clamp tight, then relax and clamp again. As she came so did he, his sperm erupting down her throat to

195

be swallowed eagerly in gulp after gulp as she bucked and writhed on his fingers. When it was over neither spoke, but allowed their senses to return slowly to normal.

They had come back late to the mine, after spending hours seeing to the injured miner, along with Peggy. As he pulled himself upright he was already thinking of the mine and whether it might be wise to slow work on the new adit. If he did it would need an excuse, either that or the absence of Reuben Eadie.

By the time he had finished breakfast and gone outside he had decided in favour of suggesting that the adit should be widened to accommodate rails for ore trucks, a system he had helped to build at Wheal Anne. At the least the discussion would delay things, and as he strode out into the daylight he was bellowing for Eadie. There was no response, but a group of men was visible around the mouth of the new adit and so he made in their direction. Among them was a tall man he did not recognise and who turned at his approach.

'You're Mr Gurney, the mine captain, I understand?' the man asked.

'That I am, Todd Gurney,' Gurney answered. 'What's about here?'

'Tom Davey, at your service,' the tall man answered. 'I'm a surveyor at Dolcombe, and I've news for you, not all of it good.'

'What's this? Where's Eadie?' Gurney demanded.

'A good way towards London by now,' Davey answered. 'Your lower vein's heavy with schorl, as I'd have thought you must know, but he took a rare panic at the news. He left last night for London, said he needed to get word to your president. But you need to come into the adit for a space.'

Gurney hesitated. It was imperative to pursue Eadie, yet he could not afford to seem alarmed in front of the man Davey. Making a casual remark about a vein of

196

schorl crossing the old shaft, he followed Davey into the mouth of the adit.

Staring from the window of Sir Joseph Snapes' carriage, Judith began to have misgivings about accepting the offer of a visit to his Suffolk estate. For hours they had been rolling through rich, open countryside, twice changing horses at towns. She had no idea where she was, while Snapes had become more and more agitated as the journey progressed. She was well aware that he had some sort of sexual escapade planned for her, and had been looking forward to it. His dinner had been close to perfect, combining erotic pain with the attentions of several men at once. Snapes had implied that she could expect more of the same, yet refused to give details.

She was telling herself that whatever it was it could hardly be unendurable, at least not for her, with her training at Mother Agie's and a long history of satisfying the most perverse of both male and female lusts. Recalling how it felt to dance naked with a pint of strong ale held up her bottom and the threat of fifty whips strokes if any spilled, she managed a sour grin. She had let go, and she had taken the whipping, and she had come under the lash. Snapes might think he was going to take her beyond her limits, but he was sure to be wrong.

'Nearly there, my dear,' he declared heartily. 'This is my land.'

Outside the window the open fields of corn and pasture were giving way to lower ground, with a great expanse of reed bed to one side and a sandy heath to the other.

'The best land for game birds in the country,' Snapes said. 'Woodcock, snipe, teal, all in abundance.'

'It seems very lonely,' Judith answered, glancing at the leaden sky and the expanse of marsh and heath.

'But we shall be in the best of company,' he assured her, 'and rest assured that dinner will be nonpareil.'

197

'Your table is excellent,' Judith remarked. 'Will we have ortolan again? It is a delicacy I greatly enjoyed.'

'Possibly, my dear,' Snapes replied. 'As to the excellence of the table, it will be truly unique, as you yourself will be responsible for it.'

He turned to lean out of the window and give an instruction to Sale, who was driving, leaving Judith to puzzle over the meaning of his remarks. For one horrible moment she wondered if they actually intended to eat her, then dismissed the idea as absurd.

In her room at the house in Petty France, Eloise lay on her bed in a sea of linen. She was near naked, with her bed-gown pulled up to her neck and her swollen belly straining upwards, a round ball of taut, glossy flesh. For some while she had been touching herself, feeling the size and texture of her breasts and belly. The bump felt huge, making her body seem ungainly but also open and female in a way she had never known before.

With Stephen on his normal round of political meetings and coffee houses and Henry off on some business connected with the mine she was all but alone, with only a few servants in the lower part of the house. As her pregnancy had advanced so her self-assurance had declined, a process brought to a peak by the Marquis d'Aignan. He had left her feeling small, vulnerable and badly in need of comfort, which Henry had done his best to provide despite not knowing the full cause of her distress. Revenge was her most earnest desire, yet it was impossible to tell Henry and with weeks or even days to go before she gave birth it was impractical to do anything else.

The worst part of it was that the awful bridle the Marquis had intended to put her in haunted her thoughts, not as a horror but as a sexual thing. Again and again she had wanted to masturbate over how it would have felt to be put in it and then thoroughly used, only to hold back as her stung pride got the better of her lust.

Now, with her hands straying over the straining flesh of her belly and her thighs cocked apart to spread her cunny to the air she was once more struggling to hold back her feelings. There had been seven servants, including the coachman and the man who had threatened to bugger her and then make her suck his soiled erection.

Given the chance she would gladly have had the lot of them hanged, with the Marquis beside them. Yet it was impossible not to think of their cocks going into her body while her head was held tight in the metal cage and her limbs were weighed down in the bars and shackles they had intended to put on her.

With a sob she let her hands go to her cunny, stroking the full, richly grown mound as she thought of being chained, helpless and taken in her mouth, vagina and anus all at once. Certainly that was what they would have done, once their master had fucked her. Remembering the spite of the peasants in her home village when the revolution had broken she knew that the men would have liked nothing better than to have a noblewoman to do with as they pleased. They would have degraded her utterly, probably urinating on her, maybe making her lick up their sperm from the floor. She would have been whipped, undoubtedly, across her naked buttocks as she crawled in her chains and her cunny and bottom-hole oozed the sperm that had been put up them.

Her fingers were on her clitty, rubbing and flicking at the little bud, then patting in the way her cousin Marie had taught her. She knew it was too late to stop, and she let her mind run. As her orgasm started to rise she was thinking of herself kneeling in a pool of pee, her own pee, which they would have made her do in front of them. The bridle would be on her head, tight and restrictive, as would be the heavy iron bars that linked her wrists and ankles. She would be nude, or perhaps in the torn, soiled remnants of her beautiful clothes. One cock would be in her bottom hole, pumping away to make her dizzy and breathless. Another cock would be in her mouth, hard and salty, tasting of man and sour leather.

The man in her mouth would have come, forcing her to swallow most of his sperm and draining the rest over her face and into her hair. No sooner would he have finished than his companion would have begun to pull from her anus, laughingly declaring his intention of having her suck his cock. It would be the coachman, the big, surly brute who had squeezed her bottom through her dress. A third man would enter her anus and then she would be gaping to take the coachman's cock in her mouth, unable to stop herself . . .

Eloise came, screaming her passion and shame out to the ceiling as her fingers worked on her cunny and up her bottom, where she had allowed them to stray as she masturbated. It went on for an age, with her back arched and her anal ring tightening again and again on her fingers as she frigged herself. As she imagined the taste of the coachman's cock she thrust her fingers into her mouth, sucking and sucking as the whole awful fantasy ran over and over in her head.

At last it was over, and all need for the scold's bridle, d'Aignan, and his vile servants was gone. She had done it, and so laid the ghost, but in doing so increased her desire for revenge to a burning passion.

Sir Joseph Snapes' carriage came to a stop. John the valet came forward and Judith allowed him to help her alight. Snapes and Sale followed and she was ushered into the house, a great rambling structure surrounded by pines and yews that created a gloom to all sides. Snapes' nervous mood had intensified as they neared the house and Judith's own unease had risen with it. As they

had approached she had heard a strange chattering
sound, which he had assured her came from his aviary
of foreign birds. Despite the reassurance she had found
it unnerving and as he began to bustle around the house
and issue orders to the servants she once more wondered exactly what was intended for her.

'Ah, Suki,' Snapes said as a girl emerged from a door
and performed a curtsy. 'This is Miss Judith.'

Snapes finished with a series of hand gestures, indicating Judith, her luggage and the stairs. Like John, Suki
was black, but small and with a pretty, pert face. A
dress of plain blue wool hid most of her body but was
unusually tight over two apple-sized breasts. She gave
Judith a smile that was not altogether reassuring, picked
up the cases and made for the stairs. Judith followed,
guessing that the maid did not understand more than
the simplest English. She also noticed that Suki was not
only the same height as herself, but of similar build, and
wondered if this was coincidence.

The stairs rose from the hall to a square balcony,
from which two corridors led into the wings of the
house. Suki chose one of these and led the way to the
end room, which proved to be a spacious chamber with
a view across a large, walled garden to the sea beyond.
Judith had not realised she was so close to the coast and
spent a moment admiring the view while Suki busied
herself behind her. Turning, she found the maid laying
out her clothes on the bed. Again Suki glanced at her,
smiling, perhaps in amusement, maybe with a touch of
awe, or perhaps sympathy.

Judith returned the smile, glad to be friendly with
someone who didn't look at her as if she were a choice
morsel of food. That, she realised, was what was
unnerving about Snapes. When most men looked at her
it was very obvious what they wanted, with their eyes
drawn mainly to her cleavage. With Snapes it was
different: his stare held plenty of desire, but it was desire

more suited to admiring a brace of roast wood pigeon than a girl. It seemed more than likely that Suki was subject to the same sort of attention, giving Judith a feeling of kinship with the black girl despite their great differences.

'Bath time, Miss Judith,' the maid informed her.

'Thank you, Suki,' Judith answered, unsure how much was understood.

Suki evidently expected her to undress, so Judith began to undo her bodice as the maid busied herself with the bath preparations. A large hip bath was pulled from a cupboard and hot water provided by Suki calling down the shaft of a dumb waiter. The demand was evidently expected, because the device immediately began to work and a large, steaming jug appeared. Four times the operation was repeated before the bath was deep enough, by which time Judith was undoing the bow on her inner petticoat. Suki had watched Judith undress in between pouring the water, showing an open interest without the least hint of embarrassment. As Judith let the petticoat go the black girl's interest turned to fascination, staring boldly at the nest of ginger curls that hid her sex.

Judith found herself colouring slightly and wondered if Suki's interest was purely directed at her pale, freckled skin and red hair or if there might be something sexual about it. It was impossible to tell, but as she stepped into the bath she was thinking that it might indeed be interesting to explore each other's bodies. The maid had taken a dish of goat's tallow and beech ash from the dumb waiter and was working up a lather in her hands, still with her attention fixed on Judith's body. Eager to be friendly, Judith began to undo her hair, showing Suki how the pile was built up from a mixture of her own hair and false extensions.

The maid watched in fascination, occasionally glancing down to where Judith's pubes showed beneath the water. When Judith had shaken her hair out to show how long it was Suki responded with a friendly grin, then began to apply the soap. Judith relaxed, closing her eyes and allowing the maid's gentle hands to soothe the stresses of the journey out of her body. Suki's touch suggested practice and, like her gaze, it was unashamedly intimate. As Judith's breasts were washed it became more so, each small globe explored and caressed with a thoroughness that Judith was sure came from more than a desire to get her properly clean. Her nipples came up under Suki's fingers, drawing a giggle from the black girl, and she found herself pushing her breasts out in the hope of more.

In response Suki made a small scolding noise with her tongue, a mannerism Judith recognised as coming from Snapes. Judith opened her eyes to find Suki giving her a look of mock disapproval, again copied from Snapes. She laughed at the imitation, feeling naughty rather than rejected at Suki not allowing her to get carried away and wondering if the maid might be persuaded to smack her bottom.

Suki gestured for her to turn over, and for a moment Judith thought it was going to happen, only to find that Suki merely wished to clean her back and bottom. Still, her kneeling position was a deliciously suitable one for punishment and also exposed both holes, increasing her arousal. The feeling became worse as Suki washed Judith's bottom with the same casual intimacy she had shown before. A finger was even slipped briefly into her anus, making her sigh and lift her hips. Having her sex washed was worse still, with Suki's thumb up her vagina as every crevice of Judith's sex was cleaned out. By the time Suki took her hand away Judith was moaning softly, drawing fresh giggles and looks of mock disapproval from the maid.

To finish, Judith was scrubbed down and rinsed with fresh, cold water that came up in the dumb waiter.

Finally, pink and tingling all over, she was allowed to get out of the bath, only for Suki to make a new gesture with her hand. For a moment Judith was unsure what she was supposed to do, until she saw what lay in the dumb waiter beside the jug. It was a brass basting syringe, highly polished and with a rounded nozzle fitted to the end.

With a resigned sigh she cocked her leg across the bath and bent, with her hands on her knees and her bottom stuck out above the dirty water. Suki smiled and nodded, then took up the syringe. Judith watched from over her shoulder, knowing full well what was going to be done to her and feeling her stomach flutter at the prospect. She was to be given an enema, which in the circumstances could only be a preparation for the sexual use of her anus.

Suki came behind her and Judith felt the sting of the soap on her anal ring. The nozzle touched her, probing the tight hole and then sliding up her bottom. Judith sighed as her rectum filled with water, enjoying the urgent, straining sensation as Suki pushed the plunger home. It was a large syringe, holding perhaps a quart, all of which was forced up her bottom. By the time Suki had fully depressed the plunger, Judith's toes were wriggling frantically and her bottom felt fit to burst. The nozzle popped free and she clamped her ring tight, squatting down to avoid making a mess of the floor. For a moment of the most wonderfully erotic pain she held it all in, then let go, gasping with relief as her enema gushed from her bottom hole into the bath water. Her eyes shut in bliss as the stream died to a trickle, leaving her bottom feeling tender and open. Suki was giggling, and as Judith turned to watch she found the maid refilling the syringe.

Four times the process was repeated, until Judith was flushed out to Suki's satisfaction. She was also shivering with arousal, her nipples stiff and her cunny wet, ripe for cock or Suki's tongue. As the maid finished cleaning her up she gave in to her feelings, taking Suki in her arms and kissing her. The maid responded, but nervously, and Judith guessed that going further was probably risking a whipping for her. Yet there was an unfamiliar, and exquisite, taste to Suki's mouth and skin, and it was hard to draw back. They held together for a moment, Judith's naked body trembling in Suki's arms. The sound of a gong rang out from elsewhere in the house and Suki quickly jumped back, immediately flustered.

Working quickly, the maid threw Judith two huge towels and then busied herself with the bath. The water she hurled from the window, making Judith giggle at the thought of Sir Joseph Snapes or a guest being below. The rest of the cleaning up was finished before Judith was dry, and Suki came to help, towelling her with the same unabashed intimacy she had shown before.

By the time Judith was fully dry she was feeling equal to a dozen Sir Joseph Snapes, and as many guests, butlers, valets and anyone else who cared to have her, especially Suki. She even squeezed the maid's bottom, finding it full and firm, but was given a gentle slap on the wrist for her efforts and then hustled towards the door.

An element of sexual indignity was added to her boiling emotions as she was led, stark naked, out into the corridor. To her surprise she was taken not down to the hall but by a back stair and into a huge kitchen. Snapes' cook was there, his enormous buttocks pushing out the back of his breeches towards her.

'Miss Judith, cook,' Suki announced and gave Judith a gentle nudge forward.

The cook turned, revealing the round, red-cheeked face that she last remembered panting into her own as she was held down to be mounted.

'And a good evening to you, Miss Judith,' he greeted her cheerfully. 'I'm Hastable, cook to Sir Joseph.'

'I believe we have met,' Judith answered. 'Although I don't recall being introduced formally.'

'Not the night for introductions, was it?' Hastable laughed. 'A merry little supper that was, but not a patch on tonight's occasion, not a patch.'

'What do you plan?' Judith asked. 'And shouldn't I be with the guests?'

'You'll be with the guests soon enough,' he answered. 'As to what I plan, why, didn't you guess? You're to be the dinner.'

Judith felt her heart go into her throat. She began to back, only to bump into Suki, then the cook burst into a gale of laughter.

'Not like that!' he roared. 'Why, you poor frightened little sparrow! You thought we were going to eat you up, didn't you! Well, peculiar Sir Joseph may be, that I'll not deny, but he's no carib!'

Judith sagged, suddenly weak at the knees. For one dreadful moment she had thought he meant it and had been too terrified to speak, and even in the face of his laughter she could find nothing to say. Suki had taken her under the arms as her body gave way and now heaved her upright. Judith steadied herself against a table and put her hand to her chest.

'Oh, I am sorry,' Hastable went on. 'Oh my, what an imagination you must have! No, it's no more than one of the master's little quirks. He and his friends like a girl as their plate, and the prettier the better. Here, have some water.'

Judith took the drink and swallowed it, relieved by his jocular tone but unable to resist looking around the kitchen for evidence of further depravity. There was none, and indeed the volume of food that had been laid out for preparation suggested that if Sir Joseph and his guests did intend cannibalism then she would be no more than a third or fourth course in a truly monstrous meal.

'Now,' Hastable went on, 'enough nonsense. You're well washed and scrubbed?'

'Thoroughly,' Judith assured him.

'Then climb on that big silvern platter on the far table, belly up and nicely spread out.'

Judith obeyed, positioning herself as comfortably as possible on the huge platter as the cook fetched a bottle from a cupboard.

'First,' Hastable declared, 'the marinade. You are to be served as the opening dish, and the sea is to give us our theme. So, cognac from the Ile d'Oléron, young, fiery and redolent of the ocean breeze! Drink some first. Shall I mix in some laudanum?'

'No, thank you,' Judith answered, restraining a giggle despite herself at the sudden change in his tone from flamboyance to concern.

Taking the bottle, she put it to her mouth, swallowing a generous gulp that burned a line of fire down her throat and then caught in it, sending her into fit of coughing.

'Young, perhaps, and a trifle raw,' Hastable admitted. 'Now, if you could lie back?'

Judith did as she was told and he began to souse her body with the cognac, pouring it liberally from neck to toes and then asking her to shut her eyes so that he might do her face. With her face soaked he withdrew, and after a pause she risked opening her eyes. Hastable had gone to the bench that ran the full length of one wall and was in the act of shelling a lobster.

'For your sweet cunt, my dear,' he said. 'Are you well enough juiced to take it?'

Judith nodded, knowing that it was true, if only from the way Suki had touched her in the bath. She spread her thighs to offer her vagina.

'Patience, my dear, patience,' Hastable declared. 'Miss Laycock will get her supper soon enough. First I must fill your breech. Lamprey, soused in claret, I have chosen. I hope you are sodomised often, or we may have some small difficulty.'

'Often enough,' Judith answered.

'Good,' he answered. 'I myself sodomise my wife once a month and throughout Lent, when we give up more normal congress. So, if you might lift your haunches?'

Judith pulled her legs up to her chest and reached down, spreading her bottom until she could feel the tension in her anus. Hastable gave her an appreciative glance and then pushed one thick finger into a dish of butter.

'Norfolk butter,' he said as he held up the glistening digit. 'From an Alderney herd grazed near Bungay, the best in my opinion. Now, as you are so prettily spread, up we go.'

He stabbed his finger at Judith's anus, making her gasp as it popped into the tiny hole, then pant as he began to work it around inside her.

'I do adore the feel of a tight anus,' Hastable remarked. 'I think I shall sodomise you when the gentlemen are finished. Yes, I shall. Suki has flushed you out well I trust?'

Judith sighed as the finger was pulled from her bottom, then nodded to answer his question. Sucking the butter from his fingers, Hastable crossed to a huge pot, from which he drew a thing like a large eel only with a grotesque head, a sucker for a mouth and a rich purple colour to its body.

'Lamprey,' Hastable stated. 'A great delicacy, of which King Henry the First died, due to consuming a surfeit. Have you tried it?'

Judith shook her head, thinking not of the taste, but that the body was perhaps twice the width of the largest cock she had every managed to accommodate in her back passage.

'You should,' Hastable assured her as he poked the thing's snout to her anus. 'They are best soused in claret, preferably from the Médoc rather than the Graves, and steamed rather than boiled. The exact preparation is my secret and something of an art. Perhaps Sir Joseph's guests will leave a little, in which case do try it.'

Judith was not listening. Her mouth was wide and her eyes were running tears as her anus stretched around the lamprey's head. It seemed impossible that it would fit, and then it had and the full thickness of the thing's body was sliding up her bottom, up and up while she gagged and panted. With a good foot of it in her rectum she was left gasping, fighting to get her breath back at the overpowering sensation of being buggered with such a huge object.

'Now the lobster,' Hastable went on. 'You may let go of your bottom cheeks now, girl, and put your legs down but keep them spread.'

Judith obeyed, feeling the lamprey squirm inside her as she moved. Hastable returned to the lobster and skilfully extracted the abdomen from within the shell. Unlike the lamprey up her bottom, her vagina accepted the lobster easily and she sighed as she felt her hole fill, with a good six inches of thick lobster meat inside her.

'Beautiful,' Hastable declared. 'This will be my masterpiece. You are privileged indeed, girl, to be the canvas for its creation. Now, a paste of crab's liver, Sauternes and spices, then crab meat, oysters, seaurchins and grigs, both in a jelly of partridge-eye and thyme.'

Judith lay back with a long sigh as the cook began to smear a rich, brown paste over her body. She badly needed to come, with the feel of her stuffed vagina and rectum getting to her as much as if they had been two great cocks. Her head was swimming and her nipples were hard and sensitive, while she could feel the juice from her cunny running out to join the butter that was melting around the lamprey up her bottom.

The cook worked patiently, ignoring Judith's aroused whimpering and speaking only to tell her not to breathe so deeply. With the paste covering her from neck to knees, he began to arrange crab meat on top, accentuating her nipples and belly button, then placing a tiny jellied sea-urchin on top of each little mound. There was a rich smell of food in the air, adding hunger to her deprived senses, and when he began to stuff her mouth with smoked oysters it was all she could do not to swallow. More sea-urchins and oysters were added, poked into every crevice of her body and built up to either side. Last came the elvers, artfully set to follow her curves and on those parts of the platter which remained visible.

'A few decorations and we are done,' Hastable declared.

The shell, claws and legs of the lobster were arranged around her cunny, making it seem as if the beast were climbing from her vagina. Seaweed and a scattering of brightly coloured shells completed the dish, which Hastable was still arranging when the gong sounded.

'Genius must not be rushed,' Hastable commented and continued with his arrangement of seaweed in Judith's hair. 'Yet I am close to the finish, so the gentlemen need have no more than a dramatic pause before you are served.'

For a further minute Hastable worked on her, then declared himself satisfied. He lifted the platter, grunting only slightly with the strain. Judith held her pose, resisting the temptation to giggle. The brandy had already begun to take effect and she felt drunk and aroused, eager for Snapes' guests to begin feasting from her body. She was taken from the kitchen, through wide double doors into the dining room, at which point she heard the mutter of voices in conversation and then a burst of clapping.

Gingerly moving her head, she managed a view of the room. A great table of dark wood occupied the centre, with Sir Joseph Snapes seated at the head and the guests ranked on either side. Luke Hurdon was visible, his powerful frame squeezed between a diminutive man with the face of a satyr and a tall, dark-haired man with a beard cut to the popular image of Satan. Two women were present, one at the table's tail, tall, exaggeratedly slim and masked, with bright, heavily painted eyes peering from the slits. The other was small, pretty, heavily adorned with jewels and seemed out of place save for the expression of utter lechery on her face. A further six sat on the near side of the table, all turned to watch her. The furthest two were typical rakes, elegant, richly dressed, one stern, one marked by an air of mildness, almost effeminacy. A smaller man sat next to them, his bright, penetrating gaze locked on the lobster between Judith's thighs. Then came a fat, obvious sybarite, a lean young man in the clothes of a priest and, to Judith's surprise, the bulky form of Squire Robson. In a life of debauchery and service to the most depraved of men, and women also, she had never seen a gathering of such obvious and lewd sensuality.

In addition to the guests, three servants were busy by the sideboard, Sale and John in full livery uniform of dark blue and gold. In contrast Suki was nude, her smooth dark skin glistening in the candlelight as she stood waiting to serve. Naked, the similarity between the ripe contours of Suki's body and Judith's own were still more striking, with breasts and hips of equal proportion and the same tight waist and well-fleshed buttocks. Judith found herself hoping that the evening's amusement might involve some sort of show between the maid and herself.

As Suki turned from her task Judith saw the thick, bushy growth of the black girl's pubic hair, with a hint of the labia at the junction of sex and thighs. There, quite clearly poked through the maid's sex lips, hung a wide ring of bright copper. Judith swallowed, thinking of how it must have felt to have the ring put in, and what it might signify.

Then Hastable was lowering the platter to the table and the maid was lost to view behind a guest. Judith lay still, listening to the compliments on her body and the food that had been arranged on it. Her head was near Snapes, with her spread thighs open to the majority of the table. Beyond the platter, just within her vision, an elaborate candelabrum supported perhaps a dozen candles of crimson wax, each alight and with tempting beads of molten wax forming at their lips.

No one spoke to her, yet the beauty of her face and shape of her breasts, belly and thighs were remarked on, compliments being passed to Snapes in the way that they might have remarked on any fine dish, or perhaps an exceptionally well-turned-out horse. A quiet cough brought an abrupt end to the chatter and Judith saw the priest rise. A brief benediction was given, in Latin, as the guests hastily tucked napkins into their collars, and, as a snatched amen rang out among them, they descended in a mass on Judith's body.

She squeaked, having expected to be served in a more refined manner, then gasped as teeth closed on a mouthful of crab meat and the nipple beneath. Other mouths were on her thighs, her belly and her breasts, licking, biting and sucking, finding her flesh as often as the food on top. She could see very little, while the sheer power of having a dozen people eating from her body was making her head swim. Snapes was licking paste from her left shoulder, while Hurdon had his mouth to a breast. Somebody had climbed between her thighs and was taking a share of lobster, direct from her cunny. Another had a tongue buried in her navel, having quickly nipped out the jellied sea-urchin. The small woman's mouth closed on hers, sucking out the oysters with her eyes closed in bliss. Two, then three people were competing for their share of lobster. Her legs were taken and pulled up and open, and she felt a mouth start to nibble at the lamprey in her bottom.

As the bulk of food reduced and lips, tongues and teeth began to fasten to her flesh more and more often she began to squirm beneath them. For one terrible moment her dread of being eaten alive returned, yet strong hands were holding her wrists and ankles and she could do nothing but writhe in the mess of food, wriggling feebly in their grip as every part of her body was sucked, licked and bitten. The bulk of the lobster was gone, and the paste was being licked from her cunny in long, wet slurps each of which ran from vagina to clitoris. Two diners seemed to be tearing at the lamprey in their mouths, as it was being dragged from her straining anus in short, sudden jerks. Both her breasts were being suckled, men's mouths pulling the nipples hard up between their teeth. Her own mouth was open, now empty of oysters but deep in a long kiss with the small woman.

The orgasm hit her suddenly, coming almost without warning. At one instant she was squirming under the sensation of being eaten alive, then the muscles of her belly and bottom had locked and she was coming, bucking and kicking in their grip, biting at the woman's mouth and thrusting her breasts up into the men's faces. She felt her anus nip at the lamprey, then its body part as it was pulled hard, a good deal remaining in her rectum. Her bumhole squeezed closed and she felt the pressure of the mass within pushing against it, adding an exquisite, filthy touch to the very peak of her climax. Nor did it end there, they kept on, feasting on her as she writhed and squirmed, lapping up every last morsel until she at last lay limp on the platter, wet and filthy, soiled with saliva and the remains of the food, totally spent. They began to stop, one by one, each taking a last kiss of her flesh or licking paste from some overlooked hollow. Whoever was between her legs finished last, polishing her anus with their tongue before pulling away and releasing her legs.

'A fine dish, Sir Joseph,' she heard a female voice say from beyond her feet. 'Exquisite, and so very exact to choose a red-head to go with the fruits of the sea.'

'I conceived it the moment I saw her,' Snapes replied. 'Yet, as you will see, she is more than a mere ornament.'

'I am so looking forward to it, Sir Joseph,' the woman replied.

'It will be quite a spectacle, I assure you,' he answered. 'For now, a compote of widgeon and truffles, served with a rare wine from the Vic Bilh hills. I think you will be amused. Sale, be good enough to clear the first course from the table.'

'Very well, sir,' Sale answered. 'Suki, prepare Miss Judith for Lord Furlong.'

Judith was giggling as Suki helped her from the table. All her earlier misgivings had fled and seemed silly in the pleasant haze of alcohol and sexual arousal. The diners clapped as Suki led her from the room and she responded with smiles and mock curtsies, then gave a final low bow as they exited by the high double doors.

She was led across the hall and into the back, where Suki took her to a large, tiled room with a great bath at the centre. There was still something in her vagina, presumably the remains of the lobster tail. While her breasts and belly had been licked clean, her skin was wet with saliva and those crevices the men had found less interesting still held food. She was also sure that at least some of the lamprey remained up her bottom.

'Scrub house,' Suki said, and pointed at the bath.

Judith giggled, wondering once more how it would feel to have sex with the pretty black girl. Giving Suki her most mischievous smile, she pointed at her cunny and then at Suki's mouth. Suki responded instantly, grabbing Judith by the arm and pulling sharply forward. They came into each other's arms, kissing and hugging together, hands going to necks, backs, then bottoms and breasts. Judith found Suki's cunny, feeling the copper ring and slipping a finger through it to tug on the labia. Suki groaned and responded in kind, sinking two fingers into Judith's vagina.

For a moment they masturbated each other, only for Suki to pull back with a giggle. Judith felt her vagina vacated and Suki lifted a hand, offering Judith some three inches or so of lobster tail that had remained in her vagina. Judith took it and they began to kiss again, sharing the rich taste of lobster along with that of brandy and excited girl. Judith found herself increasingly eager to taste Suki's cunny and to explore the ring that held the lips closed. On swallowing the lobster she began to kiss Suki's neck, then her chest, lingering on each nipple before moving down to the belly.

Suki gave a deep moan as she saw Judith's intention. Judith's hair was caught in the black girl's grip and her head was pushed lower. Suki opened her knees and Judith found her face against crinkly black hair, then moist, musky cunny flesh. Judith began to lick, lapping up Suki's juices and running her tongue over the metallic ring, teasing the pierced labia. Suki's clitoris was big, protruding from under the hood like the head of a tiny cock. Judith licked at it and felt Suki's muscles stiffen and the grip in her hair tighten.

With her face pushed hard into Suki's cunny, Judith set to work to make the black girl come. Her hands went around the girl's bottom, cupping the fleshy cheeks and pulling them open. One finger found Suki's anus and began to tickle the little knot of muscle. The firm thighs started to lock around Judith's face. Suki started to grunt, then scream over and over as she came, grinding her cunny into Judith's face.

Judith was too badly in need of her own orgasm to stop. Kneeling at Suki's feet with her bottom stuck out, she urgently needed the sort of treatment for which the whole evening had been setting her up. Her hands went down, one behind, one to the front. Fingers went up her bottom and into her vagina and she began to masturbate, using the ball of her thumb to stimulate her clitoris. Suki sank down, kissing Judith on the mouth then on her breasts, with her teeth nipping at one taut nipple.

Lost in ecstasy, Judith had begun to smear the remains of the lamprey up between her buttocks, dipping into the open, greasy hole of her anus again and again. Most of one hand was in her vagina, the hole stretched tight as her clitty burned under her thumb. Suki was suckling her, kissing as if feeding from Judith's nipple. The muscles of her sex and bottom clamped tight and for one, long moment she was at a blinding peak of utter bliss.

They came apart, giggling and sticky, to share a conspiratorial wink. Two great urns of water were already stood by the bath, which Judith helped Suki to pour. Giggling and sharing kisses, they climbed in, then began to soap and scrub each other. Cleaning what remained of the food from Judith's body meant fingers going into both her vagina and anus, starting her pleasure rising again. Even when fully clean they went on soaping each other's bodies, exploring the feel of each other's flesh. Their touches quickly became caresses, with Judith's desire to be subservient becoming slowly stronger once more. Her hand was under Suki's bottom, and as she found the anus she realised what she wanted to do: to kiss and lick the black girl's bottom hole. She began to finger it and Suki gave a soft moan, wiggling her bottom into Judith's hand.

Judith stuck her tongue out, indicating a willingness to lick the little hole her finger was toying with. Suki giggled and turned with a splash, presenting her bottom. Looking back, Suki gave a wicked grin and pulled her back in to make an elegant arc and spread her buttocks. Judith admired the meaty black rear, delighting in the

216

full, dark moon of Suki's bottom and the womanly spread of her hips. Most charming of all was the crevice between them with its rich growth of glossy black hair and the bare skin of the girl's very rudest details, those parts to which she intended to apply her tongue. Suki's anus was a tight knot of flesh yet darker than her skin, almost true black. Lower, her vulva was swollen, thick dark lips parted to show a centre of rich pink and the wet hole of her vagina.

Leaning forward, she puckered her lips, waited for a moment to allow the full pleasure of the dirty act she was about to commit to sink in, then planted a gentle, meek kiss right on the ring of Suki's anus. The black girl giggled, then sighed as Judith began to lick her bottom hole. Putting her hands on Suki's hips, Judith gave her full attention to Suki's anus, kissing, licking and probing with her tongue until the black girl had began to sigh and wiggle her bottom. Suki began to masturbate, but at that moment the door opened and both girls jumped up, finding the valet looking down at them with a mixture of lust and annoyance.

Judith smiled and stuck her tongue out, quite happy to have John's impressive cock to add to the fun. He hesitated but then shook his head and jerked his thumb back to indicate that they should get out of the bath, then started to talk. He spoke fast, in a language entirely unknown to Judith but which they evidently shared. Suki met what was obviously a rebuke with her head hung down and then gave a shocked squeal and put her hands to her bottom. Judith guessed Suki had been threatened with a beating or told she was to get one later and at once decided to intervene.

'It was my fault,' she address the valet, 'and really no more than a game. Pray spare Suki, or if you must whip someone, make it me.'

'The master will decide.' John answered her. 'Get yourself dry. Scent yourself with this.'

217

He put a tiny vase of blue china down on the floor, then settled back against the door to watch the girls dry. Judith hurried, determined to do her best to have Suki spared a beating. Soon she was dry and she picked the vase up, removing the plug to sniff the contents, then pouring a little into her hand. It was a scented oil, musky and rich, distinctly animal, not unpleasant and certainly in keeping with Snapes' sensual tastes. She began to oil herself, rubbing drops on the insides of her wrists and behind her ears.

'All over,' John ordered. 'Do your cunt well.'

'Is it not expensive?' she queried.

'It is for Lord Furlong,' he answered.

Judith shrugged and began to oil herself more fully, first on her neck, then her breasts, belly and legs. Suki helped with her back and bottom, while what remained she rubbed into her mound, avoiding only the most sensitive parts of her vulva. When complete the heady scent was strong in the air, making her head swim.

John nodded and gestured for both girls to follow him. They returned to the dining room, where Sale was carving meat from a suckling pig that lay steaming on the sideboard. The valet went to speak to Snapes, saying what had been happening in the bath and asking to whip Suki.

'Pray spare her, Sir Joseph,' Judith pleaded. 'The fault was mine. I was too eager for pleasure after the privilege of being served to your guests. If you feel discipline is needed, by all means whip me, but not Suki.'

'Absolutely,' Snapes answered. 'Spare the poor girl. She was only doing what comes naturally. Besides, she has worked well. When I saw Lord Furlong earlier he was simply bursting with enthusiasm. As to you, Judith, my dear, a whipping would not be appropriate at this stage of festivities. If you wish to make a display of yourself, you may show my guests your edifying trick with the candles.'

218

Judith gave a small curtsy and climbed on to the table, feeling thoroughly pleased with herself. Not only had she spared Suki a beating, but she was likely to be given one herself, which she felt would be a fitting climax to the evening. Determined to be naughty, and to continue doing so until they interrupted the meal to punish her, she took up a bottle from the table and drained a good half of it down her throat without pause.

'My dear girl,' the small, satyr-faced man addressed her, 'that is a Lafite of the 1765 vintage, pray show it a little respect.'

After giving him an arch look, Judith turned, pushed her bottom close to his face and boldly stuck the neck of the bottle into her vagina. She felt herself fill, pulled the bottle out and squeezed, sending a spray of claret over the man and both his neighbours. Turning abruptly, she stuck her tongue out at him as he sat, arms wide in a gesture of shock, mouth open, face and front spattered red with wine. She laughed and crawled quickly away before he could react to the outrage. Several of the other guests had found her trick amusing, notably the soft-looking man.

'I'll take a drink from your cunt, girl!' he called. 'Come, and bring another bottle!'

Judith jumped to her feet and walked down the table, swinging her hips to make her bottom wiggle behind her. He smiled as she approached and she dipped down to collect a bottle, took a deep draught from it, pushed her belly out and released the full pressure of her bladder into his face. He gave a shocked cry and pushed himself away, unbalancing his chair and collapsing to the floor. Judith laughed and continued to pee on him where he lay, only for his companion to move in and deliberately take the stream in his mouth. The others watched, some egging him on, others laughing, some exclaiming in astonishment.

'Somebody take a stick to that trollop!' a voice called out.

Cries of agreement went up immediately. Judith's ankles were grabbed and she was speedily pulled down to the table. Laughing and pretending to struggle, with her pee still gushing from her cunny, she was forced on to her face and held spreadeagled. Hands began to smack her bottom, making her cheeks wobble and bounce but only increasing her laughter. There was a pool of pee beneath her belly, along with various items of silverware and dishes. She squeaked as something was pushed unexpectedly into her vagina, and turned to find the small woman with an arm between her legs. Judith gasped as the whole of the woman's fist went into her, then squealed as Sale brought a thick cane hard down across her buttocks.

'Good man, Sale,' Judith heard Snapes say, and then a wadded napkin had been forced into her mouth.

Sale beat her well, laying the cane hard across her writhing buttocks again and again until she was blubbering and squirming on the small woman's fist. Not only her bottom was beaten, but also her thighs, once the hand had left her vagina. She had quickly lost all idea of how many cuts she had received, but eventually it stopped, leaving her lying gasping in the pool of her own pee.

'Now behave a little better,' Snapes ordered. 'Come, you were going to play with the candles.'

Judith climbed shakily into a kneeling position. Her bottom was hot and sore, and as she ruefully put her hands to the cheeks she felt the risen welts. With her lower lip set in a sulky, but fake, pout, she took two burning candles and began to play with herself. Crawling slowly down the table she made a deliberate show of sucking the candles, rubbing them on her breasts and sex, penetrating herself again and again in both vagina and anus. A good deal of wax went on her skin, more on the table and into the food. Sale and John had begun to serve the suckling pig, and Judith continued to flaunt herself and tease her senses with the candles as they ate and drank. Soon both breasts were encased in wax, with her stiff nipples showing as little bumps at each peak. Her belly was also liberally covered, and her beaten buttocks. Dripping the wax on to the fresh welts stung even more than usual, and as her excitement rose again she began to concentrate more and more on her bottom.

With her head down and her cheeks stuck high she began to bugger herself with one candle, the hot drips running down it to catch her anus and cunny. The other she held over her back, dripping wax on to her punished cheeks and into the crease between them. As the guests ate they watched her torture herself, finishing their pig one by one until all attention was on Judith's body. Her senses were full of pain and arousal, along with the pleasure of showing off and the knowledge that she had just been beaten in front of all of them. For a while she held back, revelling in the situation, until her need for orgasm became simply too strong.

Rising into a squat, she spread her thighs to Snapes and wriggled her bottom down into a dish of vegetables. A carrot went into her vagina, while her buttocks were spread over a satisfyingly slimy mixture of more carrots, potatoes and peas. Sat splay-legged in the mess, she began to masturbate happily, using one candle to drip wax on to her sex and the other to rub at her clitoris. They watched, sipping claret, some stroking their crotches, one man absentmindedly fondling the tall woman's left breast.

'Ten guineas says she can't come more than twice,' the devilish man offered.

'Taken,' Luke Hurdon answered.

Judith shut her eyes, on the edge of coming, then, putting the candle directly over her vulva, she let herself slip into orgasm. It came slowly, a hot blend of pain and ecstasy as her fingers rubbed half-molten wax into her

221

sex. She heard herself scream as if from a distance, and then it was fading, but only enough to make her want more.

As she opened her eyes she saw that Snapes had gone, and felt an irritation that he had not stayed to watch what she had thought to be an unmissable spectacle, especially for such a dedicated voyeur. Piqued at his attitude, she began to masturbate again, wondering what she could do to leave an impression on her debauched audience. The gong sounded three times and at once the guests went quiet and turned to the door. Judith looked up and froze.

Sir Joseph Snapes had returned, and was standing in the open doorway. His face was beaming and red, his expression set in a manic grin, and with him was a companion.

'Allow me to introduce Lord Furlong,' Snapes said.

Judith sat aghast, unable to find words or do more than edge slowly back on her bottom. Lord Furlong was not a man at all, but a squat man-ape, with black beady eyes peering from beneath an overhanging brow and thick, protrusive lips in a face the colour of coal. Rich and well-cut clothes covered its upper half, a coat of hunting pink with gold frogging, a waistcoat in an elaborate design of black, gold and scarlet curlicues, a cravat of red silk and a linen shirt. Below the waist it was naked, or rather he, as was plain from the dangling scrotum and dark, crooked penis.

'Lord Furlong,' Snapes was saying, 'is an enschego, or chimpanzee if you prefer the term, that beast described by the learned Doctor Johann Frederich Gmelin as *Simia troglodytes*, in 1788. You need not fear. For all his ferocious aspect he is of a gentle disposition, and well trained to boot. Entirely harmless, unless you should deny him his sport, that is.'

The candle dropped from Judith's nerveless fingers, rolling beneath the table. Nobody paid the least attention. All were watching either her or the chimpanzee, some amused, some lustful, some openly malevolent, but all, without exception, clearly delighted by the prospect of watching her mated by the beast.

'It is my theory,' Snapes continued, 'that the scientific establishment is wrong in supposing these creatures to be no more than a grotesque parody of man. Would the Lord God have permitted such a semblance to exist? I say no, and that the enschego is a cousin to man, if degenerate. Thus man and the enschego should able to breed, a hypothesis I intend to put to the test, now!'

His voice had risen in pitch as he spoke, ascending almost to a screech. As he addressed them the chimpanzee had fixed its attention on Judith and began to masturbate its cock for a purpose all too obvious. She felt the candle in her vagina slip free and her sex was open to the rapidly stiffening penis of the chimpanzee. The drink was making her head spin, while she was aroused almost to the point of orgasm, yet of one thing she was absolutely certain – she was not about to submit to having her body invaded by the penis of the grotesque animal in front of her.

'Come, my dear,' Snapes was saying as he advanced, hand in hand with Lord Furlong. 'He would prefer you on your knees, with that delightful bottom of yours held high and wide. His hands are soft, so do not be scared should he grab your breasts when he mounts you. He may lick you first, and you should let him, but if he tries to sodomise you then pull away, it would not do to have him spend in the wrong orifice!'

Lord Furlong's eyes were on Judith, taking in her face, her chest, her belly and then her open thighs and the hairy triangle between with its wet, open centre. His thick, leathery lips peeled back from yellowing tusks and he gave a quiet, chittering noise.

At that Judith broke. Scrambling desperately backwards, she made to flee. For a moment her bottom stuck in the mess of vegetables in which she was sat, then she was up, only to slip in the soggy mixture with which she had coated the table and fall headlong. A hand gripped her ankle but she kicked out with the strength of panic and broke free. The kick sent her sideways and she found herself falling, landing across someone's lap and then on the floor, face down and winded with her upturned bottom towards the chimpanzee.

Struggling to rise, she realised that the action was presenting the animal a fine view of her sex an instant before it was too late. Strong, leathery hands were closing on her hips, the turgid tip of its cock nudged her thigh and then she was scrambling under the table, kicking and yelling as she went. She had turned and found herself looking into the beast's face, increasing her desperation to get away. Wrenching herself out from the far side of the table she stood, only for the chimpanzee to bound up and face her, knuckles scraping among the debris of her masturbation as he came slowly forward.

She stopped, not knowing what to do. The door was blocked by the massive figure of Sale, while John was edging around the table to cut her off from the window. Not one of the guests showed sympathy for her plight, but were either egging Lord Furlong on or calling out wagers on how long Judith could hold out. Even the two women were no help, both staring in horrified fascination at what was about to happen to her but neither showing the least inclination to take her side.

Beyond Sale the door opened and Judith saw Suki, bearing a great dish of steaming puddings. Lord Furlong turned his head at the noise, saw the naked black girl and paused in his advance. At the same instant a flicker of fire showed beneath the table where the candle flame had caught the rug. Sale saw it and grabbed for a bottle, hurling the contents out in an arc that missed the flames but caught several guests and also the chimpanzee.

Judith seized her chance as Lord Furlong gave a chattering scream of rage. Racing for the door, she dodged the clutching hands of first the satyr-faced man and then Luke Hurdon. The satanic man held back, but Snapes grabbed for her, only to let go as her fist drove into his nose. Squire Robson made no attempt to stop her and as Judith reached the door Suki stepped away and then threw the tray of puddings down, catching Sale as he caught up with Judith. Judith fled down the nearest corridor, ignoring an impassioned cry from Suki only to realise that it had been meant to stop her going the wrong way. She was in the dead end that led to the kitchen, but a glance behind showed Sale rising to his feet, only to go back down as Lord Furlong leaped on to his back.

The chimpanzee glared at Judith from on top of the butler, its erect cock held in one hand. She hurled herself through the kitchen door, finding Hastable sat sipping claret in front of the only other door. He looked up, starting at her obvious terror, then rose, calmly opened a window and sat back. Judith was already racing for the opening as the door crashed open behind her. Leaping to the workbench, she forced her torso through the narrow aperture, poised to leap and then stopped hard as a grip like a vice tightened on her ankle. She turned in terror, finding the hideous chimpanzee face grinning into hers as it drew her back into the house. Beyond, Hastable had retreated into a corner, clearly in no mood to tackle the beast. Sale was stood at the door, and Suki, with Snapes beyond.

Pure terror welled up inside her and she screamed. She heard Snapes' cruel laugh and Suki too screamed out in a long ululating call. Snapes' laughter immediately turned to a bellow of rage but the chimpanzee's grip slackened. Judith hurled herself outwards, felt her ankle slip from Lord Furlong's grasp and landed hard on the lawn. Scrambling to her feet, she stumbled, then ran in blind panic, not caring in what direction she was going or that she was naked, just so long as she was putting distance between herself and the dreadful house.

Ahead was a moonlit jumble of confusing shapes and a flat expanse of dull silver that seemed to shift and waver in the light breeze. She ran towards it, her lungs bursting with the effort, her feet stumbling drunkenly over the lawn. She slipped as the ground fell away beneath her in a bank. Her feet found sand and she was dashing out on to the flat, which vanished beneath her feet, sending her headlong into the reed bed she had mistaken for a field.

She hit the water with a splash and struggled upright, coughing and choking. There were noises behind her, angry shouts and calls for dogs, all accompanied by the furious screams of the chimpanzee. Striking out in blind terror, Judith plunged through the reeds, coming into deeper and deeper water until at last she tripped and went headlong once more. The cool water hit her face and she went under, felt a moment of panic when there seemed to be no direction but only a world of dark, cold water and then she was up again, clinging to handfuls of reed stems and gasping for air. With the air came reason, enough to make her stop thrashing and lie still, listening.

The clamour from the house had increased if anything, and was no more than a wild mixture of shouts and curses. Sounds became clearer as she listened, one voice demanding to know where the key to the kennels was, another shouting that the chimpanzee was loose. At that Judith began to move again, pushing slowly through the reeds at an angle she hoped would take her away from both the house and the open sea.

Presently she came to open water, a broad, calm mere across which the moon cast a thin trace of silver. Pushing out from the reeds, she began to swim, propelling herself with little, soft kicks below the surface

226

of the water. As she came out from the shadow of the reeds she managed to make out the house and the surrounding trees as black shapes against the sky with a scattering of windows showing light of a rich yellow and one, the dining room, of a flickering red-orange. Seeing that the fire was taking hold Judith fought back a demented urge to laugh, then stopped kicking and let herself float free. Feeling strangely calm, she listened to the wild, rage-filled screams of Lord Furlong.

Nine

Sir Joseph Snapes strode across Bedford Square away from his house, swinging his cane in short, deliberate jerks. His anger had scarcely lessened since leaving Suffolk. Not only had the wretched Judith ruined the climax of his magnificent dinner party, but the fire had destroyed a considerable quantity of fine furniture and blackened the main part of the lower floor with smoke. Only by forming a bucket chain from the sea had it been possible to extinguish it. Furthermore, in the general confusion Lord Furlong had taken panic, run from the house and was now roaming Suffolk. As he had left for London a report had come in of the animal pursuing a woman in a blue dress, presumably in the belief that it was Suki. Of Judith there had been no trace, save the crushed reeds where she seemed to have stumbled into the mere. It seemed unlikely that she could swim, and considering how drunk she had been he could only suppose she had drowned. The probability gave him a certain satisfaction, yet also unease at how Charles Finch and Henry Truscott were likely to take her disappearance. Suki also had gone missing, although in her case he was sure she would quickly return with her tail between her legs.

He had left his staff in Suffolk to find the chimpanzee and driven the gig to London alone, determined that at the least he would complete his plans for Wheal Purity.

* * *

Reuben Eadie drew hard on the reins, pulling his horse to a halt outside the house in Bedford Square. Leaping to the ground, he made for the door, taking the steps at a run despite his exhaustion. The door knocker crashed against the plate, creating a hollow boom, and he stood back, expecting Sale to answer. There was no response, nor to further knocking, and after a while he stood back to stand, fidgeting and uncertain, on the pavement.

The vein in which his master had put so much faith was nothing but schorl, which Tom Davey had described as a black form of tourmaline useful only for the cheapest of jewellery. He had immediately realised that the entire mine was a fake, and that the fine cassiterite they had taken as a sample had in fact been taken from Sevenstones Mine by Peggy Wray. Only by picking up another of the false stones had he prevented Davey from learning the full truth. When shown the crystals side by side the difference had been clear, with the true cassiterite showing large regular crystals with a peculiar, greasy lustre, very different from the schorl with its long spikes like black glass. It had become crucial to get the news to Sir Joseph before it broke. Leaving Tom Davey to complete his survey when Todd Gurney returned, he had ridden for London, yet with Sir Joseph not in residence he had no idea of what to do next.

Henry Truscott sat at ease in what had become his favourite seat in Le Roy's coffee house. Charles was with him, both men prepared for the flood of demand for Wheal Purity shares once Sir Joseph Snapes had delivered his report to the Royal Society. Through the bowed window he could see much of the length of Thames Street, along which a man was approaching at a fast walk.

'Sir John Church, unless I am much mistaken,' he said. 'The first of many, no doubt.'

A minute later Church had entered Le Roy's, but rather than return Henry's friendly greeting he planted his fist on the table with a scowl.

'Damn you, Truscott,' Church snapped. 'I want my money back, and no business about the price having fallen. I want every last farthing!'

'Why?' Henry demanded in surprise. 'Whatever is the matter?'

'Ha!' Church answered. 'You know full well. That mine of yours is not worth a tenth of what you said.'

'Nonsense,' Henry said, although a nasty suspicion was already forming in his mind. 'Did your hear Sir Joseph Snapes speak at the Royal Society?'

'Indeed I did,' Church answered him, 'and that is the reason for my being here. It is a mine of moderate worth, with the potential for perhaps ten years production of middle-grade ore! Facts you knew well, no doubt. You have tricked me Truscott, and a good many others besides . . .'

'No, no,' Charles cut in, 'we never put a value on the stock, but merely sold at what the market would bear.'

Church answered with a snort of contempt and Henry saw two more of their erstwhile investors entering the coffee house, both looking around angrily. They saw him immediately and came to remonstrate. As Henry and Charles attempted to argue yet more disillusioned investors poured in, until it had become impossible to present any argument whatever against their demands for restitution. Still Henry held his ground, becoming ever more stubborn until Augustus Barclay forced his way to the front of the crowd. Henry had been pretending to study the share certificates in an effort to buy time and found himself looking up into the twin barrels of Barclay's pistols.

'Ah,' he said quietly, 'well, possibly we might come to some arrangement.'

An hour later they were in a private room at the bank, paying out money for share certificates while

Barclay kept a menacing watch by the door. Only when every last share had been bought back did the men leave. Henry walked weakly from the bank, his wad of shares clutched to his chest. He shook his head, looked either way along Fleet Street and then turned to Charles with a shrug.

'What have we left?' he asked.

'Damn little,' Charles answered. 'Some of Snapes' money, what you had from Mrs Cunningham and a few may not have made Le Roy's, French mainly. That is all.'

'Damn,' Henry answered. 'So, do we seek out Snapes?'

'No,' Charles stated, 'I know his game.'

'Damned if I do. He would seem to have ruined himself as surely as we.'

'Not so, by driving the price down he seeks to buy the entire mine stock and so take the full fortune for himself. Doubtless he will seek us out, produce some long-winded explanation and offer us a pittance for the shares. Faced with ruin, we would have little choice but to accept.'

'So that is why he allowed us all rights to trade, he did not wish the investors demanding restitution from him at the full price! It is also why he did not want us selling before his presentation. The bastard has us caught, yet he'll be the fool when he finds the mine worthless.'

'A poor pleasure when we too are in debt.'

'True, Charles. What say we thrash the bastard to an inch of his life and have done with it?'

'Be calm, Harry. For now we still have the money from the Cunninghams. Snapes will want to ensure that they too demand restitution before he can approach us, else he'll end up partner to Saunder Cunningham. Do you think Cunningham would buy the mine if you offered it before news gets to him, perhaps saying May had pleaded with you?'

'I dare say, but he's gone to Cornwall to lick his wounds.'

'All the better. Ride hard for Cornwall and we may yet save at least a part of our gain.'

'And leave Eloise in London to face the anger of the French investors? I cannot, but you could. Besides, Cunningham is more likely to listen to you.'

'Very well, so be it. Meanwhile you must keep low, and avoid both Snapes and the French.'

'Sound advice. I will send Eloise to her cousin's. She should be safe enough as they didn't buy.'

'Where will you be?'

'The last place anyone will look. At the Cunninghams' town house!'

Eloise lay on a bed in the house rented by the Vicomte de Blagny, feeling her swollen stomach and groaning softly at each of the gentle contractions that had started that morning. Henry's sudden demand that she move had come as more of an annoyance than a surprise. He had refused to give an explanation, but it had been clear that events with the mine were reaching a crisis. Another matter had also been exercising her mind, so she had gone with the minimum of fuss.

The other matter was a letter she had received that morning from Saunder Cunningham. It had been sent from Winchester, and had been so clearly intended to cause friction between herself and Henry that she had laughed. In unctuous tones he had stated that he intended her no grief but that he felt it his moral responsibility to inform her of the extent of Henry's infidelities. Had Henry seen it he would have been driven to rage, which explained why Cunningham had waited until he was half way to the West Country before daring to send it. Yet Eloise had not shown it to Henry, nor mentioned it. She, aware of his infidelities, used them to justify her own and had even, on occasion, shared Peggy with him. The details expressed by Cunningham were new to her, although she had known that he had won the right to buy Trethaw Wood as the result of a bet. Cunningham spelled out every detail, including Judith's part, expecting to horrify Eloise with not only Henry's debauchery. By the end of the letter Eloise had been laughing aloud.

She had heard of Mother Agie, and knew something of the bawd's reputation, also of how Judith had been trained and punished. The details had provided many an exquisite orgasm, imagining herself in Judith's shoes. Of one thing she was certain, the old bawd would be keen to know who Judith's accomplices had been. As Henry had not been set on by roughs recently, it seemed reasonable that his identity had not been discovered, which had set Eloise on an interesting train of thought. On reaching her conclusions she had called for Marie and asked for a stylus and paper, then carefully drafted a letter. It now lay beside the bed, Marie having promised to see it delivered without fail.

Marie was in high spirits, having missed a period and being sure she was pregnant. Eloise had responded warmly, which had turned their conversation to the night they had shared Henry at the house of the Comte de Breuil. In turn this had led to reminiscence of bitter-sweet memories of their days in Burgundy and so Marie had locked the door, climbed beneath the bed covers and gone down between Eloise's thighs.

Eloise stroked her belly as she was licked, thinking of the guilty pleasure they had taken in each other's tongues before and of how things had changed. Marie was teasing, licking Eloise's sex and fingering her vagina, but avoiding the clitoris. Only when Eloise's pleasure had risen to the point that she started to beg did Marie apply her tongue to the little bud. Eloise began to come almost immediately, moaning with pleasure as her muscles clamped on Marie's face then giving a louder and very different cry as her whole belly locked tight in a powerful contraction that could only mean the onset of giving birth.

As Sir Joseph Snapes crossed Bedford Square towards his house he was surprised to see the lank figure of Reuben Eadie standing at his door. Immediately he increased his pace, certain that his man would not have made the trip from Cornwall without good reason. Eadie saw him and began to hurry across the square.

'What news?' he demanded, as they came within earshot.

'Terrible, sir,' Eadie answered. 'The mine's a fake!'

'A fake?' Snapes demanded.

'There's no vein,' Eadie went on, 'nothing but schorl. They'd salted the mine from Sevenstones and . . .'

'Calm yourself, man,' Snapes demanded. 'You are making no sense.'

'Your pardon, sir,' Eadie answered, more slowly. 'The samples we had assayed, sir, they weren't from Purity at all. They were from Sevenstones Mine on Hingston Down, one of the best in the county. The vein at Purity is some stuff by the name of schorl, a crystal like black tin but next to worthless. You've been played for a fool, sir, good and proper.'

'You're sure of this?' Snapes demanded.

'It's plain, sir,' Eadie answered. 'Tom Davey came over from Dolcombe to look at Purity. He's sharp, sir, I've known him years. He says it's this schorl, but he doesn't know it's all the same, so you've time, perhaps.'

'Damned little,' Snapes answered. 'I've just delivered a report that'll have the buyers at Truscott's throat. I must get to the bank and drain the account, else I'm ruined!'

Mother Agie sat in her chair, her huge thighs spread to accommodate the head of the girl kneeling before her.

234

The pretty brunette wore no more than stockings and an open chemise, while her pert bottom was decorated by a dozen thin red welts, the result of a caning. Having been beaten, she was giving her mistress the traditional apology with her tongue and Agie was beginning to approach orgasm. Two of the bullies stood by the door, both with hard cocks sticking out from their breeches, ready to take their turns with the punished girl once Agie was finished.

A knock sounded at the door, to which Tom responded, opening it only enough to allow him to stick his head out. Agie cursed, annoyed at the distraction, but pulled the girl's head harder into her cunny. As soft lips pursed around her clitoris and began to suck at it she felt herself coming, shutting her eyes to prevent herself being distracted. The orgasm was good, long and slow, as always under one of her girls' tongues, but ended poorly due to the interruption.

'What's this about, Katie?' she demanded as Tom allowed another of the girls into the room. 'And it'd best be pressing, or I'll have your arse redder than Jinny's here!'

'There's a lady asking to see you, Mother,' Katie answered with her lip trembling. 'A real fine lady, and two servants with her.'

'No doubt some high-bred piece who wants her arse whipped in front of her husband's fart catchers,' Agie answered.

'No, Mother, I don't think so, not this one,' Katie stammered. 'She's a French lady, Mother. She says she's something to say on account of what happened with Judy Cates a while ago.'

'See her in,' Agie answered immediately, 'and you needn't fear for your arse skin, not for now.'

Katie disappeared and quickly returned with a small woman wrapped in a heavy cloak. Her nervousness was obvious, to Agie's amusement, and her eyes went immediately to the half-naked Jinny, who was standing in the corner with her reddened buttocks on show to the room.

'Don't mind Jinny,' Agie said, making her best effort to sound soft and friendly, also respectable. 'She was naughty and had to be corrected, as I'm sure you'll understand. I'll not ask for your name, but I hear you have news for me?'

'I do,' the woman replied. 'It concerns an outrage that was perpetrated in this house. By Judith Cates and another.'

'So I hear,' Agie answered. 'But tell me, what is it to you that you come to tell me?'

'I . . . I was treated badly by the man,' the woman stammered, 'and I dare not seek redress myself, not in my position.'

'I understand,' Agie answered. 'If you make a fuss then pop goes your precious reputation, so you'd rather have my boys set on him. Well, that's no trouble for me, so who is he?'

'A fellow exile of France,' the woman answered. 'The Marquis d'Aignan.'

As the barge bumped against St Catherine's Stair Judith jumped ashore. Responding to the bargees' merry farewell with a grunt, she climbed the steps and made for the Tower, judging the quickest route to Thames Street and Le Roy's coffee house. There she expected to find Charles, Henry and, with luck, Sir Joseph Snapes. Her journey to London had been far from pleasant. On climbing from the mere, naked, muddy and shivering, she had spent hours stumbling through the dark before finding a barn as the first light of dawn began to show. Purloining an ancient sack, she had contrived to cover herself, then pressed on. As the sun rose she had made out sails in the distance across the flat fields and headed towards them. By luck these had belonged to oyster barges bound for London.

One crew had agreed to take her, only to demand their cocks sucked as soon as they had cleared the estuary. Judith had obliged, going down on her knees with her bottom showing beneath the edge of her sack to take them in her mouth, one by one. Once she had swallowed each man's come, the inevitable questions had been asked about the livid welts that decorated the skin of her bottom and thighs. Seeing no reason to protect Snapes' reputation, she had told the truth, although it had been plain that they did not believe her, but thought her simply a wife on the run from a violent husband.

Nevertheless they had become affable and allowed her to share their breakfast and choose from various bits of old clothing that were about the barge. She had dressed in filthy, grease-stained trousers, a shirt that came to her knees and a pair of huge boots with holes in both soles. The shirt seemed to have been used as a rag, while the trousers had to be turned up at the ankles but were uncomfortably tight across her bottom. For all the discomfort, she had felt more gratitude than anything as she at last fell into a deep sleep on the cabin floor.

She had woken stiff and cold with the barge already well into the Thames estuary and making good way. The men had provided tea along with bread and dripping, which had made her feel at least vaguely human. At last they had reached St Catherine's Stair, at which the barge was to unload, and Judith had disembarked, along with an oyster knife she had concealed in the pocket of her trousers.

Walking through London with her mass of tangled red hair loose and her breasts and bottom rounding out her male clothes, she attracted no shortage of witty remarks and half-serious propositions, all of which she ignored. Her main need was for comfort, for soothing words from Charles, decent clothes and the feeling of being protected. Second came revenge, and her mind was full of ways in which Charles, and more especially Henry, might be persuaded to deal with Snapes for what he had done. Rather, what he had tried to do, she corrected herself, for if there was one crumb of comfort in her condition it was that Snapes had failed.

On approaching Le Roy's she braced herself for the confrontation, only to find it empty of all those she had expected to be there. Discovering that Henry and Charles had been marched away by angry Wheal Purity investors, and had been going to the bank, she left Le Roy's and headed towards Ludgate. The proprietor had been less than garrulous, shocked not only by her clothing but by a woman being in Le Roy's at all. Yet it was obvious that something was amiss, and Judith was sure that whatever it was Snapes would be at the heart of it. Then, as she came in sight of the bank, she saw Snapes himself emerge. Another man was with him, a thin, sharp-faced individual she did not recognise. Both seemed agitated, while Snapes held a thick black case in his hand.

Snapes hailed a cab. A crooked smile twitched up one corner of Judith's mouth. She ran, keeping the bulk of the vehicle between herself and the men, then, as it started off, she jumped, catching hold of the back and stepping on to the tailboard. With several urchins employing the same manoeuvre within view, nobody took the least notice. As the cab turned north into Shire Lane she slipped her knife from her pocket. A single motion slit the rear cloth of the cab, an action familiar from her days as a street urchin around the Seven Dials. She reached into the rent to the space beneath the seat, grabbed the case, jumped down from the tailboard and ran into a yet narrower alley even as Snapes' yell of fury sounded behind her.[13]

In the master bedroom of the Cunninghams' Bruton Street house, Henry sat on the edge of the bed, his anger at being cheated by Snapes fading slowly in the face of the open lust of May, Alice and Caroline Cunningham. They knew nothing of Snapes' address, but were keen to further the pleasures he had introduced them to in return for allowing the sale of shares. He had known they had enjoyed it, but was still surprised at their sheer enthusiasm for more of the same.

They had stripped for him, one by one, practising the art of teasing him as they peeled. May was in stockings and had her chemise pulled wide to display and support her breasts. Alice was bare but for her stockings and a bonnet, giving her a charmingly coquettish look. Caroline had gone nude in her enthusiasm, but had put her boots back on at Henry's request.

They now kneeled at his feet, each flushed with arousal as May and Henry taught the two younger girls the art of sucking a cock. His penis was in Alice's mouth, while Caroline leaned close to lick at what little shaft was still exposed. The two girls were greedily competing for their share of cock, sucking with more enthusiasm than skill but still bringing Henry rapidly towards orgasm.

'It is my turn, Alice!' Caroline complained when she felt that her sister had had more than a fair share of his penis. 'Tell her, May!'

'Come, Alice, let your sister have her fair share,' May said gently, 'and I shall teach you a knew trick.'

Alice's mouth slid reluctantly from Henry's cock and he shifted his hips to make it point at Caroline's face.

'Make a moue,' May instructed, 'as if you were in a sulk. Yes, just so. Now take it in and let it open your lips.'

Henry groaned as the firm ring of Caroline's lips opened around the head of his penis and then slowly engulfed his shaft. He knew he was going to come before long, but tried to hold off, not wanting to bring the experience to a close. Alice had begun to tickle his balls and had her face pressed cheek to cheek with her

239

sister. It was an irresistibly pretty sight, and as Caroline pulled back to allow her lips to be penetrated once more, he felt himself coming.

'Many men prefer a girl to swallow their seed,' May was saying. 'I think it makes them feel in command. Others prefer . . .'

Henry came, his cock jerking in Caroline's mouth. She squealed and threw up her hands as the first spurt went down her throat, his erection slipping from her lips, more come splashing across her face, and her sister's. He grabbed his cock and tugged hard at the shaft, sending another eruption of thick white fluid full into Alice's face, then more into Caroline's and the last trickle down over his own fingers.

Both girls had sat back, squealing in shock and delight at what had happened. Bubbles of white froth were spilling from Caroline's lips, while a long streamer ran across one cheek, yet she was giggling. Alice's pretty face was set in a look of disgust. If anything, she was in a worse state, with one eye closed beneath a thick blob of viscous white, more on her lips and a piece hanging from the very tip of her nose. Henry reached out and wiped his hand on Caroline's clean cheek, then sat back with a contented sigh.

'As I was saying,' May said, 'some men enjoy decorating a girl's face, perhaps to prove to her their virility. Now be good girls and lick it all up. What would the servants say if you were to soil the carpet?'

The two sisters looked at each other doubtfully, then Caroline's tongue flicked out and caught the strand of come that was threatening to fall from her sister's nose. She swallowed her mouthful and then began to clean Alice's face, lapping up the sperm with every sign of relish. Only when she was clean did Alice open her eyes, make a protesting face and then begin to lick, cleaning up Caroline's cheek and lips, then swallowing the contents of her mouth with a grimace.

'It is so dreadfully salty,' she protested. 'Will our husbands often make us eat it?'

'That all depends upon who you marry, Alice dear,' May replied. 'Now, we shall have a little rest, I think.'

'Oh, but I did want Henry in my bottom!' Caroline whined.

'Time enough, my dear,' Henry answered.

'We must allow Mr Truscott to rebuild his strength,' May explained. 'Perhaps you would care for a glass of claret, Mr Truscott?'

'It would be my pleasure,' Henry replied.

'We have a moderate green seal in plenty,' she continued. 'Saunder had it at auction, although I feel he has put value before quality. Then there is a little Lamission from his father's old stock.'

'The Lamission will do nicely,' Henry answered, 'and perhaps a little exhibition of your charms?'

May rose and walked from the room, Henry admiring the swell of her bottom and the way her stockings and chemise tail framed the cheeks as she went. His cock lay flaccid in his lap, but he made no effort to do up his breeches, instead starting to stroke it as he admired the two near naked girls. Neither seemed entirely sure of what to do, but both were flushed and clearly excited.

'How may we please you, Mr Truscott?' Alice asked.

Henry paused, seeing the mischief in her eyes and determined to make the best of it. Caroline was giggling behind her hand, also clearly willing. Yet his cock needed a little time to recover and it seemed foolish to make the girls come before he was ready for his second orgasm. Struck by a sudden inspiration, he ducked down to reach beneath the bed. Sure enough, a large chamberpot of green china stood beneath it. He pulled it out and both girls dissolved in giggles at the sight.

'You may fill this,' he declared. 'I enjoy watching a girl's blushes as she pees for an audience. Alice may go first, as she is the elder.'

241

Alice was certainly blushing as she stood, and Henry knew that he had guessed correctly in assuming that being watched as she performed such an intimate natural function would cause her more embarrassment than a purely sexual display. Not that she hesitated, but sank into a squat with her neat little sex spread over the potty. Henry watched the muscles of her vagina and belly tense as she pushed, then a spray of pale golden pee burst from the tiny hole at the centre of her cunny. As it splashed into the pot she gave a sob that mingled pleasure and shame, making Henry's cock twitch in his hand. Caroline also watched, giggling as the pee ran from her sister's cunny. Alice's stream was splashing into a good few inches of her own urine by the time she finished, giving a little wiggle of her bottom to shake loose the last few drops, then rising and performing a brief curtsy to Henry.

'A most charming display,' Henry said. 'Caroline?'

Caroline had already risen, taking her place over the pot as her sister vacated it, only with her bottom towards Henry rather than her belly.

'I shall go backwards,' she declared, pushing her bottom out over the pot, 'as I have quite the finest behind.'

'I have quite the finest behind,' Alice mimicked, sticking her own bottom out in a parody of her sister's pose.

There was a meaty smack as Caroline's hand struck her sister's bottom. Alice squealed and made to retaliate. Caroline attempted to dodge, but only managed to sit firmly down on the potty as Alice's hand smacked the upper part of one plump cheek. It left a red mark and Caroline squealed, but Alice had already jumped back out of range.

Throwing her sister a resentful look, Caroline composed herself, rising to allow Henry a fine view of her bottom with the cheeks spread wide to show off her stretched anus and the open rear view of her cunny. He could also smell the rich scent of her sex, and his cock began to respond. Like her sister she tensed and then let go, her pee gushing out into the potty beneath her to splash into what Alice had already done. Unlike Alice there was no shame to her action, only a blissful sigh of release as she emptied her bladder in full view of Henry.

'It'll be a lucky man who gets you,' he remarked as her pee began to die to a trickle. 'Either of you for that matter. It's a damned shame bigamy is against God and the law, or I'd have you both.'

'You are kind, Mr Truscott,' Alice answered.

Caroline simply wiggled her bottom, making the plump cheeks quiver as she finished her pee. As she rose she put her arm about her sister's waist and threw Henry a coquettish look, as if to demand further instructions. He could feel his cock starting to swell and decided that he would be ready by the time the girls came to their own orgasms.

'What of your own pleasure?' he asked, recalling the intimacy between the two and hoping to see it explored further.

'I had so hoped to do as we did before,' Caroline said, still sulky, 'it was simply splendid.'

'Then you shall,' Henry promised, 'but if you want me in your pretty bottom I shall need a moment to recover. Do you often behave so warmly together?'

Alice blushed and looked down; Caroline giggled. Henry was sure he knew the answer, but could think of nothing more stimulating than hearing the two girls confess to pleasuring each other in a way that was doubly forbidden.

'Now and again,' Alice admitted shyly. 'It is . . . it is comforting.'

'Comforting?' Henry answered. 'Well, I dare say there is a measure of comfort in such play. Take a little comfort now, then, and I shall watch.'

Caroline giggled and kissed her sister, to which Alice responded. Henry gave a satisfied sigh and continued to stroke his cock. The girls came together, their kisses becoming more intimate as Alice put a hand to Caroline's breasts. Henry watched the soft globe of flesh move as Alice stroked it, running her fingers under the curved underside and using a thumb to bring the nipple to quick erection. However inexperienced the girls might be with men, it was clear that they understood each other's bodies well enough.

Henry's cock had already begun to rise when Alice pushed Caroline down to the floor, mounting her as a man might have done. Caroline spread her thighs to her sister's body and they cuddled close, their cunnies rubbing together as they continued to kiss and caress. Henry found himself licking his lips as the girls rolled on to their sides, limbs entwined. The new position left him with a fine view of Alice's trim bottom, with the cheeks spread over her sister's thigh. He could see the girl's anus and the way her cunny was hard on Caroline's leg, rubbing to get friction to the clitoris. He watched Alice rub herself off on her sister's leg in fascination, delighted by the way the girl's sex squirmed and opened with each movement. Her anus was moving too, winking lewdly at him in an invitation that sent more blood to his cock.

Alice came, bucking her hips hard and scratching Caroline's back in her ecstasy, but without sound, as the two sisters' mouths were locked together. As Alice's climax subsided she lay back, and Caroline was already scrambling on to her. Henry watched as the younger girl spread her chubby, puppy-fat bottom over her sister's face, wiggled it and then leaned forward, resting on her arms with her full breasts lolling forward beneath her. His cock was hard, and he could see Caroline's bumhole. It was wet with saliva, showing that Alice had kissed her sister's anus, the thought of which gave his erection its final impetus to full readiness.

244

Caroline's beautiful bottom was spread before him, her thighs open over Alice's face as she was licked. The anus that he had so recently been invited to bugger was stretched and a little open, too good a target to waste. Sinking to his knees he got behind Caroline, resting his cock between her fleshy buttocks. He began to rub himself in her crease and her moans became louder, while his balls were slapping in Alice's face to add to his pleasure. He exercised his cock in the crease of Caroline's bottom until the need to bugger her became overwhelming, then put his hand down and pressed the head to her anus. She gave a sob as she realised she was to be buggered, but relaxed her hole as he had taught her. He pushed and saw the head of his cock engulfed by her spit-soaked bottom hole. The neck was sliding in, and the shaft, only to stop as her protesting anus pushed in beyond the wet. Henry pulled back, leaving just the tip in Caroline's bum-hole, then spat between her buttocks.

The saliva landed between the open cheeks and trickled down, wetting his cock. Rubbing the wet in with his fingers, he pushed again. Caroline gave a little choking cry, but his erection pushed deeper up her bottom. Henry could feel the hot flesh of her rectum on his cock, wet, warm and deliciously slimy. He began to bugger her, moving in a little deeper with each push until Caroline was grunting and writhing her bottom on his erection and her sister's face. He felt her start to come and her bum-hole tensed on his cock, squeezing the shaft hard as her muscles spasmed in orgasm. As she came she set up a frantic, pig-like grunting. Henry had been watching his cock move in Caroline's anus, but as she came he leaned forward, kissing her neck and scooping a fat breast into either hand. They felt heavy and the nipples were hard, moving him to pinch and tweak them as she continued to grunt her passion out and squirm her buttocks on to him.

It died, slowly, her noises stopping to be replaced by a deep, regular breathing. Henry felt Alice shift, and then the wet cavity of her mouth engulfed his balls. She began to suck, licking his scrotum and drawing his balls deep into her throat. Henry took a firm grip on Caroline's breasts and increased the pace of his cock in her anus. She gasped, then cried out in pain, but he was already coming, what little sperm he had left dribbling out into her rectum as wave after wave of ecstasy flooded his brain.

For a while he left his cock in Caroline's bottom hole, then began to pull out slowly. As it flopped free Alice took it in her mouth and Henry let her suck despite the agonising sensitivity of his penis. The act seemed more a service to Caroline than to him, cleaning a lover's cock as a gesture of sisterly affection. Henry waited until Alice had finished her task, then climbed off, allowing the girls to disentangle themselves.

By the time May returned the two sisters were giggling together on the bed, while Henry was slumped exhausted in a chair with his cock back in his breeches. May smiled knowingly but poured the claret without remark. Henry accepted the glass and took a gulp, allowing the flavour of the old claret to fill his senses before swallowing. Rising, he went to the window and took another sip of his wine, looking out over Bruton Street as he wondered what further tricks it would be amusing to have the girls perform. It was a fine day and the street was busy, thronged with pedestrians and a wide variety of horse-drawn vehicles. Most of those people in view were either clearly genteel or servants, with four obvious exceptions. Surprised, Henry moved closer to the open windows.

'I say, the estate is going downhill already,' he declared to May and her sisters-in-law. 'That's old mother Agie across the road and one along, with three of her flashmen to boot. They're going up to a house, of all the confounded brass!'

246

May joined him, staying in the shelter of his body to hide her nakedness.

'That is the house taken by a French marquis,' she said. 'Whatever can such rough-looking men want with such a noble gentleman?'

'Skipped off without paying, I dare say,' Henry answered. 'Mother Agie's not one for the niceties. Maybe we'll see some sport?'

The door of the house opposite had opened, revealing a servant. There was a brief discussion, and Henry leaned out of the window in an effort to catch the words. Mother Agie had come forward and was arguing with the servant, demanding to be admitted. The servant seemed equally determined that she should not be, and as Henry watched three more men came out from the house.

'Four to three, but my money is on the bullies if it comes to a scrap,' Henry said.

'I shall wager a guinea on d'Aignan's men,' May said. 'He has many more servants.'

'D'Aignan, eh?' Henry answered. 'I know the fellow, vaguely. He's a wicked old goat with an eye for Eloise. I'll take your guinea and I hope Mother Agie sits on his head.'

'I shall chance a half-crown on those men with the awful-looking woman,' Caroline put in. 'They do look so frightfully rough.'

'Rough indeed,' Henry answered. 'The tallest of them's Tom, who I've traded blows with before now. I'd not care to again.'

'He looks quite ferocious,' Alice said from behind Henry's shoulder, 'but I am sure I have seen the Marquis with at least six most burly fellows. I shall match your half-crown, and add a spanked behind for the loser.'

Caroline giggled at her sister's suggestion, while Henry smiled at the prospect of one girl or the other

247

being spanked regardless of who won if the argument became a fight. It was certainly becoming heated, with Mother Agie standing with her massive arms on her hips and her face red with anger.

The Marquis himself appeared in the doorway, looking down at Mother Agie with an expression of haughty dislike. She held her ground, demanding something that Henry was unable to catch above the general noise. The Marquis issued a stout denial and Mother Agie hesitated, then turned a question to Tom. Tom shook his head and shrugged. Agie again spoke to the Marquis, only now her manner seemed apologetic rather than aggressive.

'Damn!' Henry swore. 'It looks like they'll not come to blows.'

Caroline made a petulant sound, expressing disappointment.

'Poor little Carrie. She did so want her bottom spanked,' Alice teased.

'She shall have it, or you shall yourself,' Henry declared and leaned fully out of the window to shout to the group below. 'Ho, d'Aignan, you've money, I know you've money. Have the decency to pay for your tail. Don't listen to him, madam, have flashman there bloody the old bugger's nose!'

The men turned and Henry attempted to duck back out of sight, only to catch his head on the window. Cursing, he pulled quickly in, then peered out again to find Tom pointing up at his window and speaking rapidly to Agie.

'Damn!' he cursed. 'Don't say they're still sore over a few garters?'

'They are coming over!' Caroline squeaked.

'Nothing to fuss over,' Henry assured her. 'Here, May, my dear, I've but a guinea and a half in my coat, lend me five.'

May went for the money and Henry sauntered downstairs, confident that Mother Agie's anger at his behaviour in the brothel could easily be assuaged with money. Opening the door, he found himself confronting not only Mother Agie and her three bullies but the Marquis and four of his servants. Tom immediately barged forward, hurling the door wide. Henry heard a frightened squeak from upstairs and he was pushed back into the hall.

'I say, there's no need for unpleasantness,' he managed as Tom's massive fists closed on the sides of his coat. 'It was a jape, no more, nothing that a few guineas won't settle, surely?'

'I don't want your money, Harry Truscott,' Agie answered him. 'I've more in mind your blood. What do you think you're about, raiding my house with that bitch biter Judy, then trying to set my boys on the nob here? And watching to boot, you've a cheek and no mistake! Do him up well, Tom, and we'll see how clever he looks.'

'What?' Henry blustered. 'No, no, I merely . . .'

He stopped, sinking his knee into Tom's groin with all his force. The bully went down, but others were already closing on him. Screams sounded from above as he crashed a fist into one assailant's jaw. The big lascar closed with him and he kicked out, only to have another man lock his arms around him from behind. Henry drove his elbow back hard and for a moment was free, leaping for the stair even as the men grabbed at him. Hurling himself up, he glimpsed May Cunningham's terrified face peering from the bedroom door. He burst through it, the men piling in behind as the three naked girls scattered squealing to the corners. Grabbing the chamberpot from where they had left it, he hurled the heavy vessel at the lascar, only to miss and send a great spray of urine across all six of the men as the pot shattered on the wall.

Two stumbled back, rubbing at their eyes, but the other four came on. Henry met them with his fists, sending one sprawling only to go down under the others as they threw themselves on to him. He fought on, biting and kicking until his arms were pinned down and he was held helpless on the bed. Beyond, May and Alice were huddled in a corner with a sheet held up to cover their nudity. Caroline was behind a chair, wide-eyed and terrified as she looked on. Mother Agie appeared in the doorway, then d'Aignan and lastly the limping Tom.

'Damn you!' Henry spat at Agie, but it was the Marquis who stepped forward and came to look down on him with a cold sneer.

'I have waited for this moment a long time, Mr Truscott,' he began. 'Do you have any notion of the distress you have caused me?'

'Distress?' Henry demanded. 'Damn't man, I hardly know you, and why in hell are you taking the bawd's part?'

'I take my own part,' d'Aignan replied. 'As to this . . . woman, at present her aims seem to coincide with my own, which is to say to bring you just retribution for your most offensive behaviour.'

'What the hell do you mean?' Henry swore.

'What do I mean?' D'Aignan snapped back, his face colouring beneath the white of his make-up. 'Death of my life, you don't even know, do you?'

'No,' Henry admitted.

'You took my Eloise from me,' he grated, 'my little girl who I had loved from a child, who I planned to marry, to make a Marquise!'

'Eloise?' Henry answered. 'Eloise! Damn't, man, you're twice her age, more, three times, you filthy old goat. Besides, she doesn't give a tinker's damn for you, never did!'

The Marquis' hand lashed out, catching Henry in the face. He kicked hard, but failed to break the grip of the man who had his leg. Drawing back, d'Aignan adjusted the set of his wig. Henry spat, but missed.

'Do it,' d'Aignan said, once more poised and cold. 'The cods. It is no more than he deserves.'

One of the men dipped into his coat pocket, drawing out a knife in front of Henry's horrified gaze. It was a foot of crude iron, stained and specked with rust but with tiny coruscations glittering on a sharp edge. Another of d'Aignan's men came forward. Henry felt a sick fear rise in his throat as the man began to unbutton his breeches' flap.

Even Mother Agie looked shocked as she realised what d'Aignan intended, but she made no move to intervene. The man grinned and held the knife up to the light in front of Henry's face. Once more Henry kicked out, putting every ounce of his strength into it but still failing to dislodge his captors. A movement caught his eye and he saw that Caroline had risen and held the claret bottle like a club.

'You shall not, you horrible person,' she said.

The men paused, looking at the naked girl with contemptuous sneers. Mother Agie reached out, feinted and took the bottle from Caroline's fingers, then turned at a sound from downstairs.

'Henry?' a voice called out.

'Here!' Henry yelled. 'Help me, damn it!'

Footsteps sounded on the stair and Henry kicked out again, thrashing his body. Two of the bullies went to the door and a moment later there was a thud and a cry of pain from the landing. Todd Gurney burst in, driving a fist into Tom's face as Charles appeared behind him. The grip on Henry's limbs slackened and he tore himself free, kicking out at the knife even as he rolled to one side. The blow caught the man's wrist and the blade spun high in the air as Henry crashed to the ground.

Struggling to his feet he found Tom down and Gurney trading punches with d'Aignan's men. To the side d'Aignan was pulling at his cane, and as Henry came forward he saw the steel gleam of a sword stick.

251

His leap caught d'Aignan in the back and sent him sprawling almost as far as the door. Henry grappled for the sword stick, only to be caught by a vicious kick from Mother Agie. Grabbing the woman's ankle, he twisted hard and she came down, crashing to the floor with a string of curses.

Henry pulled himself up. Charles was wrestling with one man and getting the worst of it. Gurney was holding three off with his fists. Tom was down, as was the lascar, lying unconscious on the landing beyond the door. The remaining bully was attempting to staunch a bloody nose, while d'Aignan was trying to get to his feet in the doorway. Henry went forward, sinking a fist into the side of the man wrestling Charles, then kicking out at d'Aignan. He missed, and as the Marquis scrambled back the sword stick came free of its cane sheaf.

Jumping back, Henry avoided d'Aignan's weak thrust. A yell of pain sounded to one side and Henry saw one of Gurney's opponents stagger sideways, clutching at his knee. The Marquis had risen and was coming forward carefully, hate written in his eyes. Henry grabbed a handful of bedding and hurled it forward, forcing d'Aignan to jump back into the doorway. Grabbing up Charles' cane, Henry held it as if it were a sword, the gesture drawing a sneer from the Marquis. Flourishing his sword stick, d'Aignan took a pace back, tripped over the head of the unconscious lascar and vanished backwards over the banisters. A boot caught Henry's leg and he went down, only to hear Agie calling for her bullies to stop. Two were down, and d'Aignan's men took no notice. The injured one made for the door, taking Agie with him. Henry called out in triumph and swung the cane at the head of the man wrestling Charles. It caught his temple and he staggered back, even as one of Gurney's opponents threw his hands up and began to back away. Two hard punches laid out the last man in front of Gurney and the others ran.

Henry laughed and helped the last of the Marquis' men out of the door with a boot. Tom still lay on the floor, also the lascar, while all four of d'Aignan's servants had managed to get clear. Henry strode out on to the landing, intending to throw a few taunts at their backs. There was no sign of Mother Agie, nor her bully, but the four servants were clustered around the prone body of their master. Gurney joined him, then Charles.

'Fanned them sweetly, didn't we?' Gurney remarked, only to stop at the sight of the Marquis.

'Damn, it seems you've cropped the fellow,' Charles said.

'Then better in hell,' Henry answered. 'The bastard aimed to make a eunuch of me!'

'My God!' Charles responded weakly.

They descended the stairs, at which d'Aignan's men fled into the street.

'Do you think they'll call the watch?' Charles queried.

'I should doubt it,' Henry replied, 'and if they do it'll be our word against theirs that the old fool didn't take a drunken tumble. Agie'll stay close, that's for sure.'

'We'd best set the room to rights anyhow,' Gurney suggested.

'Leave it to the girls,' Henry answered. 'They know better than us what to do and what belongs where. Anyway, I'm damned grateful to the pair of you, but why are you here and not in the West Country?'

'I met Gurney at Staines,' Charles answered. 'There's news on the mine. It seems to be of value after all.'

'That's true, sir,' Gurney agreed. 'The new adit's been driving through red cuprite, a vein thicker than this house, and who knows how wide and deep. I thought it no more than rust.'

'Cuprite?' Henry queried.

'Copper ore,' Gurney replied. 'Rich copper ore.'

'Splendid!' Henry exclaimed. 'We'll even leave the fellows who sold their shares back with egg on their faces! Hey, did you hear that, May, the mine is rich after all. I mean to say, richer than we thought. They've found copper.'

May Cunningham managed a weak smile from where she was stood on the landing, looking rather doubtfully at the unconscious lascar. She had pulled her dress over her head, but still had the bodice undone and clearly wore no petticoats. At the sight Henry felt a surge of relief that his cock was still intact and found himself suddenly weak at the knees.

'Shame we'll have Sir Joseph Snapes as a partner,' Charles said. 'Although his man Eadie found us out, so it may be he thinks the mine a fake.'

'We shall see, no doubt,' Henry answered. 'For now I'm content to have my cock and balls still about me.'

Looking up at a sound he saw that Tom had appeared in the bedroom doorway and was helping the lascar to his feet. May was halfway down the stairs and hurriedly joined them, standing behind the reassuring bulk of Todd Gurney. Neither bully showed the least inclination to pursue the fight, Tom helping the other down the stairs and out with several worried glances at Gurney.

'British army douser, best there is,' Henry taunted them as they left. Neither replied.

'We'd best be away, sir,' Gurney stated.

'Doubtless,' Henry replied and then glanced up to where the two Cunningham sisters were peering down from between the banisters of the first-floor landing. 'Ladies, you must excuse me.'

He turned to May, and together they looked down at the Marquis' lifeless body.

'It would appear,' May said evenly, 'that the Marquis has sustained an unfortunate fall.'

With a brief kiss of May's lips and a bow he followed Gurney.

* * *

Judith's stomach was fluttering as she looked out from the seat of Charles' high-perch phaeton over the London traffic. Portugal Street was crowded, both with those leaving work and those on their way out to enjoy the fine evening. Her spirits had risen on robbing Snapes, and more on discovering just how much money the case had contained. For the first time since being faced with the chimpanzee she had managed to laugh, yet even depriving Snapes of such a sum had not satisfied her thirst for revenge.

Griggs had admitted her to Charles' house and tactfully refrained from asking why she was dressed as a barge boy. He had also drawn water for her to bathe, following which she dressed, deliberately choosing all her finest clothing in an effort to make up for the indignities of the night. Neat boots of fine leather, silk stockings, ruffled garters of a rich blue, a chemise and three petticoats of heavily laced silk, a heavy underskirt and a dress of magnificent blue brocade with gloves and a bonnet to match made her feel female again and a good deal less vulnerable.

By the time that she was fully dressed she had been able to accept the fact that at some future point she would want to be put back in the filthy old clothes and thoroughly used by Charles and perhaps two others. To turn the worst indignities into fantasy had always been her way of dealing with them, from her first days at Mother Agie's onwards.

When Charles, Henry and Todd Gurney had arrived she was ready to tell the story of her abuse in glowing detail. They had reacted as she had expected, Charles outraged, Henry damning Snapes yet secretly intrigued, Todd coldly angry. Nor had it been hard to persuade them to pay Snapes a visit, especially when she showed them the money she had taken from him and it proved to be the remaining funds of Wheal Purity. They had set off without delay, Gurney riding alongside the phaeton.

Charles had explained how Snapes had sought to cheat them, driving the stock price down and then attempting to gain full ownership of the mine. When it became clear that the man Judith had seen with Snapes had been Reuben Eadie, his actions had become clear.

'So he changed his game,' Charles was saying. 'Knowing the vein for schorl, he drained the account, which would have left us in a pretty pass.'

'But he knows nothing of the new vein,' Gurney put in. 'Davey didn't get to that until after Eadie had left.'

'Then,' Henry stated, 'we must go softly, but look, didn't you say Bertie Robson was at the dinner, Judith? There's his carriage.'

Henry pointed to a heavy landau with both its half-hoods raised to entirely conceal the occupants. With every overhooded carriage open to the warm evening sun, the landau looked highly out of place. Only the driver was visible, a small, round man perched on the seat and holding the team.

'Damn peculiar fellow, Bertie,' Charles declared. 'D'you suppose he's in there?'

'Let us see,' Henry said, and hailed the driver. 'Ho, you there. Is your master in?'

Robson's driver gave them a worried look and tried to make the horses speed up, only for Gurney's hand to close on his wrist as they drew level. The landau came to a stop as Todd drew on the lead rein, and Charles pulled up the phaeton beside it. Judith leaned forward, peered between the hoods and found herself looking directly into the face of Lord Furlong.

Her scream echoed back from the houses of Portugal Street and Piccadilly.

The scent of smelling salts was the next thing she was conscious of. Charles was holding them under her nose, while Squire Robson was seated in the phaeton in earnest conversation with Henry. Of the chimpanzee there was no sign.

'I came upon them on the London road,' Robson was explaining, 'not far from Woodbridge. I had intended to take them back to Sir Joseph's estate, but on making in that direction the young girl set up such an outcry that I was forced to turn again. Now I am at a loss for what to do.'

'She's coming to,' Charles said as Judith opened her eyes fully.

'Good,' Henry answered. 'Well, I think you owe the lady an apology, Cuthbert.'

'I . . . I do apologise,' Robson stammered, 'but believe me, Judith, it was no doing of mine. We had been told to expect a remarkable entertainment, but knowing your . . . harumph . . . reputation, I expected no more than an erotic exposition. Believe me, I was as surprised and as shocked as you yourself.'

'That, sir, I doubt,' Judith managed, then realised the implication of what Robson had said at first. 'Who else is with you, other than the enschego?'

'The pretty dark girl Snapes has for a servant,' Robson answered. 'She seems terrified of her master, and I do not feel it would be the Christian thing to return her. Yet she has no English, nor any clothes. What am I to do?'

'I'm sure a place could be found for her,' Henry answered quickly. 'Eloise can always make do with a new maid. Pretty, you say?'

'Devilish pretty, and devilish exotic,' Robson answered, 'but, I say, would you take her?'

'Certainly,' Henry answered.

'And the damned beast too? It seems devoted to her in any case.'

'No!' Judith exclaimed.

'Yes,' Henry answered Robson, then addressed Judith. 'Don't worry, my dear, this encounter may prove fortuitous.'

* * *

257

Sir Joseph Snapes sat at the table in his dining room in Bedford Square, clutching a bottle of port in one fist. He had dismissed Eadie and returned to the house in a black rage, cursing the street urchin who had robbed him. They had seen only a glimpse of a boy of perhaps twelve or thirteen, dressed in rags and with wild red hair flying behind him. Eadie had given chase but lost the thief in the maze of alleys to the north of Fleet Street. In the case had been what remained of the Wheal Purity funds, enough to compensate at least partly for the failure of his scheme. Now all he had was the stock and chairmanship of a worthless mine.

Taking a swig of the bottle without caring about the bitter taste of dregs, he cursed aloud, including the street urchin, Henry Truscott, Charles Finch and Judith Cates. Each he felt to have done him a personal wrong. Judith in particular aroused his anger, having failed to display the wanton reaction he had expected to Lord Furlong. In doing so, and in causing the chimpanzee to escape, she had ruined years of carefully planned scientific work, and it seemed likely that another trip to the Bight of Benin would be necessary if he was to continue his experiments. Thinking of the effort he had expended in the attempt to prove the chimpanzee a degenerate form of man he cursed again, then took another draught of port.

A movement outside caught his attention and he looked up to see a fine high-perch phaeton drawing up at the house. He recognised it as belonging to Charles Finch and immediately his anger was replaced by fear. Neither Finch nor Truscott were likely to be pleased with him, and he was alone in the house. Yet when the two men alighted from the vehicle their attitude seemed anything but vengeful. Truscott was laughing, and pointing out some amusing sight across the square, at which Finch also laughed.

Gathering his wits, Snapes hid the port bottle, then stood to arrange his dress, wondering if something might not, after all, be salvaged from the debacle. Certainly the men's attitude suggested that they knew nothing of Reuben Eadie's visit, nor of events in Suffolk. The door knocker sounded and Snapes went to answer it, forcing his face into a beaming smile.

'Good evening, gentlemen,' he greeted them. 'Do come in. As you see, my servants are at my country place, but may I offer you some refreshment?'

'A glass of port would do nicely,' Henry answered, sniffing the air.

'Port, certainly, capital,' Snapes replied. 'Come, make yourselves comfortable, I have an excellent vintage in the cellar.'

He went to fetch the port, all the while wondering how much the two men knew and why they seemed so friendly. He had discovered how much they had paid back to investors at the bank, and so it seemed likely that in place of crude revenge they had decided to come to him for further investment. This made his own intention, to get rid of his stock for as much as possible, somewhat awkward. Still thinking hard, he climbed the stairs from the cellar.

'I fear that my report may have been misunderstood by some of our investors,' he said as he began to decant the bottle. 'I gave what I felt was a balanced account, designed to impress serious investors rather than mere speculators. Sadly, those to whom you had already sold had expectations that were, frankly, extravagant. I do apologise if this caused inconvenience, but I cannot but point out that I did warn you of the hazards of selling early.'

'No matter,' Charles Finch replied. 'Doubtless the input from industrial investors will make up our loss. You were right, a sound footing is of more importance than immediate profits.'

'Quite so, quite so,' Snapes agreed. 'Nevertheless, I do feel I acted hastily, and not in accordance with the

259

express wishes of the board. If you feel this is the case, I would be willing to resign my position. In return, needless to say, for the sum of my original investment plus a disbursement for my assistance, securing the Watts engine and so forth.'

'Resign?' Charles queried.

'Quite so,' Snapes answered. 'In fact, gentlemen, I will be candid. Owing to a recent setback in another, quite different, field, I find myself in need of substantial funds to finance an expedition to the Bight of Benin. I would be grateful if you would accept my offer.'

'If you insist, Sir Joseph,' Henry replied. 'Yet can you not delay this expedition? Within a year, at most two, the mine will be paying the most handsome dividends.'

'When you reach my time of life you may be less inclined to accept such a delay,' Snapes answered with a sigh. 'No, I entreat you to accept, at, shall we say, twelve thousand pounds?'

'An increment of three parts in nine?' Charles queried. 'Henry, what do you think?'

Snapes sipped his port while the two men conferred, listening intently with his attention apparently directed to the slowly gathering dusk outside the window.

'We are prepared to offer ten thousand,' Charles eventually stated. 'Indeed we carry this sum now, in case of further demands for the return of shares. That fellow Barclay actually drew his barkers on us, you know.'

Avarice warred with caution in Snapes' mind, but only for a moment. Thrusting his hand out, he forced his face into a smile of agreement. Henry took it and they shook.

As he ascended the stairs to his study, Sir Joseph Snapes felt light-footed for the first time in years. Truscott and Finch had fallen for his story and offered more than he had originally put into the mine, showing an extraordinary naivety. Doubtless they had some new scheme, but it was nothing to him. The paperwork was completed quickly, Snapes opening his safe and exchanging his shares for the money, then signing off as chairman. When business was completed they returned downstairs.

'You must excuse me now, gentlemen,' he stated as they reached the hall. 'I am somewhat tired and was just about to retire when you knocked. I trust you leave with no ill feeling?'

'Absolutely not,' Henry answered, 'I am glad the affair has been settled amicably, and now, we are going to lock you in the coal cellar.'

'What?' Snapes demanded.

'We intend to lock you in the coal cellar,' Henry repeated. 'Pray do not be unduly alarmed, this is simply in order to allow us to trade without interference. You see, after your presentation at the Society we are not absolutely certain of your intentions. You understand, I'm sure?'

'This is an outrage!' Snapes bellowed as Henry took a hold on his coat.

Throwing the arm off, he made to defend himself, sure that his bulk would serve him well despite his greater age. Henry grappled him, but Charles made no move to join in, instead opening the front door. The massive figure of Todd Gurney appeared against the evening light.

Still protesting, Snapes was hustled below stairs and out into the coal cellar. The heavy door clanged shut behind him and he was left in total darkness. He waited as the men's footsteps retreated, angry but sure of escape as soon as they had left. The coal hole was too small by far to admit a grown man's body, yet by climbing the shoot he would be able to stick his head out into the street and call for help.

As soon as he felt enough time had passed he began to feel for the shoot, cursing as he stumbled among the lumps of coal at its base. He gripped the sides, then put

261

a knee on it, at which point the cover lifted with a grating sound and light flooded in.

Sir Joseph Snapes looked up, blinking. For a moment he glimpsed two faces, both female, one black, one white. Then something had been thrown into the hole to shatter among the coal. Girlish laughter sounded from above and the cover clanged shut, then creaked as some great weight came down on it. He cursed, guessing that the wheel of a carriage had been driven on to the hole. Behind him the door opened and he turned, only for it to shut with a thud almost immediately. A smell caught his senses, which he recognised as the musk used to excite Lord Furlong even as the chimpanzee's intrigued snicker sounded from the darkness.

Henry Truscott sat with his feet up on one of Sir Joseph Snapes' dining-room chairs. In one hand he held a glass of Snapes' fine old port, in the other an exceptional cigar he had discovered in a humidor. Opposite him Charles was also sat at ease, drinking his third pint bottle of port while he studied Snapes' notes on the creation of a chimpanzee-human cross. Occasionally his eyebrows would lift or he would utter a quiet exclamation, then take another swallow of port. Upstairs Gurney was at work picking the lock of Snapes' safe in order to retrieve their money. Judith and Suki were in the adjoining room, giggling together over the collection of strange erotic artefacts.

Henry had begun to work on the neck of his second bottle of port by the time Gurney appeared, clutching a sheaf of bills in his hand.

'Good work,' Henry declared. 'Do we have it all then?'

'Seems so,' Todd answered.

'All but the Cunninghams' part,' Charles put in, 'and Bertie Robson's, which makes little enough. What the French have we can doubtless buy back.'

'I can live with that,' Henry replied. 'I suppose I shouldn't begrudge Saunder a penny or two when it was his in the first place. Beside, if May pups the heir'll be mine anyway.'

Charles smiled and went back to his reading. Todd Gurney put the bills down and poured port into a pewter tankard. He took a draught then sat down, at which point Henry caught his eye and nodded in the direction of the two girls. They had broken the lock on one of the display cabinets and taken out a monstrous double phallus. It was made of some dark wood and highly polished, with one mock penis of reasonable size and little detail. The other was thicker than either girl's wrist and carved with writhing veins and a huge, bulbous head. An equally exaggerated scrotum sprouted from the base, to which were attached an assortment of leather straps. Both girls were giggling over the thing and seemed keen that the other take it.

Suki gave in, and Henry and Gurney watched in fascination as she quite casually peeled off the maid's dress they had bought her. Henry had already glimpsed her nude in Robson's landau, but was more than happy for another chance to admire the firm, dark curves of her flesh. Showing no concern for her nudity in front of an audience, she eased the smaller phallus into an evidently already moist vagina. This left the larger one projecting from her crotch in a grotesque, yet enviable, imitation of excited male genitals. Judith's giggling became louder as Suki fixed the straps up over her belly and buttocks and fastened the waist belt. Henry found his own cock stirring at the sight.

For a while Suki showed off, imitating cock proud male postures until both of them were convulsed with laughter. First she simply strutted up and down with her hands on her hips and the cock thrust out before her. With her breasts bare and her undoubtedly feminine bottom she looked anything but male, yet the parody was clear. She began to pretend to masturbate herself as a man would, then to bully Judith, pointing in mock anger to the phallus and to the ground. Judith feigned first shock and then reluctance, but got down on to her knees. Suki took Judith by the hair and pushed the cock out. Judith gaped wide, just managing to accommodate the width of the thing in her mouth. Watching Judith struggle with the oversized carving had Henry's cock hard in his breeches, but he held back, keen to see how far the girls would take their game. Suki forced Judith to keep sucking and the act was clearly proving arousing, only for the black girl to suddenly seem to lose interest. Pulling back, she danced away to a chest of drawers at the far end of the room.

Henry craned round to see what was happening. Suki had opened a drawer and was pulling out something black and hairy. Judith's hand went to her mouth and she gave a cry of shock. Henry realised why as Suki drew the thing fully out, and it became visible as a chimpanzee skin, complete with the head. Judith had frozen to the spot with her eyes wide at the sight, and as Suki began to climb into the thing Henry realised that it was a suit rather than a simple skin. It even fastened with large, horn buttons and Suki was quickly engulfed, hidden save for where her long legs failed to match the short, bowed limbs of the chimpanzee.

Judith had stayed rooted to the spot, still kneeling, but as Suki approached her and started to make chattering noises exactly like those of Lord Furlong, she began to move. With slow, deliberate motions, as if moving in a dream, she opened her mouth and once more took in the huge phallus, sucking on it. Suki gripped Judith's head with the chimpanzee hands and Henry saw Judith's whole body shiver. With part of the table blocking the view of Suki's legs it looked to Henry as if Judith really was sucking the cock of a grossly overendowed ape. Her face showed a mixture of bliss and submission, and Henry found himself wondering just how strong her feelings were at what she was doing, and also if she had told the full truth of her encounter in Suffolk.

Reaching out to tap Gurney's hand, he gestured towards Charles, who was still absorbed in Snapes' notes. Gurney in turn tapped Charles' hand. Charles looked up, saw what appeared to be a large male chimpanzee making his mistress suck its cock and for a moment his face froze in horror. On realising the truth he reached out for his port and swallowed the contents of the glass, then poured another and repeated the action.

Henry had began to squeeze his erect cock through his breeches, but made no move to interrupt the girls. Suki was doing her best to imitate Lord Furlong's actions and obviously enjoying herself, while Judith seemed to be in a trance. Suki bored of Judith's sucking and pulled back, then began to paw at her. Judith responded, allowing her breasts to be fondled, then turning under Suki's pressure. Kneeling, now with her bottom to Suki, Judith began to turn up her skirts, lifting each layer until her round white bottom came on show. Suki began to paw the cheeks of Judith's behind. Judith stuck her bottom up, clearly inviting penetration. In response Suki thrust her muzzle in between Judith's thighs and Henry heard the sound of a wet tongue lapping on flesh. Judith groaned, then hung her head low, accepting yet seeming in a state of deep shame. Suki licked on, her little pink tongue just protruding from the thick lips of the chimpanzee head as she cleaned Judith's bottom, first the crease and then both pouted cheeks.

Judith's buttocks were glossy with Suki's saliva by the time the black girl finished licking. As Suki pulled away it was clear what was going to happen, and Judith put her face to the floor with a resigned groan. Suki kneeled back, took hold of her massive phallus in one hairy paw and prodded it at Judith's cunny. Judith accepted the cock moaning and grunting, with her mouth hanging open and her eyes shut. It went up slowly, bit by bit, the fat, gnarled stem easing into Judith's gaping vagina until at last the balls nudged up to her thighs and the full length of it was hidden inside her.

Suki began to fuck, holding Judith's sweetly turned-up hips and chattering in a gleeful imitation of Lord Furlong. Judith seemed lost to everything beyond what was being done to her, panting, grunting and scrabbling at the carpet, one moment moaning in ecstasy and the next sobbing. Before long she had reached back under her skirts and started to masturbate. Henry watched, thinking of the hairy man-ape humping away on Judith's up-turned bottom, huge cock in her vagina, hands mauling the soft flesh of her bottom and hips. Undoubtedly it was what was in Judith's mind, and as he imagined her thoughts he began to free his cock, no longer able to hold back.

Judith's noises had changed to an unrestrained grunting and Henry knew she was coming. Rising to his feet, he rounded the table to come up behind Suki, intrigued by what he had seen of her fine, dark bottom. Judith was screaming and crying out, her boots drumming a frantic rhythm on the carpet as she came on the thought of being filled with a chimpanzee's cock. Suki too seemed to be coming, squirming her front on to the mass of the phallus. Henry licked his hand and put the saliva to the head of his cock as Suki started to give a series of sharp screams. Gripping the rear of the animal skin, he lifted it, exposing Suki's beautiful dark bottom with the buttocks clenching and opening as she fucked Judith and came at once. The base and balls of the phallus were visible, baring her vagina from entry, yet the straps parted from the base, crossing each buttock to leave the crease clear. With each push her anus would wink at him, a knot of darker flesh in a tangle of jet black fur, a target too good to resist.

He waited, judging his moment. Then as Judith's orgasm began to die and Suki's reached its peak, he squatted down on her bottom and pushed his cock between the cheeks. Suki grunted and pushed her bottom back, eager for penetration. Henry felt her anus against his cock head, soft and wet, then opening as it spasmed in orgasm. She cried out as her ring stretched open around his cock, and then he was in, pushing himself up her bottom bit by bit as she rode her orgasm. When she had finished the full length of his penis was in her rectum, with the ring clenched tight on the base of his shaft.

She made no effort to stop him, accepting her buggery well, and even bending to make a more open display of her bottom. The phallus was still in Judith, now moving with Henry's pushes so that he was effectively buggering one girl and causing another to be fucked. As he rode her, his eyes were on Suki's bottom, admiring the full, spread globes of dark flesh and the way her anal ring went in and out as she was sodomised. That she seemed to be a grotesque chimera of woman and chimpanzee he tried to ignore, concentrating on her lower half.

Todd Gurney had approached Suki's head, evidently with no such scruples as he pushed his erect penis into the open mouth of the beast's head for Suki to suck. She took it willingly, then reached out to take Charles' in one hairy paw, allowing most of her weight to shift to Judith's back.

Henry paced himself, enjoying the feel of Suki's hot rectal flesh but keen to make the most of her. Judith had began to grunt with the effort of being ridden by Suki while she was fucked, at which Charles ducked down, supporting his mistress, also fondling her breasts. She took over the task of masturbating him, holding his erection to her face, kissing it and rubbing the head on her cheeks as she tugged on the shaft.

Suki had begun to squeeze her anal ring on Henry's cock, ruining his efforts to hold back. He gave in, increasing his pace up her bottom. She pulled back from Gurney's cock, giving her full attention to working her anus. Gurney sank down, sliding a hand beneath Judith to support her and rubbing his cock in her hair. Charles came, spraying Judith's pretty face with come to leave it dripping and soiled. She turned immediately, taking Todd Gurney's cock into her mouth.

With a final deep shove into Suki's rectum, Henry came, the wet of his sperm engulfing his cock and then bursting from the ring of her anus as he pushed in once more. Suki cried out as she felt her bottom fill, then Judith had sucked in her cheeks and begun to make an odd gagging noise and Henry knew that Todd had come down her throat. With his knees aching but blissfully content, he pulled from Suki's bottom, then sat back as Suki in turn dismounted Judith.

The others disentangled themselves and together they returned to the front of the room. Judith began to strip, showing off in a lazy, sensuous manner and then curling herself into Charles' lap with nothing more on than her stockings and boots. Suki, having thrown off the chimpanzee skin, also made herself comfortable, seated on the floor between Henry and Todd, unashamedly naked.

'Well then,' Charles announced as he filled his glass from yet another bottle of port. 'Here's a toast, to Purity.'

He raised the glass, put it to his lips as the others echoed the toast, then swallowed the port. As he did so his face took on a beatific smile and he slumped slowly down in his chair, unconscious.

'Gurney,' Henry remarked, 'pray remove Mr Finch, and then bring another bottle of the port.'

Epilogue

Sitting in the warm sunlight of a summer's evening, Henry and Charles were sipping a hock that had been cooled in a nearby stream. On the hillside above them the sound of axes could be heard, where men were clearing woodland for the construction of a house, a house that Henry was determined would be finer than that in which he had grown up and which was now his brother's. A little way away Eloise was fussing over a large baby that was attached to a nurse's wet breast, while Peggy stood to the side with a happy smile. Further off two white parasols marked where Judith and Suki were walking by the brook.

'Goes for the teat well, young John, don't he?' Henry observed.

'A family trait, no doubt,' Charles replied. 'There is a wonderful gentleness to that sight, don't you think?'

'Perhaps,' Henry answered, 'though gentleness is not a virtue I've ever really linked with Eloise. Do you know, when I told her I'd cropped that fellow d'Aignan she was absolutely dancing for joy. I mean she never liked the fellow, but still.'

There was a pause, each man sipping his drink and reflecting on the calm Devon scenery.

'Talking of fellow's dying,' Henry said after a while. 'Old John's headstone is up.'

'Are you pleased with it?' Charles asked.

'Not really,' Henry admitted. 'I mean it's good thick slate, ought to be good until Judgement Day, but Stephen insisted on some piece of Christian rodomontade for the inscription. The guv'nor would have hated it.'

'What did you want?'

'Something truthful, but Stephen and old Bamford wouldn't even let me have "Accidentally smothered between the buttocks of a thirteen-stone lady's maid".'

Notes

[1] Today's political scandals seem tame indeed by eighteenth-century standards, with many parliamentary seats effectively for sale and others held by families on a hereditary basis. Parliamentary reform was hotly debated across this period but did not come about until well into the nineteenth century.

[2] This was the 'Escape' scandal, which involved a horse of that name, ridden by Samuel Chiffney and owned by Prince George. On 20 October 1791 Escape ran and lost poorly. The following day odds of five to one were offered and the horse won easily, resulting in the loss of large sums of money while the Prince and Chiffney were both supposed to have gained. The subsequent scandal ended with the sale of the Prince's stud and his angry withdrawal from Newmarket, but did nothing to decrease the popularity of racing.

[3] Hellgate (the seventh Earl of Barrymore) was a boon companion of Prince George and a notorious drinker. The two of them, along with other companions including the exiled Duke of Orleans, were notorious for drunken practical jokes, including arriving at respectable middle-class houses in the dead of night bearing a coffin and demanding to be given an imaginary corpse.

[4] During this period and well in the next century, virginity was so highly prized that a virgin prostitute

271

would earn many times what she might otherwise expect to receive. So lucrative was this trade for the madams that young girls might be 'repaired' several times by a variety of ingenious techniques, a thin membrane of gut and a tiny bag of pig's blood being just one of these. Such an incident occurs in *Fanny Hill*.

[5] Mining in Cornwall had begun to increase dramatically, with the new Watts beam engines allowing shafts to be dug far deeper than before. Speculation was rife, with many fortunes lost and made, and the county continued to lead the world in production of copper and tin until the later part of the nineteenth century.

[6] In the spring of 1791 war with France was still two years away, although it was widely regarded as inevitable. Stocking up on fine French wine to last out periods of war was a frequent necessity during the eighteenth century; claret, Sauternes and to a lesser extent burgundy and champagne were in high demand despite disproportionate taxes. The practice ceased to be necessary after the Napoleonic wars, but did not vanish. On the eve of the Second World War, Magdalen College stocked up with so much cognac that it was still on the college list in the '70s.

[7] The open, sparsely inhabited heathland of Surrey and northern Hampshire was notorious for highwaymen, mainly operating on the post road from London to the West Country. Their number supposedly included at least one woman and a priest.

[8] James Watt (1736–1819) was responsible for improving the steam engine from a clumsy, inefficient device useful only for crude pumping to a powerful industrial machine. Until his retirement in 1800 he made a practice of overseeing the installation of his engines as often as possible, although it would have been rare in the case of an existing engine being moved.

9 Tuthill Fields was an open area beside the Thames to the south of St James's Park. It was a popular promenade at the time, particularly among the military, with barracks and an artillery ground nearby. From the 1820s onwards it began to be built over, and now no more than a trace of green remains.

10 It was in fact not the Prince of Wales, but the Earl of Barrymore who did this, putting on his cook's skirts and bodice in order to serenade Mrs Fitzherbert from beneath her window at three o'clock in the morning.

11 Between 1780 and 1857 the Royal Society made its headquarters in rooms in the new Somerset House.

12 For a lady to ride any way other than side-saddle was considered scandalous at the time. To suggest to a girl that she might have done so would be a provocative remark and teasing if not actually insulting.

13 A common crime of the period, where the thief would quickly slash the fabric at the rear of a cab and extract whatever had been pushed under the seats. Like picking pockets, this was a crime best suited to young and nimble thieves.

NEW BOOKS

Coming up from Nexus and Black Lace

Surrender by Laura Bowen
August 2000   Price £5.99   ISBN 0 352 33524 6
When Melanie joins the staff of The Hotel she enters a world of new sexual experiences and frightening demands, in which there are three kinds of duty she must perform. In this place of luxury and beauty there are many pleasures, serving her deepest desires, but there is also perversity and pain. The Hotel is founded on a strict regime, but Melanie cannot help but break the rules. How can she survive the severe torments that follow?

An Education in the Private House by Esme Ombreux
August 2000   Price £5.99   ISBN 0 352 33525 4
Eloise Highfield is left in charge of the upbringing of Celia Bright's orphaned daughter, Anne. Disturbed and excited by the instructions left by Celia for Anne's education, Eloise invites Michael, a painter of erotic subjects, to assist her. As they read Celia's explicit account of servitude to her own master, they embark on ever more extreme experiments. But Anne is keeping her own diary of events . . . Celia, Eloise, Anne – three women discovering the pleasures of submission; three interwoven accounts of a shared journey into blissful depravity. By the author of the *Private House* series.

The Training Grounds by Sarah Veitch
August 2000   Price £5.99   ISBN 0 352 33526 2
Charlotte was looking forward to her holiday in the sun. Two months on a remote tropical island with her rich, handsome boyfriend: who could ask for more? She is more than a little surprised, then, when she arrives to find that the island is in fact a vast correction centre – the Training Grounds – presided over by a swarthy and handsome figure known only as the Master. But greater shocks are in store, not least Charlotte's discovery that she is there not as a guest, but as a slave . . .

Grooming Lucy by Yvonne Marshall
September 2000   Price £5.99   ISBN 0 352 33529 7
Lucy's known about her husband's kinks for a few years, but now
she wants to accommodate them herself. She knows it won't be easy
– she has heard how extreme his tastes are – and she's asked some
special friends to arrange a unique training course for her. But her
husband's not the only man with extreme tastes, and some of his
friends have their own ideas about how to train Lucy.

The Torture Chamber by Lisette Ashton
September 2000   Price £5.99   ISBN 0 352 33530 0
Catering for every perverse taste imaginable, The Torture Chamber
is an SM club with a legendary reputation. Inside its exclusive walls,
no fetish is too extreme, and the patrons know how to make the most
of every situation. When Sue visits in disguise, she realises that she
cannot visit again – the intensity of her reactions frightens her. But
others at the club will stop at nothing to share in her special
education.

Different Strokes by Sarah Veitch
September 2000   Price £5.99   ISBN 0 352 33531 9
These stories celebrate all aspects of the pains and pleasures of
corporal punishment. Disobedient secretaries, recalcitrant slimmers,
cheeky maids – dozens of young women, and a few young men too,
whose behaviour can be improved only by the strict application of a
hand, a slipper or a cane. A Nexus Classic.

BLACK
lace

Wicked Words 3 various
August 2000   Price £5.99   ISBN 0 352 33522 X

Wild women. Wicked words. Guaranteed to turn you on! Black Lace
short story collections are a showcase of erotic-writing talent. With
contributions from the UK and the USA, and settings and stories
that are deliciously daring, this is erotica at the cutting edge. Fresh,
cheeky, dazzling and upbeat – only the most arousing fiction makes
it into a Black Lace compilation.

A Scandalous Affair by Holly Graham
August 2000   Price £5.99   ISBN 0 352 33523 8

Young, well groomed and spoilt, Olivia Standish is the epitome of a
trophy wife. Her husband is a successful politician, and Olivia is
confident that she can look forward to a life of luxury and prestige.
Then she finds a video of her husband cavorting with whores and
engaging in some very bizarre behaviour, and suddenly her future
looks uncertain. Realising that her marriage is one of convenience
and not love, she vows to take her revenge. Her goal is to have her
errant husband on his knees and begging for mercy.

Devils's Fire by Melissa MacNeal
September 2000   Price £5.99   ISBN 0 352 33527 0

Destitute but beautiful Mary visits handsome but lecherous mortician
Hyde Fortune, in the hope he can help her out of her impoverished
predicament. It isn't long before they're consummating their lust for
each other and involving both Fortune's exotic housekeeper and his
young assistant Sebastian. When Mary gets a live-in position at the
local Abbey, she becomes an active participant in the curious erotic
rites practiced by the not-so-very pious monks. This marvelously
entertaining story is set in 19th-century America.

The Naked Flame by Crystalle Valentino

September 2000   Price £5.99   ISBN 0 352 33528 9

Venetia Halliday is a go-getting girl who is determined her trendy London restaurant is going to win the prestigious Blue Ribbon award. Her new chef is the cheeky, over-confident Mickey Quinn, who knows just what it takes to break down her cool exterior. He's hot, he's horny, and he's got his eyes on the prize – in her bed and her restaurant. Will Venetia pull herself together, or will her rough-trade lover ride roughshod over everything?

Crash Course by Juliet Hastings

September 2000   Price £5.99   ISBN 0 352 33018 X

Kate is a successful management consultant. When she's asked to run a training course at an exclusive hotel at short notice, she thinks the stress will be too much. But three of the participants are young, attractive, powerful men, and Kate cannot resist the temptation to get to know them sexually as well as professionally. Her problem is that one of the women on the course is feeling left out. Jealousy and passion simmer beneath the surface as Kate tries to get the best performance out of all her clients. A Black Lace special reprint.

NEXUS BACKLIST

All books are priced £5.99 unless another price is given. If a date is supplied, the book in question will not be available until that month in 2000.

CONTEMPORARY EROTICA

THE BLACK MASQUE	Lisette Ashton	
THE BLACK WIDOW	Lisette Ashton	
THE BOND	Lindsay Gordon	
BRAT	Penny Birch	
BROUGHT TO HEEL	Arabella Knight	July
DANCE OF SUBMISSION	Lisette Ashton	
DISCIPLES OF SHAME	Stephanie Calvin	
DISCIPLINE OF THE PRIVATE HOUSE	Esme Ombreux	
DISCIPLINED SKIN	Wendy Swanscombe	Nov
DISPLAYS OF EXPERIENCE	Lucy Golden	
AN EDUCATION IN THE PRIVATE HOUSE	Esme Ombreux	Aug
EMMA'S SECRET DOMINATION	Hilary James	
GISELLE	Jean Aveline	
GROOMING LUCY	Yvonne Marshall	Sept
HEART OF DESIRE	Maria del Rey	
HOUSE RULES	G.C. Scott	
IN FOR A PENNY	Penny Birch	
LESSONS OF OBEDIENCE	Lucy Golden	Dec
ONE WEEK IN THE PRIVATE HOUSE	Esme Ombreux	
THE ORDER	Nadine Somers	
THE PALACE OF EROS	Delver Maddingley	
PEEPING AT PAMELA	Yolanda Celbridge	Oct
PLAYTHING	Penny Birch	

THE PLEASURE CHAMBER	Brigitte Markham		
POLICE LADIES	Yolanda Celbridge		
THE RELUCTANT VIRGIN	Kendal Grahame		
SANDRA'S NEW SCHOOL	Yolanda Celbridge		
SKIN SLAVE	Yolanda Celbridge		June
THE SLAVE AUCTION	Lisette Ashton		
SLAVE EXODUS	Jennifer Jane Pope		Dec
SLAVE GENESIS	Jennifer Jane Pope		
SLAVE SENTENCE	Lisette Ashton		
THE SUBMISSION GALLERY	Lindsay Gordon		
SURRENDER	Laura Bowen		Aug
TAKING PAINS TO PLEASE	Arabella Knight		
TIGHT WHITE COTTON	Penny Birch		Oct
THE TORTURE CHAMBER	Lisette Ashton		Sept
THE TRAINING OF FALLEN ANGELS	Kendal Grahame		
THE YOUNG WIFE	Stephanie Calvin		May

ANCIENT & FANTASY SETTINGS

THE CASTLE OF MALDONA	Yolanda Celbridge		
NYMPHS OF DIONYSUS	Susan Tinoff	£4.99	
MAIDEN	Aishling Morgan		
TIGER, TIGER	Aishling Morgan		
THE WARRIOR QUEEN	Kendal Grahame		

EDWARDIAN, VICTORIAN & OLDER EROTICA

BEATRICE	Anonymous		
CONFESSION OF AN ENGLISH SLAVE	Yolanda Celbridge		
DEVON CREAM	Aishling Morgan		
THE GOVERNESS AT ST AGATHA'S	Yolanda Celbridge		
PURITY	Aishling Morgan		July
THE RAKE	Aishling Morgan		
THE TRAINING OF AN ENGLISH GENTLEMAN	Yolanda Celbridge		

SAMPLERS & COLLECTIONS

NEW EROTICA 3		
NEW EROTICA 5		Nov
A DOZEN STROKES	Various	

NEXUS CLASSICS
A new imprint dedicated to putting the finest works of erotic fiction back in print

AGONY AUNT	G. C. Scott	
THE HANDMAIDENS	Aran Ashe	
OBSESSION	Maria del Rey	
HIS MISTRESS'S VOICE	G.C. Scott	
CITADEL OF SERVITUDE	Aran Ashe	
BOUND TO SERVE	Amanda Ware	
SISTERHOOD OF THE INSTITUTE	Maria del Rey	
A MATTER OF POSSESSION	G.C. Scott	
THE PLEASURE PRINCIPLE	Maria del Rey	
CONDUCT UNBECOMING	Arabella Knight	
CANDY IN CAPTIVITY	Arabella Knight	
THE SLAVE OF LIDIR	Aran Ashe	
THE DUNGEONS OF LIDIR	Aran Ashe	
SERVING TIME	Sarah Veitch	July
THE TRAINING GROUNDS	Sarah Veitch	Aug
DIFFERENT STROKES	Sarah Veitch	Sept
LINGERING LESSONS	Sarah Veitch	Oct
EDEN UNVEILED	Maria del Rey	Nov
UNDERWORLD	Maria del Rey	Dec

Please send me the books I have ticked above.

Name ....

Address ....

....

....

.... Post code........................

Send to: **Cash Sales, Nexus Books, Thames Wharf Studios, Rainville Road, London W6 9HA**

US customers: for prices and details of how to order books for delivery by mail, call 1-800-805-1083.

Please enclose a cheque or postal order, made payable to **Nexus Books**, to the value of the books you have ordered plus postage and packing costs as follows:

UK and BFPO – £1.00 for the first book, 50p for the second book and 30p for each subsequent book to a maximum of £3.00;

Overseas (including Republic of Ireland) – £2.00 for the first book, £1.00 for the second book and 50p for each subsequent book.

We accept all major credit cards, including VISA, ACCESS/ MASTERCARD, AMEX, DINERS CLUB, SWITCH, SOLO, and DELTA. Please write your card number and expiry date here:

....

Please allow up to 28 days for delivery.

Signature ....
